Praise for the John Linwood Grant's
A Persistence of Geraniums

"The stories in John Linwood Grant's *A Persistence of Geraniums* would not have been out of place in the pages of Pearson's magazine, alongside those of E.F. Benson. Indeed, it's easy to picture Benson reading Grant's stories approvingly. Grant skillfully evokes the sensibility of Edwardian Britain in a series of supernatural tales distinguished both by their elegance and by their wit."
—John Langan, author of *The Fisherman*

"In the stories collected here, Grant has managed to create one of the most interesting and exciting characters to come along in some time: the enigmatic assassin, Mr. Dry. Possessed of great criminal and murderous ability, Mr. Dry is a power unto himself, moving like an unstoppable force of nature against evil and, sometimes, justice. These stories present a writer who has a strong narrative voice, a keen mind and a masterful ability to create characters that stay with the reader long after the book is finished. Brilliant and exciting, my only regret upon reading these stories is that I cannot hire Mr. Dry to remove Mr. Grant so that I could steal these tales for my own."
—Sam Gafford, author of *Whitechapel* and *The Dreamer in Fire*

"Each of the stories in this collection is utterly steeped in that bygone era, both in terms of setting and style. It's one thing to believably transport readers through space and time to immerse them in a vividly realized historical environment. It's a whole 'nother thing to be able to meaningfully evoke the tone and language of the writers from that period, all while still retaining a viably modern sensibility and enough of a unique voice to rise above mere facsimile. Through seven tales of mystery, murder, madness, and mysticism (plus a couple conversational interludes), Grant does exactly that."
—Ginger Nuts of Horror

Praise for Alan M. Clark's Jack the Ripper Victims Series

"*Of Thimble and Threat* is a terrifically absorbing read. A mature novel and superbly researched. The image of silver in the blood was woven expertly and made the ending luminous and poignant."
—Simon Clark, author of *Vampyrrhic* and *Night of the Triffids*

"Clark proves himself to be the ultimate double-threat, his prose every bit as evocative and compelling as his art. Steeped in Victoriana *Say Anything but Your Prayers* is a worthy edition to Ripperology."
—Steven Savile, author of *Silver* and *London Macabre*

"*A Brutal Chill in August*, one of a series wherein Alan M. Clark masterfully recreates the sorry lives of the Ripper's victims, is awash in atmospheric detail of those dark days in 19th century London. Exhaustively researched, Clark brings to life the plight of London's poor, and the extremes to which they must go in order to merely survive... or succumb as victims to disease, abuse, alcoholism, or worse. A great read."
—Elizabeth Engstrom, author of *Lizzie Borden* and *York's Moon*

"In *Apologies to the Cat's Meat Man,* Clark's skill shows through in terms of bringing the era and setting and characters to vivid life. Not a feel-good read, not a fun read, but another powerful one, and a stirring memorial for a woman who was more than a mark on a killer's scoresheet."
—Christine Morgan, author of *White Death* and *The Raven's Table*

Alan M. Clark has given us a great gift with his Jack the Ripper Victims series. I no longer care who the murderer was, for I know who his victims were. Exhaustively researched and true to period, Clark artfully relates their stories with clarity and compassion. *The Prostitute's Price* is the crown jewel of the quintet.
—Stephen T. Vessels, Thriller Award nominated author of *The Mountain and the Vortex* and *The Door of Tireless Pursuit.*

"I regard the five books that make up this series as unarguably one of the high points in Ripper fiction over the past 130 years."
—*Ripperologist* magazine

13 MILLER'S COURT

◈ - Comprised of - ◈

The Prostitute's Price

A novel of Mary Jane Kelly, the Fifth Victim of Jack the Ripper

by Alan M. Clark

◈ - and - ◈

The Assassin's Coin

The True History of the Deptford Assassin

a novel by John Linwood Grant

IFD Publishing
P.O. Box 40776, Eugene, Oregon 97404 U.S.A.
www.ifdpublishing.com

13 Miller's Court

This is a work of fiction. Although the novel is inspired by real historical events and actual human lives, the characters have been created for the sake of this story and are either products of the author's imagination or are used fictitiously. Any resemblance to actual events or locales or persons, living or dead, is entirely coincidental.

Cover art, Copyright © 2017 Alan M. Clark
Interior illustrations, Copyright © 2018 Alan M. Clark

ISBN: 978-0-9996656-7-1
Printed in the United States of America

Acknowledgments

Alan M. Clark—Thanks to Elizabeth Engstrom, Matt Hayward, Melody Kees Clark, Jill Bauman, Lisa Snellings, Mark Roland, Eric Witchey, Ross Lockhart, Michael Drewek, Cynthia Clark-Drewek, Margaret R. Clark, Cameron Pierce, Kirsten Alene Pierce, David Conover, Michele Green, Michael Green, Amanda Lloyd, Mad Wilson, John McNichols, and, most of all, his collaborator, John Linwood Grant, who graciously allowed him to write about his character, Mr. Edwin Dry, the Deptford Assassin.

John Linwood Grant—Thanks to my partner Sarah, who may have been driven insane by my late career choice, Sam Gafford, whose excellent 'Whitechapel' reminded me this sort of thing could be done, James Bojaciuk who first believed in 'Tales of the Last Edwardian,' Elizabeth Engstrom for her valuable comments, and of course Alan M Clark, who initiated this entire project and introduced me to the real Mary Jane Kelly.

AUTHORS' NOTE

The novel, *13 Miller's Court* is a combination of two novels, *The Assassin's Coin*, by John Linwood Grant, and *The Prostitute's Price*, by Alan M. Clark.

We originally conceived of this project as one novel that we would write together. We discussed writing from the point of view of two different characters. Alan M. Clark would be writing from the POV of the prostitute, Mary Jane Kelly. John Linwood Grant would write from the POV of a young woman, Catherine Weatherhead, who was seeking success in the growing spiritualist trade in Victorian London. In part, we intended this approach to help account for our different writing voices. The chapters of the story would alternate between the two characters' different perspectives.

Not long after plot discussions began, we became intrigued by the idea that we could write separate novels, centering on the same events, that would each stand on their own, but also fit together, and that's what we decided to do.

Alan M. Clark's novel, *The Prostitute's Price*, represents the final book in his Jack the Ripper Victims Series. The novels in the series are not meant to satisfy curiosity about the identity of Jack the Ripper. Instead, they exist to take readers back in time to experience the circumstances in which those he preyed upon lived and suffered his crimes in Victorian London. The author has depicted what history tells us about the women the Ripper killed as much as seems reasonable, while also trying to tell good stories.

John Linwood Grant's *The Assassin's Coin* explores the early days of his series 'Tales of the Last Edwardian,' focusing here on Catherine, the powerful but unreliable psychic, and the exploits of the lethal Mr Edwin Dry, who rose to prominence as the century waned. Fictional and historical figures intertwine as events come to a head during the 1888 Autumn of Terror, and we witness their judgment on the brutal and worthless Whitechapel Murderer.

Many of the place names in the novels—Stepney, Spitalfields, Shadwell, Whitechapel, Southwark, Clerkenwell, Deptford, Poplar, Shoreditch, Limehouse, Chelsea Embankment, Knightsbridge—are in the greater London area. Some are the names of districts or parishes or what were towns in their own right until they were swallowed up over time by the expansion of the city of London. They are all within ten miles of one another, most of them within easy walking distance.

The Assassin's Coin and The Prostitute's Price share the same timeline, some characters, and certain scenes. Though they are standalone stories, a broader experience of each can be had by reading both. And, so, here they are together, their chapters alternating. The chapter structure differs from the way they appear in the separate novels, but presented as one in this manner, the entire picture is available from every angle.

—Alan M. Clark and John Linwood Grant
October, 2018

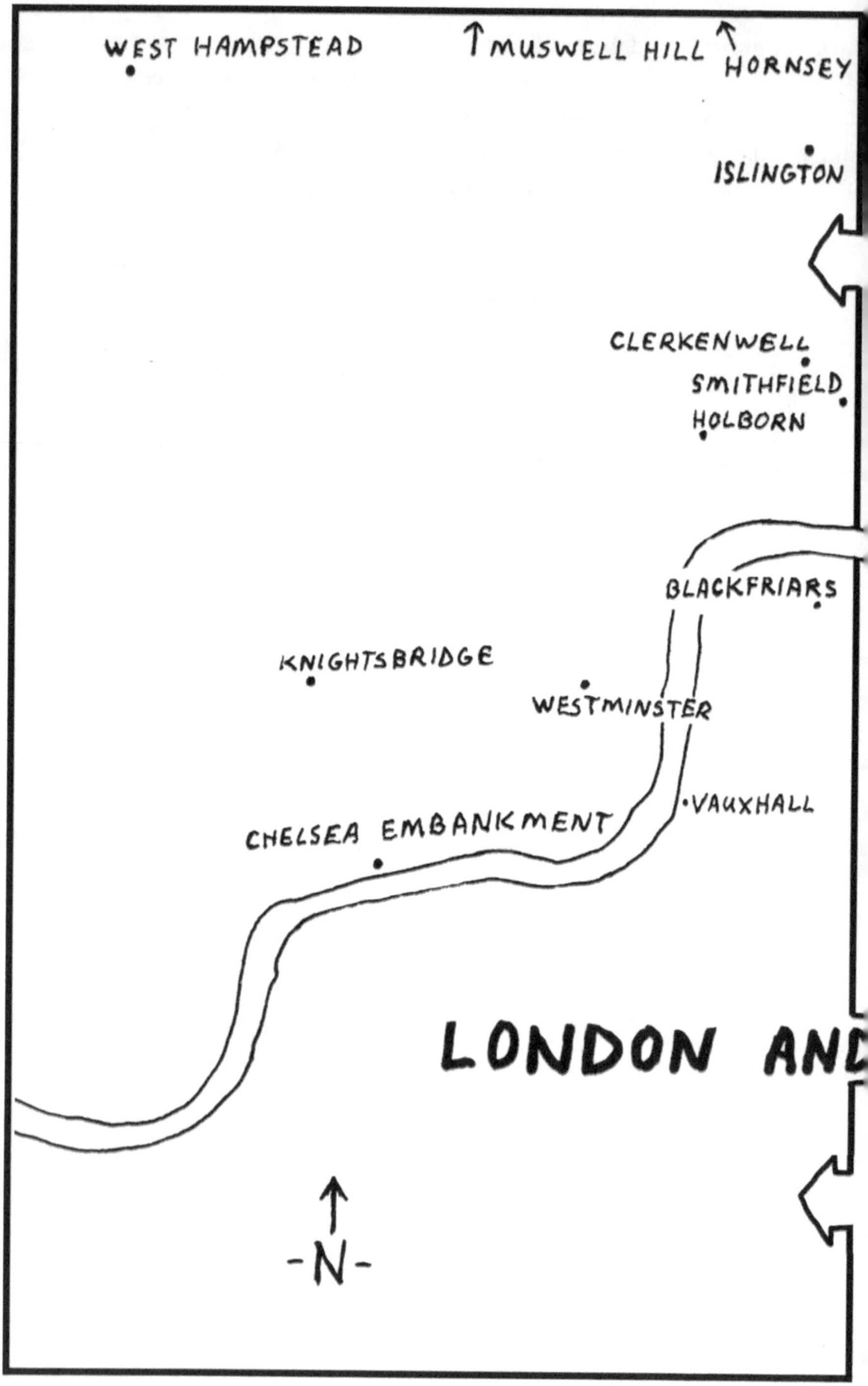
WEST HAMPSTEAD
MUSWELL HILL
HORNSEY
ISLINGTON
CLERKENWELL
SMITHFIELD
HOLBORN
BLACKFRIARS
KNIGHTSBRIDGE
WESTMINSTER
VAUXHALL
CHELSEA EMBANKMENT
LONDON AND
-N-

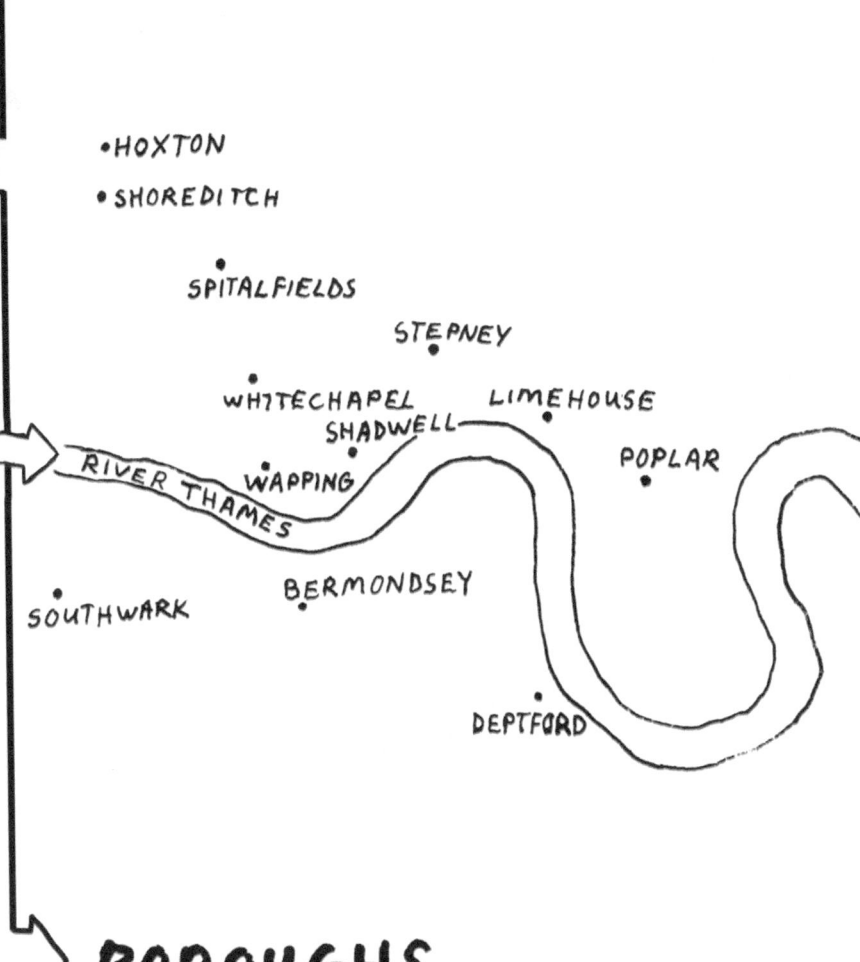

HOXTON

SHOREDITCH

SPITALFIELDS

STEPNEY

WHITECHAPEL   LIMEHOUSE

SHADWELL

RIVER THAMES   POPLAR

WAPPING

BERMONDSEY

SOUTHWARK

DEPTFORD

BOROUGHS

CATFORD

13 MILLER'S COURT

John Linwood Grant
and
Alan M. Clark

IFD
Publishing

Eugene, Oregon

PRELUDE

Mary Jane Kelly, I am.

I am not the woman that died at 13 Miller's Court.

And I will speak ill of the dead.

The haybag what died there were as wretched and filthy as the crib itself.

A bit of jam, she'd been a toffer in a fine West End gay house. Were so mouthy, the Abbess of her house turned her out in the street. Fell to common tail, she did. Would bed any cove with enough chink. A blower, chaunting to the bleeders, she hurt a lot of women just trying to get on. Her street cokum would have her put down on a friend, or sell her own.

'Tis anger what brings out the street cant. I am capable of much better.

Difficult as it is, I must become calm enough to consider carefully.

I argue with myself. Because I did indeed find the end of my life there in that squalid room, I have confused myself with that horrid buor, I've hated and even loved her. Yet, for all that makes us alike, I refuse to accept that we are one and the same. Hers is not a life what should make one proud.

Does that mean I am not proud of who I became when alive? Perhaps. The haze that surrounds my thinking on the matter obscures the truth.

A desire for independence and adventure were my undoing.

In life, I knew both opulence and squalor.

Should the religions of the East be right, and I live again in some possible future time, give me a life of hardship and hatred or one of comfort and love, but not both. The knowing between the two is where true cruelty lies.

PROLOGUE

Keighley, West Yorkshire, January 1876

Young Cath turns, whimpers.

The attic room is hot and airless, and a sheet, damp with sweat, clings to her legs. It twists around bone-thin ankles and long feet which might be cleaner; it confines her.

She twists onto her back. Her eyes are the shining grey of the ice on Redcar Tarn, high above the town, and they are wide open. The girl, however, is asleep—or beneath sleep, her mind wandering through phantasy and fever. The Night Mare presses on her chest.

She should be seeing the plaster which flakes on the ceiling, the patch where a rotting roof joist shows through. Instead, she is elsewhere...

Another room nearby, a plain enough room with solid, old-fashioned furniture. Dark furniture, crouching against brown walls—dressers, side-cupboards, and crooked, over-stuffed chairs.

And in the centre of that other place, a man's hands tighten.

The hiss of the woman's breath is gaslight and regret, forced through a windpipe that will soon have no purpose.

Again the man's hands tighten.

The legs of the woman spasm and jerk under a plain grey dress, their movement mirrored in a girl's bedroom, not so far away. And then they stop. Two bodies relax.

In the small attic, grey eyes close and true sleep comes at last. The girl presses her face into her pillow, and draws in deep, slow breaths.

But now the woman's eyes—hazel-brown—are wide open. They will stay that way until rough thumbs close them.

This night will be remembered...

ONE

Stepney District, London's East End, September 1886

In the drizzling early afternoon rain, Mary Jane left Thomas Morganstone's apartments in Harford Street intending to make the rounds of several pubs until she found a client.

As she turned west into Bale Street amidst several others using the footway, a hand came out of nowhere, grabbed her left arm and twisted it. Mary Jane cried out, and went to her knees on the damp flagstones, trying to relieve the painful pressure.

"Let me go!" she cried.

Those walking nearby stopped and faced her; startled, fearful, some appearing ready to take action against possible threat.

She turned enough to see out of the corner of her eye the stocky man who had seized her.

A constable?

No, not a blue bottle, nor even a police detective, not in such fine clothing: a worsted blue suit and a black felt bowler.

"Help me," she said to those watching.

"This is a matter of crimes committed," the man said loudly.

In his fine clothes, he had the authority. Many of the pedestrians were already moving on, the increasing rain driving them away. Two men remained. They looked Mary Jane up and down. Her clothing and hair distinguished her as a ladybird. They seemed to decide she wasn't worth the trouble and went on their way as well.

"They have no care for a harlot," her assailant said. "They know *you* are truly the danger."

She recognised his voice, got a better look at him, and saw his ginger hair and whiskers. He was probably the same man she'd seen on the street months earlier, questioning a friend of hers named Bell. Mary Jane had been hidden from his view at the time, and had seen only his back. He'd asked about Andriette's whereabouts. Her friend didn't know Mary Jane had once gone by that name. When Bell offered nothing useful, he'd struck her to the ground and kicked her viciously.

"Get up," he told Mary Jane, pulling her up by the wrist with his left hand.

If indeed he was the same man, she'd heard his name. Just prior to his attack on Bell, Mrs Buki, the proprietress of the Laughing Magpie, had warned Mary Jane that a red-haired gentleman had come to the brothel looking for her.

"The look of him told me he meant you harm," Mrs Buki said. "I told him I had nothing for him without knowing his name. 'Stuart Brevard,' he told me. In return, I gave him a lie."

With the warning, Mary Jane had left her employment at the Laughing Magpie. She'd worked briefly at another brothel, Gander's Bush, before going to live with Thomas Morganstone. She'd been avoiding ginger-haired men since.

Most likely Stuart Brevard was related to the man, Harris Brevard, a client who had attacked Mary Jane in Paris. Defending herself against the attack, she had accidentally maimed Harris. She'd then robbed him of a valuable emerald and platinum necklace and escaped. No doubt, those were the offences her assailant referred to. He, Stuart Brevard she presumed, wanted her to pay for the crimes.

He reached with his right hand to take her elbow.

She quickly moved toward his left shoulder, pivoting her wrist to parallel his. His rain-slicked grip loosened, and she nearly got away.

With his other hand, he grabbed her by the hair, just as his brother had done in his attack. He got behind her. His left hand let go of her wrist, moved out of sight for a moment. When it returned, she saw that it held a knife. He moved the blade up to the base of her ribcage, and pushed her toward the brick face of the nearest building, where the eave of the structure two stories above provided some protection from what had become a heavy downpour.

"I should gut you here and now," he said, "leave you swimming in your own blood."

"I would not do that, sir," she said. What arguments did she have? "Y-your fine suit."

He laughed with obvious delight.

Mary Jane sucked in her gut, swallowed hard, and held her breath. She would close her eyes so she didn't see what happened, but what little hope to get away she still possessed kept her from doing that.

"These people know you for what you are. They won't help. I can kill you and walk away."

"I passed a constable at the crossing." She tried to point westward.

He made a quick slice with the knife, cutting the underside of her left arm through the fabric of her chemise. So sharp was the blade, she didn't feel it until she lowered the arm and blood dripped from her elbow. Mary Jane stood trembling within his embrace, helpless.

He became still, and sighed softly. She'd heard that tone before from cruel clients—he savoured her fear!

No professional bludger, this one. Too much emotion. A sudden move while he remained quiet might win her release, perhaps an elbow to his thick gut. Yet, if such a move didn't work, she'd be hastening her death.

"Oh, what I've been through trying to help my brother. Hopeless! Then the long search for you."

Harris's brother!

"You will die here today." Mr Brevard said.

Mary Jane saw a woman, somewhat older, taller, dark-haired, approaching swiftly along the footway while adjusting her hands around the neck of a heavy laundry sack.

"No one will stop me," he whispered in Mary Jane's ear, clearly relishing his power over her.

As the woman moved, she lifted and swung the sack around. The burden lifted in an arc over her head.

Seeing what was coming, Mary Jane raised a leg and brought the heel of her boot down on the man's right foot. Her strike and the impact of the laundry sack occurred simultaneously. Mr Brevard, a large man, bounced off Mary Jane, shoving her toward the brick wall.

He let go of her. She gasped for breath and tried to regain her balance.

"Run," came the woman's voice.

Leaning away from the man, glancing back, Mary Jane saw him teetering. Several leaves of paper spilled from his coat pocket in a spray upon the footway. He fell backwards onto his arse while reaching for her unsuccessfully.

She saw the woman lift her skirts and run away, having abandoned the laundry sack. The glimpse Mary Jane had of the woman's face stuck in her mind's eye, and she didn't know why. Her features seemed familiar.

Printed on the leaves of the paper on the footway, Mary Jane saw a sketch of a woman that looked much like herself, with the name, "Andriette," underneath. She grabbed one and stuffed it into her bodice.

Mr Brevard tried to rise as Mary Jane leaned into a mad dash away from him. Her skirts tacked to lift seductively in front to show a bit of ankle when she walked, she ran easily without gathering her hems.

She looked back again, saw Mr Brevard rise and take a few stumbling steps on his injured foot. With his pained expression, she knew she'd get away. The look in his eyes told her he would keep his word to gut her if he caught up with her again.

Mary Jane wanted to thank the brave woman who struck the man, but she'd gone in the opposite direction.

TWO

Islington, September 1886

His hands are not large, though they have an unusual span and the fingers are most dexterous. He knows each sinew, each vein, even the slight resistance to torsion at the base of one thumb. That is being addressed. The nails are pared clean at every opportunity. He knows that you do not let your tools, your instruments, fall into disrepair.

His hands are the cornerstone of his trade, and what they might hold is largely irrelevant. Wire, blade or gun; a boatman's hook or a carpet needle. The requirements change with every commission. If necessary, his hands can do the work themselves, without further assistance.

And it is work. It is his only claim on the city.

From spattered fluids on brothel sheets to the brandy which drools from a politician's lips; from the fine walks of St James's Park to the Southwark stews—it does not matter to him where they live, or how they comport themselves. Vice does not make a target, nor Virtue a shield. Let bishops debate whilst the workman does his job.

London town must provide…

The way down to the cellars was poorly lit, the steps old and heavily scrubbed. Madame Rostov moved as quickly as she could, aware of the urgency, but nevertheless she halted at the foot of the stairs, unsure. The air held a smell that was visceral, crouching like a beast in its own right between the low ceiling and the stone-flagged floor. All was clutter, and only two small windows let in a glimmer of daylight. One of the pale muslin blinds was speckled with blood.

The woman with the cleaver seemed oblivious to her arrival. The blade slammed down, the fat of the woman's arms shook with the impact, and some slippery piece of flesh was tossed onto a tray more bloody than the window blind.

Madame Rostov coughed. "I need…"

The woman in the cellar turned with remarkable speed for her bulk, cleaver in hand.

"Who are you, then?"

"Mr Carlton returned early, to pick up…papers, maybe? I was told I needed to…"

19

Understanding softened the lines on the woman's face. She put the cleaver down on the block, and wiped her hands on a stained apron.

"Keep out of the way? Sorry, madam. Can I make you a cup of tea?" She looked almost apologetically at the chopping boards, trays and pans behind her. "The master is perticular about his cuts, and the butchers round here can't tell a Barnsley chop from a short rib. Has me at it, the master does, to put their mess right."

"You must be Mrs Greath, the cook."

"I am so. I heard we was having a visitor, one of them spiritualist ladies. I suppose that—"

"Madame Rostov."

"Pleasure, I'm sure." The cook wiped her hands, and went to place a kettle on the range in the corner. "Not that I hold with it, especial, but the master—he's always railing against such things. No wonder the mistress wanted you down here. You'd think we had them Paris postcards in the house, to see his face when the mistress gets out her pamphlets."

Madame Rostov looked around. Underneath it all, there was an order of sorts. Mrs Greath might be accounted a creative rather than a traditional cook.

"Don't mind the mess on the blind," the woman said. "I had an accidental with some liver, getting the stringy bits out for the cat."

"Yes, I see."

In the house above, a door slammed.

"There," said Mrs Greath. "He's off again, and the coast's clear. I'll bring the tea up. Maid's day off." She winked. "She'd tell the master what had been going on, as soon as scratch her surface, she would."

Elspeth Carlton, thin and breathy, was already on the stairs. "So sorry, Madame. My husband has certain views—"

"Mrs Greath tells me."

"Do come up to the parlour."

"Tea's on its way," the cook called after them.

The large parlour was no brighter than the cellar kitchen, but it smelled of lilac water, and the blinds were clean. The gloomy paint was broken up by a mismatched selection of photographs in silver frames, and an excess of white lace doilies and silhouette portraits. A table and four seats had been prepared in the centre of the room; a small harmonium stood ready by the empty fireplace.

"An intimate sitting," said Mrs Carlton. "My cousin Grace, and a Miss Cobb from the next street. They are on their way."

Madame Rostov inclined her head, a tangle of black hair almost hiding her eyes.

"They are believers," added the hostess.

Small talk accompanied some excellent almond biscuits and a cup of tea which seemed to bear the tang of raw liver. A faltering discussion on Blavatsky's The Secret Doctrine, which Mrs Carlton clearly had not read, was relieved by the arrival of the others.

"We have an hour and half, at least," said the hostess as she let them in.

Madame Rostov was grateful that Mr Carlton's disapproval meant for a short session, fitted in before he arrived home for an early dinner. Miss Cobb, a squint-eyed woman in an expensive dress, sat at the harmonium and sought to raise what she called "sympathetic vibrations." What the indifferent playing might be sympathetic with, Madame Rostov forbore to say.

And then they were to table, the spiritualist opposite her host, the others eager on either side.

"Does someone—something—always come, madame?" asked Grace Carlton, a mouse voice in a mouse body, as thin as her cousin.

"No. But I feel that you three ladies, you understand the ways of the Aether. I am being hopeful." There was a touch of the East European in her voice, as if despite her proficiency, English might not be her first language.

In the half-light through the blinds, Madame Rostov threw back her head and began to speak, a low mutter which clearly conveyed nothing to the others. The harmonium creaked, making Mrs Carlton jump.

"Will you come to us? There are those here who would have word of the Beyond."

"We are supplicants," added Elspeth Carlton. "Only guide us to—"

Madame Rostov cleared her throat before the woman could continue. "A dear one is near," she said. "He—no, she—flutters on the edge of this place, anxious to move on. A mother, old with care…

she waits."

Grace Carlton gripped her sister's hand. The room darkened, though it might have been the passing of an omnibus outside.

"My mother, Elspeth's aunt, yes. Is she here?"

"She waits. A name…Meg?"

The three women craned forward, gripping each other.

"Aunt Margaret." Mrs Carlton's breathy voice was almost a whisper. "Uncle Edgar called her Meg."

Miss Cobb's squint intensified. "But surely your aunt died five years ago, Elspeth."

"She waits," repeated Madame Rostov. "There is a task undone."

"Can we speak to her?"

The spiritualist turned her head slightly, towards Miss Cobb.

"Five years, yes. Her earthly voice is gone—only her will remains. And those who should remember her…"

Grace Carlton gave a small shriek. "We haven't been to the grave this year, or left flowers for her. Oh, Elspeth, we forgot!"

Her cousin paled. "That must be it. The 'work undone.'"

"Those who have passed must be remembered." Madame Rostov lowered her chin to the dark silk which covered her breast. "Remembered. Ah, now that you understand, she has gone."

"I shall take a vase to Aunt Margaret's grave tomorrow." Mrs Carlton said, decisive.

The four of them sat in silence for some minutes. After an awkward cough, Miss Cobb spoke up.

"Madame Rostov, are there others who might come to us today?"

A keen observer might have seen a twitch of irritation at the corner of the spiritualist's mouth. Beneath the unruly black hair, sharp blue eyes regarded the woman with less than charity.

"I will ask," she said. "But if the vibrations are no longer right, do not expect too much."

Her eyes closed; her head came forward. Madame Rostov's breathing slowed—long, deep intakes and a wait before her hair fluttered with the exhalation.

"A man."

The women waited.

"Grandfather, perhaps," said Mrs Carlton, when nothing else was forthcoming. "He was—"

The spiritualist gave a shudder, half-rising from her seat.

"A man, and water…"

She could see no one in the parlour, nothing around her, only another place, which had nothing of fanciful Aetheric planes about it.

"A man…a dreadful man with dark intentions…"

The bathroom is spacious, tiled in the Italian manner and dominated by a claw-foot bath of great proportion, dwarfing the slim figure of the occupant.

"Who in God's name are you?" asks the man in the bath, his hair slick with soap, his left eye half-closed. He places one hand over his half-erect member, the other on the side of the bath, preparing to lift himself.

The visitor steps into the room. Small, careful steps. The air is full of steam, the tiles slippery. He is not a tall man, nor is he as slim as the bather, though his dark suit is well cut. A black felt bowler shades his eyes, incongruous in these surroundings.

"My name is Edwin Dry." An even, neutral tone.

"But what are you doing here? Get out at once, man!" There is a shrill note in the bather's voice.

"I fear, Mr Tether, that you are no longer required."

A small revolver appears in Mr Dry's left hand, which is very steady. He draws a length of soft cotton material from beneath his jacket.

"You're not one of my clients."

"No, I am not. Hold out your arms, Mr Tether."

"I'll do no such thing."

"Then I will have to shoot you in the head, which would be an annoying development. Annoying, but nothing more. Plans can be changed."

Tether trembles, the water slopping from side to side. After a moment, he holds his arms out.

"Why…why are you doing this?"

Mr Dry comes forward, the revolver aimed still at the bather's forehead.

"You are a solicitor, Mr Tether. You are paid to undertake certain tasks, according to your talents. Your work for a Silas Smith, of Chelsea, has become troublesome. And so, you are no longer required."

"But…" Tether watches as the other man works deftly, wrapping

the material around Tether's forearms one-handed, binding them gently but firmly together. "Are you to take me somewhere? What is to happen to me?"

Mr Dry pauses, tugging the material a little tighter until he is satisfied. The revolver disappears. He takes off his jacket, and removes his cufflinks, placing them side by side on a washstand. He rolls up his sleeves.

"What happens to us all."

The solicitor does not have time to cry out as Mr Dry grabs his ankles and tugs, sliding Tether down so that his head goes under the water. It is at that point that he tries to scream, but the water is already in his lungs. With his arms bound, the man can only writhe and kick; the grip on his ankles is relentless. Bathwater splashes the tiles once, for a second and then a third time, until Tether is motionless. His face, wide-eyed, open-mouthed, is a mask beneath the water. His erection has passed, and will never return.

Mr Dry bends forward and unwinds the length of cotton, which has left no mark on the man's forearms. He takes a towel and mops the tiles, making sure to leave no boot-print as he works away from the bath. The cotton goes into an oiled canvas bag at his waist; the towel into the laundry basket, beneath others. At the last he retrieves his cufflinks and his jacket.

"Good afternoon, Mr Tether."

The solicitor does not reply.

Madame Rostov stood up, ending the séance abruptly. She pushed aside twitters of curiosity and concern, refused all offers of refreshment.

"A mischievous spirit," she managed to say to the powdered faces around her. "Pay it no heed. But I can do no more today."

Making her apologies, she left the Carltons' house in a rustle of silk, almost forgetting to grab the battered case with which she had arrived.

Away from the house, still unsteady, she checked that she was unobserved and turned into a quiet side street. There, under the shade of a plane tree, she bound back her hair, placed a simple grey bonnet over it, and found a long, light jacket from her case, obscuring much of the black silk that typified Madame Rostov the medium.

Catherine Weatherhead strode more evenly back into the late afternoon traffic, though her heart pounded. Each man she saw, on the pavement, on the omnibus, in shop doorways, was a neat, bowler-hatted figure with murder in his hands.

"It is not true. It is not true," she muttered as she crossed the river, seeking diversion in the sight of the great sluggish Thames.

But she did not believe herself.

THREE

In August, 1885, a year before Stuart Brevard's attack in Bale Street, Mary Jane had found work at the Phoenix gay house.

The four-story stone building of the elegant brothel had a kitchen with dining tables, indoor plumbing with porcelain baths, basins, and flush toilets, a common room, several plush parlours, and twenty beautiful bedrooms. She was given one of the bedrooms with a feather mattress on a fine wooden frame, an eight foot tall armoire, a vanity and chest of drawers, the furniture all a matching walnut, finished with French polish.

On her first day there, a house seamstress named Bridgid took her to a room filled with fine clothing, said, "Please choose what you'd like to wear."

The woman made alterations to the pieces Mary Jane chose so they fit properly, and placed them in the armoire in her room.

Mrs Elouise Arseneau, the elderly proprietress of the gay house, encouraged Mary Jane to set the limitations of what she would endure with clients. Mrs Arseneau wrote down her subordinate's preferences in a book on a desk in her office.

"Those I send you shall engage only in the practices you allow," she said, gesturing toward the book. "Should a customer overstep his bounds, you shall give him warning that you'll call the house warders. Should he persist, cry out for help immediately."

Mary Jane got a sense that the proprietress valued her safety and service.

"May we call you Andriette?" Mrs Arseneau asked.

"Yes," Mary Jane said. That became her name in all business with the gay house.

Her duties began with meeting clients in the parlours. Unlike her previous experience in Cardiff, price wasn't discussed. Within a month, she was attending gentlemen as a companion at events outside the gay house.

She learned that the self-made man, whose wealth brought him into demand socially, could take a prostitute who had sufficient ability with etiquette and language into certain social situations. Mary Jane had gained her position at the gay house by demonstrating her knowledge of social graces and the Queen's English in her interview with Mrs Arseneau.

Some among the aristocracy held events to draw the well-to-do, self-made men into their circles. Among the peerage, many had too much debt, and had sold off so much of their holdings that little but their titles remained. They needed investment to rebuild the strength of their family lines. Those willing to compromise the standards of their kind in order to meet new, rich blood, looked for spouses with fortunes among the wealthy families of the self-made at home and abroad. Others had schemes to win money off the unsuspecting self-made men by drawing them into rigged gambling, or, through connections in the courts, manipulations of the legal system.

Of course, no one mistook Mary Jane for one with wealth. She had little more than the fine clothes on loan from the Phoenix gay house and the education she'd received when a child. Still, Mary Jane did get looks from titled toffs. She did not look or act out of place at the social events.

Was she happy? That would have been difficult for her to answer. She had certainly become impressed with herself and how far she had risen from humble beginnings. Mary Jane had a fascination for her new world and an eager willingness to be a part of the life around her.

Some of the peerage, once introduced to those of a lower station gained a fascination for what they called "slumming." She tried to steer clear of them, as they were known to turn cruel if they thought one didn't show the proper respect. That happened most unexpectedly at times to some of the women she knew.

The self-made man could also be cruel. Something in his outlook seemed to make his anger more predictable and manageable, though. He often had a sense that his money and influence should buy him whatever he wanted. Yet, whilst his wealth and power had been gained through his efforts, the circumstances of his birth did not suggest to him that he was a superior being. A spate of cruelty might easily be quieted with a few well-placed compliments to his character, appearance, or manner. As Mary Jane found out, that didn't always work, and sometimes the tactic made things worse.

Within a few months of joining the women at the Phoenix gay house, she made a trip to Paris with a gentleman. Mary Jane had met Harris Brevard, a bridge builder, on several occasions. She'd seen him eyeing her with obvious fascination from a distance, but each time, thankfully, she had been engaged with another gentleman. Round, thick-skinned, pink and balding, he had a porcine look, even in the best clothing. One of the self-made toffs, he carried a look of defiant pride, as if that helped prove his worth.

Through the gay house, he hired Mary Jane to go to Paris with him for two weeks in December of 1885. He had a large, two room apartment, a parlour and bedroom, on the fourth floor of Le Muerice in Rue de Rivoli, in the heart of the French capital. The fourth floor balcony, which ran the length of the building, gave a perfect view of the beautiful Tuileries Garden just across the lane. Though winter time, and most of the trees had lost their leaves, Mary Jane wanted to explore.

Gardens didn't interest Harris Brevard.

The first day, they shopped in delightful boutiques, where he bought her several small pieces of fine jewellery and a fur muff.

On a visit to the Musée du Louvre, Mary Jane discovered to her astonishment that each painting was as much a portal onto the soul of the artist as it was a window to a view.

"Too much yellow," Mr Brevard said of the many worlds of vision they inspected that day. Upon leaving the museum, he said, "Shameful that they don't repair the damaged ones. There are painters who could touch up all those cracks." He stuffed his ugly head back into his silk top hat, and they strolled along the Seine while he tried to look important.

In bed, Harris Brevard was unremarkable. Mary Jane must have unwittingly revealed her lack of interest the first night because he looked at her sternly after his release. "You *must* do better," he said, pulling his stiff sinew from her notch with a sudden, angry jerk that left the sheath inside.

"Yes, Mr Brevard," she said. "I beg your pardon. I don't wish to disappoint. I mean to do my best."

His features softened somewhat. "You are desirable in most every way. The look on your face needs work."

Less yellow? she wondered. *Fewer cracks?*

"Yes, sir," Mary Jane said.

He rolled over and slept.

At just ten o'clock in the evening, she couldn't sleep, spent a restless couple of hours listening to him snore and wishing she were not in his bed.

The next day, he presented Mary Jane with a beautiful rosewood box. "The emerald and platinum beauty you'll find inside is yours if you can earn it," he said.

Within, she discovered a gorgeous necklace of cut green jewels set in large white metal beads. She knew the sparkling delight with the glowing gems had to be worth hundreds of pounds.

Mary Jane's astonishment must have shown. He smiled, even as he took the box away from her.

"I did not tell you because I hadn't yet decided that you would be the one. I still have not decided, but thought you might need an incentive to earn what I have to offer."

She had the irrational fear that he was about to propose marriage. "What do you mean, pray tell?"

"This is the beginning of what will be for me a months-long tour of the continent. Although I have seen much here in my work, I have been too busy to see the sights of Europe before now. Should you improve the look you give me in bed, you may accompany me on the tour, attend to my needs, and, when all is done, you may have that necklace in addition to what I shall pay your house."

"Oh, sir," Mary Jane said, "that is generous. Yes, I most gratefully hope to earn your favour."

He seemed pleased with himself.

She was excited to have the opportunity to earn the treasure.

Her expression that afternoon in bed must have been persuasive. He displayed a better mood.

That evening, they saw a show at the Folies Bergère; beautiful women in scant, colourful costumes performing gymnastics and dance. Bawdy at times, the tunes playful, yet grand, the graceful, supple bodies moving in time with the music took Mary Jane's breath away, while Mr Brevard, seeing so much female flesh, sat with a boyish leer on his face.

The magical establishment itself, a fancy beyond anything she'd imagined, filled her senses until wonderment overflowed. The bright colours, the chandelier lighting, the variety of fascinating people, their elaborate dress and wild costumes, the rich food and drink—all had become a waking dream. The sounds of voices and music drew

Mary Jane's attention in many directions. Turning this way and that, not wanting to miss anything, she grew dizzy.

With that, the experience began to sour. Expressions on the faces of those around her, especially the painted ones of the women, became pinched with a savage hunger of some sort. The odours of the place turned Mary Jane's stomach. The loud noises coming from the orchestra and audience confused and unsettled her. She fell ill, and knew she must find a privy quickly.

Mr Brevard did not slow her as she excused herself. Mary Jane moved through the tables, fearing she might let go the contents of her stomach there in the hall, perhaps soiling some poor patron enjoying the show.

She did not speak the language, and was in too much of a hurry to ask where to go. Mary Jane stumbled out of the entrance of the establishment and vomited there in the street. Embarrassed, she glanced around. Thankfully none of the people coming in or going out took much notice of her.

Then a hand under Mary Jane's shoulder lifted her gently.

"Poor girl," said an English voice. "Let me help you."

Mary Jane thought the woman looked to be close to her age, possibly a bit older. She had a fair, pretty face with too much rouge, lip colour, and eye shading. Her dress was that of a Parisian whore. "Miss Blanche Sayers," she said. "Did you come from inside?"

"Yes," Mary Jane said, "and I must return. A gentleman…"

"No need to explain. I see that you know life. The Demimondes are not to your liking, I take it."

She meant the hedonistic gathering in the cabaret, a word used to describe it. At the time, Mary Jane didn't know what she meant.

"Let's get you something for your stomach," Blanche said.

She helped Mary Jane, led her inside the cabaret to a marble-topped bar. "Warm rum and ginger," Blanche said.

The woman in lace and black velvet behind the bar seemed to understand her. While she moved about among the many bright bottles, preparing the drink, Mary Jane tried to locate Mr Brevard. He sat where she'd left him, still watching the show. He glanced around a couple of times, presumably to find her, a look of irritation on his face.

Mary Jane turned back to her companion. She watched Blanche

pour a few drops of amber liquid into a steaming cup that the barkeep must have placed on the polished surface. "Your drink," the woman said, lifting the cup and handing it to Mary Jane.

"How much shall I pay?" she asked.

"I've paid," Blanche said. "I put laudanum in your drink, a tincture of opium. With that, all this shall be much more fun." She waved her arms to include the entire cabaret.

Mary Jane knew of laudanum, but had never tried the drug. She also knew that some destroyed their lives with too much opium, yet she didn't worry that might happen to her.

"Perhaps I'll see you after the performance?" Blanche asked.

"Possibly," Mary Jane said, though she had no intention of seeking her company. "Thank you."

She took the cup with her back to the table where Mr Brevard sat.

"You went for a drink alone?" he asked with a scowl.

"No," Mary Jane said. "I became ill. A woman helped me, gave me this to settle my stomach."

He gave her a look of disgust—may have thought she drank medicine—and turned his attention back to the women on stage.

Mary Jane sipped the drink until she'd emptied the cup. Strong flavours. Blanche was right, the laudanum made the rest of the evening much more tolerable. In truth, Mary Jane enjoyed too much the feeling the narcotic gave her.

Again that evening, when they had returned to his apartment at Le Muerice, she must have had an acceptable expression in bed.

And, again, after he turned over and went to sleep, she could not find slumber.

Thinking of the garden across the lane, Mary Jane decided upon an adventure. She rose, dressed in warm clothing, and quietly slipped out the door of the apartment.

By the dim gaslight, she explored Tuileries Garden. Alone in the night, there in that strange city, Mary Jane should have been afraid, but she wasn't. That may have been because of the laudanum. She had the impression no one saw her. That was to her liking.

She lifted the hem of her skirts and slipped from shadow to shadow in the chill air. The black limbs of the trees, with twigs like withered fingers, reached for the crescent of the moon. The stars, mere smudges high overhead, winked lazily to let her know they would keep her secret.

Looking up at them, Mary Jane tripped over something, and her knees struck the ground. She kept herself from falling all the way. The turf, dead that time of year, had blackened her stockings. Somehow, the stains seemed a badge of honour for her tidy adventure.

Mary Jane slipped back into Mr Brevard's apartment, quietly undressed, hid her soiled stockings, and returned to bed without him noticing.

~⚓~

The afternoon of the next day they joined giblets again. Harris Brevard was crushing her. The fire on the hearth had been set too large, and the room had become sweltering hot. His sweat ran freely. As he pumped in and out, he gasped, groaned, and sprayed a bit of spittle. She pretended to find her pleasure with him, until he accidentally blew a clot from his nose into her face. She tried to relax, but all that was piggish and disgusting about him—perhaps all that Mary Jane had found loathsome in the men she'd serviced over the years—came back to haunt her in that moment. She panicked, and struggled under him in spite of herself.

He must have seen the soil from his nose on her face because he had a brief look of embarrassment.

Then he pulled away, jerked the sheath off his truncheon, and got up. "You've spoiled my coming bliss!" he said, his anger probably put on, not quite felt entirely.

"Me?" She regretted the one word question immediately because of the accusation it implied.

"You dare to blame me?" His embarrassment, possibly an unendurable blow to his pride, had quickly turned to rage. His eyes, menacing red-rimmed orbs, bore down on Mary Jane. "You disgusting whore!"

"No, o-of course you're n-not at fault," she said, stumbling on her words. "I-I should have aired out the room. 'Tis too hot. A fine gentleman such as yourself ought to be better served. I apologise."

"You patronising pinchcock," he shouted. "Don't pretend to have respect for me. The look in your eyes tells me I'm not what you want. All I've wanted is a good show for my money. But I see that if

I'm to have my pleasure, I must take it."

He struck Mary Jane in the gut. She rolled with the pain and tumbled off the bed. Trying to get away, she crawled toward the French doors that let out onto the balcony. He followed, struck her in the arse and back. She collapsed upon the floor, curled up to protect her middle. Mary Jane's head jerked back with a terrible ache in her neck as he grabbed her hair and yanked her toward the bed. Pinning her left arm up behind her back and holding the limb there painfully, he steered her onto the edge of the mattress. With his right hand, he savagely tore at Mary Jane's lower cheeks to open her. Wearing no sheath, he rammed his root deep inside. She feared he'd break her with the painful pounding her arse took. Mary Jane wailed and cried out until he shoved her arm up harder, the pain silencing her.

She would not, *could* not think. Trapped in a merciless agony, the need to get away from him could only eat at her. While she tried not to reason, unwanted memories came forth. She was back in her room in Cardiff, where a man had beaten her insensible and raped her. Should she survive Brevard's attack, another year of illness and convalescence might lie ahead. No, she would not think of that. All she could do was to endure.

Brevard had wanted to be cruel all along. He would have got to the brutality somehow eventually, no matter how Mary Jane acted. She knew those things later as she recalled him spitting in her hair, digging his nails into her back and neck, gasping out guttural, half-formed curses.

Eventually, he stiffened. His flying, slapping flesh ceased to pound against her. He cried out in his release.

His grip on her arm weakened in that moment, and she twisted around hard to her left toward him. He seemed surprised to be looking her in the eye. He still quaked in the flood of bliss, and had little control of himself. Mary Jane got away, and hurried through the bedroom door into the parlour.

He got his feet under him quickly enough, and followed. She turned as she moved, saw that he was almost upon her again, saw the hatred in his eyes and his meaty hands clawing for her. Mary Jane swung wildly to fend him off, and her right hand struck him in the throat.

A long moment passed while he stumbled forward. She moved

out of his path. His eyes grew large in his red face. He clutched at his neck, turned toward her with a frightful look of anger turning to fear. Wheezing with a pleading, childlike face, he flailed. Mary Jane dodged out of his way again and returned to the bedroom, shutting the door between them and holding it. He pushed from the other side. The latch tongue clicked into the frame, and the pressure let up. A pounding on the wood commenced, became weaker until it ceased.

Mary Jane dressed quickly, gathered her things into her travel bag. Taking the necklace from the rosewood box, she added that to her bag. She pushed to open the door, hoping he had fallen insensible. His right shoulder kept it from opening. He lay unmoving on the floor, his wheezing a thin reed of sound. Pushing with all she had, she created a gap large enough to pass through with the bag.

She left the door to the apartment open. Walking swiftly, but as casually as possible, her heart pounding, limbs shaking, fearing that he'd somehow catch her again, she fled the hotel.

Mary Jane had some money and the small jewellery Mr Brevard had bought for her on their first day in Paris. She hid the necklace inside the stuffing of the fur muff he'd given her. Over the ensuing days, she used all her money and the small jewellery securing passage to the coast, bribing a sheep smuggler to return her to England, and making her way back to London. She arrived at the Phoenix gay house two days before Christmas, believing she had some time before word of what happened in Paris got back to Mrs Arseneau. Once that happened, Mary Jane knew she'd no longer be welcome in the establishment.

She hid the muff with necklace still inside atop the eight foot tall armoire in her room, a dusty spot clearly too high for the charwoman to bother cleaning. The decorative parapet around the top of the piece of furniture totally hid her prize from sight. Mary Jane began to pack her things, leaving room in her travel bag to add the muff and necklace. She would add those just before she left.

Word of what happened to Harris Brevard arrived faster than she expected, two days after Christmas. Mrs Arseneau came to her room with two of her punishers, big fellows with hard faces. Standing by in case they were needed, the men looked uncomfortable in their fine clothes. They didn't choose to look at Mary Jane.

"We cannot be seen to help you in any way," Mrs Arseneau said, a stern look in her hooded blue eyes. The old, white-haired French woman stood stiffly and somewhat unsteadily in her finery. "If you leave now, we will tell the police nothing, should they come for you."

Mary Jane thought of the muff atop the armoire. "May I have a moment alone to gather my things? I have not finished packing."

"No," Mrs Arseneau said.

The two men turned toward Mary Jane, their sharp eyes a clear warning.

"All of the gifts you've received are forfeit as recompense for the damage we've sustained by your actions," the proprietress said. "I see you've packed clothing. I assume you have your push."

Mary Jane had little money after fleeing Paris. Still, she nodded.

"I shan't go through your bag," Mrs Arseneau said, "but you must leave now with what you've already packed."

Mary Jane had a sudden desire to strike the old woman, to tear her beautiful pink silk, to undo the white, matching curls of hair arranged so perfectly on her wrinkled brow. What might have been follow-me-lads in Mrs Arseneau's day, were just jug loops now. As stylish as the woman was, why did she wear her hair in such an ugly, old-fashion manner?

Mary Jane held in her rage, knowing that to show the anger would do no good. Nothing more could she do at that time to retrieve the muff and necklace.

She allowed the two men to escort her to the door of the establishment.

FOUR

Some women survived.

They survived despite everything set against them—disease, the injustices of society, and the casual ease with which a body could trip and fall under an omnibus or a carrier's horse. They avoided the blows of a man's grimy fist, the scratch of another woman's claws, and the lawyers of the rapacious rich; they remained strangers to the poorhouse or the prison.

To Catherine, Mrs Bessovitch was one of those women.

Swathed in perpetual mourning, she used black lace and brocade to dissuade gentlemen callers, and sharp glances to see off the few who nevertheless persisted. She flaunted tragic memories of her husband, and when it was useful she shed onion tears for his loss, years long gone, in some distant naval conflict. Only her closest confidantes (and her lodger) knew that Mr Aaron Bessovitch had leaned too far over the rail of the Dover to Calais packet ship whilst inebriated. Tragic, possibly, but not of great value to the Empire.

Catherine looked on her landlady as a safe harbour, and thanked God (with whom she was not overly familiar) for guiding her to Gilda Bessovitch's lodgings in Southwark.

"Madame Rostov, she was success?"

Mrs Bessovitch clattered at the sink, her accent thicker than usual. Catherine knew that she was concerned.

"I…yes, it all went well. At first." She sat down at the kitchen table.

"These ladies, they had doubts about you?"

"It isn't that. I'd done the usual work—picked up details on them from the local shops as myself, gossiped a little. You know."

That part had gone smoothly. It had been easy to check the local cemetery and see that Margaret Carlton's grave was untended. For backup, she had a rumour about the family's time before they came to Islington, and a tale from a garrulous greengrocer. Catherine knew how to read people, without needing her unreliable gift. The Aether did not need to stir itself to satisfy most séance goers.

"So…what is matter?" The landlady peered at a smudged glass, wiping it with her cloth.

"Something…something that reminded me of the past, that is

all. It's nothing."

"Da. Nothing, that is always frightening."

They shared a smile.

"I'll tell you some time, Mrs B. For the moment, I should rest."

"No dinner?"

"Later, if I may."

Catherine trudged up the stairs, her feet sore. Her imposture as Madame Rostov, the psychic from somewhere vague in Eastern Europe, involved far too much walking. Hansoms were expensive, on the little she had made so far, and she had always to make sure she wasn't observed in her transition between roles. She had learned far more than she wanted about the streets of London in her first six months. More comfortable boots would have to be her next major purchase.

Her bedroom on the first floor was too tidy. Mrs Bessovitch's work, but she could hardly complain. The rent was modest, nor were there any other lodgers at the moment, which made it a peaceful place.

"Is my home," the landlady said when Catherine asked about this. "If I wish company, I let my rooms. You are company. So..."

In the ancient, creaking wardrobe hung Mrs Bessovitch's cast-offs, ideal for Madame Rostov. Furs—not grand, even slightly moth-eaten, but with the right look for the part. Old-fashioned clothes, easily tacked (by the landlady) to approximate Catherine's taller, leaner figure.

Madame Rostov had been her landlady's idea, in a sense. Catherine, after her first winter in the capitol, needed shelter. Her savings were low, and previous lodgings had been unsafe, plagued by drunken fights. Then she had seen a notice in the paper. Quiet room available. Single lady only.

She walked to the address in Southwark on a raw March morning, and presented herself. With her black hair in disarray and her face scrubbed red by the wind, Mrs Bessovitch approved.

"You look like good Russian woman," she said as she made them a pot of tea. "I will like you."

"The room is still available?"

"Da. A young woman, she comes but she is pretty. She smiles too much. I do not think she knows life."

"And me?"

"You are not so pretty."

The blunt comment took Catherine by surprise, and she laughed, spilling her tea.

"You see?" said Mrs Bessovitch. "You understand."

When the landlady discovered that Catherine was earning her money, such as it was, as a medium offering herself for sittings and séances, she considered the matter seriously. Questions of spiritualism and psychic matters seemed to be of no interest to her, but she confessed a long love of performance, and the theatre.

"Who is this Miss Weatherhead? She is nobody." She reached into a sideboard drawer, eventually pulling out a sheaf of ancient theatre handbills. "The Flying Farinis. The Great Tai-Kin. Maskelyne the Magician." She waved the handbills at her lodger. "And here is young woman, no one knows her."

"Perhaps I should be Madame Bessovitch, the Russian Mind-Reading Miracle?"

Her landlady frowned. "Name is too long. Bad for spelling, also."

After some days, they settled on Madame Rostov. Catherine was introduced simply as the new lodger to some of Mrs Bessovitch's European friends. Polish women who worked on the markets, other widows whose time was spent laundering or on street barrows. A rabbi from St Petersburg, and a number of small children who seemed to belong to everyone. Some were Jewish, some were Orthodox, which Catherine didn't quite understand. Her landlady didn't make any obvious religious observance.

Catherine learned quickly, picking up useful words, comments on faraway lands—enough to pass casual muster and to know when she was out of her depth. A friend of Mrs Bessovitch had, for a small fee, provided various papers establishing Rostov's credentials, including a forged recommendation from a genuine minor member of the Polish nobility, now deceased.

"It's still easy to be caught out," Catherine admitted one night. "If they ask too much…"

"You have troubled past," said Mrs Bessovitch.

The comment had startled Catherine, until she realised Madame Rostov was the person under discussion.

"Yes," she managed to say, aping a faint Russian accent. "One that I do not care to discuss."

Which was true for both of her lives.

◦◦◦

Sleep did not come, not in the wave of exhaustion for which she had hoped. It brushed her, caressed her, but would not stay. Each time she was on the verge of nodding off, she slid into a blur of unwanted visions. Some were nonsense, but of the two particular scenes which came again and again, she saw a man drowning—and a woman being strangled. The former was the session in Islington, turning itself over inside her head again and again; the latter was something she had hoped to bury, to lose sight of forever.

Islington had uncovered it once more.

At three in the morning she got out of bed and paced around the room for a while, but that was no help. She went downstairs.

The landlady was at the kitchen table, a pan of milk on the stove.

"I hear you walk up there, I think maybe warm drink."

There was a small bottle of brandy on the table, waiting.

"I didn't mean to disturb you," said Catherine.

"Is no matter."

She sat down opposite Mrs Bessovitch, the stone slabs of the kitchen floor a welcome coolness for the soles of her feet. The woman cocked her head, staring.

"Is yesterday, da? When you sit for these people. This 'nothing' you speak of."

"I saw…a death, I think. Images of one, I mean, during the sitting."

"A death. Tch, this is not so much." She stood up and went to fuss with the pan and two large stoneware mugs. Bringing them over, she added a generous shot of spirits to both. "My grandfather, he was shot by Prussians. My father, was a tavern fight. Drunk." She shrugged. "Two of my sisters, they die of cholera, and last month, you remember my friend Yentl Przkowski? She fall on stairs, break her neck."

"That's…dreadful."

"Is what we are. My other sister, she has six children, all healthy, one a doctor. So, I say Tch, we accept it."

"It's not that." Catherine let the brandy ease her. "I 'saw' a murder

40

being committed, as if I stood there in the room."

"Death to come?" Mrs Bessovitch looked more interested. "Now you are, what is word, fortune-teller...clairvoyant! That is it. You know them, these people in picture your head makes?"

"No, not at all. Nor could I tell where this dreadful thing took place, nothing beyond the immediate surrounds. It could have occurred years ago, it could be yet to happen. How can I know? It... shook me."

She described the scene in the bathroom, slowly at first, but the details came back more easily than she had expected. It was as clear to her as if the bathwater was swilling around her feet. She omitted only the names she had heard. Tether. Silas Smith. Edwin Dry.

More brandy found its way into the milk.

"I am not spiritual woman," said Mrs Bessovitch when the story was complete. "Not hearing ghosts or such things. Maybe this is from head of one of your ladies, at sitting?"

"Possibly."

"Katerina, whatever is gift you have, you should trust. You are true cake. Madame Rostov is, what we say, icing. Decoration for ladies and their purses."

Catherine nodded. "I suppose so."

"Anna Bessovitch is like stone, she has no thoughts to give away. So with me, you must listen with your ears. These others, I think their heads are soft, like sponge."

They laughed together.

"I'll try and sleep now."

"Good. I get brandy to myself. And you forget man with hat. What is your tomorrow?"

Catherine winced.

"Family," she said.

Mrs Bessovitch knew enough to need no elaboration.

FIVE

Mary Jane ran from the site of Stuart Brevard's attack for at least a quarter of a mile. She took a northeastward direction through Stepney, across the Regents Canal at Bridge Street, to become lost in the neighbourhoods of the Holy Trinity Liberty. Finally, Mary Jane slowed to a walk. Still trembling in fear, she continued to look back frequently, making certain the man hadn't caught up with her. Larger and no doubt faster than Mary Jane, he could be anywhere among the many using the footways and streets. Hidden behind the reflections on the glass of a carriage window, he might watch her that very moment. She could only hope that her heel had damaged his foot enough to slow him.

She took the bottle of laudanum from the pocket under her top skirt, pulled the small cork, and took several tiny sips of the bitter amber liquid. Though some time would pass before she felt the effects of the tincture, she became calmer even as she put the drug away.

Mary Jane continued through Holy Trinity at a slower pace, northward at one crossing, eastward at the next, wanting even more distance from the site of the attack, while confusing her trail. She did her best to tidy her disheveled hair as she walked, and used a handkerchief moistened with saliva to clean the blood from her arm.

Putting the handkerchief away in her bodice, she discovered the leaf of paper, now wrinkled, with the sketch of the woman printed on it. The name beneath the image, Andriette, had been Mary Jane's name while at the Phoenix gay house. She decided the woman depicted looked more like Gabriella Gorse, a beautiful flaxen haired prostitute she knew. Like Mary Jane, Gabriella had once worked in a fine gay house in the West End. With her angry mouth, she had burned all her bridges and now worked the streets. Mary Jane didn't trust her.

The attack having come so close to Thomas Morganstone's apartments, she assumed Stuart Brevard had somehow tracked her there. Relentless, the man would keep coming for her until he succeeded in making her pay for what she'd done to Harris.

In Mile End Road, Mary Jane began to feel less unease and turned around, trying to think of where she might go. She couldn't return to Thomas Morganstone's apartments or Mrs Buki's Laughing

Magpie because Stuart Brevard had tracked her to both. After leaving employment at the Laughing Magpie, Mary Jane had gone to live at Gander's Bush, a brothel belonging to Mrs Buki's sister, Mrs Carthy. Despite the amount of time Mary Jane had spent in recent months away at Thomas Morganstone's apartments, she remained on good terms with Mrs Carthy and could return to her brothel anytime, but her run-down house was a place of last resort.

Joseph Fleming's beaming face appeared ahead on the footway bobbing up and down as he walked. The two walking in front of him moved off to the left, and she saw his full form, dressed for labour. He was a handsome fellow, despite his slightly bowed legs.

Clearly he'd seen her.

Mary Jane looked about for an excuse for her appearance, saw the low limbs of trees along the verge, and came up with a lie.

Joseph Fleming, a criminal of all work and associate of Thomas Morganstone's, also worked as a plasterer. She'd made love to Joseph several times while staying at Thomas's apartments. Fleming had always been good to her and anything but demanding. Despite knowing her profession, he had shown a romantic interest in her and had recently asked her to come live with him at his room in Globe Road. He'd made it clear that if she did, he wouldn't expect her to cease her soliciting activities. That had surprised her.

Mary Jane had no interest in romance. She did want possible protection from the likes of Stuart Brevard, and a place to stay since she resisted going back to Gander's Bush.

"Mary Jane." Joseph said. Moving closer, he gained a look of concern. "Did you meet with harm somehow? There's blood on your arm, and your beautiful hair…"

"Yes," she said, "Clumsy, I were, allowed a low-lying limb of one of these trees to snag me as I walked past." She gestured toward the verge.

"Well, I'm glad it wasn't worse."

"I ought not to have given you my true name." she said with a playful, chiding tone.

"Oh… yes," he said, looking chastened, "Pardon me, Ginger."

"I forgive you," she said with a chuckle. "If your offer still stands, I would be delighted to come share your room."

His smile, like that of a little boy, knew no bounds. He laughed and caught her up in his arms.

Though Mary Jane giggled for him, she hoped she'd not just made a terrible mistake. Something about the man was too appealing. To her vexation, she'd found herself thinking about him when he wasn't around.

"I'm on my way to a job site," he said with a slight frown. "My lodgings are at 200 Globe Road, number 2. 'Tis at the crossing with Green Street. I can give you my key. I'll need to return shortly after seven o'clock this evening. I'll get you your own key as soon as I can."

Mary Jane didn't relish the idea of being alone with her fears in Fleming's room at such an hour, waiting to let him in.

"No," she said after consideration, "I have a place I can stay for the night. Shall I find you tomorrow, then?"

"Yes." He bent forward and gave her a delightful kiss.

Mary Jane didn't want to enjoy it as much as she did.

He walked away, glancing back with a smile.

She would go to Gander's Bush, after all. At least then she'd have a crib to satisfy a client if she found one.

Walking southwest along Mile End Road, Mary Jane seriously considered for the first time removing from London to make a start elsewhere in a place of safety, somewhere Stuart Brevard wouldn't easily find her.

Perhaps she would do well in America. Wherever she went, she'd need funds to make that fresh start.

The stolen necklace was worth two hundred pounds, if not more. Unfortunately, she could not get it from atop the armoire in her old room at the Phoenix without alerting those who would want to claim it. Still, if she could get the necklace, sell it to a fence, and combine the funds with what she had saved, about twenty-five pounds, then she'd have what she needed. Mary Jane had never had dealings with a fence, but thought that she'd gain at least half of the worth of the necklace. One hundred and twenty-five pounds would be enough for her to feel comfortable making the move. Of course she might go with less, since soliciting would always see her through, yet she would miss much about London, and the funds would be a small compensation.

When a child, I had no need of money to go on an adventure.

With fear still dogging her, she willingly retreated into pleasant recollection.

Always the same, Mary Jane's earliest memories came to her from a time in Ireland. There, she found Mum's beautiful green eyes and musical voice, Papa's stern gaze and hard mouth, her sister's petulance, and her five older brothers, each one a different mystery.

She also found rain so gentle it didn't fall, just hung in the air beneath woollen-grey skies. The complaints of long gone sheep and crows came to her magically out of morning mists that hugged the ground. She smelled the thick brown odour—like dirt burning—of peat smoke rising from chimneys. The vapour of Papa's breath on cold evenings, carrying the sweet-rotten aroma of whiskey, lingered there still.

Of Mary Jane's own concerns of the time, only the green stains on the knees of all her white stockings came to her. They were badges of honour, from slipping in the dew and falling in the weeds. Mum wasn't pleased, but the patches of colour reminded Mary Jane of escapes from family, and her tidy adventures in the fields around their lodgings.

A small girl with few worries, Mary Jane had been happy and fearless.

"Do you know what danger is, girl?" Papa asked. Tall and thin, with straight, sandy hair and a pocked face, Papa could have been a frightening scarecrow.

Mary Jane's brother, Johnto, had captured her on that day and carried her home. He stood holding her head so she faced Papa and couldn't turn away.

She didn't understand Papa's question then. At the time, the word, *danger*, seemed a curious one. Beyond the stern look he gave her, Mum, behind him, smiled. For all Mary Jane knew, danger was the spanking she got, and still it was worth the pain to go missing.

No further recollections remained of Ireland. A grey body of water passed beneath her, separating Mary Jane from the land of her birth, and life had begun anew in Wales.

Though, we start as such foolish and vulnerable creatures, so often that is our time of greatest happiness.

A child may not need to earn, but I most certainly do. I must work to gain what I'll need in case I fail to recover the necklace.

Mary Jane turned south into Burdett Road, paused to use the

urinal near the cabmen's shelter, and considered hiring the Hansom cab that stood at the kerb. To ride would be faster, more pleasant, and safer than walking the nearly two miles to Gander's Bush in Breezer's Hill.

No, her fear had diminished. She felt confident that she'd lost Stuart Brevard for the nonce, and she had to save her funds.

Having turned southwest into Bridge Street to cross back over the Regents Canal, Mary Jane saw the woman who had helped her earlier, walking along the other side of the road with what looked like the same sack of laundry she'd wielded as a weapon. Something about her large eyes and full mouth were hauntingly familiar.

Recklessly, Mary Jane hurried into the road, almost falling beneath the wheel of a fast-moving growler. She dodged by the vehicle and got to the other side of the road in time to catch the woman.

"All my thanks to you!" she said, somewhat breathless from her dash across.

Startled, the woman dropped her sack and stopped, her hands out to the sides, as if reaching for balance. "Oh…my," she said, "you're…"

"I'm Ginger," Mary Jane said. "You saved me from that bludger in Bale Street."

The woman appeared to be forty-something years old. Her dark hair had greyed at the temples. She stood a good six inches taller than Mary Jane.

"Miss Jennifer Weatherhead," she said a bit reluctantly, her beautiful grey-green eyes looking Mary Jane up and down.

A good thing she didn't take the time to look me over before deciding to help! She recognised in Jennifer the discomfort people often displayed when confronted with a fallen woman. Mary Jane didn't hold it against her.

Then it occurred to her why the woman seemed familiar—she looked much like Mum!

Mother had died a couple of weeks before Mary Jane's eighth birthday, less than two years after the family arrived in Wales and settled in Carmarthenshire. Recollections of Mum had always been precious. Her happy expressions, her laughter, and her warm and graceful bearing still lived in her grown daughter's memory.

Mary Jane beamed at the woman, and that seemed to make Jennifer *more* uncomfortable.

"I did what decency demanded," she said. "I'm glad to have helped." She bent to pick up the sack of laundry.

"Is that the same sack?"

"Yes," Jennifer said. "I went back for it. Had to wrestle it away from a woman who tried to claim the clothing. It holds my evening's work...." She paused uncomfortably. "...Mending for Bryte's Laundry." Again she paused, looking at the pavement. "Now, I must be on my way. I'm expected at home."

"Again, I am most grateful. You are truly brave to have helped. Good day."

"Good day to you."

Mary Jane watched her go. Looking at the woman brought her delight, as if she were seeing her mother alive again. She had a desire to follow, but didn't want to frighten Jennifer any more than she had already.

Instead, still thinking of Mum, she continued southwest toward Gander's Bush.

SIX

The house where Catherine's cousins lodged in Stepney had once been as respectable as that of Mrs Bessovitch's, but here the mortar was crumbling, the roof tiles in disorder. The roof itself sagged, making the top floor uninhabitable, and bold red brick had long since blackened. Cramped between other tenement houses in a similar condition, it never failed to depress her by its very nature.

She knocked on the ill-hung front door, and waited. Already she was being noted by passers-by, and she imagined them trying to fit her into a suitable category—tradeswoman or dolly-mop, regular or stranger. The looks were not friendly.

Clarissa Weatherhead answered the door at last.

"Catherine? I did not expect you."

The woman's face was narrow and care-worn. Pale skin clung to high cheekbones and wrinkled around thin lips which never quite closed, making her seem far older than her forty or so years.

"Don't let me disturb you. I merely thought I'd enquire—"

"Come in. She's no better." Clarissa glanced upwards as she ushered the younger woman into a narrow hallway. "She sleeps more today, which is something."

"Might I see her?"

Clarissa smoothed down her patched sewing smock. "If you must."

They climbed the dimly-lit stairs with caution. Catherine could smell the damp, and see faint blooms on the wallpaper where mould was finding its own residence. In places the paper had been scrubbed with some form of bleaching agent, which only served to expose the sad state of the plasterwork beneath.

There were two shabby rooms on this floor, barely habitable. Whilst four people shared the bedroom to the right, the other had only one occupant, the dying matriarch of this branch of the Weatherhead family. Whether this arrangement was out of respect, or fear of disease spreading to the others, Catherine did not know. As Clarissa herself was hardly healthy, she inclined towards the latter.

Levinia Weatherhead lay in relative comfort under the only coverlet in the house, pillows stuffed with rags and off-cuts to prop up her head. Fine grey hair spread in tangles on the patched pillowcases, and her nightgown, a memory of better days, was in disarray, exposing one shrunken breast. Clarissa hurried forward and re-arranged her mother-in-law's clothes, drawing the coverlet higher.

"Who is there?" A weak, querulous voice from the bed.

"Mama, it's Cousin Catherine, come to see you."

"Joshua's girl?"

Closed eyelids flickered, but did not open. Catherine sat on the edge of the bed, ignoring the tang of sweat and stale urine. She began to smooth out her aunt's hair, but Clarissa stopped her.

"It sets her off," she warned. "The coughing."

Catherine drew back her hand.

"How are you, Aunt Levinia? Comfortable, I hope?"

"I must…have words with Joshua's girl. Before…"

Clarissa leaned closer, cold-faced.

"Before what, Mama?"

But the old lady was asleep again, her breathing ragged. The air was cold, the window-pane cracked. There was no fire in the small hearth.

"I had some good fortune the other day," said Catherine as they went back downstairs. "Mrs Merson wished to be rid of some trifles from her jewellery—paste and the like. I had no use for them, so I sold them to a costumier." She reached into her purse, and brought out three half crowns. "Coal is so expensive now, and with the children, and Aunt Levinia's chest…"

"We manage."

Catherine bit back a retort. "I feel so guilty," she said, "And I'm kept so busy, I can rarely call on the old dear. Please, to assuage my conscience."

Clarissa took the coins, feigning reluctance. "Well, as you say, it is the devil to get good coal. The cheap stuff spits so."

It was a charade all the more painful because both knew the truth of it. Any coal was a stretch for her cousins.

Her entry fee paid, Catherine accepted the offer of a cup of tea, to be taken whilst her cousin continued at her labours, sewing and mending for those who could afford it. Workmen's overalls and aprons were heaped in one corner of the small front room—a bounty from a local factory, Clarissa explained.

"All to be patched by Thursday—at a fair rate, as well. There may be more to follow, God willing."

"That sounds promising."

False smiles flashed between them. They exchanged news, such as they wished to share. The weather had been mild; cheese was not of the quality it had once been. The children, Benjamin and Maisie, were in good health. As was Clarissa's sister-in-law Jennie, who lived with them.

"And how is your Mrs Merson?" asked Clarissa.

Non-existent, Catherine wanted to admit. Part of our usual game.

For months she had constructed the pretence that she was companion to Amelia Merson, a widow from Streatham with adequate means. It was a story which gave her both an excuse to visit her relations as little as possible, and a convenient explanation as to how she could offer small but regular amounts towards her aunt's care. Towards the family's care. Most importantly, it allowed her to conceal her work as Madame Rostov from her family—here in London and back in Yorkshire.

"Oh, you can guess," said Catherine. "Temperamental, as the elderly can be. Why, only the other day…"

An invented tale of marmalade and missing spoons followed, raising the occasional nod from the woman sewing. Her fingers were nimble, but the tips were red and cracked from the work, and occasionally she paused for a hollow cough.

Had Catherine liked her relative at all, she might have felt more pity. The woman had married Catherine's blood-cousin Charles, but Catherine doubted she would ever have become friends with this lean and waspish soul, even if Charles had lived.

The photograph was on the mantelpiece, as always. A plain man, made more interesting by his naval uniform. A little old for a lieutenant, a place-holder rather than a climber. As an officer aboard HMS Penelope, on Harwich guard-duty, he had provided for his family and engendered moderate respect. And though Charles had been eighteen years Catherine's senior, she remembered the young man who played hoops with her when she was a child. The young man who had slipped her toffees during occasional visits to Keighley, despite her father's disapproval. He had seemed more handsome back then.

"I shall never forgive any of them," said Clarissa, following the direction of her cousin's gaze. "Caille, the business partners, the lawyers."

Spoiled rations had killed Lieutenant Weatherhead the year before. War and the perils of the sea had spared him; the shoddy practices of a victualling company had ended him. One of the many companies of Frederick Caille, a name which was spat out at Brantridge Street.

"Not a shilling, not a penny did we see. Not even an expression of regret."

Catherine, who had heard the tale many times, nodded vaguely, her eyes still on the photograph. His half-pension barely fed and clothed the surviving family. The buckled silver frame, the only thing of value in the house, would be the last thing Clarissa would sell. Catherine gave her that—Clarissa retained some genuine affection for her dead husband. Or defiance in the face of the family's misfortune. It might also have been defiance.

She finished her cup of tea, placing it noisily back on the saucer. She needed to get away from this place.

"I am so very sorry—you know I am."

"Charles was fond of you," said Clarissa, but the words were tight, ungenerous, from those lips.

"And I of him...of you all." She added the second part, the lie, because it was what she had learned to do. "I fear I need to get back to my own work."

The other woman titled her head, eyes narrow. "She has nothing to leave you, you know."

They stared at each other, and then the older woman lowered her head.

"That was wrong of me," she said.

Silence paced the cluttered parlour, inspecting the cobwebs, until Catherine shuffled her feet.

"I could stay and sew with you for a while, if that would help."

"We both know that you're no seamstress." The shadow of a smile came with the words. Clarissa stood up, and they walked to the front door.

"Will you write to me if there is any change—in Aunt Levinia?"

"I shall, if I have time. At the post office, as usual?"

51

"Mrs Merson prefers it this way." Better that than the Weatherheads find out where she really lived, and what she did for those half crowns.

Catherine did not look back to see if her cousin remained at her door, watching. The morning was gone, and so was most of the money from her purse. There would be donations after tomorrow's sitting, if it went according to plan.

If. There were ways to assist the spirits, and it would do no harm to check her homework.

She found an omnibus heading south of the river, and after a short walk, bought a sixpenny bunch of roses from a flower-seller near St John's. Sad, late blooms, but they would serve.

Rain was coming, and the comet-shaped weathervane spun on the spire, high above the streets. Inside the musty church, three or four women were seeing to floral arrangements. The mid-week changeover, an ideal time for talk. It was her second, carefully planned visit.

"Hello, dear," said a woman by the font. "Nice to see you back."

Catherine held out her own floral donation and made over-kind comments about some of the others. There was a hierarchy here, and a set of rules more closely adhered to than those of a palace. Modesty, and open ears. She accepted a few menial tasks, as befitting a relative newcomer, and listened as closely as she could.

Confounding her drab initial appearance, the short, round Mrs Glebe, in her second-hand clothes, was a mischievous woman. Her eyes were sharp, and her smile gave her face its own attraction. She was a fine source of local gossip, and had no fear of listing the various peculiarities of her neighbours.

One of those neighbours was a "too good for her own cat" spinster who had engaged Madame Rostov to sit the following evening. Miss Bournelle had bunions, a rebellious cook and a niece in India. By offering to fetch a fresh pail of water, and by assisting with certain minor arrangements of stems, Catherine soon had Miss Bournelle's details fixed, with one or two corrections on what she had heard during her last visit.

These details were the meat and drink of the jobbing medium, unless she or he were too proud to have a little earthly assistance. The name of the niece's milliner in London; an unfortunate incident with a dog-trap some years ago, and more of Miss Bournelle's medical history than might be had from a personal physician, were all offered gratis by Mrs Glebe over an hour's work in the church.

"She 'as one o' them mediums coming t'morrow," Mrs Glebe confided. "A Roosian, or somethink like."

"Really?" Catherine snipped a dying rosebud from its stem.

"'Struth. Mind you, many o' them's no better than swindlers. Tell you any old tale, they will, 'bout Uncle Alf meaning to leave 'is will in the sideboard, but being mistook of 'isself, like."

Catherine laughed.

"I'm sure you're right, Mrs Glebe. Let us hope that dear Miss Bournelle has more sense than to fall for any old nonsense."

Counting her time well-spent, she made her apologies and quit St John's to face the bluster of rain outside. A September shower, not yet cold enough to trouble, and an easy walk back to Mrs Bessovitch's. Yet as she faced the grey pall of rain, her good humour failed her.

Aunt Levinia would die soon. Clarissa and Jennie would lose the force which had driven them for the last year and a half; poor Benjamin and Maisie would be stripped of another face they knew.

She slowed, the rain soaking her coat, and her mind in conflict.

To flee the North, having managed to escape expectations there, only to end up with ties here in London, seemed unfair, unjust. It was her own fault, in part. She had looked up her cousins when she first arrived, not knowing the precise details of their circumstances, only that Charles was dead. It had been intended as a politeness, and no more.

That first sight of the decrepit house on Brantridge Street, an address which meant nothing to her beforehand, had told her much. Matters had not improved when she stepped inside and learned how low this branch of the family had sunk, for it was then that affectionate memories of Charles had trapped her...

A bicyclist swerved across her path, swore, and then apologised as he careened on down the street. Southwark reared around her, churches and tenements challenging the pewter sky. There would be blood-pudding at the lodgings. Dumplings sour with turned milk and caraway; cabbage stewed in butter.

There was no conflict in knowing that you were hungry.

SEVEN

In 1869, when the family arrived in Wales and settled in Carmarthen, Mum would have been about the same age as Jennifer Weatherhead. That year, Mary Jane became six years old.

Papa took a gaffer position at the Morganstone Ironworks.

The Kelly family—father, mother, and seven children—lived in a two-room, company-built brick cottage on the River Towy, alongside five other identical homes. The children had the back room. Their beds shared the chamber with six chairs and a table large enough for the family to all sup together. When that happened, three stood. Mary Jane and her older sister, Ruth, slept together in one bed, their brothers, Johnto, Jack, Dylan, Kevin, and Iason, wedged together like oiled herring in a tin, slept in another. Their parents had the front room, which also served as kitchen.

They had come from much humbler single room-lodgings in Limerick, Ireland. In the new house, Mary Jane felt smaller.

Papa warned of the River Towy, fifty yards down the hill behind the house. "Don't go within ten feet of the water. At least one child each year drowns in that river. Hasn't claimed the year's victim yet. Don't tempt it."

Alive with light and movement, with strange smells, swelling with the rains or running low in dryer weather to expose hidden treasures, the River Towy was home for all manner of fish and birds. The Kelly children had not known so much life before, and they all wanted to play in the water.

Papa away at work one day, Mum told them, "Want the adventure all the more, you will, to have it denied. Even if he does not know this, I do."

She helped her children find shallows where they could wade in the water safely.

They all kept the secret from Papa, a strict and demanding man.

Mary Jane's brothers found work so they might add to the household income. Johnto, Jack, and Kevin went to work at the ironworks with Papa. Dylan and Iason worked in woollen mills. Ruth and Mary Jane considered themselves lucky since they stayed home to help Mum with the housekeeping. She taught her girls to read and write, something denied her sons because they spent so little time at home.

Mary Jane enjoyed a good life in Wales for almost two years, until a day shortly before her eighth birthday, in the spring of 1871.

In the breezy afternoon of that day, she and Mum worked together hanging laundry out to dry. Ruth was spending the day with her beau. The clothesline, strung from posts, was protected from the strongest winds in a flat spot halfway down the slope behind the house. The fat clouds above started low and built high and fluffy into the bright blue sky. Good daydreaming clouds. A beautiful day in a lovely life.

"And what will you be wanting for your birthday," Mum asked.

Just as Mary Jane decided upon her wish, a frivolous desire for a yellow bonnet she'd seen in a shop window, the wind shifted and came down the hill. A damp bed linen lost its pins, billowed out in the stiff breeze and seemed to swallow Mum. She cried out, fell, and rolled downhill. The linen cloth twisted around her, pinning her arms to her sides. Running after, Mary Jane could not catch up until they reached the upper edge of the steep river bank. She leapt, gripped an edge of the linen. Though addled from a hard fall, she'd caught the cloth in her hand.

She knew some small relief, then saw the fright in Mum's eyes as she rolled out of the sheet, clawing for the verge. She caught the linen in one hand, and the cloth slipped from Mary Jane's grasp.

Hope turned to horror. Mum and the linen flew over the embankment. Falling several feet into the river, she went under, again, wrapped in the cloth.

Neither of them could swim. Too afraid, Mary Jane did not jump in to help Mum.

She struggled to the surface, but the current carried her downstream.

In a panic, Mary Jane followed along the bank, trying to find a way to help, looking for a way down and a shallow where her mother might come out. Mum rose to the surface several times, gasping for air, weaker each time. Mary Jane could not keep up. Her mother disappeared around a bend. Fallen brush and a thicket of small trees stopped Mary Jane. She turned back for help.

No one answered her frantic knocks upon the neighbouring cottage doors. Those who lived in the homes, men, women, and children, were all away trying to earn a crust. Mary Jane saw no life on the river that day, no fish, no birds, just the cruel water and lifeless rocks. The wind had blown the daydreams out of the fat clouds in the cold blue sky. She returned to the fallen brush and tangled thicket, pushed through, and searched farther downriver to no avail. Passing through the thick wooded patch had not been as difficult as she'd imagined. With that realisation, the child knew the depths of shame and regret for the first time, a pain greater than any she'd known before.

Johnto discovered where exhaustion had left Mary Jane, in a patch of violets growing beside the water. A few weeks earlier, she and Mum had picnicked there because they loved the violets.

Johnto carried Mary Jane home.

She wept for weeks, it seemed, hid herself away whenever she could.

Then came the blame from Papa. He didn't say how he felt, but she saw the anger, the accusation in his eyes.

Mary Jane had an accusation of her own.

Mum died because I didn't try hard enough. If only I'd pushed through the thicket instead of turning back for help.

Johnto moved into the front room with Papa. Ruth left home, married a cooper named Evans in Swansea. Mary Jane slept alone.

Life took a dark turn, and she thought her days would never truly recover their light.

On occasion, she went back to the flowering patch where she and Mum had picnicked. Mary Jane picked violets, and threw them into the water for her mother.

⚜

Papa sent Mary Jane to work for Mrs Margaret Morganstone in 1872. Her husband, Douglas P. Morganstone, the owner of the ironworks where Papa worked, had gone missing in 1870 when the passenger steamship, The City of Boston, "disappeared" somewhere in the Atlantic between Halifax, Nova Scotia and Liverpool. Mrs Morganstone had managed her husband's enterprises since.

She had asked those in trusted positions at the ironworks if any had a child about her daughter's age, ten years, willing to work as a live-in housemaid.

Papa offered Mary Jane, a girl of nine years at the time. The day he told her of her fate, she heard him saying "good riddance" though he did not indeed say those words. Of course, he would collect her wages for the family and Mary Jane would receive none that she might spend as she chose.

Even with a dread of displeasing her future mistress and the cruelty that might follow, she felt glad to leave home and go to live at Bryn Haearn, the Morganstone home. Not that Papa harmed her. Well…, one willow switch whipping that stung awfully for a lie she told. But worse, Mary Jane suffered his cold silence, the disapproving looks, his never once wanting the best for her. Even if Mrs Morganstone whipped or starved her, that would be better.

A conversation Mary Jane overheard between Papa and Johnto sometime after Mr Morganstone went missing gave her some hope that she'd be treated fairly in her future position. Home from the day's labour, they sat together sharing a pail of bitter Papa had brought home. Ignored, Mary Jane kneaded dough for dinner biscuits on the counter beside the pump.

"I thought to myself," Papa said, "a woman, a fine mess she'll make of the ironworks. Yet, she's done well."

"I much prefer the Missus," Johnto said shaking his head. "A hard man, Mr Morganstone."

Papa nodded. "Rode me like a bit of blood." He shook his head slowly, staring perhaps into recollection. "I won't miss him."

"The men are much happier under Mrs Morganstone."

"Yes, production is up. From Mr Collins I hear she'll share some of the wealth with us this year." Papa paused to look Johnto in the eye. "You didn't hear that from me."

Bryn Haearn, a great two-story granite house of many rooms built on a hill, had projecting gables and a high, steep roof containing several dormer windows. The interior held ornate woodwork, decorative plaster relief, and leadlight windows, each a different design with stained glass at the top in blues and greens.

On Mary Jane's first day at Bryn Haearn, she had expected the housekeeper to greet her. Instead, she found herself with Mrs Morganstone. Standing before the finely-dressed lady of the house in the marble vestibule of her beautiful home, Mary Jane suffered embarrassment for her worn clothes. Her heart in her throat, ringing her sweaty hands behind her back, she couldn't think how to act.

"Please call me Peggy," Mrs Morganstone said.

"I couldn't do that, Madam."

"Yes, but you may."

The girl didn't know what to make of the woman.

"You may call me Mary Jane, should you choose to, Madam," she said sheepishly.

"Thank you. I'd be delighted to do that."

Though short and small, Mrs Morganstone had a confidence about her. Her brown eyes had a youthful warmth. A single dimple appeared in her left cheek with her lopsided, slightly mischievous smile. She kept her nearly black hair with tidy pins. Among her sensibly drab clothing, one small brightly coloured piece always stood out, perhaps peacock-blue cuffs, a new-leaf-green collar, or the edge of a red handkerchief poking out of a breast pocket. That day, she wore a purple enamel brooch of columbine blossoms.

She showed Mary Jane to her chamber, a cozy room in the below-ground area. The room had a chest of drawers, a coal grate, a small bed that looked soft and warm, and a window high in the wall that looked up toward a flower garden. A coral-coloured rose in bloom stood outside the window in what she'd later learn was a walled garden behind the house.

"The water closet down the hall you'll share with the other servants."

An indoor toilet that Mary Jane would be permitted to use? She could not believe her good fortune.

The woman seemed an angel for a moment. Then, having heard adults in her life speak of their misgivings toward the well-to-do, and remembering Mrs Morganstone's crooked smile, a deep suspicion of her set in, and Mary Jane wondered what sort of mischief she were up to. Had the woman made her out to be a fool somehow?

Trying to discern the truth, Mary Jane looked Mrs Morganstone in the eyes.

The woman allowed the child's piercing gaze, smiled easily, comfortably. No mischief did Mary Jane see.

She set aside her misgivings, at least for the moment, and followed Mrs Morganstone back to the ground floor and her daughter's chamber.

"Elen," she said. "We have a new housemaid, Miss Kelly."

"Mary Jane, please," Mary Jane said, and winced at her boldness.

She saw in one corner of the room a girl about her age, sitting at a small desk. She had an impression that the girl had been reading before she looked up. Elen had long brown hair and dark eyes, like her mother.

"So pleased to meet you," she said in a proud, crisp voice.

She didn't get up, which Mary Jane thought strange until she rolled out from behind the desk in a wheeled contraption.

Later, she would learn that Elen's legs never grew properly, yet a happy child she seemed. She had seating with large wheels in front and small ones in back. Below the seat, a foldout footrest rode high to support her little feet. The large wheels had pushrims so she could propel herself about.

"Will you play with me?" she asked. "I have lots of toys."

Mary Jane's eyes took in the rest of the room, the small bed in one corner, in the other a trunk and a set of shelves loaded with toys; dolls, stuffed animals, and miniatures, including a chandler's shop and a fine home.

Her eyes must have grown large, and she imagined her mouth dropped open. Mrs Morganstone's dimple appeared with her broad smile. Elen giggled.

"Do you like my doll house?" she asked. "The wee housekeeper and the tiny valet are in love."

Mary Jane found herself frowning at the thought.

"What's the matter?" Elen asked.

"Domestics most often have to leave service to marry," Mary Jane said carefully, thinking she might regret the words. "How shall they earn?"

"Oh, I shan't worry," Elen said, "the master and lady of the house are not entirely stuffy. They approve. They shall permit the servants to stay on and live in the guest house."

Mary Jane looked for a smaller house, and didn't see one.

"The guest house is in the trunk," Mrs Morganstone said. Her voice dropped to a whisper. "She pretends they have not built the dwelling yet."

"It is a surprise," Elen said, shushing her mother with a forefinger across her lips, "a nuptial gift. Now, be quiet, lest they hear."

Since Mary Jane could tell that Mrs Morganstone was willing to play along, she made a show of vigorously nodding her support for Elen's admonishment. "You don't want to spoil it," she told Mrs Morganstone.

Elen beamed at Mary Jane.

"Of course, you're right," Mrs Morganstone said, smiling.

Then and there, Mary Jane knew she liked Elen.

Her mother seemed pleased that the two girls got along.

Back in the area, Mrs Morganstone took Mary Jane to the housekeeper's office, and introduced her to Miss Mateland, a grey-haired woman with a pointy nose and something of a dewlap beneath her weak chin. Though all business in her black and white uniform, she had warmth in her tone when she spoke. Mary Jane was given two sets of a black and grey uniform. Miss Mateland explained the household rules and housemaid's duties, then gave Mary Jane a leaf of paper with all that she'd explained written down in a manner easy to read and understand.

Mrs Morganstone stood by, listening.

All was much as Mary Jane had expected except for a curious two hour period after luncheon each day. For that time, the instructions read, "Help Elen with anything she desires."

"Get settled in today, and be ready to start tomorrow," Miss Mateland said.

"Yes, Miss," Mary Jane said.

The housekeeper left her office to attend to other duties.

"If you'd like," Mrs Morganstone said, as they took the stairs back to ground level, "go play with Elen. Ask her to show you her collection of stereograms. My favourites are the ones of American Indians. Such interesting faces."

Mary Jane stood staring at her, not understanding. "Won't Miss Mateland become upset with me?"

"We have a special understanding."

"But the help doesn't play with members of the family they serve," Mary Jane said, feeling awkward to be telling Mrs Morganstone her business.

"Do you like Elen?" she asked.

"Oh, yes," Mary Jane said.

Mrs Morganstone grinned. "I'll tell you a secret if you won't tell

Elen."

Mary Jane's vague suspicions about the woman returned.

"My beautiful daughter doesn't leave the house because she doesn't like feeling different from other children. She says they look at her funny. I have had companions brought to the house for her, ones that have a crippled family member and are accustomed to the limitations. Elen complains that I hire them to be her friends, and she shies away from them, embarrassed. We had a young scullery maid, Bethany, who became Elen's best friend. With the kitchen staff, I worked out adjustments to the schedule to allow Bethany time to play with Elen. My daughter was broken-hearted when the poor girl died of grippe nearly a year ago. Elen retreated from life afterward and lost interest in her lessons, especially those concerning social graces. 'I shall never need to know how to be with people,' she said. Nearly broke my heart."

"You brought me here to be her friend?" Mary Jane asked.

"Only if you want to be. I leave the decision up to you. You'll work so she doesn't believe I pay you to be a companion. Should you choose to take the time in the afternoon to play, please promise not to tell her."

Although unsure of the arrangement and still concerned that such a thing would draw the ire of the housekeeper, Mary Jane nodded her head. "Yes, I promise."

You mustn't let Papa find out, she thought, uncertain why that seemed good advice. Intuition told her that he wouldn't want her to have fun while toiling for the family.

She played with Elen that afternoon. Mrs Morganstone invited Mary Jane to attend the lessons she gave her daughter in the early evening before dinner. The lessons had three parts—reading and writing, maths, and one concerning speech and social graces: elocution and etiquette.

During that first lesson at Bryn Haearn, Elen drew the new housemaid into the work at hand. They both read, competed to solve their maths, and practiced pronunciations with tongue twisters that made them laugh.

Their favourite was by an American woman named Carolyn Wells.

Betty Botta bought some butter;

"But," she said, "this butter's bitter!
If I put it in my batter
It will make my batter bitter.
But a bit o' better butter
Will but make my batter better."

"You'll be fine ladies yet," Mrs Morganstone told the girls.

"Yes, we nearly have all the ingredients," Elen said, giggling. "We need but a—"

They laughed themselves to tears.

Elen insisted that Mary Jane attend all her lessons. Allowances were made in the work schedule to permit her even more time in the afternoons with Elen. As housemaid, Mary Jane did little work. While she feared the resentment of the other help, most of the domestic servants were so pleased to see Elen come out of her shell, they readily accepted Mary Jane's absence from duty.

Thus began the second happy period of Mary Jane's life. Four carefree years passed by too quickly.

⌁

When Mary Jane was twelve years old, Elen's cousin, Thomas Morganstone came to live at Bryn Haearn. His parents had perished when their home in Pembroke caught fire and burned to the ground. Thomas had jumped from a window to escape the fire, had spent months in hospital, and had come to Bryn Haearn with his limb healed.

Mary Jane found him handsome, his smile spellbinding. He had light brown, curly hair, grey eyes framed with dark lashes, and lively eyebrows. Though a sixteen-year-old boy, he became a companion for the girls. He loved making things. With tools he'd brought with him, he made a stable for Elen's miniature horses from the wood of crates discovered in one of the outbuildings.

"Would you make a gazebo for the lovers?" Elen asked.

"Yes, I'd be happy to do so," he said, bowing low as if he were not her equal.

Mrs Morganstone bought better wood for him to use, hand tools, and a miniature lathe and saw, powered with a treadle.

When done building the gazebo, he said, "Let's make a whole village."

Elen and Mary Jane heartily agreed to help. Thomas did most of the work. The many buildings he made matched the scale of her doll house, guest house, and chandler's shop.

Mrs Morganstone bought new pieces for their effort, furniture for the homes and businesses, small wagons, carriages, animals for the streets, and tiny people. Elen and Mary Jane sewed curtains for the windows, and clothes for the figures that populated the village. Mary Jane learned to paint, and created portraits, landscapes, and still lifes to hang on the interior walls of the houses and some of the establishments. One of the largest rooms at Bryn Haearn—what had been Douglas P. Morganstone's study—became home to their project. Most of the furniture was removed from the chamber to make room on the floor for the miniature village. The streets of the tiny town wide enough, Elen wheeled through them in her seating, careful not to upset the inhabitants.

Mrs Morganstone brought in tutors for Thomas, and allowed him to go to worksites in Carmarthen to watch construction and learn from what he saw. He would tell the girls about what he learned and show them how he used the knowledge in constructing the miniature village.

Mary Jane fell in love with Thomas. Though he treated her sweetly, he never seemed to look upon her in the manner she did him. Still, she knew happiness just being in his company.

Papa never knew how her circumstances had improved until one day after her thirteenth birthday when he arrived at Bryn Haearn to collect her wages and discovered her playing badminton in the front yard with Thomas Morganstone while Elen cheered them on. Mary Jane knew he came once a month to collect her wages, but he had not asked to see her. She had not seen him in several years, except for brief moments each Christmas.

By the look in his eyes as he watched her playing, she knew she was in for trouble.

Papa took Mary Jane from Bryn Haearn. Having no choice in the matter, she lost all semblance of dignity. She fought, wept, and cursed him as she was taken away. Ashamed that the Morganstones witnessed her wild tantrum, she became quiet on the way to her family's home, the company cottage on the River Towy. Once there, she withdrew further into herself, while anger and sadness in equal measure roiled within.

At first, Mary Jane had hoped to return to the Morganstones. She fancied they might come quickly, perhaps in the night, and take her away with them. Somehow, she knew that could not happen, and that she'd have to wait out Papa's anger.

Still a girl full of fancy, her most troubling concern was that Thomas might go on with his life without her, and she'd miss her chance to one day become his.

Papa found work for Mary Jane at the woollen mill where Iason had a position. Sister and brother walked the mile and a half to the mill together each morning at five o'clock along a deeply rutted dirt lane with a few stands of sturdy ash and oak trees here and there along its length. Until her feet became used to such a long walk, Iason let her ride him piggyback some of the way. She found a bond with him that she didn't have with her other siblings.

He had advanced over time to a comfortable position at the mill. A doubler, he operated a machine that made two-ply yarn. Mary Jane became a bowlminder, and cleaned raw wool, a malodorous and filthy job. She was miserable, having little strength for such labour.

After years of many comforts with the Morganstones, to coarse living she had returned. Mary Jane's oldest brothers had left home, Johnto for the army, and Jack for Australia. With Ruth married and gone to Swansea, Papa gave Mary Jane the task of cooking and cleaning for the family. The cottage had become a filthy hole, the privy a reeking horror. Iason saw her unhappiness and helped with the work when Papa couldn't see. She prepared plain food, made cruder still by her inexperience. To fend off complaints from the family, and in defence of her own palate, she learned to do better.

Mary Jane continued her education by reading anything she could get her hands on. Those who could read at her place of employment shared their books and periodicals with her. When done reading copies of Charles Dickens's periodical, *All the Year Round*, a woman at the mill, Mared Jones, loaned them to Mary Jane. In their pages she read short fiction stories, and some longer, serialised fiction. She also read articles involving international affairs and cultures, and social criticism.

Whenever Papa found her reading material, he disposed of it.

"Women with idle hands need books," he said. "I mean to see that you have too much to do."

Mary Jane hated her father.

Mrs Morganstone visited the Kelly home on three occasions after Mary Jane left Bryn Heaern, each time asking Papa to allow her to return. Mary Jane didn't hear their conversations. Iason told her something of what had been said during the woman's last visit.

"She offered to raise your wages and his," he said. "Surprised, I were, by what he turned down, as if he hadn't heard her. He were polite enough to keep his position at the ironworks, but later he grumbled about the insult of her visit. I cannot say I understand."

Then Thomas Morganstone came to the cottage. He arrived in the coarse clothes he wore to visit worksites.

"Please sir," he said, "at least permit your daughter to visit us."

Papa blocked the door so Mary Jane couldn't go out to greet him. "My daughter, she is," he said. "and I have decided that life with her family is best for her. One of us, she must endure what we do. Otherwise, my sons will not see the need for fairness."

Mary Jane could tell he didn't believe his own words. Obviously, he blamed Mary Jane for the loss of his wife and wanted her to suffer.

As Thomas went away, she cried.

Mary Jane missed her mother more than ever.

EIGHT

Catherine was relieved that the séance at Miss Bournelle's in Southwark offered no surprises, no gruesome visions. She played her part as the medium by filtering snippets of what she had heard on the streets and in the church, clamping on to the small slips and betrayals of the old lady's face, the nervous twitch of fingers on hearing a particular piece of information. It was easy enough, with some background, to steer a session in the right direction.

"Your niece reaches for you across the ocean…she has the finest bonnet, trimmed with blue Madras silk, which she so wants to send you…"

Because Catherine had heard that Miss Bournelle loved blue silk, and if a bonnet did ever arrive from India, the entire concept could be put down to Madame Rostov's insights. If it turned out to be red, then there must have been "disturbances" in the Aether. But she had seen into their souls and their desires, obviously. Safe enough ground.

She fielded an enquiry about a dead relative, picking up from the questions put to her by Miss Bournelle and an elderly sister that this relative had not had an easy life. The usual talk of a soul at rest, peace at last, served to meet that one.

During the two hours Catherine spent there, from the first wheeze of a harmonium to the patter of applause for her at the end, she kept herself closed, making no real attempt to use her gift. Islington had disturbed her. She concentrated on performing, and her approach worked well enough.

She left Miss Bournelle's not long after four in the afternoon, and still posing as Madame Rostov, treated herself to half an hour in a nearby ABC teashop. In the busy establishment, her poise and her loose, raven-tinted hair drew attention. The waitresses considered her with respect, and gentlemen touched their hats to her. Settled into a suitable corner-seat, she made a show of placing a book of Russian romantic poetry (barely readable) on the table, and chose to enjoy herself.

It was unfortunate that Madame Rostov took tea with lemon, but Catherine didn't let this spoil the moment. She even ordered cake. Miss Bournelle's had yielded one pound and seventeen shillings, and a recommendation to a Miss Chambers, who apparently dwelled in far fancier circles of society. A week's wages, if she were careful. From this she had to maintain her appearance and standing as a medium—and pay out the occasional gratuity to garrulous parlour maids and other servants or tradespeople. Of the remainder, some had to be put aside for the Weatherheads. All went down in her pocketbook at the end of each week. Part of her was still, reluctantly, a merchant's daughter.

Prices in the capitol were steep compared to her home town, and she had to rely on donations at the end of each sitting. Such donations were not always forthcoming—and there was always the tiresome game of pretending not to require anything.

Catherine had "seen" things since she first bled. There had been, with one terrible exception, little sense to the visions. One month it might be women sewing in a house she did not know; the next, nothing—or the sight of a dead bullock being dragged from the canal. What she saw was unpredictable, never under her control. At first it had seemed normal. She had assumed other people were the same—until children of her own age pulled away, older ones mocked her, and her father began taking his belt to her for talking "nonsense."

Keighley taught her not to mention what she saw.

As she slid unhappily into her twenties, serving in one of her father's shops, cooking and cleaning at home, she grew restive. Rebellious, he called it. Her initial idea had been to capitalise on her unreliable talent as an extra source of income, one which she could keep from her parents. Discreet sittings in nearby Bradford or Leeds, possibly, under the guise of a night out with friends.

For weeks she worked her way through borrowed spiritualist literature—her home town was awash with pamphlets and screeds, testimonials to miraculous voices from beyond the grave. Or "Beyond the Veil," as many preferred. She asked questions of those who attended spiritualist groups and chapels, and those who sat awaiting word from planchette or slate.

When much of the literature turned out to be sentimental tosh, fit to be dismissed out of hand, yet even the newspapers reported flights of fancy as genuine cases of ghostly visitation, she came to an unexpected conclusion. If the majority of spiritualists were deluded, mistaken or fraudulent, if not all three, then why miss out on the game?

She had dared a far larger thought. This could surely be done not for pin money, but for higher stakes.

A summer of scheming had tempted her; another autumn of family strife had decided her. Her beloved grandfather had died the year before, and there was nothing in Keighley which was bearable, let alone of any promise. There was only betrayal—and subjugation.

The clink of tea-cups; fragile laughter from another table in the tea-house. Catherine smiled, shaking free of her thoughts. She sipped her tea, and had the pleasant conceit of coming here again one day, and hearing someone say "Why, is that not Madame Rostov herself over there!"

She was working her way up carefully, seeking out better clients as she went. Already her name was being passed round middle-class women who sought, she suspected, release from long boring afternoons. A chance to avoid "good works" and to titillate themselves. A scare or two in the process did no harm, if properly managed.

There were other clients, though, more difficult ones. They mourned lost relatives and friends, and were desperate to make contact with those who had passed on. When she sensed genuine grief, she changed her act. Sometimes she would say, with regret, that she could find no trace of the departed. That not everything Beyond the Veil was open to scrutiny. If delivered in appropriate tones, it usually served.

If not, there were those rare sympathetic—or unguarded— moments when she truly touched the Aether, whatever that was. It was as good a word as any for the cloud of voices and images which brushed her in those moments when her mind opened and she "saw." Occasionally her visions seemed to have relevance to those gathered around the table, but she knew that most were fooling themselves, finding only what they wanted to find.

It was always about the audience's expectations, not her own. At one sitting she had uttered words which meant nothing to anyone there, prompted by the image of a confused child in a crimson dress. Rather than being disappointed, the participants had taken it as a sign of something rare and strange, enhancing her reputation for a few weeks.

All that truly mattered to Catherine was that here was a route to influence and a steady income. In the villages and small towns of her childhood, she had been Mardy Cath, the girl they taunted for her moods and daft thoughts.

In London, she was whatever she chose.

The end of that same week brought a letter. Not to her lodgings, but to the Southwark post office where Catherine collected such mail as there was for either of her personas.

The envelope at the post office was cream and of quality, as was the brief letter inside. She read it twice on a bench outside. "Would Madame Rostov consent to take afternoon tea on Sunday, and to discuss the fascinating subject of spiritualism? A small but attentive audience eagerly awaits such an opportunity."

It was signed by Charlotte Chambers, Miss, and the reply address was a well-to-do neighbourhood near the Chelsea Embankment. The session with Miss Bournelle had borne fruit, and sooner than Catherine expected.

Catherine hurried home, penned her assent, and had it posted within the hour.

Her elation did not last. As night clutched at the lodgings, so she began to drift back to the vision from Islington. Mrs B was out, playing cards with friends, and Catherine was left to toy with needle and thread over the kitchen table. A fur collar was coming loose from one of Madam Rostov's coats. Slightly impoverished was an acceptable look, but down-at-heel was not. Clarissa would have made a better job of it, but Clarissa would have wondered at such a garment being in her cousin's possession.

Without Mrs B's presence, the kitchen was an empty snail shell found in a garden, a reminder only that its true occupant was gone. The Dutch plates on the dresser had no purpose; the pots and pans were too idle. Even the fire which burned in the small range seemed to give no heat. Taking one of her landlady's aprons from behind the door, Catherine put it on. It smelled of cooking fat and caraway seed, of Mrs Bessovitch. Solid, comforting things.

Attacking the sewing, she jabbed herself twice, pinpricks of blood. The thread broke at a crucial moment, and she came close to sewing part of one sleeve to the collar. The hide beneath the fur was stiff and old, a memento mori for all small, furred creatures.

Death in all things. She knew what was bothering her. Her mind kept flickering back to Grace Carlton's parlour, and that unwanted, unexpected vision.

The stranger steps into the room. Small, careful steps. The air is full of steam, the tiles slippery. He is not a tall man, nor is he as slim as the bather, though his dark suit is well cut. A black felt bowler shades his eyes, incongruous in these surroundings…

So specific, down to the smallest detail—the gleam on the killer's boots, the careful replacement of his cuff-links…she would not think of it.

Nothing else had come to her since, not the glimmer of such a scene. But that was how it had been before, cut clear as glass; brutal and direct. She tried to tell herself that she was ten years older, and her own woman now.

The sound of the front door opening was a blessed one. She dropped her work and rushed to fill the kettle. Tea for both of them, and perhaps a slice of seed-cake, even though it was late.

"Did you have a pleasant—" Catherine stopped at the sight of her landlady's face as she entered the kitchen. The usual worldly-wise smile was missing.

Mrs Bessovitch placed her large bag down on the sideboard, and drew out a newspaper, laying it next to her bag.

"I have been with many people, Katerina. We play whist, we chatter. Like many birds, we chatter. We discuss what is to become of this fine country; what has become of our old countries." She frowned. "And there is Sadie Gerstein. You know her?"

Catherine shook her head. "You might have mentioned her once or twice. I'm not sure."

"Ah. She cooks for good family, maybe talks too much."

"Has something happened to her?"

The landlady glanced at the sewing, saw that the kettle was on the hob. She hung her outdoor coat on the back of the kitchen door.

"Sadie Gerstein, I say she cooks for good family—in Islington." She handed her lodger the newspaper. "This she had with her."

The Gazette, from the week before, was folded over to page three. "A Tragic Accident" was the main headline there. Catherine read the article beneath, already sure of what she would find.

> We regret to report the loss of a promising young legal mind. On the evening of 3rd September, shortly after ten o'clock, Alfred Turner, manservant to Mr Philip Tether, solicitor, returned from an errand on his master's behalf to find the house silent. Ascertaining that Mr Tether was not in his bedchamber, Turner was shocked to find his master lying in his bath, deceased.
>
> Thomas Merchant, a doctor resident four doors away, was summoned, but it appeared that death had occurred some hour or more previous to the discovery. An inquest is to be held, but we are reliably informed that the police are satisfied as to the accidental nature of this sad event.
>
> Dr Merchant confides to our reporter that he found no signs of foul play. He conjectured that Mr Tether had fallen asleep during his ablutions, or had suffered some minor fit, and, confused, had failed to prevent his own demise, which came about by drowning. The doctor further warned of the practice of hot baths after the ingestion of alcohol...

She put the newspaper down slowly.

"The address...this is the street behind Mrs Carlton's house. The séance was held that same night, virtually next door."

Next door.

Exactly as it had happened ten years ago in Keighley—a murder, and Catherine open to every sensation. If a man screams ten miles away, you are none the wiser. If he screams on the other side of a brick wall, then you cannot mistake it. For the second time in her life she had been yards from violent death...

"Da." Mrs Bessovitch patted Catherine on the shoulder, and eased her into a chair. "You did see this, like you are camera. It is not dream, or ghost, or thing in other ladies' heads."

"It is worse," said Catherine.

"How so, worse?"

"I know his name. I know who killed this solicitor, Tether."

The kettle hissed on the range; the old house settled around them. It should have been comforting. It was not. The older woman began to tidy away the sewing things, tutting at a loose stitch, avoiding the obvious question.

At last Catherine looked up, and when she spoke, it was close to a whisper.

"Dry. His name is Edwin Dry."

NINE

Following the dreadful incident involving Harris Brevard in Paris, and her fall from her prized perch at the Phoenix gay house in December of 1885, Mary Jane had found a position at the Laughing Magpie, a brothel run by Mrs Sarah Buki.

Standing two stories tall in St. George Street in the East End, the establishment had rooms for ten women, a kitchen, one parlour, and outdoor privies. Mrs Buki hired two women to do the charring, and the place remained fairly clean, though much of the furnishings had fallen into disrepair.

Mary Jane settled in to seeing clients there in early January of 1886. Her second floor room felt draughty and cold. The once extravagant flocked red wallpaper had faded and peeled from the walls in places. The ceiling, which leaked when rain came, had a large brown bruise growing in its plaster. After the Phoenix, everything at the Laughing Magpie seemed difficult, especially waiting her turn for hot water.

In early February, 1886, Mary Jane made an attempt to get the necklace, going to the Phoenix gay house with the pretence of wanting a visit with a friend there, a prostitute named Dorothy Wostmann.

"Dorothy isn't here," Mrs Arseneau said. "You may not come back here, Mary Jane. They say Mr Brevard suffered too little air for so long that he's now an idiot. I suspect he deserved what he got, but I cannot help you. I'll tell Dorothy you asked after her, and you may leave your address with me."

Mary Jane had no concern for the man's condition, and turned away before her anger got the better of her.

A gloom settled into her outlook, one she could not shake as she went about the business of the Laughing Magpie; satisfying a much coarser clientele than what she had known at the Phoenix. The hardship and a sense of failure wore painfully on her spirit.

Following that first taste in Paris, Mary Jane gained a laudanum habit that helped her endure the hardship. She needed the drug to help her feel better or to at least feel less. Food held little interest for her, and she began to lose weight. Mrs Buki treated Mary Jane with kid gloves, brought her extravagant meals, sat with her, and encouraged her to eat, "just a bit more."

In early March of 1886, Mary Jane had a chance meeting in Cable Street that brought about welcome changes. She was on her way to one of the pubs she frequented in Shadwell to find clients, dressed the part she intended to play. Her green bodice had panels of scarlet satin that matched the flounces of her green top skirt. She wore a shortened petticoat. As she did with all her ladybird skirts, Mary Jane had gathered and tacked the fabric in such a way that the garment swayed seductively when she walked and lifted in the front to show her slim ankles. The skirt lifted further still when she sat and crossed her legs. She wore no hat and allowed a few follow-me-lads to dangle from her coiffure.

"Mary Jane Kelly!" she heard a voice cry.

She looked toward the owner of the voice amidst the foot traffic. Seeing a grinning face stopped her in her tracks. Emotion caught in Mary Jane's throat, a sense that something good and hopeful, long since lost, had been found. She couldn't put a finger on the memories at first. Mary Jane stared at the figure in the fine double-breasted frock coat and curled-brim bowler. While his jaw appeared squarer, forehead higher, and brow heavier, she saw a young man from a past life, one with curly-hair and beautiful, pale eyes.

Sudden recognition forced his name to her lips. "Thom—," she began, and tears sprang from her eyes. Mary Jane stepped back, not understanding her response. He couldn't be real. That life had been dead and gone for a long time. Reborn, she'd been given the life of a whore.

"Pardon me," he said hurrying to her. "I didn't mean to frighten you."

Mary Jane took another step back, though she wanted to wrap her arms around him and never let him go.

He became still, with his palms out to his sides, his face open, concerned.

In recent years, she had rarely let herself dwell for long on her time at Bryn Haearn and her feelings for the Morganstone family, but not a day had gone by since she was taken from them that Mary Jane did not lament the loss of what she considered her second family.

"Thomas," she said, her weeping loud and open, "I have missed you *so!*" She folded up and collapsed on the footway.

Thomas lifted Mary Jane, held and supported her. She got an impression that Mrs Morganstone and Elen also held her.

As people strode past on the streets, some turned to watch. And with the stares, the realisation that Thomas must see her for what she was dawned on Mary Jane.

Again, she shrank away from him. He let her go. Under her own power, she got to the face of a building, and leaned against the brick.

Approaching cautiously, he asked "Are you ill?"

Mary Jane considered several lies, not liking any of them. He deserved better.

In the years she'd spent with him at Bryn Haearn, he'd never treated her with anything but respect, though she'd held a much lower station. As a child, four years his junior, she'd quickly realised that her crush on him would go unrequited. He and Elen had been Mary Jane's world, her family for a precious and magical time in her youth.

She realised that her feelings for him had not changed. Mary Jane still loved Thomas. Considering the many men she'd known since she'd last seen him, the fact that such sentiments endured took on the proportions of a miracle.

"No, not ill," Mary Jane said, "…*ashamed.*"

He looked at her with his mouth agape, clearly dumbfounded.

"You must see how I'm dressed," she said, her gaze cast toward the pavement. "Surely you recognise…"

His silence finally drew Mary Jane's eyes toward his. He had a troubled expression. "Yes, but you don't know what I am because I hide the truth so well," he said. "I am no better, and perhaps much worse." He shook his head, looked away.

Mary Jane didn't know what to make of his words. The world held people of all sort, so many of them worse than a prostitute. Not Thomas, though. Surely—

"Come with me," he said, taking her by the hand. "We'll take a meal together. You haven't known Thomas Morganstone for many years. I'll introduce you to him. There's nothing *much* to fear."

His smile, spellbinding still, encouraged Mary Jane. They walked to Shadwell Station, where Thomas hired a hansom to drive them to the Cock's Comb tavern in Whitechapel Road. Inside the establishment, he asked for a drinking box, paid the fee for the more private seating, and they were escorted to the booth for their meal. Thomas ordered from the barmaid a plate of cold meats, bread, and two glasses of bitter.

Over their meal, Mary Jane asked, "How are your aunt, Peggy, and Elen?"

"Elen is well. I think she's as happy as she can be. You know her, a little soldier, always clear-eyed and looking for the best. Still quite an imagination."

Mary Jane smiled, her heart swelling with a desire to see her one-time friend.

Impossible. I could not let her know me now.

"My aunt's business manager invested heavily in a company that developed new mining equipment. When that company collapsed in scandal, she lost a fortune. She sold Bryn Haearn and several other holdings."

"I'm saddened to hear that," Mary Jane said, finding the words hollow.

"They are quite happy in a smaller home. Some money remained from my parent's estate, more than enough to send me to school. Then I had an apprenticeship here in London with a wonderful master in the building trade, a man named Treecle. He died suddenly and I was on my own, my term with my master incomplete. Though he had spoken to some of my abilities in glowing terms, I had no letters of reference from him. No one wanted to hire me. I took what jobs I found, all the while losing funds I could not replace quickly enough. Should things have got much worse, I knew I'd have to leave the city."

Mary Jane understood the feeling of failure in the midst of a bustling city full of money, food, and other comforts; the frustrating sense that all one needed for a good life lay so close at hand, if only the treasure could be taken.

"I had made the acquaintance of a man in the Metropolitan Board of Works," Thomas said. "I went to him, asking if he could help. He did find me work, but it was secretive stuff, repairing a small bridge. The job went on forever, used inferior materials, and far more workers than necessary. When I discovered that I'd helped him commit fraud, I threatened to expose him. 'This is how the business of building is done in London,' he said. 'You can take my bribe and stay silent, or become known for your betrayal, in which case you will find no further work in the city.' He told the truth. I learned that even Mr Treecle helped professional criminals to commit such crimes in order to have work. Since then, I have done no end of things for which I'd feel shame should my aunt or Elen find out."

Thomas took a drink of his bitter, set the glass down and looked Mary Jane in the eyes. "Now that you know something of me, please tell me something about you."

Mary Jane began a disjointed explanation of what had led her to soliciting, her words quickly turning to sobs. She looked down, and hid her face in her hands.

Thomas lifted her chin, and looked her in the eye. "Please tell me what happened after your father took you from us."

Mary Jane composed herself, took several deep draughts of her bitter. "Papa blamed me for my mother's death and life with him were unendurable."

"Your father is a beastly fellow, if you'll forgive my saying so."

Mary Jane laughed. "Thank you for saying that. Never has anyone described him so tidy. I've rarely allowed myself to judge him harshly because I suffered the same terrible loss—my mother—that took the hope and kindness from his heart, and turned him against me."

"Her death didn't turn you into a beast."

"Yes, well, I didn't have anyone to blame."

Mary Jane took more of her bitter.

"I married at sixteen to get away from Papa. My husband, Evan Berwyn Davies was a lushington, always drunk when home. A collier in Penygraig working the Pandy Coal Pit, he died in '81 in a mine explosion."

Mary Jane struggled to rein in the familiar pang of loss. The strong sentiment that came with thoughts of Berwyn had always confounded her. Either he represented a longed-for time of lost innocence or she'd loved him more than she was willing to admit to herself. She said no more about him to Thomas.

"My bitterness toward Papa stood in the way of clear thinking. I would have been better off if I had returned home. Instead I went to live with my cousin Carryl Hughes in Cardiff."

A pittance Mary Jane received from the fund that she and Berwyn had paid into for protection against mine accidents. She could not remain in Penygraig alone. Nor did she want to stay there with the memories.

She wrote to her cousin, Carryl Hughes, who lived in Cardiff, asking if she might come and lodge with her for a time. Mary Jane had met her cousin twice before when much younger and with Mum still among the living. With Carryl's pretty dark hair and eyes, and her clever way with words, Mary Jane had always thought well of her.

She received the answer she hoped for. In 1881, at eighteen years of age, less than two months after poor Berwyn's death, she removed to Cardiff.

With Carryl four years her senior and living on her own, Mary Jane thought she'd learn something from her about how to get on in life. Her cousin had better togs than what Mary Jane had become accustomed to since leaving the Morganstones. Carryl's home, two rooms in a three-story wooden building near the Cardiff Docks, with upholstered furniture, papered walls, and a metal bed, was grander than Mary Jane had expected. The building housed a number of unmarried or widowed women, all rather neighbourly, given to standing on the landings and talking. The doors to lodgings, including Carryl's, often stayed opened, perhaps to encourage the chumminess. Mary Jane worried about thieves taking advantage, but realised that never did a time come that someone wasn't about. As they might have done with any newcomer, Carryl's neighbours became quieter when Mary Jane drew near. She had confidence that, with time, they'd warm to her.

Carryl took Mary Jane to eat a fine fish dinner at a tavern her first night in the city. Several times during the meal, men and women approached their table to make small talk with Carryl. One gentleman, rather fashionably dressed, left her his calling card. Her popularity dazzled Mary Jane, and that encouraged her feeling that her cousin would indeed make a good guide to her new life.

Until Mary Jane arrived in London much later, she would not see so many kinds of people. Those living and working together around the Cardiff docks were of all sorts. New faces appeared often, as seaman came and went, some from far-flung parts of the world, of different colours and creeds. Along with the dockworkers and merchants, most of those in the city laboured in positions that in some way aided the shipping of coal and iron. From its posh homes to its beggarly hovels, Cardiff remained a stew of activity. Mary Jane found the city exciting, yet unsettling too, a dirty and at times dangerous place.

Sitting at dinner in the noisy tavern, she made a confession to Carryl. "With the loss of Mum, the cruelty of my father, and the mine explosion taking Berwyn, I have become fearful of life itself."

"There *is* much to fear in life," Carryl said, "but taking control of your own fate will help you bear up. What happened to your mum, your poor husband's death—those were accidents. Your father chose to handle you roughly. That is the sort of cruelty one finds in most employment."

"I'll find it again, then, should I find work," Mary Jane said, shaking her head.

"No woman should be a slave to man," Carryl said, "as long as man's desire for union with womankind is so strong. You are gifted with a clever head and a beautiful form. Your father is perhaps the only man immune to your charms. All others you might twist round your little finger. Use your wiles and your bosom to better your lot in life." She gave Mary Jane a piercing look. "Use them to get your way."

She welcomed the idea that she possessed gifts that could win her the better things in life. Carryl had said the words with such confidence that, although Mary Jane didn't understand fully what her cousin meant, her fears were calmed in that moment. She felt grateful to Carryl for that. Mary Jane had a sense of power over her future, something she needed so desperately that she became willing to overlook what rigours might stand in her way.

A mystery, Carryl slept through most of the following day. Mary Jane was not in a position to question her cousin, but wondered if she did that often, and if so, what that meant about how she earned her living. Possibly Carryl worked a nightshift somewhere.

That evening, they made their way through a light rain to her lodgings after eating a meal at a pub. A voice beckoned to Carryl from a carriage waiting at the kerb.

"A moment," Carryl said, and went to speak with one Mary

Jane presumed to be an acquaintance inside the carriage. With the increasing rain, the driver on the exposed seat of the vehicle bundled into his blanket and pulled his hat on tighter.

The one inside the carriage, a man, leaned on the door sash, his head, shoulder, and arm emerging into the light. His clothing told Mary Jane that he had wealth. The brim of his fine woollen hat had been pulled down low over his face, possibly to keep the rain off. Carryl spoke briefly to him before returning to Mary Jane. The man called to his driver and the carriage moved off.

"Would you be a darling and bide on the street for an hour to allow me to satisfy a client?" Carryl asked.

No explanation did she have ready, and no shame appeared on her face. Clear as day was her meaning, though. If Mary Jane had not been so naive and guileless, she might have seen the truth before that. She must have stood with her mouth agape too long because Carryl asked, "Would you do that for me? 'Tis how I earn my keep."

"Yes," Mary Jane said simply, her voice unsteady. Her cousin left her standing in the increasing downpour. Others on the street moved around her. She watched Carryl go until she'd slipped from sight.

Confused and feeling oddly wounded, Mary Jane sat in a coffee shop and sipped a cup for well over an hour, thinking about her situation. Had she taken up with a fallen woman? Would she have to return to Papa? Could she quickly find another situation in Cardiff so she wouldn't have to?

No good answers came for the questions.

Then Mary Jane began thinking about what she'd just learned of Carryl in light of what she'd said the night before: "No woman should be a slave to man, as long as man's desire for union with womankind remains so strong." She'd made a business of satisfying that desire. Mary Jane didn't know why she'd never truly thought of prostitution in such simple terms until then.

Carryl had said that Mary Jane was clever and beautiful, and that she might use those qualities to gain what she wanted from men. Her cousin spoke from experience, because Carryl had made a life for herself by those selfsame means.

Pondering these things, Mary Jane's view of the world changed. Some might have thought Carryl a fool, who would end her days in misery for going against the common notions of goodness. Mary

Jane began to see her cousin as one with enough brains to see past the prosaic day-to-day concerns and stifling morals of most folks.

With the protection of a sheath, what was sex but a bit of lather, one that when done well felt very good indeed? And to get paid for it too—what was to dislike?

The management of the coffee shop asked Mary Jane to have another cup or leave.

The rain had stopped and she thought she might walk for a while with her thoughts.

She discovered Carryl outside, casually leaning against the worn grey stones of the establishment's exterior.

"You found me," Mary Jane said, not certain what else to say in that moment.

Her cousin nodded.

"Why didn't you come in?"

"I saw you lost in your own thoughts" Carryl said, "and knew you would find your own way out with time."

Mary Jane was past judging her. Still, she didn't know how to look at her cousin, and kept her eyes downcast.

"His name is Martin Bowers," Carryl said. "He give me this." She lifted her right hand to show that she wore a beautiful silver ring with a bright ruby. "Supplies iron mongers, he does, and he's getting richer by the day." She laughed. "Says but for my coarse mouth, I'd be on his arm once his wife has gone."

Mary Jane frowned, not understanding.

"Consumption," Carryl said. "He says her suffering is almost at an end."

Although what Mary Jane had learned that night troubled her, she did want the best for her cousin, especially as Carryl seemed to have Mary Jane's best interests at heart. "I can teach you how to speak the Queen's English," she said, making a clear change in her voice.

"Where did you learn?"

"I became a companion for a young lady in Carmarthen, and shared her lessons."

"Yes, that would be a fine thing!" Carryl took Mary Jane in her arms and hugged her like a sister.

Even then, she could not seem to look at her cousin.

"What troubles you, my dear?" Carryl asked.

Mary Jane's thoughts ran too fast to answer at first. Finally, she had what she wanted to say, and the words surprised her. "Can you teach me how to do it safely?" she asked, hoping she would not have to explain herself.

Again, Carryl nodded. "First lesson," she said. "Never go by your true name. How do you like the name Ginger?"

"I *do* like it."

"Well, then, Ginger, come with me." Carryl took Mary Jane's arm and led her home.

She remembered her father asking when she was a small child, "Do you know what danger is, girl?"

Still, Mary Jane had no answer.

⚓

She paused to give the impression she'd finished her tale. Her shame had returned, and she wasn't certain she wanted to tell Thomas more.

He gave her an expectant, warm look, placed a hand atop one of hers affectionately. "There's more because you are now here."

"Yes," Mary Jane said. She took more of her bitter. "Would you excuse me?"

"Of course."

Mary Jane got up and went to find a privy. The tavern had stalls indoors. She slipped into one, relieved herself, then took several sips from her bottle of laudanum.

Exiting the privy, she considered fleeing the tavern, though she knew she could not do that to Thomas. Instead she returned to their drinking box. A fresh glass of bitter stood at her place. She sat, took a couple of deep draughts from it, and continued her tale.

"What little innocence remained to me, I quickly lost…"

⚓

Carryl made certain Mary Jane had safe and pleasurable experiences at first, the men she serviced handsome and kind. That changed with time as her cousin foresaw a certain toughening of Mary Jane's spirit. Rarely did she enjoy the sex. Much of the time she found it merely disgusting. Many of the men, if not openly cruel, had a cold disregard for her. Every now and then, she'd have a man who played some sort of role for himself, one that had little to do

82

with her, and she had the frightening feeling she was just another object in the room for him.

Carryl had many ways of managing the dangers of the business, her weave of friends and business associates a great help. She and Mary Jane paid protection to the Beloved Ratters, a gang like the High Rips of Liverpool that preyed upon prostitutes. The payment was demanded under threat of violence. Most not soliciting on the streets didn't know that the gang would do little to protect prostitutes. Mary Jane did as Carryl suggested, and mentioned the Beloved Ratter's when talking with new clients to put a fear into them so they'd behave.

Mary Jane felt safe enough.

The earnings did not amount to much, since the competition on the streets of Cardiff set a going rate. That unspoken starting point dragged down the price for even the best of ladybirds.

Mary Jane often stopped on the landing outside Carryl's rooms to talk with Daphne Michaels, who lodged across the hall. "My sister what lives in a London gay house earns at least two shillings a customer," she said one day. "That's after the cut as goes to the house where she gets free room and board."

Perhaps overhearing the conversation, Carryl came from her room. "That's quite a tale, Daphne," she said, rolling her eyes.

Indignant, Daphne said, "'Tis God's honest truth,"

"Spoken by a pious member of the Church." Carryl made a mocking face for Mary Jane to see, one hidden from Daphne, and returned to her room.

"I don't doubt you," Mary Jane said.

"She's afraid I'll put grand ideas in your head and you'll leave her. Her business was never so good 'til you come."

Mary Jane couldn't complain. What she earned was better than Berwyn's wages had been and might have been as good as Papa's. That thought made her feel good.

Of course, she did dream of earning more, and tucked away the idea of one day going to London to seek her fortune in a gay house.

To all appearances a generous heart, Carryl shared her room and her clientele with Mary Jane, all but Martin Bowers.

"He asks about you," her cousin said in passing one day. "'Who's the flaxen-haired beauty I've seen with you?' Mr Bowers asks. 'My uneducated cousin, Ginger, from Carmarthen,' I says. 'She's my personal maid,' I tell him, 'still a virgin, worse mouth than my own.'"

They laughed together at that. Mary Jane had no desire to compete for his attentions.

The cousins looked out for one another and had good feelings between them for at least two years.

Hard feelings began to come between them when they entertained clients together and a time came for a man to choose which one of them to bed. Carryl had been comfortable enough the first few times a man chose Mary Jane. As the choice came more often, something in her cousin's gaze turned dark.

In a foul mood after waking late one afternoon, Carryl said, "Time you took a room of your own."

Mary Jane felt stung, though she did look forward to having more room. She removed to one recently vacated in the building on the same second floor landing. Still, the cousins came and went from both lodgings often enough that the doors remained open much of the time.

One night, the evening's clients had gone away satisfied. Carryl and Mary Jane were straightening the rooms before bed. They'd finished with Mary Jane's single room, and had started on her cousin's bedroom. Carryl had begun to undress for bed when she looked up with that dark gaze.

"'Tis you wearing my best silk and velvet bodice what gives you the advantage," she said. "Ginger ain't nothing without my borrowed flash."

Mary Jane had fewer fine clothes. Carryl's much grander dunnage fit them both, and she'd been generous with lending. Indeed, Mary Jane had done most of her borrowing at her cousin's suggestion. She thought Carryl's words a jest of sorts, a way of admitting her pettiness and getting it off her chest at the same time. Mary Jane simply smiled.

"Think it's a delight, do you?" Carryl asked. She spit on the floor, bent to loosen the laces of her boots. "Well, you stay away from my armoire from now on. Spend some of the money I've taught you how to earn."

Recognising true anger, Mary Jane felt embarrassed and upset. "Yes, I will," she said. "I didn't mean to trespass."

"Mr Bowers saw you again when he came for me at the Sea Anchor," Carryl said. "Should you know he's about, keep out of sight."

Mary Jane had tried to show her sorrow, and her cousin had come back with more anger. Now, she was angry too. But for her efforts, Carryl might not have had him at all.

"Too bad I can't take away that tidy language you wear like an ill-fitting gown," Mary Jane said, a bite in her tone.

"Oh, the cat's out of the bag, is it?" Carryl said. "The reduced cat, I see, mere pussy. Little Ginger shows her claws. Isn't that cute?"

Her words did their job—Mary Jane felt small.

She'd done her best in giving her cousin lessons in elocution, yet hadn't managed to break Carryl's worst habits of speech. And, like Mary Jane, in moments of high emotion, the slang spilled forth. She had learned at a younger age, and could control herself with a minimum of concentration. However nicely Carryl dressed and held herself with good posture, at the first distraction, she'd lose her way. Mary Jane might have felt the same trying to gild a wooden spoon.

"If you'd done a better job teaching, the gents wouldn't think I were putting on airs."

Carryl spoiled for a fight, so Mary Jane tried to put some of her anger away.

"Hasn't the better language helped with Martin Bowers?"

"He knows me for what I am," Carryl said bitterly. "There's no fooling him."

"You might have known that."

She glared at Mary Jane. "I have little time left before he takes a new wife."

"Mrs Bowers has passed away?"

"Last month. Took her long enough." Carryl threw her right boot at the wall, cracking the plaster. "You stay out of sight when he's about. If by chance you speak with him, Ginger ought to sound like a labourer."

She threw her left boot at Mary Jane.

She dodged in time.

"Get out!" Carryl cried.

Mary Jane left her cousin with her bad mood and went to bed.

Hoping Carryl's feelings would mend, Mary Jane wore only her own clothes and kept her distance for a time.

⌁⌖⌁

Carryl interrupted Mary Jane in the midst of seeing a client. The door to her room had been open and they'd not got to business yet. They sat together, talking, enjoying glasses of wine.

"He wants you now!" Carryl shouted. "You've been seeing him behind my back."

Her angry words drove the client away. No great loss, Mary Jane thought, as he slipped through the door. He'd been a rough one.

"Who?" she asked, though she knew the answer.

"Bowers, of course."

"He found me in the Sea Anchor, a chance meeting. Bought me a drink, he did, and I spoke to him briefly. I made certain to sound like a muck boot. Gulped down my gatter, then made my excuses quick as I could. "

"Weren't no chance meeting—he's been looking for you."

"Why didn't you tell me so I could avoid him better?"

Carryl had no answer for that. She bared her teeth. "He were my chance to get out of this life," she shouted.

"I thought you liked the business."

"Nobody likes soliciting for long."

"Yet you brought me into it."

"You had nothing else, you ungrateful wretch!"

"Ungrateful? I've had only the best intentions toward you. I've offered nothing but kind words."

"Oh, that's the way, use the jemmy mouth. Makes you out to be my better, doesn't it?"

"Better than your bloody bone box, what can't help you land a floundering fish."

Carryl struck out with a metal-toed boot, kicking Mary Jane in the shin.

Though she thought she deserved the blow for her cruel tongue, the pain enraged her. She lifted an empty wine bottle from the floor and threw the thing. It hit Carryl on the forehead, glanced off and broke against the open door beside her. A shower of green glass shards fell in her hair and on her shoulders. Her eyes went wide, and she stumbled back against the wall, pieces of glass falling from her hair into her clothing and on her face. She moaned and clutched at the collar of her bodice.

Mary Jane saw blood at her cousin's neck. "Don't move," she said, horrified at what she'd done.

"You wicked child!" Carryl said, her tone vicious. The pain must have been more powerful than her anger. She became still.

Without a word, Mary Jane shut the door, and helped her cousin out of her clothing. Carryl didn't speak, merely stood, red-faced, staring into the distance. Mary Jane carefully picked the bits of glass off the bare skin of her cousin's face, neck, and right shoulder and gave her a dressing gown.

Carryl gathered up her clothes, and paused at the door before leaving the room. "I'm done with you," she said. "Don't come in my room again. Don't try to talk to me. Stay away from Mr Bowers."

With that, she left, and Mary Jane never spoke to her cousin again. She was glad for that. Still she wept for the loss.

⚓

Less than a month later, a new client turned on her. She'd picked up a pillow, buried her head in it, and hung on for dear life through the horrible dewskitch. He struck her in the head so many times, and so hard, she later had no clear memory of what happened.

Mary Jane seemed to recall her cousin coming into the room afterward and standing over her with a gloating look. Mary Jane couldn't be certain of that, though.

The man would have had a written reference. She took no clients without one. Again, uncertain as to the truth, she seemed to recall it was from Carryl. He must have taken the reference away with him because later she couldn't find the piece of paper to confirm that.

He'd used a sheep's gut sheath, something Mary Jane didn't accept because they'd seen a bad batch come through town. They leaked, and the ladybirds had taken to calling them broxy sheaths. Word was that even when whole, the ones made of sheep's gut weren't reliable at keeping disease away.

Daphne Michaels told her about the sheath. She had found Mary Jane and helped her get to the infirmary. Daphne said she discovered the thing lying on the floor beside Mary Jane's bed. Since her falling out with Carryl, most of the Cardiff ladybirds had turned against Mary Jane due to her cousin's lying gossip. Daphne had stayed friendly, though, and was trusted in return.

Since Mary Jane did not accept the sheep's gut with clients and had plenty of the rubber ones, her assailant must have forced himself on her before the beating, or he'd done so afterward.

Mary Jane remained in the Cowbridge Road Workhouse infirmary for nearly a year, from March, 1883 to November of the same year. One infection followed another. She lost the ability to bear children. Once they'd had enough of her at the infirmary, she found herself destitute and still not fit.

As a fallen woman, she was sent to the Monmouthshire House of Mercy to be reformed. Mary Jane heard from other inmates there that if she'd been much older, they would have considered her too hardened to save, and would not have taken her. For all the hard work they gave her, though, she knew they merely wanted strong, young backs.

They spoon fed Mary Jane religion with every meal, something her parents had thankfully neglected. In the house where she spent her days as a lavender, Matron Moss told her, "Doing laundry without pay is one of the best forms of contrition. Endless scrubbing to remove stains reminds us of the hard work needed to remove the taint of sin from our souls."

⌒⚶⌒

"Her prater mouth made me feel a right mark, it did," Mary Jane said. "I played the role of the penitent until I could lie no longer. Once I felt fit enough, in March of 1884, I left the House of Mercy and spent a month working my way to London."

Thomas released a shuttering sob, struggled to hold himself together. He took her in an embrace. "Oh, Mary Jane, how after all that is your warm heart still whole?"

His response set her off. She bent into his shoulder, biting down on her lower lip to push the pain and shame away. Her eyes dampened his jacket.

Finally, having composed herself, she sat up. "It got better," she said, and laughed through her tears. "Perhaps my memories of life at Bryn Heaern helped. I dreamed often of returning to my second family there."

Thomas seemed lost in memory for a moment. Then, for all the sadness expressed, he let out an odd, short laugh.

Throughout the telling, Mary Jane had looked to him each time she'd revealed what she considered a lapse in her character. His steady and caring gaze had assured her each time that he didn't judge.

Another laugh, and his handsome lips bent almost to a smirk.

"What do you find humorous?" Mary Jane asked.

"We were *indeed* your family," he said, "and you never truly left us. Even after your father took you away, I saw you in the corner of my eye from time to time flitting among the rooms of Bryn Haearn. On my last visit, I caught a glimpse of you in the great mirror in the main hall."

"Such fancy," she said.

Did he miss me that much? The thought gave Mary Jane a thrill. She wondered if he'd like to take up with her, though she considered such fancies on her part unwise.

"Seems you've shown great resourcefulness in the face of adversity," he said at last.

Mary Jane scoffed, said, "I'm considered a fallen woman."

"Yes, but I frequently work for criminals who do much worse." He paused and sighed. "Misery loves company. Criminals need coconspirators, and they'll get them by hook or by crook. Once you've worked for them, they'll hold it over you or find some other way to make you do it again. I grew more willing with time. Having gained a tidy reputation among thieves, I am kept busy and live quite well now."

Mary Jane nodded her head. "Just so, I've discovered that to get on in life, I must break the rules of polite society. I have nothing else. Of course, my crime involves sex, a thing hidden away as beneath human dignity, even when the engagement is innocently used to get children."

Unexpectedly, Thomas laughed. His laughter persisted, and, again, Mary Jane thought he must be laughing at her.

He saw her confusion, and calmed himself. He clasped her hands between his own, leaned in, and gave her a warm smile. "You ought walk in my shoes for a time," he whispered. "Should the wrong person find out that I'm a homosexual, I could go to prison. That's if I'm truly unlucky. As it is, I often find I have a fight on my hands."

Startled to silence, Mary Jane stared at him. Then, remembering her adolescent daydreams of a tumble in bed with Thomas, she laughed.

"Do you mock *me?*" he asked, grimacing slightly. "I don't admit that to *just* anyone."

"Not in the least," Mary Jane said. "Surprised, is all. I…well, … when we were young, I had *such* a crush on you."

"I knew that, and love you still for your affectionate smiles."

She felt herself blushing.

He rolled his eyes and his smile grew larger, showing a gap in the lower left jaw. Perhaps he'd lost the tooth in a fight.

"Do you get in a lot of fights?"

"Sure, but I'm good with a bunch of fives." He made a comically fierce face and showed a fist. "I'm a bully trap."

They laughed, and held each other, rocking together in the drinking box.

The spell of shame broken, Mary Jane told about her employment at the Phoenix gay house, losing the position, and her situation at the Laughing Magpie, leaving out the most unseemly details. Surely his imagination filled in the rest. She did not tell him anything about what had happened in Paris with Harris Brevard.

"I have apartments near the Stepney Gas works," he said. "You have a standing invitation to escape the Laughing Magpie and stay with me whenever you want."

Mary Jane's crush on him had not gone away. She understood that her amorous sentiments would remain unrequited. The knowledge stung a bit. With all that, she felt glad to have him back in her life.

Following that chance meeting, the beginning of spring brought warming weather, and Mary Jane's heart became much lighter, her mood lifted.

During one of her stays at Thomas's apartments in Stepney, she had met Joseph Fleming. The fellow began to flirt with her the moment they met. Although she usually found that sort of thing irritating, something about the way he went about it made for a fun game. He came to the Laughing Magpie a couple of times to take Mary Jane out to a music hall performance. On the occasions she stayed at Morganstone's apartments and Fleming was present,

Thomas encouraged him to stay over. She got the impression that the two had been lovers at one time, but Fleming always spent the night with her. She said nothing of her suspicions. Thomas didn't seem the least unhappy that Joseph bedded Mary Jane.

Since she spent much of her time in Stepney, Mary Jane located cribs that let by the hour, where she could satisfy clients. She made an effort to get to know the local Ladybirds, and found a coffee shop that made for a convenient place to organise them. "A weave of friends," Carryl had called her own similar efforts to organise the prostitutes of Cardiff. The idea was that, with a meeting place and a willingness to communicate their experiences, ladybirds might work more safely.

TEN

Madame Rostov, ice-eyed and haloed by loose black tresses, sat at one end of the long oak table. Her fingers glinted with rings, not ostentatious but curious—dark red enamel on silver for the most part. They had that quality of another place, and might have been seen on hands of painted icons—Greek, Russian, or passed down through some Serbian family of limited wealth but much history. Her lips held the same shade as the enamel—port wine and garnet, not the modern reds.

Her sitters were of a different world. Young and in the latest fashions, sipping sherry and smiling knowing smiles. They seemed slender and bird-like in comparison.

"It is such a pleasure," said Charlotte Chambers, heart-faced and open of manner. Loose, straw-coloured ringlets made her seem girl and woman at the same time.

"Oh, indeed." Amelia Baring-Smith, a slim blonde in the same green taffeta as her friend, giggled. "Most of your profession, Madame Rostov, seem so—"

"Plain." Lady Seldon said the word without hesitation or obvious offence, as she might remark on a length of cloth at a haberdashery.

Catherine was at a loss as to how to respond. This house in the Chelsea Embankment was grander, and Lady Seldon a far more important figure in society, than she was used to. A liveried butler had welcomed her; a housekeeper in grey silk had shown her into the drawing room. It occurred to her within minutes that she might have made a mistake taking up this invitation.

"But we are entranced by the idea of hearing from beyond the Veil," added Lady Seldon. She brushed back a dark tress which had escaped one of her ornate hair-combs. "Lottie has herself toyed with the board and planchette—"

"And we saw that Indian man on the stage, remember, Lucy?" Miss Chambers leaned forward, elbows on the table like a schoolgirl. "With his levitation, and his 'electric grip.'"

"We did," agreed Lady Seldon. "Mirrors and wires, Harry says."

The three young women were clearly close. They made in-jokes, and finished each other's sentences like sisters. The speed of the invitation meant that her usual research had been rushed.

Charlotte—Lottie—Chambers was the daughter of a banker, and by all accounts likeable enough, courted by several young men who saw more than marital partnerships in their futures. Amelia Baring-Smith was a complete unknown.

As she watched them chatter, Catherine considered the third woman to be the most likely to cause problems. She gave Lady Seldon only three or four years on the other women; there was a sharp intelligence there.

"I meet them, of course, these people." Catherine put on a dismissive tone. "They entertain, which is enough for some." Passing entertainment would probably be enough for these three, she thought, but to be lumped amongst the frauds and mountebanks would not suit Madame Rostov. She needed better than that to prosper.

"Miss Bournelle speaks highly of you, Madame Rostov." Lottie contemplated her empty sherry glass. "And a girl always trusts her nanny."

That was something Catherine had missed, nor had Miss Bournelle confided it to her. So the old lady had been Charlotte Chambers's nanny. A very useful connection.

Amelia Baring-Smith giggled again. "My nanny was on the gin most of the time."

Lady Seldon frowned. "I don't think Madame Rostov will be staying long with that sort of talk, Amelia."

Catherine considered it time for Madame Rostov to take centre stage. She turned the conversation to an entirely imaginary occurrence at a séance that had also never happened. Stitching together various stories she had read, and altering a few names, she soon had the three women thrilling to a tale of communications from the dead.

"And this is what you do, Madame?" Lottie handed round a plate of tiny almond biscuits. "You communicate with those who have passed on?"

Catherine offered an expression which she hoped was one of thoughtful consideration, and not hasty invention. "I do not know, Miss Chambers. The nature of that which travels the Aether is beyond me. The departed, possibly; the hopes and wishes of many minds in communion...who can say?"

"The Devil?" suggested Amelia. "I've heard some scorching sermons on the subject of consorting with spirits. The Witch of

Endor, and suchlike."

"I am not whispered to by daemons, Miss Baring-Smith, if that is what you imply."

"Oh, no, Madame, I didn't mean…"

In the awkward silence that followed, Catherine stared at her hands, pale fingers pressed against the dark, polished oak. The rings she had borrowed from Mrs Bessovitch glinted in the soft light from outside. What had whispered to her in Keighley, and then in Islington? Who sent such visions, without apparent purpose? She doubted God, and was reasonably sure that the Devil too was a construct of church and chapel. Evil was done by man's hand, and drawn from man's mind.

Lady Seldon coughed. "Amelia is excitable—she reads too much."

"Well really, Lucy!" Amelia reddened. "They're Lottie's books I borrow, after all. Especially those shocking French ones"

All three laughed, and Catherine smiled, not sure of her place.

"Literature is a gift," she said, "As is imagination." She found that she was unsettled—two of the women here at least were much of an age with her, and Lady Seldon could not be thirty. "I am not so old that I do not understand amusement," she added quickly. "If I am too…formal, forgive me."

In the look which Lady Seldon gave her, an intelligence passed between them. Another woman playing a role, then, one way or another.

"We will not ask you to 'perform' for us today, Madame Rostov." Her tone was decisive, but not unfriendly. "It has been a pleasure to meet you, and Lottie was quite right to seek your acquaintance. Would you consider a small sitting, say, next week? The four of us."

She had passed a test, it seemed.

"With pleasure" said Catherine. "I am at your disposal, Lady Seldon."

She was trembling as she waited for the omnibus, hair pinned, and covered with a plain, drab shawl; another shawl hid the fur trim of her coat. Foolish, foolish—and fortunate. She should never have taken up such an invitation without time to study those who would be there. These were not middle-class mourners or bored women trapped at home, but people of more influence, more knowledge about the world. It was conceivable that they had met Polish and Russian nobility, and highly likely that they were far more widely read than Catherine.

As she stepped on the omnibus, a man jostled her—a well-dressed man of moderate stature, with a black felt hat pulled low. She gasped, and then pretended she had come close to losing her footing. The irritated face she glimpsed bore no similarity to that in her Islington vision.

I am not whispered to by daemons.

It was Sunday, and she wished for rest, for sleep, but there was only time to return to her lodgings and change. Out came the dull dress that made her Mrs Merson's dowdy companion, and borrowed rings were slipped into their box. She wiped her lips clean of any adornment, tied her hair into a tight bun, and set out for her cousins, bound by a thread of duty which felt more like a chain with every day. Five shillings she could spare, which would be presented as a contribution towards Aunt Levinia's medicines. Why she and Clarissa had to keep this charade was beyond her. She nodded at Mrs B's talk of lamb cutlets for dinner, and was out of the door again.

This was not a day of rest, whatever the pulpit might demand. Some still worked; others paraded with their sweethearts or paid fawning court to their enemies in tearoom and tavern. The process was much the same. Evening services would begin soon, and churchgoers lined the parks, showing off how proud they were of being so modest and Christian. Across the river, the beggars increased in number the closer she came to Stepney. The blind and the limbless on one side of the street, the palliards with their artfully applied "wounds" and woeful falsehoods on the other.

She knew deception when she saw it. The bent, straw-haired man by the closed butcher's shop—she had seen him changing his clothes in an alley not five hundred yards away, putting torn fustian on over a clean shirt and experimenting with his limp. With a good act, he would make more than a factory worker, and drink it down as quickly as any one of them. Two prim, tightly-buttoned women passed him as she watched, tossing coin into his cap. She could shout after them, and explain that the man was a fraud, but what was Madame Rostov?

The sight depressed her, and as she approached the Weatherhead's, she felt the weight of lies on her. Lady Seldon's had been exhausting. Now here she was at Clarissa's door, ready for another round.

It was a relief to have the door answered by Jennie Weatherhead, the same age as Clarissa but with a friendly, honest appeal.

"Why, dear Cathy!" said Jennie, smiling.

They embraced, a reminder that they were blood. Jennie had taken her brother's death badly. The last of the family money had been lost in court fees, and the spirit had left the family. The move away from Harwich, to cheaper lodgings in London, had stripped Jennie of much of her life. Promised jobs never materialised; Clarissa's health did not improve. It had been a mistake. Laundry and mending was all that was left to them.

"You look well," said Catherine. She did not; she looked drawn and tired, despite her greeting smile.

"Mama has been asking for you."

Catherine paused in the hall. It was an oddly direct thing from Jennie, before they had even exchanged news and pleasantries.

"She is worse." Jennie bit at her lip. "We intended to write to you today."

"The doctors—"

"Have pronounced, Cathy. There is little hope."

In the parlour, Clarissa looked up from her patching a long gingham dress in an old-fashioned cut.

"You've heard?" No warmth, no welcome.

"Yes. I have some money for medicine. I thought—"

"Keep it. Mama won't need it."

Jennie looked shocked at the bitterness in her sister-in-law's voice. "Clarissa! Catherine only seeks to help—you are too harsh."

"I know." Clarissa let the dress fall to the floor. "I know. Everyone seeks to help, but what good does it do, any of it?" She looked to the discoloured wallpaper. "I had my nice little house in Harwich, with flowers at the door. The vicar's wife would call, as if I were her equal, and there would be fresh scones, brought in by a maid…"

"I remember, dear." Jennie sighed.

"That was a home. And all we entertain these days is 'Joshua's child.'" Clarissa spoke in mimicry of the invalid in the room above, her eyes now on Catherine. "Your father should have helped us. He has wealth aplenty, enough to buy this house and raze it to the ground."

"Oh, he does," said Catherine, a red heat coming to her cheeks. "Write to him this day, and be welcome. Let him list the whys and wherefores of how it would not be reet to assist thee." Anger stripped her talk back to the open sewers of Keighley. "Of how we mek our own way, of the perils of charity. Aye, have to it, cousin, and read the sermon he sends instead of coin!"

Panting, she stared the two women down, even as she knew that Jennie deserved better.

"I meant—" began Clarissa.

"You meant what you said." She took a deep breath, seeking to find some composure, to return to herself. "You try your hand with that lying prater of a man. I'd not ask a penny of him, nor take one, neither—not if I was lying like Aunt Levinia in his very front parlour."

The sudden heat was spent. Jennie stood astonished; Clarissa Weatherhead put her long face in her hands and wept. Unable to risk another word, Catherine went upstairs on her own. Where were the children, Benjamin and Maisie? Waiting at some laundry, probably, for mending work to bring back to the house. Or hoping to cadge half-bars of soap, a collar that no one would miss. She would leave them a gift, what change she had—Clarissa could not refuse that.

The smell of the old lady's room was worse than before, the tang of incontinence and something else beneath the lavender water. There was a small fire this time, but Catherine thought she smelled fever. Her aunt's lined face was too pink, her eyes too bright.

"I heard you," she said, struggling to prop herself higher in the bed.

"I'm sorry, Aunt Levinia. My temper."

"The only thing you got from him, God be praised." Levinia wiped discoloured spittle from her lips. "You have your grandfather's sharp mind, and sense of duty. You have his iron in your jaw, and in your eyes. Be thankful."

And with that at least, Catherine agreed.

"You wanted to see me, aunt."

"I did. Time is short—I have weeks left, maybe less." She waved aside a murmur of denial. "Time is short, I said, and you are the only one to whom I can talk."

"What is it you wanted to say?"

"I want revenge. Frederick Caille caused my son's death, and then laughed at us in court. I was there to see him smirk to his fine and noble friends…" The old woman paused, strained for breath. After a brief coughing fit, she continued. "He brought us to our knees, and lower, yet it meant nothing to him. I doubt he remembers our names. I want the man who killed my son to suffer."

Catherine had often heard it said that one should humour the dying. She didn't subscribe to the belief. What was the value of false hope?

"Aunt Levinia, it cannot be done," she said. "If it could, some other would have done it long before. I hear he has no shortage of enemies and detractors, as he has his allies and lickspittles."

"Reach under my bed. There is something for you there."

Next to the chamberpot sat a large pasteboard box, which Catherine pulled out. It felt as damp as the house, its lid held down with faded blue ribbon.

"I have kept everything," said Levinia. "That which was said of Caille in the papers and the courts. What little I found out, before and after. One day it may be of use—now it is yours."

The wind through the cracked window was an echo of her aunt's laboured breathing. Levinia's eyes had closed, but Catherine felt her still awake.

"Someone might spread calumny, or expose more of his false dealings, I suppose," she said after a minute or so had passed. "They might seek further ways to besmirch his name."

It was possible, though it was a task beyond one in her position. There were people like Lady Seldon, and maybe others, if Madame Rostov was fortunate enough to get closer to them. Should she rise in renown, and be courted…there were surely spider-webs of gossip and influence in those fine drawing rooms, and each wealthy man had some consort to whisper in his ear. Would that make any difference to a man of Caille's standing?

"I charge you, Catherine Weatherhead, to hold this in your mind. If opportunity comes, if Caille's black armour cracks…" The old woman's voice was stronger, steadier, than before. "The grave has not been dug that can hold me, if you deny me this one last hope. I want ruin to come to Frederick Caille, for him to sink to the level he has driven the Weatherheads. Swear."

"No," said Catherine. "I will not swear."

She was astonished to see a weak smile form on her aunt's lips.

"Iron in the jaw, and in the eyes," said Levinia. "You see, that is why I have you alone left to me. Clarissa, Jennie—they would have sworn, and lied, to please me. And it is how I know that you will remember my charge."

"I did not say that," Catherine protested.

"I know. But you will take the box."

Catherine lacked the energy to argue. There would be her cousins to placate downstairs, and then the long journey back to her lodgings in Southwark. The lamb cutlets would be cold. And on Monday, she must find sources which told her more about those three young women of Chelsea, before she sat with them.

"I will call again in the week, Aunt Levinia, if that suits you?"

The old woman coughed, and lay back to rest. She did not answer.

ELEVEN

Stuart Brevard's attack having come mere hours earlier, Mary Jane continued to look back in worry that he would find her even as she arrived at Gander's Bush in Wapping and Mrs Carthy welcomed her at the front door of the brothel. Mary Jane took one more glance back before entering.

A woman in her late thirties, Mrs Carthy had prematurely grey hair, almost white, framing a sweet face. In silhouette, her figure cut a pear shape: small bust, thin arms and shoulders, large backside. Over her rather plain, white calico chemise and grey top skirt, she wore a kitchen apron.

"My sister has finally done as you suggested," the proprietress said, walking into her kitchen, "and gone to the Phoenix after your things."

Excited by the news, Mary Jane followed, almost stepping on the small woman. "Did Mrs Buki come away with anything?" she asked. Although so hopeful she could hardly contain herself, Mary Jane shut her mouth before saying more. She had confided in Mrs Buki about the necklace, but not Mrs Carthy.

"I don't know. I'll send my boy around to ask her here to tell us. I'm sure she'll come—I have a new recipe for plum duff to try out on her."

Both proprietresses had a love of puddings and enjoyed sharing recipes.

"You can use Bell's room," Mrs Carthy said. "She's finally gone to the infirmary, poor girl."

The young woman had suffered stomach pains for the four months since Stuart Brevard kicked her. Ashamed that she hadn't gone to the young woman's aid at the time of the attack, Mary Jane made a promise to herself to go to the Whitechapel Union Infirmary to visit her friend.

"You're third in line for bath water if you want it," Mrs Carthy said, bustling about her kitchen, beginning preparations for the pudding. "You're welcome to look for something in the wardrobe."

"Thank you, Ma'am," Mary Jane said. "I'll look for clothing, but I shan't be wanting the water."

She went to a room off the entrance hall, one that housed a

large wardrobe, picked out clothes that would fit her, and took them upstairs to Bell's room.

Mary Jane currently knew with a certainty that the fault lay with her for Bell's injury at the hands of Stuart Brevard.

Returning to the Laughing Magpie following a stay at Morganstone's in early May, she had heard from Mrs Buki about Stuart Brevard coming to the brothel to ask about her. Not long after that, hidden from the man in shadows, Mary Jane saw him injure Bell. When the violence began, another man nearby came to Bell's aid, while Mary Jane remained hidden. Even though the Good Samaritan had stepped in to help, the poor girl had been severely harmed. Mary Jane had retreated before she was seen. She felt cowardly doing so. Returning to the Laughing Magpie, she told the proprietress about what happened.

"You shall both go stay with my sister, Elsa Carthy, at Gander's Bush," Mrs Buki said, "Just until this bludger has given up on you. You'll be safe there. She is married to John McCarthy, a landlord of some reputation."

Mary Jane remembered being unable to look Bell in the eye on the day they both removed to Mrs Carthy's rotting two-story wooden house in Breezer's Hill off the Ratcliffe Highway. After settling Bell into a wretched little bedroom upstairs, the proprietress took Mary Jane to a similar room down the hall.

A cell for labour, she thought, looking at the tiny, ill-furnished chamber. Yellow and grey with stains, the exposed ticking of the sagging straw mattress on the small rope bed disgusted her. Roughly folded, frayed bedclothes lay upon the foot of the bed. A battered washstand with ewer and basin sat against the rear wall, a small mirror above. Mary Jane believed she could smell the odours of the men and women who had struggled for release together in the room over the years, their sweat, their now rancid sexual fluids absorbed into the wood, the cloth, the plaster. The atmosphere gave a dizzying emptiness to the pit of her stomach.

To fall even farther from the heights of the Phoenix gay house brought back the melancholy that had lifted after she found Thomas. The room would do as a crib for satisfying clients, but she would spend as much time as she could at Thomas's apartments.

"I understand you were at the Phoenix for a time," Mrs Carthy said.

Mary Jane swallowed hard before answering. "Yes, for a short time."

"My sister has always been a good friend to the abbess there."

"Mrs Arseneau?"

"Yes. Mrs Buki knows everyone in the business in London. Mrs Arseneau has depended on her several times for information and introductions."

Now that was good news.

Shortly thereafter, Mary Jane had a talk with Mrs Buki about the hidden necklace.

"We could share the earnings from a sale of the jewellery, should you succeed in retrieving it," Mary Jane told her.

At the time, Mrs Buki had seemed doubtful about the idea.

Four months after making that offer, Mary Jane saw recovery of the valuable item as necessary for her escape from harm. She vividly recalled the violence of Stuart Brevard's attack on her earlier that day, his apparent glee at having her under his control. Relocating to some place where Mr Brevard would not find her had to be her ultimate goal.

Since Mary Jane had been staying so often at Thomas Morganstone's apartments, her room at Gander's Bush had been given to another ladybird, and her possessions put in storage in the cellar. In Bell's room, she undressed and cast aside the damp clothing she'd worn on the walk from Stepney, then dressed in a Prussian-blue linen skirt and bodice she'd taken from the house wardrobe with Mrs Carthy's permission.

Waiting for Mrs Buki to come to Gander's Bush for plum duff and conversation, Mary Jane began to worry that the woman's cut of the necklace might reduce the possible earnings too much.

Too late to change the bargain now.

She took out her bottle of laudanum and took a sip.

"Mrs Buki has arrived," Mrs Carthy called up the stairs.

Mary Jane joined the two sisters in the kitchen.

At forty-five years of age, Mrs Buki still had the figure of a young woman, and might have easily been mistaken for one if not for her heavily lined face. She looked good dressed as a ladybird, and with her dark hair done up with pins. As far as Mary Jane knew, she did not seek clients of her own.

While Mrs Carthy was gone from the room, fetching cream from the cellar, Mrs Buki spoke. "I recovered some dunnage and paste jewellery that Mrs Arseneau said belonged to you. They are bundled in a blanket in the entrance hall. I was not able to secretly get to the top of the armoire."

Mary Jane did not like the news.

Mrs Carthy returned and served the pudding.

Downcast and thoughtful, Mary Jane took little notice of eating the fruity delight.

Of course, London is a great, frightening labyrinth, filled with many people and goings-on. Stuart Brevard shall not find me as easily a second time. I have survived the violence of men before. Should I be careful, I'll avoid him. His red hair stands out like a sore thumb. Moving south of the river might be all that's needed.

Again, she remembered how she'd felt, the urgency of her earlier fear.

No, across the river is not *enough. Those thoughts come from my desire to stay in London! I just need the chink to make a fresh start elsewhere.*

"That was truly delicious, Elsa," Mrs Buki said when finished with her plum duff.

"Thank you, sister." Mrs Carthy said.

"Yes, quite tasty," Mary Jane decided, tasting its remnants on her tongue as if for the first time.

"Excuse me for a moment," Mrs Carthy said, and she stepped out to take the cream back to the cellar.

Once she'd gone, her sister placed a warm hand on one of Mary Jane's. "Of course, I said nothing of the muff and necklace to Mrs Arseneau, so that you might still have the opportunity to get them one day." She paused for a moment as if considering something. "That man what came to call on you at my house, the bow-legged one with the spattered togs—he a plasterer?"

"Fleming?" Mary Jane asked. "Yes, he is."

"The Phoenix has shoddy plaster, needs work, possibly near the ceiling beside the armoire in your old room there."

"Thank you," Mary Jane said, clasping and squeezing the woman's hands.

"Look at your face!" Mrs Buki said, "your shining eyes!"

Mary Jane's mood had improved.

When Mrs Carthy returned, Mary Jane said, "I'll just get my things from the cabinet in the cellar and be off. Thank you for the delicious pudding."

"You're welcome, dear." Mrs Carthy said. "You know you are always welcome here."

Mary Jane retrieved her belongings from the cellar storage cabinet, picked up the bundle Mrs Buki had placed in the entrance hall, and left Gander's Bush, headed for the crossing of Globe Road and Green Street. With so much to carry, she decided to pay for a cab to take her there. She would arrive well before Joseph Fleming did—he'd said after seven o'clock in the evening—but the idea Mrs Buki had given her awakened new hope in Mary Jane, and she was too excited about the possibilities presented to wait.

⚓

Mary Jane waited at the Green Man pub across the street from Fleming's room for two and a half hours before he arrived home after his day of labour.

He proudly showed her his crib. The new brick tenement at 200 Globe Road had water closets on each landing. His room, a large one in the corner of the first floor, had a bay window, built-in shelves, and counters.

"The flue draws properly," Fleming said, "In colder weather, the room holds its warmth well."

Although Mary Jane knew better than to present her pressing need right away, she could not wait to speak of it. She told him about the necklace and the difficulty in retrieving it from the Phoenix gay house. His brow rose at the name of the fine brothel, and she got the impression he knew the place.

"The necklace were a gift from a client when I worked at the gay house. The proprietress holds that I owe her, and would claim the jewellery if she knew it were there."

Thankfully, he did not pry into why her circumstances had been reduced to the likes of the Laughing Magpie and Gander's Bush, and what had led to her leaving the necklace at the Phoenix.

"Surely your treasure will be found in short order, if only by the

104

charwoman."

"The decorative parapet around the top of the armoire hides it," Mary Jane said. "Even should one stand on a chair, the place cannot be seen, and is difficult to reach. I had to toss the necklace and muff there. The spot is so high and dusty, I don't believe anyone has ever cleaned it. We would split the proceeds of the sale of the necklace, should you succeed in retrieving it." She described a plan she'd developed on her ride to Globe Road, one based on Mrs Buki's suggestion involving his services as plasterer.

"Is that why you accepted my offer to come stay?" Fleming asked with a look of worry.

"No, certainly not," she said persuasively, since that had indeed not been her initial reason.

He seemed to accept her answer as truth.

"I see your cokum," he said. "The lurk will have to be considered carefully. It shall be more difficult than you suggest."

"But you'll think about how the job might be done, won't you?" Mary Jane said, leaning in to give him a deep kiss.

He responded with enthusiasm. Then, in the midst of the kiss, he seemed distracted. When he pulled away, she worried that he was not sufficiently charmed.

"If Mrs Arseneau owns the building," he said, "I'll have to come up with a fakement to account for offering a bid low enough she cannot refuse."

Indeed, I do have his interest.

"Should she have a landlord… well, that is a matter Mr Morganstone might best handle, should you be willing to cut him in."

"Yes, I would do that."

He shook his head. "No, no, my dear, I cannot work on that yet. We'll sort out your necklace later. I do one piece of *what-if* at a time. You're right to think the dust says no one cares about the top of that armoire."

But not well enough.

When he said, "what if," he meant a criminal scheme. She knew little about his work, only what he and Thomas spoke about openly.

"I thought you two worked a job bona fide."

"Oh, no, we're working again for family people. Nothing

dangerous, mind you, and it shall pay well enough."

Mary Jane knew he meant professional criminals, a family of such.

At least he'd thought about her proposal. He saw no urgency in the matter because he didn't know about Stuart Brevard.

She didn't want to say anything about Brevard for fear that Fleming might break with her to avoid exposure to danger.

"You can see clients here if you wish," Joseph said, "as long as I'm not here. I'll be sure to let you know my schedule."

He continued to surprise her with his tolerance of her profession.

With time, I will persuade him to retrieve the necklace.

In the meantime, the Globe Road address was far enough removed from Thomas Morganstone's apartments for her to feel that Stuart Brevard would not find her easily. She also appreciated that Fleming's room was close to her haunts in Stepney; she could continue to earn soliciting, while remaining within the area where she had organised a protective weave of ladybird friends.

Mary Jane grew so busy over the following month that she never took the time to go see Bell in the Whitechapel Union infirmary. Shame welled up in her every time she thought about that.

TWELVE

The first few sittings for Miss Chambers and her friends did not pay, not directly. These were women who bought everything on their accounts at various stylish stores. They carried money when issuing forth to the theatre, or some other performance, but even then they rarely had to open their purses. That was the function of men—to order another bottle of champagne, to offer purchase of a bauble on display in a shop window. Catherine would not have called the women spoiled, exactly. They knew the worth of things, and they knew especially the worth of someone else footing the bill. It placed her in an awkward position, as little able to ask as they were likely to think of offering.

At the same time she was burdened with her aunt's words, and could not help but wonder if she might find out more about Caille through such circles. She was determined not to let the old woman's phantasies of revenge become her niece's obsession, but she could at least be observant. Even banking magnates and wealthy industrialists must make mistakes.

Her own income was still an issue, and so two or three times a week she offered her services to the Mrs Carltons and Miss Bournelles of middle-class London. The lower the status of her sitters, the more they understood that she, too, needed to eat. It was ironic that those who worked hardest would cover her fees willingly, but had the least money available to do so.

Miss Bournelle was content that her dear Lottie was being well served, though the former nanny might have been surprised at the nature of the sittings, which involved more gossip and discussion of literature than it did psychic enquiry. Catherine, who had been a precocious girl and an avid reader, had heard of few of the books which Miss Chambers held in esteem. Miss Chambers, on the other hand, would have never read *The Rearing of Chicken for Profit*, or the *Creed of the Congregational Church*, not that Madame Rostov could admit to those. Catherine's grandfather had been generous with his books and a man of eclectic tastes, but those tastes had not often run to fiction.

In such fields as spiritualist enquiry, theosophy and similar areas, however, Catherine held her own. Her months of candle-lit reading in her room had not been wasted. She had also devoured those works debunking various mediums and clairvoyants. Each sceptic who penned his exposure of deception added to her own knowledge of how to deceive—and how not to be caught. A recent article concerning dubious practice by Madame Blavatsky had warned her away from posing as a physical medium—the methods were tedious, requiring much training, and could still be detected by a researcher or sceptic with a good nose. Wires, extendable rods and trumpets were not for her.

Catherine's line came from lean hill farmers, men and women able to wrestle down a truculent ram or raise a dry-stone wall, who did their own slaughtering and walked a dozen miles in a morning. Some of that lived on in her, in a strong face and a figure which would never be called dainty. It amused her that even Lady Seldon thought her older than the others, a convenience when she was posing as Madame Rostov.

"You will understand, Madame," Lady Seldon would say, as one wiser head to another. There was potential there, she was sure. She feared, however, that she would have to start dropping hints about the expense of hansom cabs, or tut-tutting at the price of good sherry. She was not a charitable concern.

It was that or "borrow" the occasional silver spoon from Lady Seldon's cutlery drawer.

⚰

Early in the month, conscious of her light purse, she undertook to sit for a Mr Arthur Brompton of Wandsworth. One of Arthur Brompton's sons had died in the Sudan, and she might have rejected the opportunity, but for chance. Elsie Brown, a Keighley neighbour and friend, had two brothers in the South Staffordshires. Both had been on the Nile Expedition the year before, and their welfare had been a regular topic in the Brown household, to the point of tedium. Catherine gauged that she had absorbed enough to produce relevant "colour," should it be required.

She had scant information otherwise. Brompton was, it appeared, a widower, described as mild and pleasant by one of his neighbours (posing as a flower-seller for a few hours gained her this, and a similar character sketch from a local policeman). His maid was sadly recent in her post, and untalkative.

It would have to do.

Number Six Harbut Road, not far from the Wandsworth and Clapham Infirmary, was a pleasant terraced house, well-kept inside and out. The dour maid let Madame Rostov in, taking her outdoor coat and conducting her to a small dining room. Brompton sat there already, in one of only two straight-back chairs at a bare pine table. He rose, and smiled.

"I appreciate your willingness to indulge me, Madame Rostov." A soft voice, London but educated, from beneath a broad moustache which almost concealed his mouth.

"There are no other sitters?" She hesitated in the doorway.

"My maid will be at hand, and the daily is somewhere about, if you fear impropriety?"

His round face had a sort of grave innocence to it, and she shook her head. "It is not a difficulty."

He offered her coffee in a delicate china cup, patterned with sad blue willows, and stood by the bay window, looking out. And he talked, as if they had known each other for many months. He told of his wife, who died suddenly of the influenza two years before, and their relative content throughout their marriage. He told of his surviving son, who worked in France as a junior architect; of his dead son, the eldest, who he had loved. He recited his boy's campaign, and his death by accident at the hands of terrified Anglo-Egyptian regulars.

"Gerald crossed a picket-line without thought, and failed to hear a challenge. The sand and dust had damaged his hearing, you see, Madame—"

"I should not have come." Catherine made to rise. "I cannot help you, sir."

Brown eyes fixed her, brown eyes and a drooping moustache.

"You do not have...the gift? They said—"

"For this, I do not think so."

The small set seemed frozen—Brompton half-turned from the light, his hands entwined; Catherine standing, with one hand on the table.

"I have been fooled so many times," he said. "They say that my boy will speak through them, that he will comfort me. They talk in vague military tones, and whisper that he is near. But he is not."

She sat down again.

"I do not know what will come, Mr Brompton. I do not control...what I see or hear. If there is nothing, or if it makes no sense, you will be grieved."

So much acting, for so long, that she had forgotten what she should feel. There was a sense of unremitting sorrow in the room. It flowed from this small man—a barrow-boy could have read it.

"Will you try?"

No, she meant to say. And in a word, she would condemn him to more searching, to tricksters and black-clad women with clickers and strings hid beneath their skirts, with stolen snippets just like herself...

"Yes."

He sighed with obvious relief, and sat opposite her, holding out his hands.

"That is not necessary."

His moustache twitched, either with humour or disapproval. She ran her fingers through her tangled hair, spreading it on her shoulders. The room was a cabinet, containing only them.

It was Catherine who sat for Arthur Brompton, not Madame Rostov. She closed her eyes, and fed all that Brompton had said to herself, each word, like the mantras of the Eastern thinkers. She remembered Elsie Brown and her brothers, until her tongue was dry with sand, her lips thick for lack of water. Men had died, far away. Gerald Brompton had died, far away...

And she knew him, taller than his father, less full of face. The uniform, down to polished buttons, and a vile-looking, unkempt beast at his side. A camel, though she had never seen one in life, only pictures in a children's book. He had Arthur Brompton's eyes, too sad and soft, and the rifle in his arms was wrong—he was not meant to kill. He missed his home, and his father...

"He should never have gone," she said, almost a whisper. "Only a boy, a gentle soul..."

Brompton was silent. She let the Aether, the terrible flux of minds, thoughts and emotions, take hold of her, lead her through images of young men spilling their blood, their intestines, into the disinterested sand—some trapped in borrowed uniforms, some choking their last in the Arab jellaba. White skin burned red, and black skin scarred with anger. All children. All sons to a stricken father…

Was what she saw being drawn from the man before her? From others who had known Gerald Brompton, or from the living brother, so far away? She struggled, screwing her eyes so tight shut it hurt. There was no soul, no voice from beyond, only the wash of sorrow and imagery.

It faded.

"He is dead." The palms of her hands were wet, and she had broken a nail gripping the edge of the table. "He was alive, and he loved you, as you did him. He has passed on beyond our cares." She almost believed the words. "I have nothing else."

When she looked, Brompton seemed radiant, even the moustache failing to hide his smile.

"Thank you, Madame Rostov."

"I have given you little enough."

"You did not lie. You did not lie, which is all I asked of the others, but they could not oblige."

She sat back, drained. "Do you have brandy, Mr Brompton?"

He poured them a glass each, and they sat, watching a blackbird on the tree outside the window. Neither spoke until the bird, startled by a passing cart, flapped off to the south.

"Would five pounds be suitable recompense for your time, Madame?"

She meant to refuse, but thought of the Weatherheads. "It would be more than generous, sir."

"I have no reason not to be." He counted out the notes from a pocket-book, and held them out. "Please take them."

They parted on the doorstep, the man with a lightness to his step; the woman with thoughts she did not like to face.

That night in her room she opened the box from Aunt Levinia. Her attention was not on the task, and she flicked through ragged clippings without great interest. She read of Frederick Caille, noting his many holdings here and abroad, his position on so many boards and committees. She went through scraps she had already seen more than once, scraps which laid out the utter pointlessness of common citizens taking men like Caille to court.

It was depressing. One law in the land, but only truly effective if you owned the land, it seemed.

There was a wife, and a young son. Was she as wicked as the husband? If not, how could she bear to be with such a man? Catherine could almost answer that, she thought. Comfort, wanting for nothing, and access to the finest of the capital's entertainments. Influence beyond that which most woman achieved.

There were, no doubt, many reasons why Mrs Caille might lay herself down next to wickedness.

THIRTEEN

Mary Jane nodded her head periodically to give the sailor the impression that she listened to what he had to say. One of three men vying for her attention in the Angel and Trumpet pub in Stepney High Street, he sat across the sticky table from her.

The dose of laudanum she'd had before entering allowed her to sit at ease in the pub. Prostitution among the coarse and unwashed became more bearable with a dose of the drug.

Soon, I'll be free, she told herself. *Once Joseph retrieves the necklace, I'll be done with the East End entirely.* She'd been telling herself that for a month, ever since taking up with Joseph Fleming.

"What shall I call you?" the sailor asked.

The other two at the table, the labourer sitting to her left, and the older fellow, perhaps a tradesman of some sort, on her right, both leaned in to hear her answer over the surrounding noise.

"Ginger," she said. As far as Mary Jane knew, Stuart Brevard didn't know her by that name, so she felt safe using the moniker.

"Pretty," the sailor said with a grin. "I like a little ginger."

She produced a demure smile and took a dainty sip of her bitter.

For a Thursday afternoon, the Angel and Trumpet had drawn a rather full house, with raucous groups at several tables. The haze of tobacco smoke helped obscure the many distracting glances and occasional stares aimed at Mary Jane from persons, mostly men, at other tables, and aided her pretence that she could see no further than ten feet. The tactic had always promoted the idea that her glances alone had value. If a man wanted to catch her eye, he'd have to approach.

The dark oak furnishings of the Angel and Trumpet, the local events ephemera decorating its walls, and the limited selection of victuals available were no more remarkable than the clients she found there. Mary Jane liked the taste of their bitter, though, and she wasn't well-known to the establishment since she'd spent most of her time in the area down the street at the Crown and Dolphin or at Dresser's Coffee Shop. That gave her what she knew to be a false sense of security. The pub stood within a quarter of a mile of Thomas Morganstone's apartments, as did Dresser's. Yet she had persuaded herself that with so many people and so much activity in the neighbourhood, Stuart Brevard would not locate her easily, even if he still searched the area.

Mary Jane had grown so weary of being hunted—the continuing sense of unease, and frequent realisation that, at any moment, she might need to run from the man—she'd looked for ways to dampen her worries. Assuming Mr Brevard would turn violent again if he caught her, or at the very least take her to the police and make her answer for her crimes against his brother, she'd got a knife that fit in her boot and asked Fleming to teach her how to use it. In her mind's eye, she'd practiced what to do in a possible future attack. She imagined that since she hadn't come up with a knife the last time, and he plainly wasn't a professional bludger, he'd be so surprised to see her blade that she'd somehow gain the advantage. Her fear of the man had faded some with time.

Two fellows approached and stood behind the three men already seated at her table, as if queuing up for their chance at her. Possessed of uncommon beauty, Mary Jane never had difficulty attracting men to her table at a pub. She would consider which of the current batch of three would be the best prospect, or dismiss them and consider the other two. If she dismissed them as well, there would always be more.

Seeing the woman who had rescued her from Stuart Brevard's attack in Bale Street, Mary Jane became distracted from the business at hand.

Jennifer. Yes, that was her name, Miss Jennifer Weatherhead.

She sat alone, four tables away. Dressed nicely in a plum-coloured skirt and a dark brown bodice, she clearly had done herself up to meet someone. She'd removed her hat and shawl so that the gloss of her dark hair and the slim shape of her shoulders could be seen. Her glances about suggested that she searched for a prospect of some kind. Even so, she obviously didn't want to talk to anyone.

A moment passed before Mary Jane realised that Jennifer Weatherhead was soliciting. New to the game, though, she wasn't winning, and had her tail down.

Because Jennifer looked like Mary Jane's mother, seeing her felt good, as if Mum indeed sat there in the Angel and Trumpet. That coupled with the way Jennifer had defended her, Mary Jane felt a great warmth toward her. Finding herself thinking of Miss Weatherhead *as* her mother, Mary Jane wanted to dissuade the woman from taking up prostitution.

She wanted to get up and go to Jennifer, but stopped herself.

I would only be frustrating her efforts, and at her age, she is surely frustrated enough as it is.

The tradesman at the table pushed toward Mary Jane. She drew away from his breath, a strong odour of gin and rotting teeth. Earlier, he had introduced himself as simply Franklin. "Give us a kiss," he said, "and I'll have the barmaid bring you another glass of bitter."

All three of the men were the worse for drink. Franklin, forty or fifty years old, had a shiny round face with a spiderweb of tiny blood vessels across his cheeks and nose.

A rusty guts lushington.

She'd decided he was a tradesman because he had no callouses on his hands and his clothing carried the confused smells of a chandler's shop of household goods. He wore a grey wool jacket and trousers, the cuffs and hems worn. The watch chain that dipped into the pocket of his faded black linen waistcoat flashed a dull brass colour. By the quality and condition of his clothing, Mary Jane judged that Franklin had met with small success in life or significant debt.

"No, thank you," she said.

Trying to avoid the tradesman's foul breath entirely, she found herself looking at the labourer to her left, a burly blonde fellow somewhat blackened with a residue of coal. With the darkness rubbed into the creases of his face and hands and his clothes made a colourless dark grey from the dusting, he reminded her painfully of her deceased husband, Berwyn. The labourer had been trying to catch her eye for some time, and she'd avoided talking to him. Possibly a coal backer, he would have few funds to spend on her.

Unbidden, she recalled a black smear of coal on her pale skin as she lay naked, holding her Berwyn. They had been married a month and she'd been so eager to make love to him on that day she hadn't let him wash after his hours of labour in the coal mine. He put up a fight when she tried to drag him to their bed. Finally, he'd relented and let her have her way.

What a mess that were to clean, but the prigging were worth the trouble.

The memory, bitter-sweet, brought more pain than pleasure.

She turned away from the coal backer. Setting aside the pretence that she could see no further than ten feet, Mary Jane focused on the one she chose to think of as Mum.

Jennifer rubbed her face, perhaps to rearrange the features and give herself a new look, one that would belong in the pub. Still, her face displayed unease. She looked up at a gentleman passing by her table with his companions. Catching her eye, the fellow quickly turned away. Although attractive enough, Jennifer's appearance held an unavoidable dread of her very pursuit. Mary Jane had seen the look before, especially in young, green tail. She'd been that way herself, five years earlier.

Franklin gripped her under the arm, trying to lift her from her seat. "You have a crib nearby, somewhere we can go?"

Mary Jane became deadweight in her chair, looked toward the sailor.

"Here, now," the sailor said to the tradesman, "I had her talking. You wait your turn."

Franklin turned slowly toward him, said, "Look at your hooks, Jack Tar."

The sailor's hands were stained black with rope pitch. Mary Jane had known worse. He looked fit enough and had a moderately handsome, if weathered face.

"You think she wants those touching her?" Franklin asked.

She knew the angry words would end with fisticuffs. Men had fought over her since her days as a mere dollymop in Cardiff. To see one suffer for desiring her seemed to make men want her all the more. She'd played that to her advantage on occasion.

"My name is *Tedward*," the sailor said, his tone cold. "*Not* Jack Tar."

Mary Jane hoped he would win. He had spoken to her with some respect. Probably of able seaman grade, he no doubt earned less than the tradesman, yet was more promising. The Royal Navy withheld much of sailors' pay until they reached home port to prevent desertion. He still smelled of his ship, the tar on his hands, and the sea, so he had likely returned to London that day. If his voyage had been long, he might be in a mood to squander his funds.

"*Tedward?*" Franklin shouted. He bellowed his laughter.

Heads turned toward the sound. Jennifer Weatherhead's eyes, four tables away, grew large with a look of concern. She obviously wasn't accustomed to pubs and loud men.

Mary Jane hoped to catch her eye, and couldn't tell if she had.

"Who would *give* such a name?" The tradesman asked. "Mum couldn't decide between Edward and Theodore?"

The sailor rose swiftly and shoved the tradesman. Franklin clung to the back of Mary Jane's chair as he fell. The legs of the rickety seat gave way, dumping her in the sawdust on the floor. Tedward fell upon Franklin, pounding with black fists.

The coal backer fled.

Mary Jane crawled under the table.

From her new vantage, she saw the beautiful blonde prostitute, Gabriella Gorse, at the entrance to the pub. The woman had always been ill-mannered, if not insulting to Mary Jane. Because both had once been prostitutes of high standing, perhaps a competitiveness came between them. Folks called her Gabby because she chatted up all the fresh tail in the neighbourhood. She seemed too helpful to the new girls; the daily crop of inexperienced pauper women of many ages that landed hard on the streets with but one commodity left to them.

Remembering that the woman in the printed sketch Stuart Brevard had dropped in Bale Street looked more like Gabby, Mary Jane had a notion that he might find and beat the churlish prostitute one day.

No, I shan't want cruel thoughts, just because I don't like her.

Gabby took half a step into the pub and stopped, holding the door open. The ugly, scarred face of Nick Shears came into view behind her, looking into the establishment over her shoulder. He'd become the most feared Demander of the Gully Bleeders. A gang like the Beloved Ratters of Cardiff and the High Rips of Liverpool, the Bleeders took protection money from prostitutes. Mary Jane had to pay what Nick Shears demanded. He carried sheep shears in his belt. Thinking about what he'd done with them to women, her hands moved involuntarily to cover her breasts.

Still in the doorway, Gabby nodded toward the table where Jennifer sat.

"No!" Mary Jane said aloud, the word drowned in the sounds of the struggle between Tedward and Franklin.

Nick also nodded, palmed something to Gabby, and they parted company without fully entering the Angel and Trumpet.

I have to warn Jennifer.

The fight between Franklin and Tedward moved in Mary Jane's direction. Out of the confusion of tumbling bodies emerged a clawing arm, probably trying to find something to grip as a weapon. The hand closed on Mary Jane's booted right ankle. Noting that the palm wasn't blackened with tar, she brought the heel of her other boot down on the hand's exposed digits, and it withdrew instantly.

Keeping her head down, she got up, and moved toward Jennifer's table. When she got there, she discovered an empty chair. Looking toward the front of the pub, Mary Jane saw the woman's plum-coloured skirt. Jennifer passed through the door to exit the Angel and Trumpet.

Mary Jane had to catch up with her.

Out in Stepney High Street, Jennifer could be seen fairly running from the pub, despite a limp. Mary Jane hurried forward to catch up. They slipped quickly between the many people using the brick footway. Drawing closer, Mary Jane reached to touch her shoulder. Not wanting to startle, she hesitated, pulled back, and said a bit too loudly, "Excuse me, Mum."

Jennifer looked back at her without breaking stride, then faced forward again as she continued. The limp became more pronounced, but whatever the injury, it didn't seem to slow her much. She had not been limping on the day she came to the rescue with her laundry sack.

Mary Jane realised she must look a mess, with saw dust from the floor of the pub caught in her hair and clothing. Still, she sped up and placed her left hand on Jennifer's right shoulder. The woman stopped and turned. Her six inch advantage in height added to the illusion that she was Mary Jane's mother.

"*Yes?*" Jennifer said, her eyes narrowed, brow furrowed. She didn't seem to recognise Mary Jane. "I saw you in the pub. Those men fighting…"

"Yes, at my table," Mary Jane said. She forced a chuckle. "Tedward and Franklin. I had to get away from them."

Mum raised her brow with a disapproving look. "*And…?*"

"I am the woman you helped in Bale Street about a month ago. You struck a man with a sack of laundry. He were molesting me, and that allowed me to get away. I saw you again later that day on the street and introduced myself."

"Yes, I remember you." Jennifer looked around distractedly, then fixed her eyes on her feet.

For what had been a brave, helpful woman, she seemed timid and uncaring at present.

Mary Jane struggled to find a way to talk to her. "You were... *ill at ease* in the pub," she began.

"I'm glad I could help. Now, I must—"

Mary Jane pressed on. "Y-you wanted—"

"I wanted *out*, just as soon as they—" Rather than finish, the woman shook her head, pulled her checked woollen shawl tighter. She adjusted her felt hat, and began to edge away.

"No, not *then*," Mary Jane said, shaking her head, "*before* the trouble started, you..." Again, she didn't know what to say.

Jennifer looked nonplussed and impatient.

"Pardon me, I've forgotten my manners. I remember your name, Jennifer. You may not remember mine. Miss Mary Jane Kelly, I am."

She immediately regretted giving her true name.

"I am Miss Weatherhead." Jennifer turned her face away from a biting wind.

Because Mary Jane had seen the woman as much like her mother, until that moment she had not thought of her as a spinster. *How painful it must be for her to learn soliciting. No wonder she is so irritable and guarded.*

I should try to persuade her to give up the trade, yet her choices are truly none of my business, and she must have her reasons.

"Did you have a purpose in stopping me?"

Mary Jane wanted to warn her about Nick Shears straight off, but didn't want to frighten her away. Instead, she said, "Street cokum, you need."

"Say what you mean," Jennifer said with a frown.

"I can help you learn—"

"Learn what?" The frown deepened.

How shall I allow for her dignity whilst...? Arguing with herself, Mary Jane didn't answer quickly enough.

"How to find *clients*?" Jennifer offered.

Her expression had turned to a defiant challenge, a common

response, Mary Jane knew, for one keeping shame at bay.

"Well…yes." she said, not knowing what else to say. *And something of the dangers of the street,* she thought, *like Nick Shears and the Gully Bleeders.*

She'd stood up to Harris Brevard and a variety of blackguards over the years. Mary Jane had kept a cool enough head to manage all that, yet with the way Miss Weatherhead looked at her, she felt cowed.

Jennifer gestured back the way they'd come. "Clients—like the ones you found at the Angel and Trumpet?"

Mary Jane felt herself blushing. "I *do* take risks." To admit such things to her mother—or so it seemed! "Exciting, I find it…" She looked down, then she raised her head to look Jennifer in the eye, "I manage the risks *because* I have cokum. Advice, I can give you. I'd like to help."

"*You* have experience?" Jennifer said. "*You* are cunning? I should think you were but a girl a few short years ago."

"Twenty-three years old, I am. I've been a ladybird for five years, five *long* years. Solicited, I have, amongst both toffs in the West End and labourers in the East End. I know my business."

Jennifer turned away and began walking again. Competing with the woman's long, limping stride, Mary Jane struggled to keep up.

"I made mistakes you might avoid," she said, "spent nearly a year in an infirmary in Cardiff healing from what a client gave me."

Jennifer kept walking. Mary Jane fell behind.

Why should I bother? I have my own concerns.

Mary Jane watched the woman stumble and recover. Holding her head high, Miss Weatherhead marched onward.

Another small blow to her dignity. She wouldn't have it, but I pity her.

I must do something to help!

What advice could I give quickly that might have helped me?

"Don't use the sheep's gut," she called. "Use the rubber ones."

Jennifer stopped and turned suddenly, her eyes wide, lips pressed tightly together.

Mary Jane grimaced at what she took for anger.

The older woman lifted a hand to her face. Glancing around to see if any others walking on the footway nearby had taken notice of the conversation, she crossed her lips with an index finger.

Mary Jane knew she had spoken too loudly. Jennifer had no doubt become embarrassed.

She approached, said in a quiet, cracking voice, "I bought the sheep's gut." Her expression had broken open to reveal that of an innocent child, the flesh around her eyes straining, her mouth small and worried. "This is *hopeless. I* am hopeless. We shall all end up seeking relief in the workhouse, I'm sure of that now." She bent forward and shook her head. Tears rolled down her cheeks.

"Come with me, Mum," Mary Jane said. She placed a warm hand on the woman's back. "I know a coffee shop where to we can talk without any bother."

Jennifer hesitated, and Mary Jane thought she might turn and flee again. She waited patiently.

Finally, the woman stood straight and turned to look her in the eye. "I am Miss Jennifer Weatherhead," she said with a return of some of her earlier pluck. "I *do* need help."

When the woman took her arm and allowed herself to be led, a thrill ran through Mary Jane.

She remembered her cousin, Carryl Hughes, offering an arm in a similar circumstance, and the distant echo of her father's question that followed: "Do you know what danger is, girl?"

I hope I am not leading Jennifer into peril.

FOURTEEN

He walks in shadow, and shadow serves him. He thinks nothing of thieves and thugees, of miscreants and murderers. He thinks of purpose. His collar is starched, and his cuffs are white as sepulchres; his black bowler is not jaunty, or angled to a fashion—it is proper. A half hunter watch is seated in his waistcoat, its chain the only visible mark of many and varied devices.

It is a tavern, as it so often is. He slips into a quiet corner, a glass of porter placed before him. He will not drink it. His guest is not far behind—a thick-necked man, overweight, whose collar is stained with sweat. The settle by the window creaks as the man sits down.

"They say you are good. That you know your business."

Mr Dry does not answer.

"I have a job, and it needs discretion."

A woman shrieks near the bar, discordant laughter. The Smithfield men are in, a scant half hour before the cleavers begin their work.

The large man is uncomfortable. His suit is of quality, his whiskers waxed back. He appears out of place in the Crown and Sceptre public house.

"You want the details, then," he mutters. "Yes, I suppose that's next. I have an inheritance due, from my brother, who won't see out the year. His heart. But he has a brat, and as his sole uncle, I would have to be his guardian."

"And?" Mr Dry moves his glass a half inch to one side, considering the dimensions of the small, copper-topped table. The large man looks annoyed.

"I can't wait, do you see? I have debts, and matters to manage. Others are pressing me. So, should there be an accident—with the boy, I mean—I would be my brother's legatee. I could put my affairs in order. These others who make demands, they will realise that I have expectations. They will wait."

"How old is the boy?" The voice is soft, but certain.

The large man scowls. "Thirteen years old."

"Then I cannot help you."

"You have a conscience?" The man laughs. "You are a killer, a man for hire. Since when did such as you pick and choose? The boy swims daily; he walks alone through woods which are known as haunts of beggars and

dross. He has no mother to watch him. Can you make nothing of this?"

Mr Dry has eyes which are dark and pale, according to what you choose. They take in the bustling tavern—the butcher's apprentice with his arm around a Judy; the fishwife who slips her hand into men's pockets. There is meat on the air. The morning markets will blossom soon, and all manner of things will be well.

"The young, like dogs, have little say in what they receive." He touches his forefingers together. "And I do not kill dogs. I am rather fond of them."

"An inconvenient hound should be put down." The large man is sweating, angry. "I've gone this far—paid handsomely to track you down. Now I've said too much about myself to leave the matter there. You'll do it."

"I will not."

The quiet, neutral tone seems to infuriate the other even more.

"Then I'll have word of this put round, and damn your choices. The Tradesman, indeed! That's what they called you, but you're a milksop and a taunt, less use than any lascar from the docks!"

He rises, and storms through the gathered patrons, pushing his way to the narrow streets outside. He obviously feels that his information has failed him, and the meeting has been a waste of time. There will be others, without scruples, who will assist him.

Dawn grows faint to the east, a blotch of rose on a charcoal sky. He takes a side-street heading out of Smithfield.

"Our business is not concluded."

The large man pauses, uncertain. The man he left behind in the Crown and Sceptre could not have got ahead of him, but he is there, by a rusting iron gate in the wall.

"You've changed your mind?"

"I have not."

"Then to Hell with you." The large man turns to leave the way he came, yet Dry is before him again, a slender knife in one hand. They are alone on the street.

"I...I didn't mean what I said. It was...bluster, truly. I'll say nothing, of course."

"I consider your word unreliable," says Mr Dry.

At ten minutes past five in the morning, approximately two hundred yards from Smithfield Market, Constable Samuel Markham discovers *an obstruction on his beat, one which yields to his bulls-eye lantern to become a body. A corpulent man in his forties, whose throat and wrists bear the marks of a blade—three long, well-placed slashes, no more.*

Constable Markham can see how deep the flesh has been cut, through artery, windpipe and gullet, down to bone. Despite his evident wish to vomit, the constable tries to do his duty, examining the wounds. The throat must have been first, for no one in the area recalls a cry for help.

The constable will conclude that the assailant must surely have been as large and powerful as the victim. The cobbles run with blood which has not had time to coagulate; the body is warm. When colleagues arrive, he tells them they seek a tall, muscular man with blood on his clothes.

A police van arrives to remove the body, and high above, gulls scream their annoyance. But there will be other carcasses...

Catherine gasped, almost screamed at a tightness which burned through her calf muscles. The candle was long down to a puddle of wax on the night-stand, the curtains grey squares of growing day. She had dreamed. She had dreamed of him, Edwin Dry, and woken with such pain in her legs, spiking up to her spine. Sitting on the edge of the bed, she massaged the muscles until the discomfort abated.

"Night cramps, nothing more." She drew the curtains back. On the Southwark streets, a faint mist mingled with smoke from early hearths. The hands of her clock showed a quarter of six.

The man in the vision in Islington had killed again. If she dared to find a newspaper, if she dared to look, she knew that there would be a report—"Man killed by unknown assailant in Smithfield."

Not unknown to her.

She gulped water from a carafe, stretching her toes, letting the last of the cramps subside. When she was fifteen years old, when she grew maddened by the taunt "Mardy Cath" from a gang of local children she had hired a man. That was how she saw it. Slow Charlie, a forge-worker who had his eye on her. His own mind was little better than a child's, though behind the steelworks she pulled on a cock larger than she could have imagined. When she wiped her hands and her dress clean of his spendings, she had him in her debt.

The leader of the gang was a spindly fourteen year old who brushed floors at the ironworks which employed Slow Charlie. He discovered that week that he was not to make fun of Catherine

Weatherhead. That he and his friends were to give her a wide berth. The boy's arm never did set quite right.

There were obviously more malevolent creatures than Slow Charlie available for hire in London. But what was the significance of that to her? Why did she see Edwin Dry? A question which kept intruding. She would drive it back for a day or so, and then it would return.

She could only pick at her breakfast kippers. Mrs Bessovitch saw the hovering fork, the lingered-over cup of tea.

"You have bad night."

Catherine smiled. "I had the cramps."

"In the..." Mrs B rubbed her abdomen, a generous curve beneath her apron. "Or lower, where you are a woman?"

"No, just my legs. I need some exercise. A gentle stroll."

She forced down the second kipper, tried to give her landlady a reassuring smile, and set out for the river.

The Thames smelled better in autumn, freshened by the breeze which carried away the stink of night-soil and sour mud. Sunday's promenaders had gone. The roads by the river-front were busy with brewery drays and coal-wagons; omnibuses nosed their way through, announcing "peerless" washing powders and Liptons Teas. The scene was normal, tangible. On the way she passed the church where her flower arrangements had brought her useful talk. She should probably go back there at some point, to keep her face known and the gossip flowing.

Office workers slipped passed her, the occasional apology if they brushed her arm. Too many dark felt bowler hats. This commonest of symbols began to startle her, make her glance beneath in fear she would see *that* face. Smooth shaven, slightly rounded; the hair dark brown and neatly cut.

In her second vision there had been glasses, possibly tinted. Circles set over circles. What colour were his eyes? She thought them a pale blue, but couldn't hold the vision. Or, more likely, some part of her did not want to see that clearly. It was a face you remembered and yet forgot. Not a single distinguishing mark.

But why had she seen a murder far from where she slept? That had never happened to her before. Nor could she understand why visions of the same killer had come to her a second time...

Gulls wheeled above, said to be the sign of storm approaching at sea. More likely they were regulars, come up river for London's waste and sewage. It reminded her of Brantridge Street and the squalid tenements there. She couldn't face her cousins when she felt like this. Later in the week, it might be easier. As for Aunt Levinia—a dying woman could scheme and hope, and if that brought some small satisfaction, what was there to say?

Catherine despised Frederick Caille for causing Charles's death, but also because she understood at least something of what he was, a detail which eluded her cousins. Her own father could have been such as Caille, given opportunity.

She herself had hurt people, physically and emotionally. And in abandoning her father, she had left behind a weak and subservient mother. But she had never killed, or caused a death to occur. She had wished for a few such occurrences, certainly…

"Help a soldier, miss? Queen and Country."

She had hardly noticed the man, tucked into an alcove between two office buildings. A torn red tunic, stained dress trousers over the remaining leg. He held out an empty cocoa tin.

"I were with Wolseley, Gawd bless him, at Amoaful."

"I don't know those."

"Ashantee, miss. 'Struth, they did fight so, them blacks. Soldiers of their King, they were."

A clerk pushed past her, and she shared a choice Yorkshire expression with his pin striped backside.

"You were in Africa, then? Is that where you lost your leg?"

"Didn't lose it, miss. It were took, sliced like rare beef by a 'Shantee spear."

He had dirt in his whiskers and under them, yet there was something about him which appealed. She reached into her bag, and found her purse. A sixpence made its acquaintance with the otherwise empty cocoa tin.

"Gawd bless you."

"I don't think he's even heard of me."

"I'll ask when I sees him," said the man in the alcove.

"You do that, sir. And whilst you are there, be so kind as to ask him why I am plagued by Edwin Dry."

"He don't sound like no Ashantee."

"No. I don't know what he is."

The stiffness in her legs had gone, and at least she had two of them. Lady Seldon would want her later in the week; there might be a sitting in Catford on the Friday evening. She bid farewell to the soldier, and turned south, back to her lodgings.

Hard work would clear both family and killers from her head.

Two unremarkable séances in Vauxhall swelled her coffers a little. Accepting that she could at least pay lip service to her aunt's obsession, she bought a notebook, and sat up late, the pasteboard box open on the bed. This time, as an exercise, she noted down every mention of Mrs Caille in the clippings. She could not say why, except that she had become curious. Lady Seldon's husband was mentioned briefly in one paper, beneath the spots of mould which had begun to confuse the text. Lord Seldon had spoken of a wish that families in another case against Caille might be recompensed, a wish shared by some others in Parliament, but not those in power. Did the Seldons know the Cailles personally? She could find nothing on that.

The banker's interests were too wide, his influence too pervasive. If she drew anything from what she read, it was that he bought and sold both men and women as he pleased.

"Nothing can be done, Aunt Levinia."

Spoken to the wardrobe in Catherine's room, of course.

FIFTEEN

Mary Jane guided Jennifer across Stepney High Street and into Durham Row, a lane running along the northern edge of St. Dunstan's Church. Trees in the churchyard had taken on yellow fall colour, the leaves beautiful beneath an unusually crisp and clear blue sky.

Entering the Ashfield Place footpath to head northward to the coffee shop, Mary Jane noted that Jennifer's limp had lessened.

"While soliciting, I use the name Ginger. If you would, please use my true name only when we're alone. You should find a name to use other than your own, one that feels comfortable."

"I'll think about what that might be," Jennifer said. "My friends call me Jennie."

Mary Jane considered the last statement an invitation.

She saw a man with red side whiskers and moustache moving toward them among the other pedestrians ahead. With the warm colour of his whiskers and the hair that poked out from beneath his brown bowler, he stood out, even at a distance.

Brevard!

Her heart beat quickened, and a tingling at the back of her neck told her to hide. She didn't want to frighten Jennie.

"Look at this hat," Mary Jane said, taking Miss Weatherhead by the arm and tugging her into the recessed doorway of a Milliner's shop. "Now where is it?"

Though clearly surprised by the sudden deviation, Jennie seemed willing to concentrate on the hats displayed in the window. "Which one?" she asked. "They're all quite beautiful."

Mary Jane hadn't got a good look at the man, and she didn't think he'd seen her.

Jennie stands out too far! He might recognise her.

"Excuse me for a moment," Mary Jane said. "I have a rock in my boot. Would you steady me?" She offered her left hand.

Jennie took it and turned toward her.

Good. Now she faced completely away from the approaching man and had her face down.

Mary Jane crouched and pretended to attend to her foot with her right hand beneath the cover of her skirts. Then she realised that if the man had noticed her, crouched down as she was might prove her undoing, since she would not be able to sprint away quickly. She gathered in her hand the hems of her skirts in case she did have to make a dash for it.

The fellow walked by, taking no notice of the women in the Milliner's shop doorway.

He was not Stuart Brevard, yet she had felt the return of the fear from a month earlier, and regretted taking a more casual view of the threat he posed.

Mary Jane realised she'd been holding her breath. With relief, she took a gulp of air.

Remaining in her crouch for a few moments to compose herself, she leaned out of the recess to watch the man walk toward the pretty trees of the churchyard and turn eastward into Durham Row.

"Did you remove the stone?" Jennie asked somewhat impatiently.

"Oh…yes," Mary Jane said, standing.

The two women continued up Ashfield Place.

Mary Jane dreaded a possible future in which Stuart Brevard tracked her to her new lodgings in Globe Road, an eventuality that seemed inevitable. She'd gone to live with Joseph Fleming initially to confuse her trail and gain some male protection. Persuading him to help her recover the necklace was taking more time than she'd anticipated. If Stuart Brevard found her in Globe Road before Fleming agreed to help, and she had to move again, she might lose her chance to get the necklace altogether.

"Here we are," she said, leading Jennie into Dresser's Coffee shop, an establishment run by a man named Sean Dresser. They served tolerably good, strong coffee, different types of tea, and a few simple comestibles. Perhaps a nod to the name of the place, many old, battered dressing screens stood between the numerous tables. The patrons were allowed to move those about to create pockets of privacy.

Mary Jane regularly visited the coffee shop with potential clients, sometimes to sober them up, but more importantly she used the place as a neutral territory to get to know a man before committing to a transaction. She had organised numerous ladybirds of the area at the coffee shop, confederates of sorts. They all used the establishment for the same purpose, and shared their knowledge of the men they met in an effort to identify and, hopefully, avoid the dangerous ones.

Around the edge of a screen, Mary Jane saw May Wildash glance up at her from her seat at a table. The woman purposely caught her eye.

"Good afternoon, Ginger," May said. She adjusted the screen as if she wanted a better view of Mary Jane. The true purpose was to reveal the man with whom she sat, a tall fellow in a dark grey jacket. His thin face held heavy side whiskers and a curling moustache. They sat with cups of coffee and slices of bread. The gentleman busied himself brushing crumbs from the table, and then from his lap. He obviously didn't want the intrusion.

"Good afternoon to you, Kitty," Mary Jane said.

She had met the man before, knew that he had hired a mutual acquaintance, and that the transaction had gone off without incident. Pretending to adjust an errant lock of hair, she pulled on her right earlobe with her left hand.

"We'll have to find time to do a tightener, the three of us," Mary Jane said, "so I can properly introduce you to my new friend." She nodded toward her companion. Mary Jane didn't want to force a name on Miss Weatherhead, yet felt awkward not giving one.

Jennie, quick on the uptake, nodded and smiled. "Emma Lizabeth Smith," she said.

"Very good to meet you," May said. "Yes, I'd like that." She smiled, and turned back to her gentleman.

Mary Jane adjusted a green screen made of spilt cane or bamboo so that panels largely surrounded a table in the corner. She and Jennie took chairs at the table.

A young girl brought cups for the two, poured coffee into them, and left without a word.

"Emma Elizabeth Smith?" Mary Jane asked.

"No," Jennie said. "Emma Lizabeth, after a strict and proper school marm I had as a child in Yorkshire." She chuckled. "A small revenge for the many times she rapped my knuckles with her stick. And Smith because, well, the name is common."

Mary Jane smiled. "A good thing that you can jest. You'll need the humour. If I were to do you kindness, it would be to persuade you not to take up the life."

"My fears alone *are* a persuasion, but there's nothing for it. My family and I have lost nearly everything. I can but try."

Mary Jane saw in the woman a kind and generous gaze, now that Jennie's fear and shame had been put away. The lines around her mouth and pale eyes, deepened from worry, formed open, pleasant expressions that further reminded Mary Jane of Mum.

Obvious from Jennie's voice and manner, she had not been poor for most of her life, and had received a good education. Mary Jane longed for more stimulating conversations than she had with most of the women she currently knew, almost all of them East End prostitutes with little if any education. She got a sense that she might eventually have that with Jennie.

"Will you tell me something of your circumstances?" she asked.

"My brother, Lieutenant Charles Weatherhead, was the bread winner for our family. He died from eating bad victuals while serving aboard the HMS Penelope. Several others onboard the ship died from the poison food. His family—widow, Clarissa, and two children, Benjamin and Maisie, our mother, Levinia, and I—tried to hold a man named Caille accountable. With help from the families of the other victims, we paid a solicitor to bring the claim in civil court. The costs to trial took what little we had and we lost the case. The other families suffered the same loss. My family now survives on my brother's pension, cut in half for a surviving spouse, and what work Clarissa and I find. Levinia, my mum, has taken ill—grippe, I think—and cannot help. My cousin, Catherine Weatherhead, visits from Southwark on occasion. She earns as a widow's companion, and is able to provide a little assistance from time to time. She is so very lucky to have found a position, but then she is young—twenty-three years old, I believe—strong, and well-spoken."

"Little worse for a woman in the East End than to be left to earn for her entire family," Mary Jane said.

"I have Clarissa. I must say, though, she doesn't have the wind for some of the labour we take in." Jennie's face reflected the frustration in her tone.

"What sort of labour?"

"You saw me with it. I used it as a weapon." She smiled crookedly. "We take in work from Bryte's Laundry. Stain removal and renovation. Clarissa cannot scrub for long, so I do most of the stains. Childhood illness stole half her breath away and she doesn't have the wind to give to the effort. She does the mending instead. Well, we both do that. The children help some, when they're not in school."

"I knew there must be hardship for you to turn to…"

Jennie nodded her head rapidly with a grim smile. Mary Jane didn't finish.

She watched the older woman sip her coffee. *Yes*, she decided, *Jennie has it in her to keep herself safe while soliciting. She needs to follow a few simple rules. She will not want to discuss what's needed, though she knows she must.*

"Don't hurry," Mary Jane said, getting down to the business. "Get to know a man a bit with conversation first."

Jennie nodded, clearly listening intently and thinking about the words.

"Bring him here, if you can. Women I know what come here will take a look at him and give you a signal." She demonstrated with a slight tug on her right earlobe with her left hand. "*Right ear should the man be right and true, left ear if he's left you black and blue.* A simple shrug says you don't know. Introduce you, I will, to those willing to show you the ropes. Once you get to know the local clientele, you can help too. When you make the signal, always use the opposite hand so there's no confusing, and do so as easy as you can. Some men are so wary, they'll flee should they suspect a conspiracy, even if it's harmless to them."

Jennie took a deep breath, sat straighter, exhaled slowly.

"Always use a sheath, the rubber ones."

Although the words had been spoken so quietly that none but Jennie could hear them, she glanced about uneasily.

She could be a virgin, still. At the least, she has little experience.

"If a man can speak only of the act…" Mary Jane said.

Seeing the question in her companion's eyes, she paused, said, "Engagement."

Still, a lack of understanding.

"*Tupping*, then."

Finally, Jennie seemed to understand, nodding with fresh embarrassment.

"Should he want to talk about the particulars at length, that is his manner of having his way with you. Should you allow such a thing at no cost, unlikely he'll be to commit funds. That, or possibly he's dangerous."

Jennie's eyes became wide, and Mary Jane placed a warm hand atop one of hers.

Poor thing. Would that I might hold her hand when her first time comes. She would have laughed at the thought if the look in Jennie's eyes had held any real sense of hope.

"The going rate for a *casual* is four pence. They are unfortunates with little or no experience."

Jennie frowned, as if confused.

Mary Jane forced a tight smile. "The muck snipes you see wandering the streets."

She immediately regretted using the derogatory term, and knew she'd revealed her unavoidable resentment toward the innumerable amateur prostitutes, something of which she wasn't proud.

Jennie's expression changed, her eyes narrowing with suspicion.

"They are, I know, just trying to get on in a hard life," Mary Jane said quickly. "The casual, she is most often a poor woman who has lost her man."

Jennie's frown deepened. "Or her brother," she said with a look of challenge, "the family bread winner?"

"I should not have called them muck snipes," Mary Jane said, speaking more rapidly still. "I do not truly look upon them with scorn. The crude term I use so there's no mistaking. You are not like them, and we intend that like them you shan't become. The casuals drive down the prices for all of us. Attractive, you are, and your tidy clothing will do for now. We'll make improvements as we can. You should ask for six pence to start. A tanner is respectable."

"*We* intend?" Jennie said indignantly.

"I don't mean to speak for you," Mary Jane said, shaking her head.

A bitterness had entered the conversation. Appearing uncomfortable in her seat, Jennie looked away, placed her hands on the table, her mouth forming a tight line. "*We'll* make improvements?"

Mary Jane knew she'd upset the woman again. She couldn't think what to say to mitigate what appeared to be a return to mistrust. "I meant only to show my eagerness to help."

Jennie ran her right hand over the stained, pitted wood of the tabletop. With a look of hurt, she rose slowly from her seat, and looked down her nose at Mary Jane. "If you know so much, what are you doing *here*? You say you have experience with the well-to-do, yet no gentleman would have a woman on his arm who speaks as you do. By your manner of speech, I should think you grew up on the streets."

"I don the voice I need," Mary Jane said calmly. "Quite capable, I am, of the Queen's English."

Jennie frowned, and shook her head. "I might need help, but I shan't need a whore's minder, nor your pity." Her eyes flashed with accusation. "Who are *you* to decide what *I'm* worth?"

She turned to leave. Mary Jane grasped her left hand. "Please, I don't wish to gain anything from you, save, perhaps, friendship. There is more to tell to help keep you safe."

Jennie pulled her hand free, hesitated. Her expression suggested that she couldn't decide whether to stay or go, that a desire for help warred with a fear of being played.

Mary Jane realised she'd been presumptuous. She had indeed somehow got the feeling that Jennie was family. That had driven her words too much. Portraying herself to be a ladybird of a higher station had set a barrier between them. The older woman's pride might not permit her to share her problems so intimately with a woman half her age.

Her face, so much like Mum's, will haunt me if she walks away.

Telling how I came to be here might put her at ease. Then she might listen.

"My story, I'll tell, if you'll sit with me. It may well be instructive."

Moments passed as Jennie shifted restlessly from foot to foot. Finally, she sat with a look of resignation, her eyes downcast.

With a sense of relief, Mary Jane sat back, and tried to relax. Unaccustomed to explaining herself and unsettled by the conflict, she wished she had whiskey rather than coffee. Better still would be another dose of laudanum, but when others saw her take the drug, they often had questions she didn't want to answer. *Jennie already looks upon me doubtfully. No sense in making that worse.* She took a deep draught from her cup of coffee before beginning.

Mary Jane told of the loss of her mother and her father's anger. "With hard feeling toward Papa, I left my home in Carmarthen,

Wales when sixteen years old and married the first man what'd have me, Berwyn Davies. He were a collier, a coal runner, killed in '81 in a mine explosion in Penygraig. I don't miss the drunkard much."

Jennie looked up at her, possibly to assess the feelings behind the words.

Mary Jane didn't mean to sound uncaring. "Difficult he made my desire to love him." The familiar sadness filled her heart. She gasped slightly and swallowed hard to keep the feelings down. Embarrassed to think that the emotion showed on her face, she gestured with her hands aimlessly.

A small flash of sympathy in Jennie's eyes said that the woman recognised the pain. She clearly knew much about loss. "Tell me," she said, a bit of demand in her tone.

Mary Jane didn't want to tell her, yet wanted to gain her trust. "A woman who worked by my side at a woollen mill in Cartmarthen, Mared Jones, introduced me to her brother, Evan Berwyn Davies. He had come from Penygraig for a visit. He worked the Pandy Coal Pit there. I saw my escape from Papa when Berwyn took a romantic interest in me. At such a young age and selfish, I thought little of the poor fellow's feelings. Because my father disliked me so and wanted to see me suffer, I knew he would accept my marriage to one of such a lowly station. Once Berwyn and I were wed, I removed to Penygraig, a village of dullards and drunkards. The colour at sun's set was the best part of each day."

Dabbing it up with Berwyn had felt good while it lasted. At that age, she had not learned how to manage a man. His pearly shower came too quickly. Afterward he got a bad case of lobcock. She became pregnant once, but lost it.

"Berwyn looked at me at times with a certain light in his eyes, as if proud to have me. Turning his lamps on me like that, I felt worth something after the poor treatment of my father. Made my heart to skip a beat. I found Berwyn handsome, if a bit rough.

"He were a lushington. Weary once home from his labours at the mine, he drank too much and fell asleep early most evenings. I missed him, even when I had him home. I wanted to talk, go out for a drink, a meal; anything to break the monotony of my days.

"Bored in a way that told me I didn't truly love him, I grew upset with myself. I'd become spoiled, as Papa would have it. Though I do believe I had feeling for him, my interest had waned quickly. I tried to talk to Berwyn about my restlessness. He wouldn't talk about it. I fought a desire to sneak out alone to the bottom of Amos Hill and drink at the Steamer Seam pub.

"On one occasion that we drank together, I cursed him, turned petulant and contrary. 'You are as dull as the others in this dirty village,' I told him. 'Take care to keep me interested, or you'll find yourself alone again.' Those words I regretted most in my short marriage. They weren't all of my ugliness.

"As time passed, I made little effort to be fair with him. I took to teasing him for his rough language, his lack of maths, and inability to read. I looked for ways to bring into our conversations things I'd learned and read about that I knew he would not understand. Enjoyed his lack of understanding, I did, and a feeling that I were his better.

"The day I lost the battle with my desire to go to the bottom of Amos Hill, Berwyn died in the mine while I drank at the Steamer Seam. The constabulary took me to see his lifeless body. The light had gone from his lamps."

Remembering the pain she'd experienced with Mum's death, Mary Jane had held in her grief, regret, and shame. Perhaps that was why the sentiments had to sneak out.

Jennie looked at her intently, squeezed her hands, but remained silent.

Mary Jane wiped the moisture from her eyes and nose with a handkerchief.

"My pride and anger toward my father wouldn't allow me to return home. I went to live with my cousin, Carryl Hughes, in Cardiff. A prostitute, she led me into that life. We had an affection for one another, with a sense that we'd taken charge of our own lives."

Mary Jane paused briefly, trying to untangle the love and the hatred she felt for her cousin before saying more about her. Her cousin's betrayals, large and small, loomed large in recollection. Impossible to sort her feelings quickly, she went on with her story instead.

Mary Jane described the attack in Cardiff and her many months recovering in the infirmary. She told of journeying to London and finding a position at the Phoenix gay house.

"Born of a low station, by twenty-two years of age, I were riding about London town in carriages with wealthy industrialists. On the arm of fine gentlemen, I've attended extravagant social gatherings where our kind is tolerated. I partook in the ways of the well-to-do; enjoyed fine food, fine lodgings, comforts of all sorts.

"But they wanted a lot in return, too much at times. Suffer abuse, I would not. I stood up for myself." Mary Jane recounted the incident with Harris Brevard in Paris. "That ginger-haired man, Stuart Brevard, what attacked me the day you helped, I believe he is the brother of Harris Brevard."

Out of shame and a desire to avoid frightening Jennie, Mary Jane offered little description of the severe violence suffered on both sides in the incident with Harris Brevard. She also held back much of the emotion associated with the memories, and didn't admit that she'd robbed him.

Held back or not, she did relive those feelings some. Following a long pause in which she struggled to compose herself, she realised that Jennie still waited for her to finish.

"The gentleman what I harmed in Paris were a client in good standing with my gay house in the West End," she said. "Because of what I done to him, they turned me out in the streets."

Jennie had covered her mouth with a hand. Mary Jane couldn't tell whether the gesture hid an expression of shock or disdain. *A good thing the full story I did not tell.* Whatever the case, she had begun the tale, and must find an appropriate end if she hoped to regain the woman's trust.

"In high society, I dare not show myself for fear of that brother. Destroyed what I had gained in life, I did, such as it was. I've returned to the dreadful work I began at age eighteen in Cardiff, yet my experience remains, and much the wiser for it I am."

Mary Jane paused for a moment, took another drink of her coffee. "I speak before thinking at times. Please forgive me, and allow me to help."

Jennie seemed to relax. When her hand moved away from her mouth, Mary Jane saw that her ire had melted away.

A wing of the bamboo screen opened outward to reveal Rachel Bowles and a handsome fellow in a pale grey suit.

"Good day, Ginger," Rachel said.

Jennie's eyes grew wide.

"Good day to you, Rachel." Mary Jane said brightly.

Jennie tugged on her left ear repeatedly, no subtlety to the effort.

"Has the earache returned, Emma?" Mary Jane said quickly. "Excuse us, Rachel, My friend hasn't been feeling well."

"Of course," Rachel said. She and the gentleman retreated and swung the wing of the screen back in place.

Placing a hand on Jennie's arm, Mary Jane raised an index finger to her smiling lips. After a moment, she said, "They're gone now, I think. You know the man?"

Jennie appeared embarrassed. "I know I did a poor job of the signal. I used the wrong hand! Please forgive me." She waved a hand before her face, as if brushing away her mistake. "He came for me in the Crown and Dolphin, just at the end of the street. He grabbed my…" Again, she looked embarrassed. "Well, I didn't expect his touch, and I complained loudly. He savagely stomped my foot."

"Ah, the limp." Mary Jane felt her smile grow as she thought of the older woman's frantic earlobe tugs.

"Yes."

Mary Jane chuckled.

Jennie gave her a cross look, seeming confused as well as indignant. "My misfortune amuses you?"

"No, just the face you made when you gave the signal." Mary Jane laughed. "You'll have to work on being nonchalant when you make it."

Jennie must have seen the humour. She smiled and burst out with her own chortling.

"But you did well to give it. Wrong hand or not, I'm certain she got the message." Mary Jane tried to quiet her amused response. "Pleased Rachel will be with you," she gasped, her laughter resuming.

"Yes, I shall practice it now." Jennie tugged both ears and screwed up her face in a foolish grin.

Mary Jane broke into uncontrolled guffaws.

Jennie covered her mouth to stifle her own growing laughter.

The good humour slowly died out, and the two women sat silently and comfortably for a time.

At length, Mary Jane said, "One more piece of advice have I for you today. If you heard nothing else I've said, should you think I am a fool or a danger, still, please, hear this well."

Jennie sat up, shaking her head. "I believe you, and am most grateful for your advice. What would you have me know?"

"The Gully Bleeders will come to you for protection money."

"Protection? Protection from whom?"

"'Tis a shakedown. You pay them to protect you. Should you fail to pay, a nobbling they give you."

"Nobbling?"

"A beating. You pay them for protection from their abuse. Nick Shears, a man with a scarred face, or one of his underlings will come for it. Don't be afraid, just pay the price. If you don't, they'll cut you badly, leaving permanent scars."

She saw Jennie's horror grow in her expression. Mary Jane had nothing for it—she had to finish the warning. "Should they decide to make an example of you, they will maim you. Find a way to pay you must. From a casual, they take a half-shilling per week. Should the Gully Bleeders see that you make more than a casual, they'll demand more."

The look of concern on Jennie's face said that she considered a tanner a dear price to pay. Carryl had paid Mary Jane's protection to the Beloved Ratters for a time. A tanner, just six pence was a small burden—she could pay that for Jennie for a few weeks. Jennie would be able to pay it herself with time.

"If you haven't the chink, find me and I'll pay for you."

"I could not let you—" Jennie began.

Mary Jane cut her off. "Yes, you can." She gave the woman her most grave and piercing gaze.

Then, something of the woman who had swung a laundry sack at Stuart Brevard emerged. "You stood up for *yourself*..." Jennie complained.

"Yes, and have someone after me for my trouble, yet he may never find me. He is an amateur. The Gully Bleeders are different. Eyes and ears, they have, everywhere in the East End. Promise me you will come to me if you cannot pay them."

With a fragile smile, Jennie nodded. "It isn't at all fair."

Mary Jane returned the smile with a grim one, chuckled dryly. "What's fair rarely visits the East End."

SIXTEEN

The watchman takes his rounds with heavy steps. The eel in his belly was none too fresh when it entered that night's pie; the woman who served the pie was none too kind in her views on her husband's prospects. The two war inside him, and instead of turning right, by the passage to the vault, he turns left towards the privy meant for bank staff only. As he strains for relief, he neither sees nor hears the cracksman at the far end of the building that night. A bad eel and a sharp tongue save him from the lead-filled cosh.

A man lives.

The civil servant's mistress has jilted him, gone with a cavalry man to play hogmagundy before the Regiment sails. Whitehall is a place of gas and shadows, and the civil servant's eyes are thick with misery. He dips his pen and signs an end to one Mr Orlesky, being held at Her Majesty's displeasure. As Left might have been Right, the man who should have been marked to dance for the hangman is a Mr Orlenski, but Her Majesty's servant is too tired to notice.

A man dies.

These are the vagaries which Edwin Dry observes. They are why he prepares each venture in detail, yet has always alternatives in mind. Small things without intention come to pass, and great plans slip out of one's hands, like fat eels that once held so much promise. Not by logic and conscious effort, but by the contents of a pastry crust, or the blotting of a single word.

Such things cannot be predicted.

All eels are grey in the dark.

Catherine attended a late supper at Lady Seldon's in the Chelsea Embankment on the Thursday of the week after Vauxhall. A light meal of game pie, a syllabub and cheese went smoothly, but as the evening progressed, she began to realise that she should earn her invitation.

They did not ask, but that was not the way these people lived. All was done by vague suggestion, and by a system of mutual obligation which was, at times, hard to penetrate. Nor was language direct. A maid who was considered "lively" or "so bright" could as easily anticipate dismissal as advancement. Favour waxed and waned easily.

Catherine sought to play safe. She provided vague imagery of foreign lands at a short sitting, and afterwards intrigued her small audience by recalling snippets from spiritualist literature, concerning the phenomenon known as automatic writing. She had determined Amelia Baring-Smith to be the most impressionable of the three, and she directed a number of enquiring looks in that direction as she spoke, drawing the girl in.

Under Catherine's direction, each of them sat with paper and pencil, whilst Madame Rostov asked if there were souls upon the Aether who wished to communicate. Eyes closed, the three let their pencils wander across the table, with occasional supportive murmurs from the medium.

The results were a mixture of nonsense and scribbles, with barely any distinguishable words, but Madame Rostov pronounced that Amelia's paper might hold some blurred meaning.

"Is that not the word 'Berlin,' below the half-circle?" she suggested, and after a few minutes she had them inclined to agree.

"I had an uncle at the Embassy there!" cried Amelia. "Uncle Freddie. He's in Budapest now, but still…I must write and tell him. Perhaps he has unfinished business in Germany."

Her object achieved, for almost an hour she sat and nodded, saying little, as Lottie Chambers read from her new acquisition, a book entitled *The Strange Case of Dr Jekyll and Mr Hyde*. Catherine knew only that the author had published some sort of pirate tale a few years before, and was somewhat mystified by Lottie's attempts to explain Stevenson's latest.

"And he takes this potion, this serum, but it no longer works, or something along those lines. So he kills himself, except that I don't think he does." Lottie beamed. "It is what Papa calls a metaphorical death—that side of him has to die, but the brutal, terrible Mr Hyde may survive."

"It sounds rather lurid," said Amelia Baring-Smith. "Are you sure it is worth the time, Lottie?"

"I enjoyed it. What if we all have two sides to us? I might take a draught, and—"

"Become a quiet, sensible young woman," finished Lady Seldon, provoking laughter all round. "What do you think, Madame Rostov? Are we all more than one person?"

The irony of the question did not escape Catherine.

"We are many persons," she said in a grave voice. "I have not read this Stevenson, but perhaps he asks, which part of what is within us will we let dominate? Do we let our monsters out?"

More sherry flowed, and Lady Seldon lit a slender cigarette.

"I know some who do," she said. "Harry considers old Salisbury a positive monster, living in his privileged past. Harry has moments where I think he should have been born a factory worker, causing agitation, not a marquess."

It seemed an opening that Catherine could use, if they did not think her speaking above her station.

"But then he might have to work in one of Mr Frederick Caille's factories. I would not envy him that."

The other women looked at her.

"It was something I read. In the newspapers." added Catherine. For a moment it seemed she had overstepped the boundaries. "Where there had been many accidents, and people hurt."

The two younger women looked to Lady Seldon, who drew on her cigarette and then nodded.

"No, that is not a fate any of us would wish on friends or relatives. Not the decent ones, anyway."

Charlotte and Amelia relaxed.

"I saw Evelyn last month," said Lottie. "I was *allowed* to see her, I should say. Her husband's an absolute horror. I could see him as Mr Hyde."

"Evelyn Caille?" Amelia sighed. "That poor woman."

"To have to share a name with that ghastly man. Intolerable. More scandal over his South African mines, and talk of a Spanish *condesa*, would you believe?"

"He all but bankrolls several peers." Lady Seldon pulled a face. "What have you heard of him, Madame Rostov?"

Catherine considered what she should and should not know.

"That he is a banker, an industrialist. Many do not seem to like him, but he has much power."

"That is the nub of it." She stubbed out her cigarette. "Do you think we should sit again tonight, Madame?"

Surely she had paid her dues? It was almost midnight.

"I would prefer not to, my lady. I am tired."

"More sherry, then. My husband's *oloroso* is far too expensive for his boorish friends."

Catherine was aware that she was little more than a diversion, an act to enliven the evenings of these young women, and yet she liked them, in their way. They were less shallow than they had at first seemed.

"This Mrs Caille…" She pretended to test out the name as she took a glass of sherry from Miss Chambers. "She is badly served?"

"Oh, indeed. They live apart," said Lottie. "You'd think she was under house-arrest, the way she's treated."

"There are no children?"

"A young boy, Beresford, trapped under his father's wing. She's hardly allowed to see him."

The spiritualist wrapped an unused deck of cards in soft black silk, and slid them into her bag.

"That is sad. And she is a good woman?"

"Absolutely! Married off young, like Lucy here—"

"Have a care," said Lady Seldon. "We should not gossip too much, or we will bore Madame Rostov."

The moment's familiarity passed. These were women of position, and where Madame Rostov fell on the spectrum between hired entertainer and honoured guest would never quite be certain.

Conversation shifted to the fashion in hats, and half an hour later, Lottie Chambers showed the spiritualist out.

"Do you think that next time, Madame, there might be word for me?"

"There are disturbances on every Plane," said Catherine, feeling inventive. "They interfere, but they will not last. I am sure that more is to come."

Lottie seemed thrilled at the words. It was clear, even after only a few sittings, that the young women of this circle wanted something a touch more visceral and exciting than organ music and soothing messages.

"Marvellous," she said. "Shall I have Merrins find a hansom for you?"

"I shall walk, thank you."

She slipped into the streets of the Chelsea Embankment an hour before midnight, leaving Lady Seldon and her friends to more *oloroso* and a round of cards. Unobserved, she pinned her hair down, turned the hood of her cloak and slipped her rings into an inside pocket. She checked her small change, and walked back into the gaslight. A hansom trotted by, and she gestured.

"Where to, lady?" The cabbie tipped his felt hat.

"Southwark St Saviour."

And home. She had much to consider.

⚶

The Chambers family's town-house was an imposing red-brick building no great distance along the Embankment from Lady Seldon's, on Cheyne Gardens. On Saturday morning she presented her card, as Madame Rostov, to a limping butler, and was shown immediately into a high-ceilinged room which still bore the marks of the nursery—a child's easel in the corner, a faded map of the Empire, and wallpaper with soft forget-me-nots. Miss Bournelle must have ruled here once. Charlotte Chambers and a girl of ten or eleven years sat side by side on an old divan, peering through an illustrated book.

"Madame Rostov, what a pleasure." Lottie sounded genuinely pleased. "May I introduce you to my sister, Jemmy."

The girl, small and with the same pale blonde hair as Lottie, stood up and curtseyed.

"It's Jemima, actually," she said, scowling at her older sister. "Most pleased to meet you, Madame."

Catherine tipped her head politely. "You are also a lover of books, Miss Jemima?"

"She is worse than I am. Go show Mama the drawings of the heron and the crane, Jemmy, there's a good girl."

"If I must." Jemima's skipping exit managed to display both insolence and reluctance. Lottie smiled fondly after her.

"A man will pay when he catches her," she said. "I hope."

Whether by common practice or by some hidden signal, a maid came in with a tray of tea-things, including scones and butter.

"A wasp has been in the jam, miss," said the maid. "I can send out for more."

It was agreed that jam was not required, and they sat on the divan, tea cups in hand.

"You are kind to see me," said Catherine.

144

Lottie looked surprised. "I think you an intelligent woman, Madame. Papa would not have me at casinos, or late card games, nor does he approve of many theatrical productions. Am I to sit alone and read until parcelled off to a son of one of his friends?"

"I do not—"

"If I did not have Lucy and Amelia, and our afternoons, our evenings, I would be mad." The words were emphatic. She leaned closer. "I am a suffragist, not that my parents know. I shall teach Jemmy accordingly, though she hardly needs it."

The subject—and the conspiratorial tone—were unexpected. Catherine had a limited grasp of politics. She smiled, nodded, and attended to her tea, hoping that this would suffice.

Lottie laughed. "But you are here for your own purposes, I'm sure. How can I help you, Madame?"

Here was the test. If she had judged Charlotte Chambers correctly, if she had understood aright the way she had talked the other evening…

"You spoke of a Mrs Caille."

Eyebrows raised slightly. "Evelyn? I don't know that she has any interest in spiritualism, or tilting tables and the like. I do not see her often these days."

Catherine hesitated. How was she to put this? She had thought it over each night since the name of Caille had come up. Of course these people knew each other, and so eventually most names would arise in casual conversation. It was no different from Keighley high street, in many ways. The wives gathered, glancing into each others' shopping baskets, seeing who had ironed their pinafore and who bore a bruise from a drink-sodden husband. They spoke of this girl who had spread her legs once too often, of that woman who no longer ordered anything but the cheapest cuts…it was the way.

She could ignore Charlotte Chambers's passing mention of acquaintance with Evelyn Caille at the Seldon's, knowing it would most likely lead her nowhere, or…

"I sense a grief about this good lady. A heavy cloud that weighs upon her. She wished, perhaps, to marry a Jekyll, but was misled?"

Lottie seemed pleased at the literary allusion. "Oh, quite so. Caille—the brute—is a man of ideas. But each idea is squeezed for profit, not for progress. Harry Seldon loathes him; even Papa keeps

145

his distance."

"Yet this man has great influence."

"Bought, all bought, Madame." Lottie broke a scone in half, then placed it back on the plate. "Not that I know that much, you understand. Though I have very good hearing. It's surprising what people will say when they think you are out of ear-shot. No, you would do well to keep clear of Mr Caille."

"I shall do so, Miss Chambers. And yet, his wife…still I have the sensation that there should be some comfort for her. I cannot say why this touches me."

"Oh, I see." Lottie considered this for a moment. "Is there a sentiment you wish me to convey to her?"

Catherine pretended awkwardness. "I do not know…without having seen her in person, you understand? It can be difficult to be sure what is required. Possibly there is a message for her, from Beyond."

"Oh." The young woman's interest was undoubtedly engaged. "I suppose…"

"Yes?"

"Lucy—Lady Seldon—*might* arrange for you to meet Evelyn. She has more influence than I."

"If it would cause you trouble…"

"A challenge. I like challenges. You see, Madame, Mrs Caille is practically confined to her place at Muswell Hill, a rather dismal old house. Caille does not wish his wife in society."

"But how can he stop her?" It was a stupid question. There would be ways, for a man of Caille's wealth and influence.

"She loves her son very much," said Lottie, sighing. "And Caille holds that over her. He will have an heir in his own image, if he has his way. A dreadful thought, really." It was one which seemed to stiffen her resolve. "I shall speak to Lucy this weekend. We will find some pretext for you to see Evelyn, and trust that you can bring her some kinder words than she usually hears. I doubt Caille knows enough of spiritual matters to question a minor diversion for her."

A shriek from the hall outside marked the return of Jemima Chambers, clutching her book. The girl's fingers were smeared with jam, and she careened across the polished floor of the old nursery looking unabashed.

Catherine smiled, expressed her appreciation, and bade the two sisters farewell.

The air outside was crisp, the sky less grey than usual. The red brick of Cheyne Walk glowed warmer in a shaft of rare sunshine.

As a merchant's daughter from a Yorkshire town, she would hardly have stood much higher in London society than the tradesmen who called at the back of these houses.

As Madame Rostov, new doors appeared to be opening for her.

SEVENTEEN

Mary Jane remained at Dresser's to finish her coffee following her new friend's departure. On her way out of the establishment, she saw a fellow named Mansfield—whom she knew to be dangerous—seated at a table. If he sat with a prostitute, Mary Jane wanted to give her a warning. She approached the screen that hid the other side of the table. Behind it sat beautiful Gabriella Gorse.

Although they didn't get along, Mary Jane thought she should warn the woman. She reached for her left ear with her right hand as Gabby glanced up.

The woman gave a scornful, lop-sided smile. "I have no need of your quaint intrigues," she said.

"You might have, without knowing," Mary Jane said, and nodded subtly toward the man.

He huffed, and glared at her.

"Be gone, Ginger," Gabby said.

Ungrateful termagant. "Suit yourself." She left Dressers to head back to the Angel and Trumpet.

The next day, while passing through Stepney Green, Mary Jane saw Gabby with a black eye.

Serves her right, Mary Jane thought, assuming that Mansfield had beaten the woman. *She's lucky she only copped a mouse.*

Gabby, seeing Mary Jane, approached. The closer Miss Gorse got, the more bruises could be seen on her face. She held out folded pieces of paper. "Is that you?" she asked.

Mary Jane took what looked like three sheets of half-foolscap, unfolded them, and saw the printed sketch of a woman with the name, "Andriette," beneath.

The pictures Stuart Brevard carried!

"No," she said, remaining calm while her brain raced.

He is still here, and could be anywhere. Has she led him to me? She wanted to look around, searching the area to see if she could spot him, and she wanted to question Miss Gorse, but decided that either effort would reveal her answer to be a lie.

If she believes that's a picture of me, did she tell him so?

She would probably not know that Mary Jane went by Andriette at the Phoenix gay house.

"The fellow what had those thought I was the woman in the picture," Gabby said, then pointed to her face. "He give me this before deciding maybe he'd made a mistake."

Mansfield hadn't given her the black eye, Stuart Brevard had.

Does she know she took a beating meant for me?

"You ought to take more care in the company you keep," Mary Jane said coldly. "Do you know his name?"

Gabby spit on the path at Mary Jane's feet, turned, and walked away.

If he is still here, at least he's confused about who he's after.

Mary Jane worried that Gabriella Gorse had detected her lie, and that she might find and tell Stuart Brevard that Andriette was now going by the name Ginger.

EIGHTEEN

Levinia Weatherhead's health continued to deteriorate, and Clarissa's moods grew worse. Each of Catherine's visits to Stepney was fraught with misunderstandings and hopeless silences.

"The doctor says she will leave us all the sooner if we try to move her to the infirmary. A colleague of his kindly came out from the London Hospital…he pronounced that there is no help except a comfortable end. The tubes and passages of her lungs are blocked; her heart cannot force her breath, and now she may have the grippe. She eats little in her fever."

"I will sit with her a while," said Catherine. Clarissa herself was coughing intermittently, a condition of long-standing. The sweating sickness would put her at risk as well.

"Good. I have mending to do, lest we do not meet the rent."

"I could—"

"Make us more beholden to you than we are already." She turned away. "I begin to mutter like Mama, and wish Frederick Caille in a cell while I can still rejoice in it."

Catherine was torn between annoyance and pity. "Have you thought of moving to Yorkshire? I know that it is not your own native county, but there are other folk there—neighbours, friends of the Two Gentlemen."

This had long been the family term for the two brothers, Joseph—Catherine's grandfather—and Charles—grandfather and namesake to Clarissa's late husband. Farmers together on the wilder moors above Keighley, who had thought two foot of snow no more than a spattering, yet who could cry at a lamb lost to crows.

"There is nothing up there for us." The words were sharp, final.

Nor was there anything in the room upstairs except the shallow gasps of an old woman. Catherine sat for two hours, reading a borrowed copy of Stevenson, but took none of it in. She left two sovereigns by Levinia's bed, and let herself out. Those would have to be earned back quickly—unlike her aunt, Catherine had a fine appetite.

An omnibus saw her down Whitechapel Road and as far as the Tower. Work had started on the new bridge, and she could see barges all around, plying to and fro from the site of two reinforced piers which were to be set into the Thames. They said in the papers that this Tower Bridge might cost near a million pounds, a sum which made no sense to her. Caille would understand it, easily.

She walked to London Bridge via Botolph wharf, where Mrs Bessovitch regularly took advantage of those crates which were damaged as they were swung from ships' holds. Oranges, and other fruit such as limes and sometimes figs, could be had there for a pittance if it were done quietly, in the shadow of the creaking and almost decrepit wharf buildings.

She was fortunate. A sleepy-eyed black sailor, his head wrapped in a silk scarf, sold her a handful of Sicily oranges for tuppence, adding a bag of sweet sultanas. They would have cost him nothing. She cut an orange with her pocket-knife, and sucked on it as she crossed the bridge to Southwark—this haul would get her an extra chop from her landlady, at least.

⌁ ✦ ⌁

Madame Rostov conducted a vexing session with two local women, and made mistakes. Catherine's intelligence on the women failed her. In seeking to recover her sitters' confidence, she let her mind wander and open, which brought blurred images of an endless leaden sea, great waves beneath a twisted sky. By useful coincidence (for Catherine did not think it had true meaning) one of the women had been married to a sailor, lost in the Baltic. The sitters pronounced themselves satisfied, but only to the tune of a shilling each.

Walking home, she settled in her bed with backache and a distinct feeling of being hard done by...

The mirror is large, a shard of the true world bound in a simple ebony frame. It needs neither gilt nor adornments. It shows a room like any other, in which stands a man of no particular interest. He might be clerk to a shipping office, or secretary to some branch manager of a modest bank. His form is that of Everyman, in essence. The thought pleases him.

He considers his reflection, long enough to adjust his collar a fraction and be sure that his jacket sits perfectly square upon his adequate shoulders. He is not Everyman, of course. He is a journeyman, and journeymen should always be presentable. To be otherwise reflects badly on the trade.

A journeyman must not be prey to appetite—of any kind. He will dine on a small pork chop, with potatoes and peas. A little cheese to follow, matured and with the faint crunch of salt. He will set out without hunger. And without malice or anger.

Those who must hate would not understand.

No death.

In the half-light of the Southwark dawn, Catherine clutched her blanket to her.

No death had occurred, and yet still he came to her, entered her dreams.

Was this how it was to be?

⚜

A visit to the post office revealed another cream envelope waiting for her. Inside this one was simply Lady Seldon's embossed card; on the back of the card, a neatly written couple of lines.

'Evelyn—I would consider it a favour if you were to receive Madame Rostov. She is most talented, discreet, and deserves due patronage. S.'

"S" no doubt for Seldon. Lottie Chambers had come through, as promised. Now she had her entrée to Mrs Caille, one which might have her received rather than turned away. And perhaps Catherine would learn more of those who ruined the Weatherheads. She would be able to say to Levinia that she had pursued the thread, if nothing else.

She hauled out the finest of Madame Rostov's clothes, borrowed the rings again from Mrs B, and asked for advice.

"I know nothing of Muswell Hill," she said to her landlady.

"Write down address you must find." Mrs Bessovitch waited, then drew on her outdoors coat and was away. She returned an hour later having questioned, no doubt, Gersteins, Goldschmidts, Coopers and Cartwrights.

"Is easy, Katerina."

A parlour maid of a friend's neighbour had once worked…and so it went. Catherine received instruction to go by rail to Hornsey, and after that she had only to walk or take a hansom up Hornsey High Street, and keep going. Grove House, where Evelyn Caille lived in apparent exile, was halfway up Muswell Hill.

If she hesitated, she might keep that card of Lady Seldon's for days, or weeks. It ought to be done…

~∴~

The Great Northern train was crowded, a situation exacerbated by a man trying to put two crates of chickens in one of the passenger carriages. People were feeling uncharitable, but eventually the guard's van was utilised, and the journey to Hornsey was simple enough. In character, she decided to take a hansom to Grove House, and sat back to enjoy the short journey from the small town centre and up the moderate incline into the wooded Muswell Hill.

Iron railings and horse chestnuts losing their last leaves; fields and men on bicycles. Recent, quite stylish houses had been raised amongst the trees, but Grove House was not one of them. Set alone down a lane to the north, it slumped between chestnuts, an amalgam of Georgian villa and later, awkward additions, as if the architect had forgotten what should be there, and had come back fifty years later to try and make rushed amends.

She paid the cab driver, and marched with false confidence to the lopsided porch which marked the main entrance. The bell-push made no sound that reached her, and so she knocked as well, for good measure. Eventually a man in a butler's uniform, but poorly shaven, answered.

"We do not wish visitors," he said.

Catherine had learned enough to know that this was an inappropriate welcome. "Mrs Caille is not at home…" might have been acceptable, but "We?" She tightened her lips and stared hard at the man.

"I come from Lady Seldon." Catherine held out the card she had been sent. "I am Madame Rostov."

He hesitated, but then took the card and read the back. "I don't…"

"It will be known," she said, "That Madame Rostov was refused at this house. Refused by you."

She spoke with her best mock-Russian edge, and it weakened him. He asked her, more politely, to wait a moment, "If she did not mind," and disappeared inside.

The grounds themselves were well-maintained, with even a spot of late colour in borders to either side. Scarlet dahlias and ivory-pale chrysanthemums still bloomed, all neatly staked and cleared of fallen leaves. It seemed an odd contrast to the apparent state of the building.

"Madame Rostov?"

Evelyn Caille stood in the doorway. Charlotte Chambers had described her. A nondescript dress, out of fashion; thin lips which reminded Catherine of Aunt Levinia. One hand played at tousled hair without colour—the other hung at her side, fingers tapping on her thigh.

"I am."

"Please, join me in the drawing room."

The house was clean enough, but its dark paint and heavy furniture absorbed life, muted it. The butler stood by the drawing room door, watching. He had much the same effect.

"We shall not need you, Tanner."

Hesitation, and a slow withdrawal. Mrs Caille went to the door, and pressed it firmly shut.

"He listens," she said. "Let us sit by the French windows. He will hear less that way."

The woman moved like an actress, each gesture exaggerated. Even sitting, her fingers tapped against her left leg.

"He is my gaoler. I think you should not have come, though God knows, I have little enough company."

Catherine had not expected such directness. "Mrs Caille, I—"

"Evelyn. All I hear is 'Mrs Caille.'"

"Evelyn, then. Miss Charlotte Chambers was kind enough to arrange this introduction, and—"

"Let me spare us time, Madame Rostov. There is no force which could make Lucy Seldon disadvantage me, and therefore I can be sure that in some way, you are a friend. You do not need to present further credentials, or promise that you mean me no harm."

"Ah. I see." For once, Catherine wished that there had been a maid with afternoon tea, just to give her a cup or side-plate with which to toy.

"And if you have spoken to Lottie, then you must know that this is my exile. I have occasional visitors. I tend my garden. I see my son,

Beresford, once a week, though Tanner watches us throughout. My husband permits this, subject to my complete compliance, and my pledge that I support whatever scheme in which he is involved. He intends this to continue, for as long as he pleases."

Evelyn laughed, a hollow sound so devoid of humour that those scripts, those planned enquiries and subtleties which Catherine had stored up over the days—they died. It almost seemed better to quit Grove House and forget that it existed, than hear this.

"I am allowed to attend very few functions. I must be bright and charming, or I will lose a week's privileges with my son—or more. Beresford is told, by a doctor in Frederick's pay, that his mother is not strong, not well."

"I…I understand."

"And do you understand that Tanner will report all he hears to my husband?"

Catherine shuddered. Frederick Caille's actions had caused the death of Charles Weatherhead and others, yes, and he had used all his power to crush the simplest wishes for remorse to be expressed, restitution to be offered. But those events were at a distance, and a year ago. Sat here, Catherine felt a new and direct horror of the man who had crushed Evelyn as well. His own wife.

Catherine was "Joshua's child." The daughter of a fragment of Frederick Caille. Control and subjugation. Veiled threats, and always something held just out of reach. A much loved son, or a chance for freedom. The same gleaming apple, never quite in reach. Do as I ask—am I not reasonable? It had produced her mother—produced her and reduced her.

It had created Evelyn Caille, as she now was.

"But come, you do not speak, Madame Rostov," said Evelyn. "Ignore my mood. I would welcome new conversation, on whatever subject you choose. I believe that Lottie mentioned you had a psychic gift, for example?"

The tapping fingers drummed out frustrated love, frustrated purpose.

"Yes, I—"

A creak at the drawing room door galvanised Catherine to act. She rose to her feet, and strode to the door, throwing it open. Tanner, the butler, started back, almost losing his balance.

"There is a darkness in this house," she said, looming over him. She thrust out her chin, and spread her fingers, like the conjuror she had seen at a show in Bradford once. "I, Madame Rostov, am here to bring release. How do I do this, when there are mice who chew the skirting boards? Do you have the gift, little mouse?"

"I am to—"

"You are to find your hole, and let me work. Do you understand?"

Tanner's face reddened, and he opened his mouth to speak again, but Catherine knew that impetus was everything. She had met his sly type before—they rarely had an appetite for direct confrontation. "Rarely," of course, was a hopeful word.

"Scurry, now. If I must speak of you to the Aether, to those who have gone before, what will they say?"

His cheek twitched, and he backed farther away. She did not yield, but watched until he left the hallway and disappeared into another room at the rear of the house.

In the drawing room, Evelyn Caille had her head in her hands, her shoulders quivering.

"I have gone too far," said Catherine. "I am so sorry to…"

The face which appeared from behind slender hands was that of a younger woman, one who had remembered, however briefly, how to smile.

"I may pay for that, Madame Rostov, but bless you, I have never managed to cow Tanner in such a way. I am in your debt."

Catherine sat down, and put her hand on Evelyn's knee. She herself was shaking slightly, not from laughter, but in realisation of what she had just done.

"You must call me Katerina," she said. "And when you are ready, we must talk more about your devil of a husband."

NINETEEN

Mary Jane asked Joseph Fleming to fetch her possessions from Thomas Morganstone's apartments. He borrowed a friend's coster's barrow and hauled what were mostly clothes over to the room in Globe Road.

She continued to see as many clients as she could. Though Fleming had allowed she might see them at their lodgings while he was out, she made a deal with Rachel Bowles to share her crib in Eastfield Street, since the place was closer to Dresser's Coffee Shop. Mary Jane had satisfied an average of twenty clients a week in the almost two months since taking up with Fleming—although some were repeat customers—earning just over sixteen pounds. Of course, the money wasn't nearly what she'd earned working at the Phoenix gay house. Fleming didn't expect her to contribute to household expenses. She added seven pounds to her savings, bringing the funds she could depend on for relocating to a new city to thirty-three pounds.

Instead of seeing clients in the late afternoon of Tuesday, October 23, Mary Jane spent time with Jennie Weatherhead at Dresser's Coffee shop. They sat together in relative privacy behind a dressing screen while the older woman told about her first successful transaction with a client and what followed.

"The act was not as bad as anticipating it," she said, attempting a brave face. "Then the scarred man you told me about came to me outside the Crown and Dolphin…" Her words caught awkwardly in her throat. "…demanding I pay a half shilling per week to…" She shook with sobs, unable to finish.

"Nick Shears of the Gully Bleeders." Feeling that further words would be hollow, Mary Jane fell silent.

"Yes," Jennie said. "That's the one. He cut me under the chin with a small knife." Quaking in renewed fear, she tilted her head back to show a small, scabbed nick. "'That's my mark,' he said, 'just like my Christian name. You'll not be wanting more of those. Each one is bigger and they lead to my surname.' He showed me sheep shears, then took the tanner I had earned."

He likes to think he's clever. Mary Jane nodded to show she recognised the ritual marking.

Two days earlier, upon passing south through the East London

Cemetery, she had seen Nick Shears, four of his bludgers, and Gabby Gorse among the grave markers. Out of curiosity, Mary Jane slowed to see what they were up to. She'd paid her protection money for the week, so she had nothing to fear if they saw her, yet didn't want them to think she intentionally spied. Fairly well hidden among uneven markers, she felt safe enough. Nick and his young men remained too quiet to be engaged in a shake down. Gabby spoke to Nick calmly. She counted out something on the fingers of her hand, said something, and Nick nodded. He gave her something, and she smiled. That was the second time Mary Jane had seen Nick Shears give Gabby something. The woman had to be working for the man in some capacity.

"If I were my young cousin, Catherine," Jennie said, "I would not be so afraid. She is a tall woman with and iron jaw. Not that I would wish my lot on her, but she would succeed on the street much better than I do. Would that I could be more like her."

Jenny covered her eyed with her hands. "Such self-pity! When I think of my mother, now on her deathbed in our miserable lodgings, I know I should feel fortunate that I have my health. She will not be with us much longer."

When Jennie's emotions had quieted, Mary Jane pressed a shilling into her friend's hand, and would not take the coin back despite protests.

Finally, the older woman accepted the gift with thanks.

They finished their coffee, and Mary Jane walked Jennie back to her lodgings, a room in an old, wooden tenement in Brantridge Street. They took a rather circuitous route to avoid going by Thomas Morganstone's apartments, just in case Stuart Brevard watched the neighbourhood.

"Please allow me to introduce you to my sister-in-law, Clarissa, and her children," she said.

"Thank you, but no," Mary Jane said.

Jennie wanted her soliciting to remain a secret, had come up with a lie concerning a position as a housemaid, and seemed fairly confident that Clarrisa believed it.

"You've changed," Mary Jane said, referring to Jennie's clothing, "but I haven't. I don't want to give your family any suspicions."

The door of the tenement opened, and a tall, young woman with some family resemblance to Jennie emerged.

"Oh, Catherine, good to see you. I spoke of you earlier, and here you are."

The woman seemed surprised, as if her thoughts had been far away. "Cousin, yes. Good to see you, also."

"My friend, Ginger."

The young woman looked Mary Jane up and down, made the merest nod of acknowledgment, then turned back to Jennie. "I don't have time to visit at present. Perhaps soon." She strode away at a fast pace.

"Your cousin, Catherine Weatherhead?" Mary Jane asked.

"Yes." Jennie shrugged sadly. "She saw you. Hopefully nothing will come of it."

"She *was* making haste."

"I will see you at Dresser's, then."

"Yes, or at the Angel and Trumpet. There is still much more for you to learn."

Jennie nodded. "Thank you," she said, and entered the building.

Mary Jane headed north and west toward home as the sun set. The afternoon with the woman had been strangely more exhausting than seeing most clients.

She had become accustomed to walking in the night. Usually she did that with other women. Stepney had dangers aplenty any time of the day. In the benighted streets, illuminated unevenly as they were with gas lamps—which oddly deepened the areas of shadow—the activities of the pickpockets, both child and adult, the mug-hunters, and various other rampsmen became easier to conceal. Though the stone streets and footways were busy with traffic and pedestrians, and a feeling of being lost in the herd came easily enough, Mary Jane knew the predators were good at singling out those walking alone. She made frequent casual-seeming glances around and behind her as she made her way toward Globe Road.

Nearing her lodgings, Mary Jane had troublesome thoughts about her situation with Joseph Fleming that she had difficulty pinning down. While the room had been comfortable enough, and she remained at ease in his company, something about the arrangement didn't sit right with her.

He paid her nothing, and treated her like a lover. The lack of payment perhaps gave him an impression that she was indeed his. Mary Jane had not been honest with him about her reasons for taking up with him. She had not told him about her need to get away from Thomas Morganstone's apartments because of Stuart Brevard. And, of course, in part she remained with Fleming because she needed his help with the necklace. Her role as lover did not mean the same to both of them.

She'd done worse, so why was she so troubled?

Possibly, the answer lay in an earlier experience of the day.

Around noontime, as Mary Jane and Joseph had left their room and walked south on Globe Road amid the heavy foot traffic, she resumed her efforts to wheedle him into helping her with a plan for recovering the hidden jewellery.

She'd made the mistake of telling him she needed the funds from a sale of the necklace to make a fresh start out of London, a city for which he'd expressed much affection.

Briefly, he'd looked hurt. She should have expected he wouldn't like that. If she left, he'd be torn between losing her or his beloved London. He wouldn't want to leave the city. Thankfully, he had not asked her why she wanted to leave.

"We'll talk about that when I return from Deptford," he said.

Thomas Morganstone had taken a job at the Deptford Victualing Yard, just south along the River Thames. The work required Joseph's presence for a few days.

Entering Mile End Road where they would part company, he leaned down and kissed her goodbye.

"I'll return late Friday night," he said.

Mary Jane saw a warmth in his expression that troubled her.

He'd been acting rather queer, and she feared that he'd fallen in love with her.

"Perhaps give poor Miss Laudanum a rest," he said. "You've been hitting her hard lately. Should she become fed up, she'll turn on you."

Mary Jane punched him lightly in the chest, gave him a stony look. Her habits were none of his business.

"And don't sell *all* your wares while I'm away," he said, grinning.

She had been neglecting him while she increased her efforts to earn from clients. They'd enjoyed sexual relations much more often when she stayed at Morganstone's apartments. Some sexual distance could make her more desirable. Too much and he might lose interest.

"Leave some for me to enjoy upon my return," he said. Laughing, he walked eastward.

Moving westward, Mary Jane felt herself smiling as she thought about his performance in bed; his graceful movements, his affectionate gaze, and the thrust of his proud instrument within her.

Then his laughter came again from a distance, his guffaws heard over the noise of a tram rolling by. She chuckled.

He would rendezvous with Thomas Morganstone in Deptford at the job site. She had headed for the Angel and Trumpet.

Blast Joseph, she had too much fun with him. From the moment they met, she'd liked the jocular fellow. He was handsome enough, attentive, kind to her, not particularly demanding. He had few nice clothes, a modest embarrassment for her when they were out together. Similar, yet strangely quite the opposite of her husband, Berwyn Davies, who had rarely been seen without a coating of black powder from the coal mines, Joseph, a plasterer, frequently had a dusting of the lime used to make plaster white. Somehow, the sprinkling looked good on him.

Mary Jane didn't want to fall for Joseph. Her mysterious feelings for poor Berwyn were quite enough unwanted sentiment. Her primary goal had to be to resettle somewhere away from London.

If he *had* fallen in love with her, she might use that to help get her way, though not quite knowing the depth of her own feelings for the man complicated the matter.

Yes, *that* was the problem, the source of the uneasy feeling about her situation with Joseph. Not understanding her feelings for the man left her troubled.

Of course, she could always leave him. She could go back to Gander's Bush if need be, yet the idea of returning to the run-down brothel held no attraction.

Mary Jane turned into Devonshire Street, and intentionally dropped some of her wariness. Why she liked doing that when close to home, she could not say. As if playing a game, she ceased to glance around and behind her, choosing instead to pretend blithe innocence to potential threat. A foolish habit, but somehow an exciting one, especially in the moments her lodgings came into view. She'd get the oddest feeling she could outrun any danger that might appear, imagining herself dashing inside her abode and slamming the door to shut out menace. Mary Jane hadn't actually run home since she was a child. The fancy, merely played out in her mind, gave her a pleasant surge of vigour. Along with the sense of danger and risk came memories of the knees of her childhood stockings stained green with adventure.

Of course, just because she did not turn her head to look for danger did not mean that she wasn't aware of what went on around her. The sound of rapid footsteps from behind startled Mary Jane. Turning, she saw shadows flitting across the dampened street, heard an odd chuckle that sounded like it might belong to Gabriella Gorse.

Is she following to find out where I live? To tell Stuart Brevard?

Mary Jane strained to make out the features of those behind her. The people she saw in the lane were mostly silhouettes in the spotty gas light and the misty drizzle of rain. None seemed suspicious of anything, yet Gabby would not necessarily raise anyone's suspicions either running or laughing, not in London.

Still, having the nagging feeling that someone stalked her, Mary Jane picked up her pace.

Turning into Globe Road, and approaching the railway viaduct, the feeling increased. She saw a dim form moving in her direction through the darkness beneath the arches toward the east. Lifting her skirts, she ran as the road passed beneath the viaduct. Seeing threatening shadows emerging from between the stone arches and the mission hall, she ran with all she had.

Those around her stared in wonder. Her skin felt tight. Her lungs burned from the exertion. Mary Jane gasped for air, and pounded on, past Portman Place and Digby Street. She knew someone was at her back, though she would not turn to look.

She saw the tenement on the left, and entered the road to cross to the west side through moving traffic. Mary Jane fouled her boots in the "mud," and came so close to a dray, its driver reined his team of horses to a halt to avoid her.

At the door to the building, she fumbled with her key, her heart pounding in her neck, vision disturbed with bright flashing stars. She got the door opened, glanced left before entering, saw a male figure hurrying toward her. Did he have red hair?

She dashed through the threshold and pushed it shut behind her.

The figure banged into the door. She saw his shadow through the small window at its top.

"Let me in," he called out more calmly than she would have expected. The voice did not sound like Stuart Brevard's. The fellow rattled the door in its frame, trying to get in.

Mary Jane rushed toward her room through the darkened hallway. The broken gas jet had not been fixed.

"Please, I lost my key," said the one outside the building's entrance.

She unlocked her door by touch alone.

Once inside, she moved to the bed and collapsed.

Her heart beat slowed, and her skin seemed to relax. The stars swam out of her vision. Had Gabriella Gorse followed Mary Jane home to find out where she lived? Had anyone at all chased her? Had there been genuine danger or had she merely played an exciting game? She had felt actual fear, yet the danger she'd sensed could have been pure fancy.

Mary Jane heard the door at the building entrance being rattled again, presumably by the man who said he'd lost his key.

Deciding she had indeed let fancy get the better of her, she felt foolish. Even so, she was not about to go find out if the fellow truly needed help.

Mary Jane missed Joseph Fleming already.

Eventually, she sat up and took a large dose of laudanum, at least twenty drops. Since the attack from Stuart Brevard, she'd increased her daily doses of the drug, often having the largest one at night to help her find sleep.

Though much of the evening remained, she needed rest. Mary Jane ate a light meal of bread and cheese, then lay down on the bed again.

TWENTY

In Clerkenwell the crows were fractious, black beaks stabbing even at each other as they vied for carrion and scraps. A dead cat provided them with amusement, as welcome as any forgotten crust of bread. Catherine wandered without purpose down Kings Cross Road and Farringdon, her mind too full to let her rest. Grove House clung to her, and all around were reminders—Clerkenwell was a land of dead prisons, from Coldbath Fields to the Middlesex House of Correction. All closed, their birds transferred to other roosts.

She knew, as she bought an orange from a barrow-boy, that she could not free Evelyn Caille. She could not harm Frederick Caille. She had heard enough to know that, truth or slander, there was nothing she could say that would affect the magnate. Evelyn told him of those who had tried. Ernest Glaive, a former partner and once well-respected, had ended up in Coldbath Fields. Court cases abandoned; reputations torn. Caille did not have all influence, nor did he always win, but he never quite lost.

The Liberals in Parliament, Evelyn had volunteered, would have had at him, but enough landed masters grew fat from Caille's purse. They said he would gain a title within the year. Many, such as Lord Seldon—Lucy's Harry—worked round the man and hoped for change.

"I might be Lady Caille, or bear some such fine monicker," Evelyn murmured, joyless at the prospect. "How grand I would be."

Catherine found a tea-room, and took strong coffee for once. Evelyn had offered to find refreshments, but there had been so much to hear. To Madame Rostov, a vouchsafed stranger, the woman poured out a history of mistakes—an ailing father who had pressed Evelyn to accept Caille's offer of marriage; the subtle way in which her father's legacy had disappeared into her new husband's schemes and factories. He was seventeen years her senior.

"Strong and purposeful men attract—at first," said Evelyn. "A pretty wife—I was pretty once, Katerina—on his arm at the ball, and then a healthy heir…"

"What happened?" Catherine had asked, wondering at this woman's fall from grace.

"After Beresford proved bright and fit, my value fell. Frederick

164

does not invest in shares whose promise is likely to diminish."

The afternoon had been painful. Catherine saw the shadow of her mother creep over the other woman at times. "Perhaps I should be grateful for…" and "There are worse lots for many, I know…" It was how she had watched her mother, Agatha, die inside, and how a precocious, rebellious girl had come to despise her own mother's weakness.

She shared none of this with Evelyn Caille. She said nothing of any Weatherhead, though she was so tempted to echo Aunt Levinia's views on Caille himself. She listened instead, and in listening, found hardly the barest hope that anything could be done, short of slitting Frederick Caille's throat…

A tea-room maid, tripping on an over-generous tablecloth, spilled tea on Catherine's green silk dress. The girl drew back, awaiting anger.

"It is not blood," said Madame Rostov. She stood up, taking the tea towel that was folded over the girl's arm, and blotted her dress. "It is not blood."

Confused, the maid fled back into the kitchens.

Catherine walked south once more—Clerkenwell Green, which had no trace of greenery upon it, and Farringdon Street Station. The streets grew busier, men leaving their places of work to return to their homes or lodgings, or to gather in the chop houses, where women could not intrude. Top hats and tweed caps. Homburgs, the occasional wide-awake, and…the dark felt bowlers that now so bothered her. It was important not to look, not to peer and see if below them sat the face that haunted her. Haunted was now her word for it.

The streets became more familiar, and yet she did not remember coming this way before. The Blackfriars Bridge and her passage to Southwark across the river lay due south of her, a simple journey. A chestnut seller cried out nearby, startling her. She looked around, only to notice that beyond the hawker's barrow stood a man in a dark brown Derby and a neat, well-tailored suit.

And he saw her.

Pretending to fumble in her bag, she closed her eyes. When she opened them, the man was still there. Pale eyes blinked, and he moved away, down a narrow side-street. She knew this place. They were near to Smithfield, and the bloodied cobbles of her vision. Catherine pressed against the wall of a bank, drawing curious looks from other pedestrians.

He could not know her. Never, in dream or vision, had there been any sign that he was aware of her presence. She was an observer, a mind on the Aether, and no more.

"Are you well, madam?" A young clerk paused.

"I...yes, thank you."

She meant to find somewhere to sit and think, but instead she was drawn to the street into which she had seen him go. Madness, an inability to let this pass. She walked unsteadily across the road, earning a curse from a cab driver. Benjamin Street, cramped shops and rooms above; Albion Place the same. A woman clad in many layers of soiled flannel tried to sell her dried rose petals in penny bags, but she pressed past. He was at the corner, looking south. Two apprentices, hardly men, kicked a tin can along the road, and were admonished by an old man in mufflers.

She had no weapon, no guard set to watch her.

Constable Markham sees how deep the flesh has been cut, through artery, windpipe and gullet, down to bone...

As the snow-bound poles called to the compass needle, his presence called to her. She had to know, to learn something of the man behind her nightmares.

In clumsy imitation of stealth, she turned with him, still well back, into an even narrower street behind a Board school. A small boy stared at her, and spat. The bowler-hatted man was not there. Too many alleys surrounded her, squalid lodgings piled upon each other. She caught her breath, knew she should leave...

"You see me."

He stood in the shallowest of recesses, a bricked-in doorway. No taller than Catherine; tidy, polished, as he always appeared.

"Excuse me, sir. I mistook my way," she said, quick-breathed. "I have friends hereabouts, awaiting me urgently."

"Come, come. We know that you do not."

The weakest toss of a child's ball separated them. Two, three yards. Surely someone would come this way soon.

He took out his watch, consulted it. "A quarter after six."

"What do you want of me, sir?"

"Want? I am as the cat. Curious. I am a man who is rarely seen. And if seen, I am not noted. Why, then, do you act the Diana, hunting me down through these narrow ways?"

She edged back slowly, towards the busier streets. "I thought...I thought you one of the friends who expects me."

He nodded. "A quick thinker. I like that. Still, your words are sadly untrue. Let me see. You are from the North of England, by your voice—it is not hidden well enough—yet dress as a Jew, a Pole or perhaps a Russian. I am never followed, and yet you follow me. Mystery is not in my nature. Can you not satisfy my curiosity?"

Catherine swallowed. Her pursuit of him had been madness, and this conversation was a worse lunacy. He did not threaten or show displeasure—they were talking as if they had met on a busy street corner, and the weather had turned suddenly. He might have been asking her why the clouds had gathered so.

"Very well. I have...I have heard of you," she said, all trace of Madame Rostov gone. "And I was told you might be of service, but I realise that I am out of my depth. We should have no quarrel," she added more hastily.

"Go on." He brushed a hair from his shoulder, hardly looking at her.

She drew on the vision from before, when she had seen another make fatal errors in his dealings with Mr Dry.

"You are called the Tradesman."

His lip twitched.

"Ah. The tedium of men's minds. Bacon the Butcher; Spring-heeled Jack. They must have their names. I dislike such cheap names and epithets. I assume that a former client of mine has been discussing me?"

If he knew for a second that she had observed his deeds, that she had touched his mind, a knife would surely be her fate. But if he believed that she was a prospective client, she might live. At that moment she was willing to clutch at any assumption which favoured her.

She tried to keep the relief from her voice, her face. "Yes. Just so." She swallowed. "But they spoke most discreetly, a chance word only."

"And thus you have a commission for me?"

His pale gaze was assessing her, she knew. Client or victim, still in the balance.

"I thought…I am not sure now. I thought I did. But it is foolishness…" Levinia Weatherhead's pasteboard box. There was one name she could use, be rebuffed and perhaps win free. "I had a man in mind," she said. "But now I realise that he is beyond reach. I will leave, and say no more."

She prayed that it might be so.

He was quiet for a moment.

"I am intrigued." He looked around. "A constable turns that corner in seven minutes. He is slow and unreliable, but he will ask what we are doing. We are not 'in our place' down these alleys."

She edged back. "Please, do you not see? I was mistaken. I will not speak of this again, to anyone."

"No," he said. "The coin has almost left the purse, and having been Diana, you must now be Athena. You must let me hear your wisdom. To say that something cannot be done is to invite interest. Do you truly wish to leave this matter unfinished?" His lips smiled. "I have your scent now."

Six minutes only to the constable's heavy boots on damp cobbles. What did he mean by her scent? She wore no fragrance, no eau-de-toilette.

"What do you propose?"

"There is a quiet room in the Crown and Sceptre, a short walk from here. It is slightly—slightly—better in quality than the public bar. We should adjourn there, so that I may learn of the task that outmatches me."

A flash of spirit came to her on hearing the name of the tavern.

"And if you do not like what I say? Do I end in some alley hereabouts, a carcass to be found and hauled away that a harassed coroner may consign me to his notes?"

She thought she saw faint surprise, though his features gave so little away.

"A colourful image, but not an outcome I anticipate," he said.

The "quiet room," barely a cubbyhole with table and benches, brought her closer than she liked to Dry. He dusted his seat with a handkerchief, which he then carefully folded and replaced in his pocket.

"Brandy and one glass," he said to the boy who hovered nearby. The tavern was half-empty, their place concealed by thin partitions. When the drink came, he placed bottle and wine glass before her. "I observe that it stiffens resolve in some." He watched as she poured herself a half-glass, and took a hasty gulp.

Heat, and temporary courage. Catherine struggled to believe that she was here, that she had gone along with him.

"I consider your word unreliable," says Mr Dry.

More quickly than she should, she refilled the glass, and spoke of Fredrick Caille. She named his position, his power, his general malignancy, as heard from Lottie and Evelyn, added to from Levinia's clippings. When she began to explain the reasons why she might want Caille served due vengeance, Dry raised one hand.

"I have no interest in others' tawdry lives. Nor do I need the details of what set you on this path. You may spare me the rest."

Bold with spirits, she stared at him. Were his eyes almost black, or was it the way that they were set, peering from shadows?

"You see my mistake," she said. "God forgive us, there is no remedy against such as Caille."

"Is there not?" He sat back, motionless; she drank again.

Her head swam, fear and excitement trying to live within the same moment. She was ensconced with a killer, an assassin. Her visions had drawn her into ridiculous folly.

"I am sorry to have wasted your time," she said when he had neither spoken nor moved for some minutes. His eyes were open, but what they saw was beyond her.

He blinked. Once.

"I have come across the name. He is powerful, yes, but it can be done. You come to a craftsman, and ask for a work that transcends the usual, that presents true challenge, an opportunity to excel. What would I be if I turned you away, young lady?"

"Human," said the brandy within her, aloud.

"Possibly. But I will do what you ask, though you have not quite asked it."

"You…you will punish Caille?"

"I will remove him. It is what I do."

"How?" She craned forward, mistrusting what she had heard,

and her empty belly griped, wrestling with the drink.

He sighed. "When you purchase bread, do you interrogate the farmer who sowed the corn? Such details are none of your concern."

Was it possible? That she had commissioned a murder almost by accident? She wondered, dazed, how such a situation could have arisen. But she was here, in this room, and Mr Edwin Dry was only feet away. Impassive, still watching.

"May I ask when, then?" Close to a croak, her throat tight. "When would this be done, if it can be?"

"Within the month. I have tools to prepare."

"And the price?"

"To be considered. Not great, I believe. What is in your purse?"

She rummaged and brought out a handful of shillings, a couple of half crowns. And then she found a sovereign, trapped in the lining. "Not nearly enough—but with time I might find more…"

He was paying no attention to her. He took up the sovereign, examining it.

"The monarch ages, but gold does not. We may call this a token, between us, of what is to come."

"My further payment, you mean?"

"The success of this commission," he corrected her. "An end to Mr Frederick Caille."

TWENTY-ONE

"…I have great affection for you, Mary Jane," Joseph said. "I do not like Miss Laudanum. Come, I've decided you *must* give her up."

Groggy from her narcotic nap, Mary Jane looked up at him somewhat confused. Moments passed before she knew she lay in her bed in their room in Globe Road. Little light came through the thinly-curtained bay window. The night had begun Friday, October 26, and Saturday might have arrived while she slept. Joseph sat on the edge of the bed, her empty bottle of laudanum in his hand. He must have just returned from the work in Deptford. She'd done little in his absence but see clients, and school Jennie Weatherhead in the ways of the ladybird.

Despite his words, his features did not suggest he made a demand. He set the bottle down.

"Before you left, you were on *her* side," Mary Jane said, "wanting me to not *hit* her too hard."

"I've tried to have good humour about your habit. The truth is, the time you spend with her is time away from me. I don't resent your clients half so much as I do her. They are not with you when I am. Laudanum is. In the grip of that stuff, you seem to have one foot in the grave. You're hardly here with the rest of us. I *miss* you."

"You were not here tonight," Mary Jane said flatly.

"I have returned, and I'd had some hope you'd be awake and in a mood for a bit of…." Joseph slipped his right hand into her chemise and cupped her right breast softly, lovingly. "Did you sell everything you had in stock while I was away?"

Though his touch felt good, he'd brought up the subject of her laudanum use again. "The hour is late." She pulled the watch from the pocket of his spattered waistcoat, held the timepiece in the moonlight coming through the bay window. "Past two o'clock in the morning."

He unfastened the chain with his left hand, took the watch from her, and set it on the bedstead. "The work is progressing, but now we have a short deadline. I'll be returning to Deptford in the coming days." He lightly pinched her right nipple, twisted the softness gently. "Seems we might need your help."

Mary Jane tried to ignore the pleasant sensation within her chemise. "In what way?"

"Morganstone took an innocent job at the Deptford Victualing Yard, the renovation of several buildings. That's where Royal Navy ships take on victuals. I'm part of his crew working the job. Then this ordinary-looking cove comes to speak with Morganstone. Oddly, I can't remember anything about the fellow. When they're done talking, we're suddenly up to a bit of *what if* that I don't understand completely. I'm certain Morganstone knows everything. He's keeping quiet about the full lurk. I *do* trust him."

Mary Jane nodded. "So you're not renovating anymore?" she asked, disappointed—he'd said that he wouldn't consider her plan to recover the necklace while he was already engaged in what he called "a bit of what if." With his near constant involvement in the shady side of Morganstone's work, she feared that Fleming might never find the opportunity to help her if she didn't keep bringing it up.

"Yes, we're still doing the renovation, and those who hired Morganstone to do the job know nothing about what the cove asked us to do. Along with the renovation, we're secretly creating a detailed map of the Deptford Victualing Yard, particularly certain parts of the buildings we're working on and the grounds around them."

Joseph slid his left hand beneath the bedclothes, caressed the soft, furred lips between her legs.

Without thinking, Mary Jane shifted her hips and legs to give his hand more room. "What's my part? What do I get paid?"

"Seems night rounders at the yard stand between our client, the ordinary looking cove, and what he's after." He paused, his face screwed up in a strain of concentration. "Curious that I cannot recall a thing about *that* man."

"And *my* part?" Mary Jane asked impatiently. If his caresses hadn't felt so good, she would have pushed his hands away.

"I don't know how it would work. You'd provide a distraction of some sort to draw the night rounders away. We'd make certain there would be no risk for you, and you'd earn a piece. I just don't know what that is yet."

As his fingers found their way into the cleft of her cunny and massaged lightly, she let out a soft moan, despite intending to show little interest.

"I'd do about anything for Thomas, I would," she said.

Again, an involuntary moan.

How did Joseph do that? What made his touch so delightful

when it felt little different from that of many men to which she responded with indifference or even disgust? To her frustration, she realised she was intent on hiding her pleasure from Joseph, the one person who should know how she felt, quite the opposite of the pretence of enjoyment she practiced with clients.

"And for me?" He inserted a finger deep inside her. "Would you do just about anything for me?"

I am falling for him, and haven't wanted to admit that to myself.

Mary Jane pushed his left hand away, gave a warning look meant to remind him that he was still earning his privileges with her. "I haven't known you as long," she said. "I'm not certain our *dalliance* is worth the risk of being *lagged*."

He seemed to take the slight of being a mere dalliance in stride. "Ah...*prison*," Joseph said. "Well, it won't do to worry about that." He looked thoughtful for a moment. "But, should you help, I would feel better about our chances if you and Miss Laudanum had parted on good terms by then."

More harping!

She pushed his right hand away, tried the warning look again.

Joseph plucked at the bedclothes in a distracted, ill-tempered fashion.

Hopefully, he is weighing what *he might risk to win my heart.*

"I'm quite troubled that you care more for Thomas than you do for me, given..."

No, he wants to compete with the man! Why can't Joseph say what he means? Does he secretly scorn Thomas?

The tattered end of her dose of narcotic warned her against starting a fight. *A message from Miss Laudanum,* she decided.

Joseph would never understand the feelings she had for Thomas.

Despite knowing better than to quarrel, Mary Jane couldn't help herself. "Given that he's a *gal-boy?*" she asked sharply.

When she had learned the truth about Thomas, she'd experienced a strange relief, deciding that she could continue to love him without sex, and the large role it had in her life, coming between them.

"Well, yes," he said sheepishly. "Although I have nothing but respect for him, I know *he* could not please you like *I* do."

"Could he please *you* as well as *I* do?" she asked, showing more anger.

Joseph gave her an innocent look.

Time is your enemy, Miss Laudanum seemed to say. *You cannot risk the hard feelings, or worse, a falling out.*

Yes, showing more anger might hinder her efforts to persuade Joseph to help her. Once done with his latest business with Morganstone, he'd be on to the next job, like as not another bit of *what if,* unless she could shift his priorities ahead of time.

Mary Jane forced a smile, guided his right hand back into her chemise to her dairy. She caressed his arm, and his shoulder.

Joseph held the fingers of his left hand to his nose, took a deep breath, and smiled. Mary Jane's entire day was there for him to smell; her moments of discomfort and emotion with potential clients, with Jennie, plus the long walk home and her frightful flight at the end. He clearly liked what he found. Was it her quim that he liked, or would that of any woman do? She suspected he liked the odour because it belonged to her. The idea pleased Mary Jane.

"Did you sell all your wares," he asked, "or did you save something back for me?"

Like it or not, she must prevent him from believing he could have her easily. To hide the smile growing on her face, Mary Jane leaned away from Joseph toward a panel of the bay window at the head of the bed.

Where do these feelings for Joseph come from? Why can't I shut them out?

She pulled the curtain aside, looked up and out through the sooty pane, saw the moon riding the coal smoke haze in the sky above.

All the emotion hopelessly confused her efforts. His touch drew her to him, while he angered her, insulting their good friend. She had to give him hope and yet keep him at arm's length; persuade him that her love remained a possibility if he offered enough, without explaining exactly what she required—all in the midst of falling for him in a way she'd never experienced with a man before. How could she sort all that out to best advantage?

Would that I could ride above it all, Mary Jane thought, considering the bright moon high in the night, *so serene and unconcerned with what happens down here.*

"You do want me," Joseph said, "I can tell. I am possibly the best you've had, else you would not find so much satisfaction. I take you to the heights easily."

Yes, he was the best she'd had in her bed—something she ought not to admit. Still, what braggadocio!

"I am no bee, but a hornet when it comes to the sting of pleasure." He spoke with good humour. "I lay you low with the agony of bliss and bring the sweet, sweet death."

Mary Jane couldn't keep herself from chuckling. Wiping her smile away, she turned back to him, expecting to see the joke on his face. His gaze had turned serious. She gave him a sour, questioning look for his boldness. At the same time, she found herself oddly pleased with him.

"Well, of all the men you might have..." he said, "*have* had..."

Now he'd gone too far. With a look of hurt, Mary Jane gave him a punch to the chest.

Again Miss Laudanum counselled her, *You don't have time for a fight.*

Mary Jane knew she wanted a return to anger *because* he was right. Not only did he perform in bed the best of all the men she'd had, he'd also been the kindest to her.

Silence stood between them for a moment.

He slowly slipped his hand back into her chemise, caressed her breasts. "I'll make a bargain with you," Joseph said. "You give Miss Laudanum her freedom, and when the *what if* at the Deptford Victualing Yard is finished, I *will* find a way to get your necklace from the Phoenix gay house. Perhaps we can go away together, after all."

Mary Jane sat up so that her eyes were level with his. "Truly, you'll help me?"

"Yes. You mean more to me than you know."

Mary Jane giggled with delight. Somehow, she'd got her way in spite of herself.

"Will you agree to my terms?" he asked.

"Yes!" she said.

Mary Jane threw her arms around him, and dragged him down into the bed with her.

His deep kisses brought her fully awake at last. She cast off the slight discomfort that had come with the ebb of the narcotic tide and responded with eager passion.

Joseph shed his clothing, pulled the chemise off Mary Jane.

She smiled to see that he'd already placed a rubber sheath on his standing root. He grinned, spread Mary Jane's soft, pale thighs, and quickly found his way inside her. As he had on other occasions, he inclined his body to keep from crushing the ripe fruit of her bosom, or possibly to see the pinkness more clearly. With the repeated warm, wet thrill of penetration, Mary Jane struggled to stay quiet. The thin walls of the building permitted sound to travel easily. She didn't want to disturb the neighbours so late at night.

His smell filled her nose, a strong odour of sweat, yet somehow fragrant and healthy, bringing with it something of his day of work, a sense of the flexing and relaxation of his muscles as he'd gone about his labours.

Her imagination revised what had led up to the moment. She imagined they stood in a shop she'd once seen being renovated in Cleveland Street, an empty, unfinished room with tall windows that allowed those outside to see in. Working naked, he'd filled a giant crack in the rear wall with her naked body, then spread warm plaster around the edges to seal her in place, all except between her open legs where a triangular gap in the lath would give him access to her cunny. Scrutinising his work from a slight distance, the intensity of his gaze brought out the best planes of his handsome face, particularly his jade-green eyes. Her eyes fell to the taper of his slim hips, and his proud instrument. Over his shoulder, she saw passersby on the street outside pausing to look in.

Positioning himself in the gap, he thrust himself into her over and over, the sensation exquisite, the idea that they were seen by others adding to the sexual excitement.

Those watching from outside became more animated, gesturing, talking, laughing, their expressions jubilant, appreciative, envious, delighted.

Mary Jane struggled silently to touch Joseph's chest, arms, head, to draw him closer, but her hands remained trapped. His face was too far away to kiss. She had to break free and take control.

She quaked in time with his thrusts, heard the plaster crack, felt the pieces begin to give way. First, her head pushed forward, the plaster falling from her ruined coiffure. Their lips touched and stayed together, moving hungrily. Her tongue penetrated his mouth to taste him, to caress his tongue.

The loving sensation of his warmth penetrating her own moist heat at both ends gained power and presence within her. A shuddering pleasure, a release more intense than any she'd known before took her out of the wall entirely, out of the fantasy, and back into their bed. She turned away from Joseph for a moment to let go of a strangled cry.

He moved atop her more rapidly, thrusting more deeply within her, his sweet mouth on hers again, the soft hairs of his chest brushing across her nipples maddeningly. She strained to touch him more fully, to leave no gaps between them. Mary Jane raised her legs across his muscular back, pressed the heels of her feet into his flexing buttocks to pull his manhood in deeper still. Her sensation of release came repeatedly, the muscles of her cunny and back avenue contracting in pulses of ecstatic, wet acceptance around the gift of his warm, thrusting steed. She turned away again, used a handful of the bedclothes to help stifle her cries.

Finally Joseph shuddered and made several small cries of his own. He gripped her arms with clasping hands. All his muscles seemed to flex at once. Inside her, despite the sheath, Mary Jane felt a slight pulsing, like a tiny heartbeat, and suddenly the bedding between her legs grew much wetter.

Her intense sensations ebbed as he relaxed atop her. Their heavy breathing slowed together.

He turned to look at her, his cheeks pink, lips open in a satisfied smile, eyes mere inches away from hers. In them, she saw something she'd not seen since Berwyn died: a look that suggested she was loved. Joseph's guileless, open gaze told her that he took pride in her presence within his life, that he had an acceptance of who she was, and that he wanted to protect her and what they had together. She'd never found anything like that in the eyes of a client.

"I love you too," she said without thought, the words coming from her unbidden and catching somewhat in her throat.

His eyes widened, he sat up suddenly, and looked down at her, a confusion of emotion playing across his face.

Mary Jane felt foolish. He had not said as much. She'd presumed. She closed her eyes, grimacing in shame.

"I-I do not say it well," he said, "so I shan't. But it's true, and you are right to say it in that manner."

She opened her eyes and looked again. The qualities she'd seen remained in his eyes.

"We'll have to decide what to do about it," he said.

Relieved and happy with his response, Mary Jane took a deep breath.

I am loved! Such a simple thing. How has that eluded me until now?

She smiled and discovered some hope, imagining the bright days to come in which the two of them continued together. The vision brought a giddiness, an out-of-control feeling somewhat disturbing. She pushed the discomfort away.

Leaning in, he gave her a long and loving kiss.

Joseph sat up, pulled the sheath off, folded it, and placed the wilted thing on the bedstead. Mary Jane got up and washed at the basin with a moist flannel. He lay back down and closed his eyes.

She donned a robe, let herself out onto the landing, and went to use the water closet.

Upon returning, she found Joseph asleep.

She lay awake next to him. Thinking of the personal and social responsibilities involved with a feeling of love frightened her. She'd treated Berwyn so badly.

Mary Jane could not find sleep and her craving for laudanum returned. Once the idea of taking another dose of the narcotic occurred to her, she couldn't shake the thought. The desire became too intense to ignore. Finally she got up and located a bottle of the stuff she kept in a small box of her jewellery.

"One last dose," she whispered to the darkness in the room, "just to help me sleep. He'll never know."

TWENTY-TWO

Safe ensconced in her Southwark room, Catherine could only turn the incident at Clerkenwell over and over in her head, without resolution. Mrs Bessovitch had a tendency to Russian stoicism, and to saying that things were "meant." Catherine was certain that the encounter with Edwin Dry would be described in such a way if she ever dared tell her landlady what had occurred.

Would Dry have killed her, if she had not come up with her preposterous suggestion, her commission? Had she escaped sudden death by the merest sliver?

If he knew that she had been "seeing" any fragment of what he did, that would surely have been the end of her. It was a realisation which sent her to the privy for some time.

Steadier, she ate toast and drank over-sweetened tea. There were surely only two outcomes. Dry would attempt the deed and fail, dying or be taken into custody in the process. Or he would succeed, and come after her for the rest of his fee. She had promised no specific sum, nor had he named one.

Would the Tradesman really work for the challenge itself?

In ignorance of what was to come, Madame Rostov had to work, and maintain a fragile position. This was Catherine's argument to herself, and how she tried to drive the matter of Frederick Caille from her mind. It was how she placed barriers around herself, thrusting Clerkenwell away, again and again. To Miss Bournelle's, and a quiet sitting in which many mysteries were explained, from the turbulent nature of the Aether to the reason why the dead may not wish to speak. All was concocted from Catherine's books and journals—or pure invention. Miss Bournelle, upright and stick-like, retained the discipline of a nanny, even if there was an affectionate nature somewhere beneath. Small errors and inconsistencies were questioned.

"Some who have the gift," said Madame Rostov, "wonder if there are influences on other Planes who may deliberately seek to confuse, to obfuscate."

As opposed to Catherine simply forgetting the name of Miss

Bournelle's late friend in Holloway, and saying Janet instead of Judith. She was still prone to these mistakes. Fortunately the talk of "influences" served for the hostess and the two elderly couples who formed the rest of that night's circle.

"Will there be a manifestation, Madame?" asked a quite tiny, stooped gentleman.

"Madame Rostov is not a physical medium," said Miss Bournelle.

She was not. The complications of producing "psychic" matter from various orifices, or parading vague images of the dear departed, did not appeal to Catherine.

She survived the afternoon, and the dry, crumbling seed-cake which followed. The circle, all quite comfortable in retirement, pressed her to one pound and sixteen shillings, which she received with her usual show of reluctance. It would pay Catherine's rent, and a portion she would keep aside, in case she found Dry at her side one chill night.

The smallest part would appear at Levinia Weatherhead's bedside. The matriarch was no better, no worse. The doctor believed this the plateau before death, a time of quiet as the body gave up its last vestiges of resistance.

New clients were not that easy to find, arising in dribs and drabs and mostly by word of mouth. Coincidence and happenstance had taken her this far, but as she extended her knowledge, she learned more of the others who traded in glimpses Beyond the Veil. Showmen, who sat in vaudeville halls and had messages from "Someone whose name is J...J...might it be a Julia?" (there always was a Julia). Self-effacing women who protested they had no gift, and then filled a house with raps and strange creaking noises. Americans, quite the worse, with their colonial determination and panoply of trick devices—how the trumpets did dance and play themselves in darkened rooms! Her competitors seemed to have the knack of drawing audiences, one way or another.

Nothing had challenged the assumption which she formed in Keighley—that most spiritualist circles consisted of harmless folk, and that most mediums, psychics and their ilk were engaged in taking advantage of such people. Not all, though. Her own gift was genuine, when it arose, but her performances in general were not.

The dead did not speak to her—but those who brought death

had certainly called, and left their cards. It was a thought that, as usual, she tried to purge from her consciousness.

⚓

Each visit to Stepney was an imposition she laid on herself. A duty.

No, not merely duty, she recognised. The fading end of her affection for Charles, the most decent of men, and a certain spite, a stab against her father, who had never lifted a finger to assist this side of the family. It was as if by clenching her teeth and doing what she could at Brantridge Street, she was challenging him. *I am better than you, Joshua Weatherhead*, her actions said.

She sat with the mostly insensate, wheezing shadow that was Aunt Levinia, whilst Clarissa patched and mended below. Jennie was usually absent. Catherine and her cousin shared few words, though she saw a little more of Charles and Clarissa's children.

Benjamin was a grave boy, isolated as the only male left in the family; Maisie, no beauty on the outside, had a generous manner and when not at school or collecting from the laundry, sat by her mother's knee and learned the ways of the seamstress. They seemed to view "Aunt Catherine," so much younger than Clarissa and Jennie, as a peculiar stranger who drifted in and out from the night, occasionally bearing gifts.

"You should not spoil them," said Clarissa.

"It was a florin. I suggested that they might have new socks for the winter, without bothering you."

"And when you are not around to attend to the state of their stockings?" Her cousin stabbed at a patch of thick hessian backing with a curved needle.

"Then they will still have warm socks for you to mend," snapped Catherine, returning to the cold, cramped room upstairs.

When she at last found an excuse to leave, and was in the act of pulling the front door shut behind her, she was surprised to find herself accosted by two women walking up the street.

"Oh, Catherine, good to see you," said the older one.

Catherine suddenly realised that the speaker was Jennie Weatherhead. She tried to gather her thoughts.

"Cousin, yes. Good to see you, also."

The other woman was more Catherine's age. Her locks dangled loosely, and one ankle was deliberately on show. A prostitute, by appearance.

"My friend, Ginger," said Jennie.

Catherine managed a polite smile. Friend, then, however that friendship had come about, but enquiry would have to wait. The last thing Catherine wanted at that moment was to be invited back into the tenement.

"I don't have time to linger at present, I fear. Perhaps soon."

And she sped on her way, eager to be free of Brantridge Street.

∼⚓∼

Her session that week at Lady Seldon's was awkward, with much unsaid at first. Amelia was oblivious to Madame Rostov's visit to Evelyn Caille; Lady Seldon and Lottie clearly meant matters to remain that way. Catherine guided them through automatic writing again, and there was consensus that Lottie had outlined not words, but the images of a giraffe and a lion. A visit to Africa in her future, they concluded.

She did not—dared not—attempt any genuine contact with the Aether. Because it was safer, and because she had few, apart from Mrs Bessovitch with whom to talk, she showed them how one might tilt and rap at a table.

"You risk yourself, Madame Rostov, showing us these tricks," said Lady Seldon, as she knelt and watched Catherine use a wooden "clicker" on one knee to make the table speak. "Might we not wonder at the nature of your own talents?"

"Lucy!" Amelia looked amused and shocked. "Madame arms us against the frauds and mountebanks."

Lady Seldon shared a look with the smiling psychic. Yes, thought Catherine, there is a mind in that slim, privileged woman. And she wondered how many of Harry Seldon's votes and party stances were informed by his wife.

When Miss Baring-Smith apologised that she had an

appointment to keep, and took her leave, the atmosphere changed. The maid who brought the sherry tray was dismissed, the doors to the drawing room closed.

"You saw Evelyn." Lottie perched on the edge of a divan, refusing a cigarette from Lady Seldon. Catherine had wanted to cultivate the habit of smoking pungent Russian cigarettes for her imposture, but her attempts so far had left her choking and slightly sick.

"Yes." Catherine stared into the swirl of her sherry glass. She had to remember that she was Madame Rostov. "It is true, she carries a great burden. Thank you, Lady Seldon, for your kind introduction."

She outlined a version of her visit to Grove House, giving them the colour of the situation, describing Evelyn's general health and demeanour as best she could, but omitting most of the conversation. She risked sharing the incident with the butler, Tanner.

"Do you think I did wrong?"

They thought on this.

"Tanner will report back to his master, or his master's closer aides," said Lady Seldon. "But no, they say that Evelyn rarely laughs these days. To be shown, even for a moment, that all is not under Caille's control will be good for her spirit. You did well, Madame." She lit another cigarette. "Amelia does not know of this, and I would be grateful if you did not enlighten her. The situation is…unstable."

"Of course." Catherine pushed away a tangle of hair from her face. "I am your servant, Lady Seldon."

Though quite what she represented in this company remained uncertain.

"I do still wish we could help poor Evelyn in some more substantial way," said Lottie. "If only we—"

"I will do what you ask, though you have not quite asked it."

"I'm sorry?" Lottie stared, and Catherine realised that her lips had spoken Edwin Dry's words out loud. Her glass fell to the floor, spreading a stain across the Persian rug. A brown stain like dried blood…

Madame Rostov struggled for words; Catherine Weatherhead fainted.

When she came to her senses, she was stretched out on the divan, and a mob-capped parlour maid was scrubbing at the Persian rug. She sought the mantle-clock, and saw that four, five minutes had passed.

"You had a turn, Madame. Lucy is arranging a carriage." Lottie sat on the arm of the divan, looking both concerned and excited. "Was that…" She leaned close enough for Catherine to smell the *oloroso* on her breath. "Was that a vision, a premonition? Did some spirit grasp and use you?"

"I…yes, yes." She sat up, smoothing down her dress. "It has passed, Miss Chambers, thank you for your kindness."

Lottie's voice was a whisper, her eyes on the vexed maid.

"Was it to do with Evelyn? That voice…it was not yours, Madame."

Catherine could not let her lives tangle like this. She could not. A practised medium would recover quickly, and would have experience enough to explain. She accepted a glass of water.

"This can happen." The water was cold, slightly metallic. It helped. "When the Aether is disturbed, when we allow ourselves to be open to difficult thoughts…all manner of influences, often the vaguest of things, may brush us. They mean nothing."

Lady Seldon returned, the butler Merrins at her heel.

"My carriage will take you where you will," she said. "Are you well enough to stand, Madame Rostov, or would you care to rest here a while longer? There is no haste, no haste at all."

"You are gracious, but I should search out my own couch, Lady Seldon." Catherine got to her feet. "Such moments pass quickly."

A chill October fog had clamped its hands around the world outside, each street light a distant star. Vague figures came and went along the street. By the two-horse carriage, its side emblazoned with the Seldon arms, Lady Seldon halted.

"I saw no giraffe, no lion. The girls are bored, and you bring stimulating new ideas to our little circle."

Catherine stood, one hand on the carriage. *But?* she thought. There was something else to come. Dismissal from her post as entertainer?

The other woman looked at her, grave-faced.

"I have sat and heard poor imitations of those who have passed, the garbled nonsense "brought" by spirit guides. There must be entire tribes of misunderstood Red Indians floating above our city, wondering at our denseness." She gave a sharp laugh. "Just now, though—you echoed a quite different sort of spirit."

"My lady?"

Lady Seldon stepped back, gesturing to the carriage driver.

"I believe that you have touched darkness, Madame Rostov, and seen into others' minds. There is no trick there, of that I am convinced. You may visit at your leisure, and be welcome here."

As Catherine took her seat, the carriage pulled away, and she pressed her mind to immediacies. Where to go? She could not be taken to Mrs Bessovitch's. None knew where Madame Rostov lived, and it had to remain that way. There was no doubt that a woman as sharp as Lucy Seldon would enquire of her coachman when he returned.

"De Keyser's, if you please," she said to the man at the reins.

De Keyser's Royal Hotel would do. There were many continentals there, and it was close to Blackfriars bridge. She could mingle unnoticed in the foyer, seem to recall something, and walk across the bridge to Southwark without notice. Or, given the weather, take a hansom from the hotel.

The Royal Hotel was a bulk of gleaming eyes, the lights from its windows struggling with fog that had grown denser, colder. When Lady Seldon's carriage had gone, she had the doorman find her transport, and was finally dropped at the end of the street by her lodgings.

She was calm, organised, and so when she gained the warm kitchen, to see Mrs B ensconced by the fire, toasting a muffin, she sat down and wept, uncontrollably.

Her hands would not hold the mug of milk and brandy she was offered; her mouth would not make words. Mrs Bessovitch went back to her muffin, turning it, and as she did so, she lent the room a lullaby, some Russian song in a low, slightly cracked voice.

At last Catherine lifted the mug, and drank deep.

"I may have done something terrible," she said. "And I have done it over a few cans of spoiled meat, and a woman I do not really know."

Her landlady gave her an enquiring look.

"It is the man, yes? The man who kills. I have seen that face of yours, when he has been in head."

"It is, in a sense. And it is about the one who killed my cousin

Charles."

Catherine wiped her eyes, and a new flood commenced, not tears but words.

She spoke to Mrs Bessovitch of Harwich, *HMS Penelope*, and the fate of her cousin Charles. Some Mrs B knew, but not the whole. The tale had come up to Yorkshire, to be dismissed by her father as nothing to do with them, but Catherine remembered all, the details drummed into her by Levinia much later, or laid out inside the box upstairs.

On November 6, 1885, a blustery evening, the *Penelope* stood off the east coast on guard-duty, no more than ten miles from Harwich. Lieutenant Charles Weatherhead, accepting the hospitality of the midshipmen, sat down to a meal. With the last of the fresh beef used up by the officer's wardroom, and a supply-lighter not expected until the morning, they shared a meal of tinned meat, peas, and turnips from Harwich gardens. This was washed down with watered rum and a bottle of German wine, brought by the lieutenant as his offering.

By the end of the following week, he and three of those midshipmen were dead, the victims of food poisoning. Botulism, the Naval doctors said—a slow and painful death for those who succumbed. Several petty officers of the same vessel were hospitalised, but declared fit for duty within the fortnight.

Catherine asked for more brandy, less milk.

"Meat inspectors gathered at the Harwich Victualling Yard and opened over two hundred cans of meat destined for the Navy." She read out the facts from memory. "Not until they opened the twenty seventh can did they found one fit for human consumption. It was in the Illustrated News, all of it. They found ligaments, offal, tendons—some from what could only have been diseased animals, where the species of animal could even be identified. They found evidence that the cans had not been heated sufficiently, nor sealed with due attention."

"Tch." The landlady scowled. "To save pennies, they would risk lives."

"They took lives," said Catherine. "It was an embarrassment to the Admiralty, not one they wished to pursue in public. The relatives of Charles and the other sailors made enquiries—spoiled food was regularly supplied by the Harwich and Deptford Victualling Yard. Regularly! The contract in question was held by Frederick Caille, a man with many such contracts, a man also involved in banking and industry at the heart of London. He denied any fault, so the families hired a lawyer to sue Caille and his company for reparation—and to expose his profiteering.

"There was no doubt. A hired investigator uncovered written evidence that Caille had a direct hand in the matter, instructing his workers to use sub-standard meat, and to process it cheaply. Temperatures were not met; the hygiene in the factories was appalling."

Mrs Bessovitch placed another muffin on the toasting fork.

"So is proof for court, yes?"

Catherine was weary, but it was the first time she had told the entire story to anyone outside the family. She made herself continue.

"No. The investigator, a retired policeman, disappeared—the day after he wrote to the relatives' lawyer, to say that he had the proof. He was never seen again. No one ever discovered if he was bribed, or threatened. He might even have been beaten to ensure his silence. The result was the same—nothing tangible that could be used against Caille."

"What is happen to case, then?"

"Dismissed after four long months," said Catherine. "Two foremen were reprimanded, another dismissed. When the factories were inspected, they were clean, and all equipment new. Very new. Caille's contracts continued. He was begged for a gesture towards the bereaved; he laughed, and told them to seek such from the foremen involved—men he had instructed!"

"These men—"

"All three found work in South America within a week of the case being dismissed, and took ship accordingly. South America, where Caille has many business interests…"

"It is sad story. This is how your people, they are so poor?"

"The families were left penniless." She took the muffin from her landlady, and made to smear it with butter, but put it down. Here, in the warm, well-lit kitchen, it seemed possible to think, again. "My aunt—Levinia—even as she lies dying, wants vengeance on Caille. She wants him to suffer, to rot, for what he did to her son. For his arrogance, his utter lack of contrition."

"Is understandable."

"But is it understandable that she passes this burden to me?"

"Tch. What is little Katerina to do, with such a powerful man? And who is this woman, who you do not know?"

"Caille's wife." She gave her landlady a much abbreviated version of the situation.

The house creaked; the hearth spat. They sat quiet for a while on either side of the table.

"I met the bowler-hatted man who plagues my dreams. I did not mean to, nor do I know quite how it came about." Catherine pressed her knuckles together. "I met him. The one who kills without conscience."

Mrs Bessovitch nodded her head slowly.

"And you tell him, Frederick Caille is no good. You tell him he should kill this factory-man."

Catherine stiffened. "I...I was scared, confused. I did say it, though I'd had no such intention. It happened so quickly..." What else could she have done? Better an inept, foolish client than another victim.

"Is what I might do," said Mrs Bessovitch, surprisingly matter-of-fact.

"You might?" Catherine's eyes wide, she took in the plump, aproned figure before her, grey hair pinned back, a smear of butter on a rounded cheek. One or two crumbs of muffin clung to a chin that was beginning to whisker.

"Da. I tell you story now, very short. You hear me speak of my Aaron?"

"Your husband? Yes, you said he died, went overboard, at sea."

"Is so. It was mercy."

"He was not well, then—or troubled?"

"It was mercy for me, not poor Aaron." Mrs Bessovitch eased herself up, wiping her chin. She smiled, a fond expression on her face.

"Meant I did not have to use arsenic I buy."

TWENTY-THREE

On November 5, Mary Jane and Joseph sat together, having a meal at the Cock's Crow Tavern in Mile End Road.

"Our efforts will clear the way for a theft at the Deptford Victualing Yard," Joseph said, pushing his plate away and finishing off his glass of ale, "the ordinary-looking cove I told you about is the client. I don't have his name to give you. On the night of the theft, there will be two night rounders, Sims Overton and Roy Nagel, who stand in our client's way."

Mary Jane repeated their names to better fix them in her memory. She took another a bite of her rump steak pudding.

"Though they are Government employed," he said, "as are the stevedores, much like lumpers, they are organised at a local pub. Their master works out of the Evelyn Arms just across Grove Street from the entrance to the Deptford Victualing Yard. They are required to eat and drink at the pub before their shifts. Often they spend breaks there as well. Their shifts are twelve hours long, eight o'clock at night 'til eight o'clock in the morning. They take breaks around midnight, one at a time for fifteen minutes. On Saturday nights, during his midnight break at about a quarter to twelve, Overton goes to the Evelyn Arms, hires a Judy and takes her back to the south gatehouse. The small building is part of the gated entrance to the yard, and has a back door, so she can slip out should anyone come. The hire is prearranged, so you'll have to attract his attention in the week before, then be available that Saturday night, November 20. Overton and Nagel each take a turn with the woman, one having his way with her while the other stays outside to act as crow, ready to signal should someone approach the gatehouse."

"They're helping us without knowing," Mary Jane said with a smile. Though she had little enthusiasm for the job, she wanted Joseph to see her willingness. She had agreed to help because of the money offered, ten pounds, and because both Joseph and Thomas were important to her.

"Very nearly. You'll spend some time at the Evelyn Arms. Some sort of story for how you wound up there will be needed."

"I'll have to talk with Mrs Buki," Mary Jane said. "She's acquainted with most of the ladybirds and their minders along the docks and can make what introductions I might need to smooth the way."

"You will hear distant alarms shortly after midnight. We'll be setting fire to a barge on the Surrey Canal that we will have wedged under the Blackhorse Bridge to the west. Also we'll set fire to a rail car on a siding in the Brighton & South Coast Railway depot just north of the victualing yard. That should draw the police of R Division away and give them something to do. You'll need to find a way to occupy both men for about ten minutes in one of the gatehouses. You ought to be out of the yard by half past twelve."

"Both men at the same time?" Mary Jane asked. "You said one watches as the other has his pleasure. They shan't both want to be in the gatehouse at the same time."

Joseph frowned, then smiled. "You are much more captivating than any of the other ladybirds in that neighbourhood. I think you shall not have too much trouble."

Mary Jane did not have his confidence. He could be a leg when need be, good at pulling a ruse. With the right mark he had no difficulty swindling. Even though he had a good heart, he'd grown up hard on the streets of London—"a gormless shit of a guttersnipe," he'd said. He expected she'd been made of similar stuff perhaps, but all she could think of was how their plan could go awry if she didn't keep her two pigeons sufficiently entertained.

After so many years of solicitation, she had little trepidation about tupping strangers for money; yet doing so as part of a scheme designed by Joseph to satisfy the needs of a client of Thomas's was several steps removed from the sort of control she preferred to have over her work. Joseph had told Thomas that her part of the lurk would not have to include actual prigging.

"If we see success," she said. "it will be because of my willingness to dab it up with the night rounders, whether it comes to that or not. Will you promise not to tell Thomas if it *does* come to that?"

"Yes," Joseph said, "but you're a bricky girl. I have every confidence in your ability to play the crooked cross. Just look at the way you've got me under your thumb." With the smile that followed, he seemed to be saying that he knew she'd been playing him, and he remained happy to have her.

Were I that obvious with my wheedling before? Well, yes, she supposed she had been. That was part of the problem with love—she'd become comfortable enough with him to allow her facade to slip from time to time.

Somehow, they had both changed after she professed her feelings for him. He'd begun to say things to her that he might have held back before. Afraid of too much familiarity, she'd found herself wanting to manage his impressions of her even more than she had before. At present, she held back her lack of confidence concerning her part in the lurk, and the continuing discomfort she experienced in her withdrawal from laudanum.

In the week and a half since they'd made their deal, she'd kept her word to herself—the dose of laudanum she'd had that night after he'd gone to sleep had been her last. She meant to stay with the decision, even though doing so had been far more difficult than she could have imagined. She silently cursed Blanche Sayers, the prostitute in Paris who had provided the first taste of the drug.

Mary Jane's part in the deal with Joseph had been compromised two days earlier when he'd discovered the bottle of laudanum she kept with her jewellery. They'd had a row. She'd left the box open—almost, she thought, as if she'd wanted him to find the tincture.

"I'd forgot about that bottle," she'd protested.

He'd given her a look that said he didn't believe her. "Should you want my help recovering your necklace," he said, "you know you'll have to give it up."

That he'd dispensed with the charming phrasing that suggested laudanum was a woman told Mary Jane how serious he'd become.

"Would you dump what remains in the privy?" he asked.

She agreed to do that and went to the water closet on the landing. *Foolish that he didn't come with me to watch.*

Standing alone beside the toilet, considering the laudanum, she decided she shouldn't waste what amounted to a couple of soothing doses. She'd paid for the drug, after all.

No, I must give it up for his help, and for my own well-being.

She had poured the tincture in the toilet and pulled the chain to wash the amber liquid away.

At present, sitting at dinner in the tavern with Joseph, she couldn't help wishing she hadn't done that. Fearing that she'd fail to keep the two night rounders entertained, an indispensable part of the scheme, left her feeling weak and cowardly. She wanted the escape from those feelings the drug could provide. The insidious craving had taken hold of her thoughts again.

Of course, she could always go to a chemist's and buy more.

No!

Mary Jane considered the remains of her meal. The bits of sodden pastry, the coagulated fat and gravy didn't look tasty now that the food and her gut had gone cold. She looked around the tavern at the other diners, most of them labourers eating inexpensive meals. She alone experienced severe unease, while those around her enjoyed their food and drink, talked, and laughed.

Earlier, when she'd expressed doubts about the scheme, Joseph's frown had told her he expected more than a smile to confirm her willingness to take part.

Mary Jane decided that if she wanted him to take a risk for her, to find a way to secretly recover the emerald necklace from the Phoenix gay house, then she should not question his plan further. She would find a way to do as he asked on November 20 at the victualing yard because that would go a long way toward restoring his trust and motivating him. The ten pounds offered would add considerably to her savings and bring her closer to making a fresh start out of London.

Being gone to Deptford for a week also had its advantages. Even though she believed the notion emerged from the realm of fancy, she couldn't help thinking that Gabriella Gorse had followed her home the night of October 23, and that the bitter prostitute might relay the location to Stuart Brevard. Mary Jane would feel better getting away from Globe Road for a while.

She gave Joseph another smile and nodded. "Yes, I can do that."

"Don't worry," he said, "we'll go over the lay again once you've been there and had a look around."

⚓

On Mary Jane's behalf, Mrs Buki made an agreement with a whore's minder and magsman nicknamed Alister the Onion, a tall, rail-thin fellow with oiled brown hair and a waxed moustache. His clothing, though that of a swell, had been tailored for someone heavier and shorter. He sported a fine new brown bowler. The Onion operated most of the ladybirds of Deptford that frequented the Evelyn Arms. He had a reasonable disposition for a cash carrier, habitually ate raw onions, and took strange pride in his terrible breath.

When Mary Jane arrived in Deptford on Saturday, November 13 to meet with the man for the first time, she asked, "Aren't you troubled that the night rounders will want to do you harm after our work here is done?"

"No, love," Alister said. "They shan't want to own that the yard were robbed while they entertained tail in the gatehouse. Even if, I have a family behind me, and Overton and Nagel are jus' little men."

Deptford by day was a noisy place, with the incessant sounds of equipment, vehicles, and ships in motion, men moving about, talking and shouting to one another as they organised their labours, the sounds of hand tools in use, the whistles and the horns from the river and the rail yards. Although the industrial area remained a busy one at night, with fewer labourers working after hours, and most of the night shifts indoors at the slaughter houses, the saw mills, the warehouses, and the factories, a relative calm came to the community once the haze-swaddled sun had set.

The Evelyn Arms was small, with a simple rail before the taps, and about ten dilapidating tables. The drinks, both strong and mild, were watered down. The hardworking men who came to the establishment stank from the sweat of their labour, and the river rot along the docks. Most of the women who came in did so to earn from servicing the men. Like any other pub, the patrons talked, laughed, and argued. They played games, got into fights, or drank themselves into insensibility.

With Alister the Onion's help, Mary Jane's reception as Fair Rose at the Evelyn arms went uneventfully well, but for one prostitute, Sally Fourth, who eyed her with mistrust.

What a ridiculous name, Mary Jane thought. She had begrudging respect for the woman's ability to spot the suspicious.

Sally Fourth was not one of the Onion's Judies. The blonde, raw-boned, and bow-legged woman had a deeply pocked face that seemed like a piece of leather that had suffered in severe weather, then dried and set up, holding its distressed shape; in her case a permanent expression of scorn.

Like Sally Fourth, the Judies that frequented the Evelyn Arms were a slatternly lot. Most had a cordial manner once Mary Jane broke the ice asking them about themselves and showing interest in their answers.

"I'm from Cardiff," she told them. "Come to Deptford to attend my sick mum. She died, poor old soul. Now I must earn enough to return home."

Monday afternoon, Sally Fourth approached a table where Mary Jane sat with another prostitute, a heavy woman named Deborah LaFluer. "Too good for the likes of us, I see," Miss Fourth said to Mary Jane. "Haven't seen you try to earn a single farthing."

She didn't answer, assumed the woman suffered envy because nearly all the men at the pub stared at Mary Jane with a frequency difficult to ignore. She'd spent much of her time fending them off.

"I suppose that's a good thing," Miss Fourth said, "You ought to go back where you come from, and leave *our* men alone."

"Leave Fair Rose be," Deborah said. "Poor manners are like a contagion. You don't want me to come down with them, now, do you?"

Miss Fourth clearly saw the stout woman as a threat. She grumbled and wandered off.

Concerned that Miss Fourth's dislike might get out of hand, Mary Jane and Joseph Fleming decided to stage a meeting at the pub, one in which she'd seem to accept him as a client. While working at the Victualing Yard, he'd spent enough time in the pub to fit in. Since the previous Saturday, he'd been meeting her following her hours at the pub one road to the west, where Windmill Lane crossed Hanlon Street. Then they'd walk across the Surrey Canal on the Windmill Bridge to catch the Lower Road tram back to the inn in Plough Road where they had a room. Tuesday night, after they staged their meeting in the pub, they left from there together.

The Onion introduced Mary Jane to both Sims Overton and Roy Nagel when they came into the Evelyn Arms on Wednesday.

"Fair Rose is me cousin-what's-died's daughter, me second cousin," Alister explained to Overton the next day. "She's a toffer in Cardiff, but is far from home, fallen on hard times, and has no push. She must earn the price to get home, and will take one and a tanner for a storm of heaves." He winked at Overton. "Though it's more than you've paid in the past, she's well worth the chink."

Mary Jane smiled pleasantly and remained silent.

The man took on a thoughtful frown, perhaps unable to accept that a woman of Mary Jane's looks would come so cheaply. He might also have been bargaining with his own willingness to pay the price.

They had anticipated he might think she could earn her fare home more easily elsewhere.

"Fair Rose has a debt she must pay before she goes," Alister said.

Overton's eyes narrowed doubtfully.

"I am under obligation to the Onion," Mary Jane said. "He paid a debt I had in Cardiff to free me up to come help my mother, then he paid for my way here. I agreed to work for him for a week, to help him rebuild his reputation."

Overton gave a skeptical look.

"Remember Little White Bumps?" Alister asked.

Overton nodded. "Glad *I* never partook."

Mary Jane knew from talking to the Onion that Little White Bumps was a prostitute who had worked for him, one with what looked like raised white freckles on her face. The young girl had made several men deathly ill, or so the story went.

"Seems her bumps," the Onion said, "cute as they made her, were a pox, an *unknown* contagion. When she left Deptford, my reputation went with her."

Overton's jaw became set in a satisfied manner—he seemed to have been persuaded. "You'll come to me Saturday night, then, Fair Rose? You have but to knock on the south gatehouse."

Mary Jane nodded.

Waiting impatiently for Alister to make the suggestion they had worked out, she saw Sally Fourth enter the pub with a labourer. The two took seats at a table in the northeast corner of the room, the woman staring at Mary Jane with undisguised hatred.

During their planning session on Saturday, when she'd arrived in Deptford, she'd asked Alister to help her come up with a plan to occupy both night rounders simultaneously.

"I've been thinking about that since Mrs Buki offered the job and described the lay," the Onion said. Then he chuckled unexpectedly. "As luck would have it, our marks have provided the solution. Overton asked me just last week to find a woman what'd take him and Nagel at the same time. Can you take both at once, Fair Rose?"

"Describe the inside of the Gatehouse," she said.

He did so.

"Yes," she'd said, "I can see a way." Mary Jane described it to the Onion.

"I like that. Would that I could watch."

Obviously, he'd assumed she'd be willing to prig the two night rounders, and had been surprised when Mary Jane asked him not to tell Joseph about it.

She'd experienced some relief with a plan in place, but at present feared Alister had forgot it.

Overton got to his feet.

"She'd take two men at once for two bob," the Onion said.

Overton's eyes grew large. He settled again in his chair, and glanced at Mary Jane. She gave him her tiniest, most charming crooked smile of confirmation.

Experiencing a small thrill of some sort, he quaked. But then he frowned. "Couldn't do that. There'd be no one to keep watch."

"I could loiter at the gate as your crow," the Onion offered, "knock on the gatehouse door should I see someone coming."

Overton's smile grew slowly, became large. He nodded toward the Onion. "I'll sing your praises, I will," he said with a laugh.

"Good man." Alister clapped him on the shoulder.

The two men rose together and left the pub.

Mary Jane found a seat at the table to her left, next to Edith Gilcrest, a friendly young woman close to her age. The spot also had the advantage of placing Mary Jane out of Miss Fourth's line of sight.

TWENTY-FOUR

Within the month, Dry had said. Catherine was left to wait and fret. She took small engagements, where she sensed that the clients were predisposed to be gulled or guided, wanting re-assurance rather than hardened fact. Was a mother safe in Heaven, would a child be granted God's grace? Yes, and yes, so many affirmations that she grew bored with her own tongue. The Aether did not tremble; the Veil did not part.

Each day she checked the newspapers—bought, borrowed, or glimpsed on an omnibus—waiting for news on the fortunes of Frederick Caille. And with each day her confidence took a blow.

At one lonely hour of the clock, after a particularly tiresome sitting, she conceived the idea that a police inspector might be the next to rap upon her door, accusing her of trying to assassinate an upstanding member of the business community. She constructed defences for anyone who might question her. She had been distraught, of course, at the condition of her cousins, and that had led her into folly.

Or, thinking on it, she could do better—all was but a phantasy to appease a dying widow, played to seem as if she had done the widow's bidding. She would laugh, and laughing, draw any officer of the law into the absurdity that Catherine Weatherhead could have anything to do with the lives of those who moved at the level of Mr Caille. Who was she but an insignificant young woman?

As proof of her erratic moods, she then became worried that Dry would come for her. An easier target than Caille, after all. He would remove her, now that she knew his face…

"I have your scent…"

When these anxieties tumbled out over the breakfast table, Mrs Bessovitch pointed out that she had given the bowler-hatted man no name, no address. They had not even met near where Catherine lived. How could he possibly find her, whether he did the deed or not?

TWENTY-FIVE

Friday night in Deptford, when Mary Jane met Joseph at the crossing of Hanlon and Windmill, she saw Sally Fourth watching from the recessed door of one of the terraced houses along the lane. Though Mary Jane tried not to worry about the ill will of the woman, the weather had turned cold, somehow raising a chill feeling that the mistrustful prostitute might be the undoing of their carefully laid plans. Needing to feel protected, Mary Jane clung to Joseph on the walk to the tram and the ride to their inn.

"I like your cuddling tonight," he said.

She didn't respond, deciding he *wouldn't* be pleased to hear the reason she stuck so close.

Saturday, Mary Jane watched to see if Sally Fourth communicated with Overton or Nagel. The men finding out that Mary Jane didn't seem to have any clients from the pub could compromise the plan. The men did not speak with Fourth. At the end of the day, as a light snow began to fall outside, she realised that her fear had been for nothing. The woman was just trying to protect her territory from an intruder. By one o'clock Sunday morning, Mary Jane would be out of her life.

Saturday, near midnight, Alister the Onion and Mary Jane stepped out of the Evelyn Arms pub together and walked across Grove Street to the south gatehouse at the entrance to the Deptford Victualing Yard. Little traffic moved along the lane at that hour.

Halfway across the road, they heard the door to the pub open again, and Sally Fourth's coarse voice cut through the cold air. "He's one of mine, Overton is."

Mary Jane and the Onion turned to face her.

The woman, drunk and stumbling, heedless of an oncoming van—the only vehicle moving within several hundred yards—stepped into the lane, forcing the driver to steer out of her way.

"Glocky buor," the driver cried angrily.

We don't have time for this, Mary Jane thought. She'd looked at the clock above the taps in the pub. They'd left the establishment with one minute to spare before midnight.

"He's never asked for you before," Alister said to Miss Fourth.

"Not so's you'd know he'd done," she said, her sloppy, scornful gaze fixed on Mary Jane. "I don't work for you, Onion Man."

"Best take a better tone with me, bunter," Alister said.

"We don't have time for her." Mary Jane edged away toward the south gatehouse.

"*She* don't work for you *either*," Miss Fourth said. "She come here from somewhere else, taking away some of *my* chance to earn."

"I have to go," Mary Jane said.

"Off with you, then," the Onion said. "I'll deal with her."

"Don't go, coward," Miss Fourth said, "we's just getting started."

Mary Jane knocked on the gatehouse door.

"Keep your voice down, Sally," Alister said.

The door opened. Sims Overton poked his head out into the chill night. "What's all this? You want to wake the dead?"

"I'm here," Mary Jane said. "Let me in."

Hearing the sound of rapid footsteps, she turned to see Sally Fourth rushing toward her. Alister caught her in mid-stride and took her to the ground. The woman's head hit the cobblestones hard.

"We can't be knocking away in here with a disturbance outside the gate," Overton said.

"I'll take care of the problem," the Onion said, "and be your crow."

Mary Jane pushed her way into the gatehouse. Inside, the air felt nice and warm. She doffed her shawl, dropping it on a chair. Overton lingered by the door with a worried look, watching the two outside.

"Come," Mary Jane said, tugging gently on the man's coat sleeve. "We have an agreement. Call Mr Nagel."

Overton gave her a look of unease. "No, h-he'd better stay without to keep watch. The Onion won't be watching."

Before the gatehouse door shut, Mary Jane saw Alister carrying Miss Fourth away. She seemed to be insensible.

"He'll return quickly," Mary Jane said.

"Perhaps we'll do it another night," Overton said.

Mary Jane broke the buttons on her bodice and chemise opening them quickly. She laughed to pretend delight. Having dispensed with her corset for the evening in favour of ease of movement and speed in dressing, her creamy breasts were instantly exposed.

Overton's mouth dropped open. His eyes wide, he reached for her.

Mary Jane backed away, shaking her head slowly. "Call Mr Nagel," she said.

He seemed to come out of a trance.

She teased with seductive poses.

Overton appeared to consider possibilities. Finally, he turned to the back door, the one that led out into the yard, opened it, and called quietly. Nagel appeared quickly, and entered.

Mary Jane doffed her top skirt and tossed it over a support beam that ran across the small room about eight feet off the floor. From a hidden pocket of her bodice, she took a small leather pouch containing coconut oil, and applied some as lubricant between her legs. She handed each of the men a rubber sheath, and they got down to business. Both ends of her skirt hung down from the beam, the hem on one side, the waistband on the other. Mary Jane clung to the ends for support as the men had their way. At the peak of their pleasure, both men had achieved penetration, and were working up a sweat. All three stood together, a beast with three backs; Mary Jane between, Overton in her cunny, Nagel in her back avenue.

The distant sound of a fire alarm came from outside, probably to the west. That would be the burning barge on the Surrey Canal.

The men paused for a moment, seemed to decide simultaneously and silently that they had no responsibility to deal with whatever disaster unfolded, and went back to their vigorous thrusting.

Shortly thereafter, another fire alarm sounded toward the north. That would be the rail car in the depot. Again, the pause, the silent consideration, and resumption of fervent activity.

Mary Jane had gained the ability to relax in such situations. All the same, she was becoming sore. She did not know how much time had passed before she heard shots fired in the victualing yard. Both men pulled away from her instantly.

"What—?" Nagel began.

"Firearm," Overton said, "In the yard."

The two men pulled up their trousers.

"Go," Overton said to Mary Jane. "Dress quickly and go!"

The men hurried out the back door into the yard.

Mary Jane did as the night rounder instructed. Her shawl hid the fact that her bodice and chemise were loose. She heard more gun shots as she left the gatehouse.

She met Alister the Onion and Joseph Fleming in Windmill Lane. Joseph was counting out money into Alister's hands.

"A pleasure, Fair Rose," the Onion said. He tipped his hat to Mary Jane, blew her an oniony kiss, and walked away toward the south along Hanlon Street.

"That's done, then," Joseph said, taking Mary Jane's arm and leading her toward the west. "I'm glad the job is over. I feared for your safety. The Onion told me what happened with Miss Fourth."

"And someone fired a gun," she said.

Joseph had a troubled look. "Yes, I heard, but don't know why."

Determined to be a good sport for him, Mary Jane shrugged, despite a sudden exhaustion, and a churning of her gut, a remnant of her fear that Miss Fourth would keep her from meeting the scheme's timeline.

"Now we can work up a plan to get your necklace back," Joseph said.

At any other time Mary Jane would have jumped for joy at his suggestion. With the unsettling events of the evening, all she could think of was having a deep, soothing dose of laudanum. She remained determined to resist the desire.

TWENTY-SIX

Work lined her purse enough to meet the rent and spare a crown or two for her cousins. The atmosphere at Brantridge Street was cheerless. Levinia's sunken eyes asked questions which she could not answer—she had not mentioned (how could she?) the vaguest possibility that Mr Dry would complete his commission. Not mentioned that such a commission existed. The longer it went, the more deranged the idea, and the entire Clerkenwell episode, seemed.

There came a Saturday of especial tedium. Mrs Combes, a shrill woman whose husband had managed to escape her via the kindness of a rheumatic heart, was determined not to let the poor man have peace. It was Catherine's third sitting with her—between obituary notices and a few pence to Mrs Combes's truculent daily, Catherine had enough to keep up the charade.

She was also experimenting with the introduction of a Spirit Guide, a ludicrous notion sparked by Lady Seldon's comments. To stand out from her peers, Catherine's imaginary guide was a Mongolian. "Temur" was a shaman from a suitably vague period in Mongolian history, and was to assist her in locating poor Mr Combes, amongst others.

Much to Catherine's annoyance, Mrs Combes pressed for more detail than was to hand, and she had to bluff her way through parts of the sitting. She abandoned Temur, and concentrated on "seeing," hoping that her genuine gift might make itself known. Nothing but an intense headache resulted, and she had to end the session.

"There are other spirits, blocking me," she said as she left. "Darker ones, which do not wish us fortune today."

Mrs Combes's hand hovered at her throat. "I can't imagine why, Madame Rostov. I certainly have no stain to draw that sort of attention, and neither did poor George." She sniffed. "Unless you yourself have…"

Catherine was unwilling to follow that line of thought.

"Perhaps another day," she muttered, and quit the house without making the usual appointment for a further sitting. As she trudged homewards, she decided to let Mrs Combes find someone else to badger "poor George."

Light snow fell from a heavy sky, and her head…the non-existent Temur was beating his drum within. A pork chop did no good, and neither did brandy or one of Mrs B's powders. Catherine retired early, unable to undertake her usual research into potential clients. The room seemed smaller than before, more mean in aspect, and again she thought of the money which had gone to her cousins. The snow had stopped, and barely a breeze troubled the lodging house chimneys, letting the fire glow peaceably in the hearth. Those coals cost extra, and winter was coming.

Lying on her bed with her boots still on, she felt the blood pound through her temples, saw the veins stand out on her wrists, and knew that something dreadful was coming. This would be Islington and Clerkenwell again, in all their painful clarity, the opening of an inner eye beyond her control. She pressed her palms to her face, covering her eyes.

She could still see.

This was not the dusty room at Mrs Bessovitch's, but a vaster swathe of night, a London of sparse gas-lamps and yawning alleys. The Thames churned, sickened by its diet of sewerage and bloated bodies; the stars were hard, uncaring dots. She had no idea where she was, if she was anywhere.

Trembling on the bed, her mind embraced the night, the vision so clear that she might have been walking through a photograph, a photograph which lived. There were night-sounds around her, and she smelled the ordure of animals in great numbers, like the cattle farms of her native Yorkshire, yet she was deep in the city.

Her hands gripped the bed-frame, and she tried to guide herself, in vain. Her self, her focus, was drawn to a set of great gates, these closed but flanked by two gatehouses, crossed anchors carved upon them. Each gatehouse had its own lesser door, and the one on the left was open. Through this she swept, insensible of any contact with the ground, and there she watched the act unfold, that act she had set in motion without truly understanding...

Mr Edwin Dry walks calm and straight through the Deptford Victualling Yard, close by the Foreign Cattle Market. He pauses beneath the ornate bell-tower, and examines his half-hunter by moonlight. Sunday tomorrow, and hardly a light in the compound. Adams, the Superintendent, is home with his seven children, wondering if there is more he can trim from the budget to satisfy his masters; only one of the Assistant Victualling Store officers still holds late vigil, alone in an office by the high-beamed bulk of the cattle warehouse.

Dry has measures in place to engage and occupy any night rounders, to draw away constables who might wonder if they should check the Grove Street beat once more, rather than head for cocoa at the cab-men's shelter further down. And once such arrangements are agreed, he leaves them to others.

His focus is on the victualling offices—their precise configuration, those small variants on what can be gleaned from maps and descriptions. To the northwest, nearest the adjoining railway yards and stores, are the offices he seeks. Quiet places in brick buildings; good places for men to discuss matters of business which should not be widely known.

The Honourable Eric Seaton will not be attending tonight's meeting with Frederick Caille. Not long after dusk his youngest son, a babe of less than two, was taken from his nursery, the nurse chloroformed. The child will be found unharmed and none the worse for his experience in the morning, but Seaton does not know this, and in his panic, he has forgotten all other engagements.

Thus Caille and his bully boys sit in an Assistant Victualler's office and await Seaton in vain. Certain adulterants, meats of dubious provenance, will not enter the Deptford Yard later this month as a result. Mr Dry has already observed another man enter the Yard, but he knows this man and his purpose. Constable Retton from the local station, deep in debt to one of Caille's associates, a policeman bought and paid for should he be needed. If he runs, and runs fast enough, Mr Dry has no interest in him.

Pale eyes capture the scene and identify the side-entrance mentioned by his contacts. He moves through shadows—there is always the chance of a late cashier or drunken boatswain crossing the grounds—towards his goal. The lock surrenders with one twist of a wire. Inside, high-ceilinged corridors are pockmarked with office doors, all firm shut save one.

Mr Dry pauses. He brushes a trace of whitewash from the sleeve of his heavy outdoor coat, and places himself within himself, aware of each fold and pocket, each tool of his trade. He cannot be excited or fearful, for this is not his nature. He can, however, be appreciative that the endeavour is far more bold than his previous commissions. His client, the curious black-haired woman at the Crown and Sceptre, is of little interest to him. There are things which he will learn from this night, however the required outcome is achieved.

Which it will be.

The soles of his boots are coated in gutta-percha, and make no sound as he approaches the open doorway. There is conversation within; the bray of one who commands, and the whine of those who serve.

It is said that Frederick Caille's men are armed, for the magnate has a distaste of the lower classes which borders on fear, and a man of his stature has enemies. Two years ago an attempt was made on his life by an Italian who had fallen into disgrace—the result of financial dealings with Caille's bank. Mr Dry does not rely on firearms. They have an indiscriminate nature, and can fail or fire regardless of the owner's wishes. He is provided for tonight, though, with two small and well-sighted revolvers. Just in case.

He reaches into his overcoat, and takes out a curiosity, an American Civil War grenade which he acquired from a collector in Paddington. The heavy iron ovoid has no charge, but it looks the part. Leaning in, he tosses the grenade into the outer office, an action which brings forth cries of horror and surprise from within.

The bully boy nearest the door is transfixed, staring at the supposed deadly object; there have been bombings in London in recent years. The other shows more presence of mind and seeks to kick the grenade from the room. Mr Dry moves in, twisting to his left and away in a smooth turn which drives his slender blade into the stunned man's jugular and out again, avoiding the resultant red spray. His silent dance across the tiled floor brings him to the second man, who hesitates between this sudden assailant and the grenade. He is dying as he falls across the harmless device, and Mr Dry is already pressed hard against the wall by the inner door, waiting.

An angry query from within; an order. Police Constable Retton appears, slack-jawed at the sight before him.

"Run," says Mr Dry.

Retton's broken-veined face pales, but some fateful instinct, perhaps gained many years past when he was young and decent enough, makes him raise his official billy club and stand, blocking the inner doorway. He manages to deflect the first cut of the knife with his truncheon. A second thrust finds his belly, but heavy serge and brass buttons foil its intent; in return, the truncheon fails to connect with Dry's left shoulder.

Unfortunate seconds have passed. Mr Dry slashes across the tendons of Retton's stick hand, slides beneath a swing and drives the point under the constable's chin. The man's scream is choked by blood and steel, and the blade is free.

The first shot from the inner office comes close to taking Retton in the head, but the constable is done. He slumps to the floor, his arms outstretched and one leg gently kicking, a pithed frog on a finely tiled tray.

A second shot, wild.

"Who's out there? Show yourselves!"

An interesting situation. Caille was not reputed to carry a weapon himself, though Dry had prepared for the possibility. He reviews his knowledge of the offices. A grand window at the far side of the inner office gives access to the grounds. Caille can hide behind the desk and wait, or he can seek to speed his way from the room through that window. Dry crouches low by the doorway, listening to catch any sounds which might provide further information—the scrape of heels or furniture, the grate of...

A window catch.

Caille's two shots have relieved the need for quiet work. Dry darts forward, gripping the small revolver which was resting in its slide above his right wrist. He fires once at the figure halfway through the open window and rolls to the cover of the large oak desk. An oath tells him that the bullet has hit home, but the thud and faltering step on the gravel outside add the likelihood of a flesh wound only—or a slow, unreliable bleed.

Retton is not a large man. Mr Dry grips the corpse and drags it into the inner office. Sliding both arms around the constable's waist, he lifts it up to the window. This time the shot, which comes from a dark mass of shrubbery a few yards to the west, takes Retton in the chest, not that it matters to the constable any more. Dry is over the sill, outside and low to the ground even as the corpse falls back.

"Name your price, you bastard!" Caille yells from the bushes.

"It will be met by another." Mr Dry fires in the direction of the voice and the muzzle-flash from before.

"I can match and beat..." The words are interrupted by a wet cough, "...any amount of coin you've been offered. And the shots will have been heard."

Caille fires back, but Dry is no longer there. He moves with economic speed, sliding into the bushes to the right and behind them. The grey hunched shape of Caille is easily seen, and then Dry is behind the wounded man, sliding his revolver back into its mechanism as he moves. There are times when it suits him that a death should be a personal one.

A skilled journeyman must be close to his trade.

The garrotte wire is cold around Frederick Caille's neck before he can sense the presence at his back. Bleeding from a shoulder wound, the magnate lets his firearm drop to the wet grass.

"Why?" says Caille.

"Must there always be reasons?"

Mr Dry holds the garrotte tight with one hand, and wipes his glasses on Caille's jacket with the other, removing a spot of someone's blood. Either the man is too weak from pain and blood loss to struggle, or he is considering, at last, the possibility that all empires fall.

"Everything…" Caille manages, "Has purpose. What, damn it, is the source of your hate for me?"

"Hate?" Dry's pale eyes widen, and for a heartbeat a smile might have been about to form. "I am, sir, utterly indifferent to you."

The wire bites deep; the throat constricts. Two, three kicks; a low choking noise. Then Frederick Caille, a fine and mighty power in the great financial labyrinth of London, becomes no more than the substandard meat that he purveys.

A whistle in the distance, and the sounds of running men, but not too close as yet. The Deptford Victualling Yard is sizeable, and has many shadows. He blends, dances in darkness, noting small details as he leaves. On Windmill Lane he sights a female figure clutching her shawl as she hastens to be elsewhere. She would be the one assigned to distract the night rounders—the prostitute Mary Jane Kelly. The job was well enough done; she may be worth remembering, assuming the pox or the casual violence of the streets do not take her.

He does not hurry. He walks the tow-path of the Surrey Canal, and breathes in the night.

Twenty three days have passed since he met a woman in Clerkenwell.

TWENTY-SEVEN

On Monday, November 22, two days after returning to their lodgings in Globe Road, Mary Jane and Joseph sat together in the Green Man pub, waking up with morning coffee, reading newspapers. She read in *The Star* that a man named Frederick Caille had been killed at the Deptford Victualing Yard on the night of November 20. Although several others were also killed, including a policeman, the emphasis was on Mr Caille, an important man. The story said nothing about a theft.

Had Joseph been hired not to aid an effort of theft, but for one of murder? The crime occurred while Mary Jane kept in gammon the yard's night rounders. She'd heard barking irons, yet Mr Caille had died from strangulation. The other men perished from stab wounds.

"What do you know of the murder at the victualing yard?" she asked Joseph, showing him the story.

His face as he read told her much about his innocence. Still, Mary Jane remained upset.

"I just saw that in *The Globe*," he said, tapping the newspaper he'd set aside. "I hoped you would not see it."

"You think I'm flat, do you?"

"Keep your voice down," he said, grimacing. "No, I'm not trying to hide it from you. I didn't know. I dare say Thomas didn't either. The map we made of the yard aided the killer. Could be the theft went awry or, as I now suspect, his plan had been for murder all along."

"I don't like it that you led me into something like that," Mary Jane said.

"All three of us were gulpy enough to be duped into taking part. We ought to hope the police of R Division are unable to put together our presence in Deptford with the murder, and find us."

The angry face of Sally Fourth came to Mary Jane's mind.

"*You* were gulpy," Mary Jane said. "You might be guilty. Victim of a second-hand flam, I haven't any guilt."

Fleming shook his head, stared into his cup of coffee. "Should the one who committed the crime be the man what came to the job site to talk to Thomas, I've seen the fellow. To look at him would not give one concern, yet something about him told me he was indeed dangerous. I should not ask further questions if I were you. I'm ill-at-ease with what little I do know."

Joseph was right about Thomas. He later professed his innocence to both of them, and Mary Jane believed him. Thomas was just a business man trying to get on. Fleming had been the one to disappoint her. He had street cokum, or so Mary Jane had believed. The realisation that he'd been tricked into helping with a murder tarnished the halo she'd placed over his head.

TWENTY-EIGHT

She had not risen from her bed for two days, except to relieve herself. She did not wash; she hardly ate. The water carafe was always full, as if some house-sprite came when she slept, or when she lay in blind consciousness. Dried spittle marked her nightdress, and her dark mane of hair was unwashed, unbrushed.

"There are letters." Mrs Bessovitch, framed against the gaslight on the landing. "Again. I pick them up this afternoon for you."

Catherine did not speak.

She had killed a man—a vile man, true, and by another's hand, but the ease of it appalled her. You spoke into an ear, gave a name, and soon the one who bore that name was dead. It did not matter who. You could name a kindly matron, or a much-loved politician. You could take against a neighbour, or an interfering police inspector. She doubted that it made much difference.

The ease of it…if you knew a certain person.

The papers glared and sparked on the day after Deptford. Boys stalked the streets with extra copies, calling out the news with glee.

"Slaughter in the Yards!"

"Four dead by murderous hands!"

"Criminal gang leaves trail of blood!"

She smiled at that one—a mad smile, which she imagined could be found in many an asylum. Had there been a gang, had she by some means organised a crew of sticker-men and common bravoes, all ready to tumble with Frederick Caille and his guards…then she might have understood what she had done. But she had only said a name.

To Edwin Dry.

Mrs Bessovitch read to her at first. Each edition carried more, most newspapers convinced that a mob of incensed workers had entered Deptford Yard that night, surely a dozen men. The police and authorities responded, denying that it could be that number. "Impossible," said Scotland Yard. Despite regrettable delays, and disturbances elsewhere which had occupied some of the constabulary, no such mob could have been involved. Three or four skilled miscreants then, responded the papers the next morning. Editors and senior officers played numbers. As for who exactly would arrange such a thing…

Fenians. Jewish malcontents. French agitators and Balkan dissidents. A rival Anglo-Irish businessman, whose corned beef trade was under threat from Caille's industries. Catholics (though no sense was ever made of this one). A senior minister of Her Majesty's Government, deep in debt to Caille. Escaped lunatics, finding themselves discovered in the Victualling Yard and panicking.

They did not suggest a young woman from Southwark.

"It does not appear," said Mrs B carefully, on the third day, a Wednesday, "That this Caille will be much missed."

Editors and reporters then began to close sharp teeth on other matters related to the event. Scandals concerning Frederick Caille, certain cases of which few had dared speak until now. Reports that two of the dead men had extensive criminal records before their gainful employment as the magnate's guards. And with great reluctance, the Metropolitan Commissioner confirmed that Police Constable Alfred Retton did not have a spotless record. That he was under investigation for possible misconduct—which many took to be a way of explaining why he had been there, so far from his beat. There was no appetite for "avenging our own" in the constabulary, apparently. Not where Retton was concerned.

Certain politicians expressed sorrow and outrage—briefly, and where it suited them; it was rumoured that others lifted brandy glasses in their clubs and cheered. Caille's business peers surveyed his empire, eager to partition that tempting sprawl between them.

Catherine lay helpless because she had been at Deptford, an unwilling observer, and had heard the final gasps of Frederick Caille.

Because she had heard that sound ten years before.

In Keighley.

It had issued from the mouth of a woman she admired, an unhappy woman in a bad marriage, who often read to a young girl, and taught her letters better than any school. Maggie Witten, the wife of Uncle Jack, her father's trusted friend.

Catherine had slept, had "seen" the trusted friend choke the breath out of his wife—and when she woke, much later, she ran downstairs still in her nightgown—shrieking the news that Uncle Jack had slain his wife with his own hands.

But no, that could not be, she was told. The Night Mare had

crouched on the girl's chest, misleading her. Jack Witten had been with Joshua Weatherhead, drinking and playing cards in the back-parlour at the Weatherheads' house until ever so late. He had slept on an old settee in there—there was the rumpled blanket which had covered him. And here was Uncle Jack, returning from the privy…

Catherine would not be silenced, not even by blows from her father's hard hand. So they must go see. They found the body in Jack's plain, gloomy back room, Maggie Witten's face mottled and half-blue, the bruising clear on her neck. The cabinet and sideboard were in disarray, the drawers turned out. Fourteen years old, behind her mother's legs, Catherine saw all this as well.

"A thief, a burglar!"cried Joshua Weatherhead. "Surprised in the act."

"By God, it's true!" cried Jack, his strong, thick fingers over his mouth.

They bustled Catherine away, and made her close her lips. The houses adjoined—a mild fever and strange sounds, perhaps raised voices, had fused into a dreadful dream. At first they were almost kind, but she was Mardy Cath, the "difficult" girl. The more she spoke, the less they heard. No one would hear that Jack had a hand—two hands—in the murder of his own wife.

Blood was not thicker than water, especially when the water was taken with whiskey and shared between two friends of long-standing. Jack and Joshua, drinking partners for many years. Inseparable. When there was a bottle around, at least.

Had Joshua Weatherhead known the truth? Or had he covered for his friend? It didn't matter. His daughter was instructed that she would not spread foul slander, nor speak of visions and visitations. She had no gift, nothing special—she was a trouble and a woe to her poor mother. Should she persist, there was always the cracked leather belt which hung behind Joshua's door…

After a suitable period of mourning, Jack Witten married a farmer's daughter, heavy-chested and without her letters. The murderous burglar was never found; Joshua and Jack were never quite as close.

"I cannot speak with the dead," Catherine moaned, alone in her Southwark room. The letters were on her night-stand; Mrs Bessovitch was gone from the doorway. "But I can watch them, hear them, being made…"

On the third day she awoke to the lullaby she had heard before, brought or borrowed from wherever Mrs Bessovitch grew up. Snatches of Russian, something else that sounded close to it, and the occasional word of English. The tune was soothing, if sad.

"Is enough, Katerina" said her landlady when Catherine opened her eyes. "Three days, is enough. Tch. How do you pay me if you do not work? How do you become famous lady this way? One man, four men, die. What is this, in such a world?"

Catherine lifted her hands from under the coverlet, looked at the pale blue veins.

"It is not Caille. Many would say that he deserved to meet his end that way. Many wished it, I think, if they could not see him jailed and ruined. It is…the sight, the knowledge that comes to me, with each death."

"Da. This I understand. But you are young woman, strong. What do you say to Mrs Gelderd, who loses seven children before any is one year old? To Pieter, who has stall by cathedral? Wife and children die from bad water, and in this fine country."

"But I…"

"You have worse than them? Because is in head, not in room where you can touch?"

Catherine searched for an answer to that, found none.

"See?" The other woman held out a clean dress. "You wear clothes, you come down for eggs. Tea. Toast. If you want be sad, go to cemetery. Tell Pieter's wife you are sad. See what she will say."

None of it was said in anger, or reproach, which might have driven her to pull the coverlet back around her. It was said because it was true, and she could not deny it.

"I will join you…shortly," said Catherine. "Truly, I will."

She took breakfast at two in the afternoon, awkward with the food at first and then ravenous.

"Enough," said Mrs B, when she asked for more toast. "Belly will burst, or get angry. Besides, where is money for this feast?" But that was said with a wink of the eye.

Fed, and then bathed, Catherine dressed herself and looked to the letters on the night-stand, not yet sure if she could face opening them. Seven were to Madame Rostov. Of these, one was the cream, quality envelope that usually marked a communication from Lady Seldon. The other six would likely be requests for her services—she thought that one of those was addressed in Mrs Combes's hand. A polite reply that she was engaged elsewhere for the foreseeable future would answer that one.

Two envelopes were addressed to Miss C Weatherhead. The uppermost was in Jennie's awkward writing, the other clearly from Clarissa. She opened the first one.

> *My dearest Catherine. Poor Mama asks for you again. I do not think she will be long with us, and I beg that you come to see her, though I know how hard this is. I reckon only too well how C can be Fractious and difficult. Apart from Mama, we are well, in our way, and B has been praised at Sunday School. I am engaged much away from Brantridge St, adding a little to the Coffers, but hope we will meet soon. Yr Affectionate cousin, Jennie.*

With less enthusiasm, she opened Clarissa's letter. It was somewhat blunter in its approach. Levinia Weatherhead would die soon, should Catherine have "time to spare" to see her before then.

She made herself read that morning's paper, with its continued speculations as to the "Deptford affair," though already this was relegated to the second page. Soon there would be other crimes, news from abroad, an announcement on butter prices, and so it went.

An omnibus; a brisk walk through November rain. The beggars and huddled figures around Stepney seemed set like statues in the downpour, with barely the vitality to call out their woes or needs. At Brantridge Street, Clarissa let her in immediately, taking her dripping coat and umbrella.

"Not long," she said. "I am...I am grateful that you came, cousin."

Catherine stood wary, but this was a genuine Clarissa, borne down by her situation and the shadow of Death in the room above. Her eyes spoke of sickness, exhaustion. Did her cousin not know that Frederick Caille was dead? Surely those would have been her first words, if she was aware of it?

"You should rest," said Catherine. "Find me some simple mending which will help, and I will sit with Aunt Levinia."

No argument, no caustic words. It was a year since Charles Weatherhead died—Charles who placed decent food upon the table, and tempered Clarissa's ways with his homely good nature. As she climbed the stairs, Catherine found herself missing him. And knowing that he would not have approved of what she had done…

Levinia's face was ready for the death-mask, the posed photograph. Her breath was hardly discernible—when it came, it was painful, laboured. Catherine sewed, addressing herself to simple tears in otherwise decent linen, and patches in inconspicuous places. Needlework would never be her strength.

The rain continued. She lit a candle rather than try to ignite the unreliable gas sconce on the wall. Her aunt turned slightly, and moaned. Catherine attended to her, and found part of the bed damp with urine. She slipped a torn tea-towel between Levinia and the linen, to take up some of the fluid. Should she lift her out of bed, try to change the bedclothes? She had no idea where fresh linen might be found in the house, and Clarissa slept in the other bedroom.

"Charles…" the old woman moaned.

"It is Catherine, Aunt Levinia. I am here."

"Catherine?" Eyes fluttered, opened a fraction. They were gummed, and Catherine wiped her aunt's face with a moistened cloth.

"Yes, I am here. Do you remember what you asked, what you demanded of me?"

Levinia looked confused for a moment. "What I…asked you?"

Sixty eight years stared at twenty four, the gap between so vast that it might have been oceans, or the sand-blasted wastes of foreign lands.

"It does not matter, aunt. You must lie easy."

The invalid's hand shot out, grasping her wrist. Catherine gasped at the unexpected touch—and the strength in that grip.

"I remember." Levinia's head turned to the window, the grey veil of rain. Some had entered through the cracked pane, droplets which caught the candlelight as they trickled down the glass. "I remember so much, Joshua's Child."

Catherine caught her aunt's wrist, returning the pressure. She felt the cold in her gut, and let it fill her eyes, her words. "I am not Joshua's Child. I am my own creation!"

Levinia coughed, shifting in the bed to look back at Catherine. An intelligence of old was awake in the old woman's face, a last flicker before eternal nightfall.

"Your own creation? What, then, have you wrought, girl?"

Catherine took a breath, a second breath, and tried to still her sudden anger. Her grip eased, though her aunt's had not.

"You burdened me, Aunt Levinia, with your pasteboard box and your hunger for vengeance. My father would have laughed, scorned such a burden and gone to his bottle or his account books, unconcerned."

"But you—"

"Frederick Caille is dead; the dogs fight over his empire. There. Are you content with what you have brought me to?"

"Caille is dead? This was by your hand?"

"By my instruction."

It was madness to say this aloud, and it would be madness if any believed it. A melodrama of ridiculous dimensions, too unfeasible to credit. The dying queen on her bed, and the faithful handmaiden who orchestrated her queen's revenge. Catherine wanted to laugh, to choke on bitter laughter.

Levinia stirred again, clutching the blankets with her free hand.

"Jennie says I will…be well, but I will not. Clarissa stitches a smile…on her face…and says all is in order, that we prosper. They are liars."

"I am also a liar," said Catherine. "All women must be. But in this, I swear I tell the truth, aunt. Caille was killed four days ago, and his men with him. My hands are bloody—though another served for the deed."

Wonder flickered across the old woman's face, and her eyes closed.

"Then I can rest," she said, more softly. "My Charles, my dearest Charles, someone has paid at last." Tears formed at the corner of one eye. "I have done a mother's duty."

Catherine felt her aunt's grip slide, and she too let go, stepping back from the bed.

She should have been relieved, her task completed. Instead she felt anger, that she had been pushed to this, had entangled herself until she could not escape. Despair, that she had crossed a street in

Clerkenwell, when she could so easily have turned and spent her time on milliners' windows, wondering about a new hat for Madame Rostov—feathers, perhaps.

Frustration, that she was not now sat in a dimly-lit parlour, murmuring about the "dear departed" and earning her way through the credulous nature of Mankind.

There were no tragic queens, no handmaidens. An impoverished old woman lay on her death-bed in a damp Stepney garret, with lice in her hair. And a wilful girl from Keighley, who had read too many cheap and fanciful pamphlets, was swimming far out of her depth. Maybe she would drown because of it.

Levinia appeared to be asleep once more. Catherine blew out the candle, and took up the completed mending. No doubt Clarissa had a basket downstairs for work that was ready to go back out into the world...

"I never liked your father," said a weak voice from the bed. "Nor trusted him. Not in anything."

TWENTY-NINE

Mary Jane saw Jennie outside the Angel and Trumpet on November 29. The older woman recounted the death of her mother, Levinia Weatherhead, a few days earlier. Then, wiping away tears, Jennie said, "The children were hungry, so I returned to the streets the next day, walking about in colourful clothing, looking for a man, whilst knowing that respect demanded I wear mourning black. Please, forgive me mum!"

Mary Jane hugged Jennie and stroked her shoulder, then offered her a shilling. The older woman refused the coin. "Thank you, but I must learn to take care of myself."

❦

Fleming had made no further mention of recovering her necklace. She pressed him on the matter on December 1.

"I am working on it," he complained. "As I told you, the lurk shall be more complicated than what you offered. I must come up with a believable flam to give Mrs Arseneau that will push her to hire me on the spot, without questioning the low price I offer. Something about a new plaster mix or process that need tests, that I'll do the work, repaint for free, and come back and repair it if it fails in any way. Why the Phoenix, though? I've thought to suggest that the plaster might be scented so that it spurs desire or some such thing. I haven't sorted it all out. I'd hate for her to step back and decide that indeed the work needed to be done, but she has a nephew what'll do it for free."

As the weeks passed, she kept at him about it, her harping coming between them at times. She began to develop hard feelings toward Joseph.

Although he'd paid her the ten pounds for her efforts in Deptford, she suspected he'd merely used her, that perhaps he'd known all along that she'd have to prig the night rounders and he didn't care because she was a whore.

The low cost of Fleming's room, the comfort, its location, and her damned feelings for the man had kept her there. Still finding her love for him frightening, the sentiments were also driving her away from him.

THIRTY

The newspapers have begun to speak of the Deptford Assassin. It is somewhat melodramatic for his taste, but it has a certain gravitas. He permits them to continue, though he would never describe himself in such terms.

For they have concluded that one man, of unnatural ability, slid in blood across the Deptford Victualling Yard. An Italian or Italian-American is their favourite suspect now, bred to the knife and the wire—a member of the "Red Circle" or some other such vicious and criminal organisation. Paid handsomely by persons unknown (rival bankers, perhaps) for his daring act of slaughter at the heart of Empire.

Giorgio Frazetti, a barber from Catford, is arrested, his razors examined and found to be entirely the wrong sort of instrument. Besides, Frazetti, it transpires, was thirty miles away that night, visiting on a sick cousin. The papers have not yet assigned the power of flight to the assassin.

The police do not comment, but it is said there have been telegrams to New York and Chicago. The Pinkerton Agency has been alerted.

Edwin Dry picks up the solitary gold sovereign that he gained by the venture. He is content, because he has satisfied himself, the only judge he recognises. It could be done, and it was.

Already he has catalogued small errors—the constable should have been removed immediately, for example. No warning. Those others who provided information and diversion had a certain value, but it might have been done without them. A journeyman must always learn.

He will keep the coin aside, to remind him. The black-haired woman will have to be watched, of course.

He has her scent…

Josiah, son of Joshua, son of Joseph. A stooped young man in borrowed black mourning, the trousers slightly too long, the jacket too large, Josiah Weatherhead had the same untamed black hair as his older sister Catherine, his temporarily plastered down with hair oil and other preparations. His face, unlike hers, was weather-tanned. Anxiety swam beneath his dense eyebrows as he held his hat, dressed with black crepe, to his breast.

"I should not have come," he said as they walked, side by side.

Catherine wanted to snap at his meekness, but she restrained herself.

"It was a kind gesture, Josiah."

"Father said…"

She waited for the rest of the sentence, until she realised that there was no more, that it was there in her brother's face.

Father said.

This was Joshua's single token, then—dispatching his son in pretence that they were all still family. There was no wreath, no letter of concern or condolence from the North. No offer of assistance. Just Josiah, thrust alone into the tangled skein of station, rail and junction, even though a pony cart from Keighley to an outlying village was usually the height of his adventures.

The mourners straggled from Bow Cemetery, with its great protective walls and its many—so many—mounds for the unmarked dead. Levinia Weatherhead lay in there now, silent in a public grave. A private plot was beyond the family's means, but the last of Catherine's money had insisted on an inscription grave. Levinia was buried with strangers, but her name was on the headstone with theirs. Better than the fate of most Stepney residents, heaped upon each other unmarked in a few feet of sour earth.

Jennie, supported on the arm of a hard-faced Clarissa, wept throughout. Her brother was dead; and now her mother. It tore the heart to see her.

"The children, they look well," said Mrs Bessovitch as they quit the cemetery.

They did—Benjamin serious but with healthy red cheeks; Maisie unsure as to her role here, more interested in the finer monuments than the mean stone over her grandmother. Had others not been watching them, they would have been playing tag between the tombs.

Mrs B, named only as a "friend of the family" to anyone who asked, wore swathes of black muslin, her dress little different from her usual outdoor garb.

"You learn much of people at funeral, nyet? Today they wear special faces."

Her eyes were on the short procession of mourners behind them. Neighbours from Stepney attending out of curiosity, ready to criticise the arrangements, the clothes, the demeanour of family members. Tradesmen watching, wondering if this would leave their bills unpaid. And then there were the women who always followed funerals, slipping into the parade in their midnight crepe and worn silk. No one knew who they were, or cared.

Few present had any real concern for Levinia Weatherhead, the almost unknown woman from the sickroom at Brantridge Street.

Madame Rostov was not there, only Catherine. Madame Rostov brooded alone, for the time being. She had read the letter from Lady Seldon, though, the night before. Its core was direct.

> *I wonder at what vision or presentiment impelled you to visit Mrs Caille, so close to her husband's bloody, and well-deserved end—and what strange currents flow beneath the surface of our lives. Because you have expressed concern, and as we find you an uncommon spirit, I am pleased to confide that young Beresford Caille is to be reunited with his mother, and Grove House is to be quit.*

The letter ended simply.

> *In due time, we will expect the pleasure of your company in Chelsea. S.*

A letter to neither a friend nor a servant. As there was surely nothing that Lady Seldon or the others could suspect, perhaps they took this as another indication that Madame Rostov's gift was genuine?

The gathering at Brantridge Street that afternoon was small, and awkward. Mrs Bessovitch, who had somehow found her way into the house without anyone asking or suggesting it, bustled about in the mean, ill-equipped kitchen, and lied fluently about knowing Mrs Merson, Catherine's imaginary employer. The children, stripped of their one set of decent clothes and back in outfits suitable for the Stepney slums, were sent out to play for an hour.

"I return…I mean, I must go back, to Keighley this evening." Josiah balanced a cup and saucer on his knee, the tea within untouched.

"To report to your father on our lowered circumstances." Clarissa's sharp voice cut across the room. "He will be content, I imagine, that he at least prospers."

Jennie's face crumpled into tears again; Josiah turned with dumb appeal to his sister.

"It is not Josiah's fault, Clarissa." Catherine tried to hold down her anger. "He lives under our father's roof, remember."

Where he did the books for the thriving ironmongery and coal trade that was Weatherhead & Son. Joshua Weatherhead the tradesman had long since become Joshua the prosperous West Yorkshire merchant. Gone were the farms of the Two Gentlemen, and with their sale, any ties to the land. Josiah was what Catherine might have become, a servant in their own home, had she learned from the belt and their mother's timidity. Had she stayed under their father's hand.

He lowered his eyes.

"To report on my sister. To satisfy Father that all is not too well with her, and that she will soon swallow her pride, return to Keighley."

"Oh." Clarissa's narrow cheeks reddened. "Cousin Josiah, I...it has been a trying day."

Mrs Bessovitch handed a linen square to Jennie for her tear-stained face, and a plate of tongue sandwiches to Clarissa, who took it, puzzled at its presence. There had been no tongue in the house, and little bread.

"To share blood is blessing and curse," said Catherine's landlady, and went to fill the kettle again.

Catherine shared a hansom with Josiah to King's Cross station. They sat side by side as siblings who had parted ways long ago. Uneven lanes and cobbled streets rattled at their teeth, the cabman too easy with the whip, the horse fractious.

"Is he hard on you?" asked Catherine as they turned from Whitechapel Road.

"No worse. He took the pledge, of course, and is a little the better for the lack of hard drink." Josiah fretted with his hat brim. He had no change of clothes, and she wondered if Joshua Weatherhead had given his son sufficient money to meet the cost of this hansom. "Better" would only be relative to how ill-tempered and controlling their father had always been.

"There are opportunities here for book-keepers—"

"Mother would not have it, not with you gone as well."

From another it would have been censure; a pointed remark

on Catherine's abandonment of family. From her brother, it was no more than what it was.

Outside the railway station she hesitated, and put her arms around him. He smelled of hair preparation and defeat.

"I do mean it," she said, forceful. "I could find you a position, Josiah, I'm certain. It might take a few weeks, but…"

He slipped from her embrace, but took her hands in his for the briefest moment.

"Jack Witten remembers you," he said. She didn't understand why he had said this, until she saw the narrowing of her brother's eyes. "The drink will take him soon—rotten inside, the doctors say. Rotten inside." This was added with a venom which was unexpected, completely uncharacteristic of the young man.

"I cannot—"

"I always believed you, Catherine," said Josiah. "About 'Uncle' Jack."

And he was gone for his train, and the long journey back to all she had fled.

~✣~

Caille's death, Bow Cemetery, and the achingly cold start to December should have been an end to so much, but that hope was dashed within the week. She visited Stepney on a Thursday morning clear for once of rain, to find a constable at the door.

"Has something happened?" she asked.

The constable shrugged. "Don't know, miss. I was set to wait—the inspector is inside."

She pushed past him. Clarissa sat stiff and hostile in her sewing chair; a uniformed sergeant waited, apparently ill at ease, by the window. An older man in a long overcoat stood in the middle of the room. He looked to Catherine as she paused in the doorway.

"What brings ye here, miss?" He spoke with the directness of a born Scot. "We need neither pegs nor heather."

"My cousins live here. I am Catherine Weatherhead. Who are you?"

"Inspector Swanson, of the Metropolitan Police."

"Is there a crime?"

"Aye…or fair to say, there was. Ye ken the death of Frederick

223

Caille."

"I read about it in the newspapers. The Deptford affair."

"Did ye? Bright lass. Then ye recognise the name well enough."

She might have sought the path of deference and a young woman's expected confusion, confronted by the bold and weighty officers of the law. She might have.

"Frederick Caille, the banker and industrialist who ruined this family? Why yes, Inspector, I 'ken' his life and his welcome death. My aunt Levinia, buried only a week past, would have had the man dragged through the courts in chains."

The sergeant, who seemed young for his rank, looked even more uncomfortable; the older man simply smiled.

"That sets us up well, then. I'm here to ask if any should have heard word, last month. Talk against the late Mr Caille, encouragement to ain gang or anither in these parts."

"The authorities still have no idea, then, who did this?" She was caustic, covering her alarm at this development.

"I wouldna ken, miss. I serve only, and have been called in to assist. My interest is ay the gangs of London Town—their feuds and the like. It was given to me to check any who had motive and interest. The Weatherheads of Brantridge Street, my colleagues say, have burned and boiled 'gainst Caille, wi' good reason."

"Why yes," said Clarissa, "We must be implicated. Because we are so powerful a family, with such influence." She gestured to the peeling wallpaper. "No doubt my late mother-in-law conceived the entire affair?"

"I did not say we thought ye were—"

Clarissa's temper was up.

"Yes, I sat and sewed my fingers down to blood and bone by day, whilst at night I ran a gang of bloody-handed villains!" She glowered at the inspector. "Or perhaps you think young Catherine here stalks the streets at night?"

The sergeant smiled, covering it with a broad hand; the inspector seemed unperturbed.

"Wheesht, now, Mrs Weatherhead. I came only to ask, to set my ear to the streets. No accusations, ye ken, none at all. In Catford and Southwark, in Spitalfields and Limehouse, my bonny boys are at it. Our duty."

"He deserved his death, and worse," Clarissa muttered. "If it had been my choice, I would have had him gaoled and rotting."

"Each must find their ain fate, madam, according to due process. There is sich a thing as the law."

Clarissa gave a derisive snort. "There was not when my husband was poisoned, nor when John Hollis and those others followed him into the grave."

Catherine swallowed, trying to remain steady.

"Inspector Swanson, you can see that there was no love for Caille here. Do you not think my cousins have been through enough?"

"Aye, maybe they have." He sniffed, and nodded to the sergeant. "We'll leave these guid folk to their thoughts, man. But..." He looked at Catherine. "If ever ye think of aught that might assist the Yard, I'm sure ye'll find me."

"I applaud your confidence, inspector."

⁕

When she arrived back at her lodgings in Southwark, she was angry, worried, and most of all, tired. Her money was gone, and she must awaken Madame Rostov that same week. Mrs Bessovitch was generous, and patient, but not a charitable board given to handouts.

"There was other letter," said the landlady. "Came yesterday."

Catherine had forgotten that Mrs B was still picking up correspondence for both Catherine and Madame Rostov at the post office.

"Oh, thank you, Mrs B. I will get my affairs in order, never fear. I shall make a list, and see about more sittings."

"Da. I know you will."

Catherine took the letter and went to her room, easing off her boots. She turned the envelope, curious as to the precise, copperplate writing on the outside.

'Madame Rostov, Blackfriars Road Postal Office, Southwark.'

She tore back the flap, extracting a single sheet of paper. The writing inside was the same hand as on the envelope, but smaller and even more precise. It might have been set by a printer.

"It is done, and your coin will suffice. No further reckoning will be required.'

That was all. No signature. It did not need one.

Catherine tore the note in half, flinging the pieces away from her. She had told Dry neither the name she used, nor the means by which he could contact her. He had not asked.

She picked up the fragments and envelope with the fire-tongs, and gave them to the smouldering fire in the grate.

He knew how to find her.

THIRTY-ONE

In mid-January 1887, coming to the realisation that she might never recover the necklace, Mary Jane had begun to neglect Joseph's needs again and resumed her efforts to earn as much as possible from clients.

In early March, having increased her savings to seventy pounds, she found herself looking for reasons to leave Fleming.

The idea that he'd used her wasn't quite the reason she needed because she was also using him.

If I were on my own, I could have laudanum again, she told herself, though her desire for the drug had thankfully diminished considerably.

The thought that Joseph had unwittingly led her into danger in Deptford became the seed she needed to grow her discontent. With time, she came to the conclusion that if she stayed with him, he'd eventually get her killed or imprisoned. She'd just about persuaded herself to pack up and leave at the beginning of spring when suddenly she had all the reason in the world to get out in a hurry.

In the late afternoon of March 15, while looking through the sheer curtain over the bay window in their room, she saw Stuart Brevard moving along Globe Road, talking to some people, searching for a while, lurking in doorways, and watching the street.

Gabriella Gorse did follow me home that night. She told him where to find me!

Mary Jane felt certain Mr Brevard watched for her. She knew he would give up if she stayed out of sight. He could not see her through the thin curtain.

If not Gorse, someone had given him enough information that he'd got close. Mary Jane didn't think she'd ever said anything about where she lived to Gabby or anyone who knew the woman.

Brevard gave up on waiting, and entered the Green Man pub across the street. He left there after a time, crossed Green Street and entered the Fire Station. Mary Jane waited and watched to see him exit. He moved along Globe Road, talking to a few more people. He tried a few doors of tenements, and entered some buildings. She watched each time until he returned to the street.

Finally, he approached her tenement. A rattling came from the direction of the front entrance. Fearful of becoming trapped if he got in, Mary Jane left her room and stood in the darkened hallway beneath the broken gas jet, ready to flee through the back of the building into the complex of small yards in the rear. Watching the door shake, fearful that he'd somehow get in, she took care not to allow herself to think what he'd do to her.

The lock resisted Brevard's prying, and he gave up on the door. Standing at the bay window, she watched him walk away toward the south.

Mary Jane packed most of her belongings into two carpet bags and left, heading west to become lost in the stews of the Whitechapel and Spitalfields rookeries. Mrs Carthy had once recommended a boarding house in New Street, Bishopsgate. "Mr Buller has both a common lodging and a boarding house," the proprietress had said. "If you want a common lodging go elsewhere." She'd grimaced, which told Mary Jane that the common lodging must be truly horrid, Mrs Carthy's standards of cleanliness being so low. "But if you give Mrs Buller my name, she'll make room for you at the boarding house. It's quite nice there."

⚊⚊⚊ 🦇 ⚊⚊⚊

Mary Jane walked southwestward along Bethnal Green Road, stopped at a tavern for a meal, then made the mistake of continuing on toward her goal after nightfall. She noted that the gas lamps on the street were dark near the crossing of Bethnal Green Road and Brick Lane. On the south side of the street, she hurried forward to pass quickly through the darkened area.

Close to Brick Lane, five creatures rushed out of a building's thin through-passage. Mary Jane let out a small cry of surprise, and backed away only to discover they had surrounded her. *Goblins!* she thought, seeing merely glowing eyes in dirty faces, and the filthy tatters of their clothing.

No, she thought, getting a better look, *children.* She couldn't determine the sex of the raggedy creatures in the gloom. The two largest, perhaps ten to twelve years old, threatened her with knives that reflected the blue-grey of the night sky and what little warm light came from nearby windows. The other three grabbed her bags and pulled her toward the passage opening.

"Stop!" she cried, still holding onto the handles of the bags.

They seemed to anticipate her, and all cried, "Stop," drowning her voice with theirs. As if playing a game, they followed that with laughter, the sound echoing up the passage.

Mary Jane wouldn't let go, and they pulled her into the darkened corridor.

"Help!" she cried.

Again, they anticipated her. They all cried, "Help the little children, Lord," drowning her out, More laughter followed.

"Let go if you value your life," came a boy's voice from her left, the tallest figure, one with a knife.

"Such drama," Mary Jane said, trying to sound calm and confident. Despite knowing better, she had decided they would not harm her if she showed enough courage.

She was losing the battle of strength.

"We get ream swag from this toffer," came a girl's voice, one of those tugging on a bag. "Too bad if we have to cut her pretty face."

Another child giggled, the high-pitched sound clearly belonging to one well below the age of ten.

Mary Jane's eyes had adjusted somewhat to the darkness.

An adult appeared in the passage, an older fellow.

"Sir, help me, please," Mary Jane said, breathlessly.

"He ain't no help to you, miss," came the boys voice again on her left. "He's got to live here with us."

The man walked by without a word.

Mary Jane prepared herself to yank her bags free with great force, to push past the children, and go on her way.

As she planted her feet firmly to make her move, the boy on her left stabbed her in the arm.

Mary Jane cried out again, and went into a slight crouch. Not a deep wound, just enough to draw blood. She could feel it running under her sleeve.

She thought of the knife in her boot. *I won't have to use it on the children, just frighten them with it.*

She reached for it. The child on her right kicked the boot where the knife was hidden. Mary Jane cringed with pain as the point of the blade punctured her ankle. The sheath she'd fashioned for it was lightweight because her boots were already tight.

The boy on her left, swung his blade in threat a couple times, with a warning look in his wide eyes, the circles of whites the only part that showed in the dimness.

Mary Jane realised she was about to lose everything she had.

"Do it now, fancy woman," he said, "or we shall take it."

They closed in.

Mary Jane let go of her bags, backed away quickly.

The one with the knife on her right let her pass. The boy on her left waved his knife and lunged toward Mary Jane to dislodge her from the passage.

She continued to back away into Bethnal Green Road, turned toward Brick Lane, and ran.

Mary Jane wept, feeling cruelly molested, and ashamed for having suffered such treatment from children. She'd been slow to appreciate the severity of the threat. Gaining distance from the nippers, she discovered gratitude for finding herself alive. Her savings and other possessions could be replaced.

Her right ankle stung from the puncture the knife had inflicted. Mary Jane slowed to a walk.

Most of the Ladybirds she knew didn't carry weapons because clients were known to take them and use them against their owners on occasion. The little bit of training Fleming had provided hadn't prepared Mary Jane to face true danger. If she hadn't been able to use the knife against children, what further disaster might come from drawing it on an adult? Another item she could add to the list of failings she held against Fleming. Disgusted, she crouched, extracted the blade, and threw it in the gutter.

Mary Jane gave up the idea of going to Buller's. Some funds remained in the pocket under her top skirt. She would find a doss house and a bottle of laudanum.

Joseph found Mary Jane a week later at Cooley's Lodging House in Thrawl Street, Spitalfields. They sat in the common room between meals with no one else about.

"Why?" he wanted to know.

Mary Jane didn't want to tell him about Stuart Brevard. Not having spoken of the man's pursuit of her before then, she'd be ashamed to reveal that she'd kept that a secret. Joseph might have protected her from Mr Brevard, if she had given him the chance. Of course, the ginger-haired man was only part of her reason for leaving.

"You hold me too close," Mary Jane said, "when you know what I am and what I must do."

"I earn enough for us both," he said. "You don't have to solicit any longer."

"I cannot depend on you forever. Life has shown that I am a fool to depend on anyone but myself."

"You don't mean that." Joseph had a terrible sadness in his eyes.

Mary Jane turned away so she didn't have to see him.

She had nothing to say because he was right. The excuse that if she'd stayed, he would have led her into danger had not held up to further consideration. Unwilling to admit to herself that she'd left because she feared the power and the worth of the love she felt for him, she had latched onto the second most plausible reason as an excuse to leave: She'd wanted her freedom purely for the laudanum.

He ought not to have told me to give it up.

As if Mary Jane needed the habit to justify her thinking, she'd returned to the drug with a vengeance, her consumption already greater than what she'd known the previous fall. Considering her plans for leaving London to settle elsewhere, she'd had to wonder what particular *elsewhere* would allow her continued easy access to laudanum. Large cities were the best candidates, yet those were also the costliest in which to live.

Given time, I will have savings again. Then I can make the big change.

"You prefer this?" Joseph asked, gesturing around at the dingy common room that served as dining hall and parlour for all the lodgers at Cooley's. The room had random stains from floor to ceiling. A smell of mildew and rancid food hung in the air.

Stuart Brevard will not easily find me in Spitalfields. She imagined he might be too proud to enter such a rookery.

"The rooms can't be much better," Joseph said. "How many strangers share your bed?" He frowned as he seemed to see the flaw in his question.

"I pay for a room of my own."

"You want me to check your hair for chats?"

231

Mary Jane shook her head, looked down at the table top, and stopped talking, though he continued.

Finally, his arguments ended. "I won't give up on you," he said, and walked out.

In her room afterward, she took thirty drops of laudanum, and enjoyed a deep, dreamless sleep.

THIRTY-TWO

Winter had swept the streets of Southwark with snow and then dark, discoloured slush; ice and then great pools of water that rose to soak pedestrians with the passing of every wagon. Catherine took to using hansoms more often, despite the cost, and the habit persisted after the long thaw. She knew why. If she spent too much time walking the streets, she might see him.

Dry.

Every few weeks she wrestled with the idea of moving to other lodgings, but did nothing about it. She did not want to lose Mrs Bessovitch, or her comfortable room, and besides, what purpose would it serve?

He would come to her if he wished, wherever she was.

For all her initial concern, the months which followed Deptford brought no visions of bowler-hatted men, no sweat-filled nights of slaughter—and no unwelcome visitors. Her fears subsided as she reasoned there would never be any other business between her and the Deptford killer. Even the most lurid newspapers had abandoned any interest in the mysterious slaughter at the Victualling Yard. She was nothing to him, merely a passing client to be forgotten, and nothing so dreadful could happen that she might ever request his services a second time.

Madame Rostov remained a quiet figure throughout. She performed for the most ordinary of people a few times a week, earning enough to get by but not enough to prosper greatly. She attempted to touch the Aether as little as possible. Her sitters heard what they wanted to hear, spiced only when unavoidable by vague images that Catherine drew from...wherever. The vaguer the better, for she did not want to see murder again.

By Easter, she was almost recovered, but her inmost thoughts were often hard to focus. In her Southwark sanctuary she sat on her bed and darned a stocking. Her cousins, the whole Caille business of the previous year—that had surely been too much. And the Weatherheads were still a shadow over her, needs and obligations which were unlooked for and mostly unwelcome. If she abandoned them, though, she would be abandoning Charles...

She finished the darn and put her sewing materials in their box, packing away her concerns along with needles and thread.

Others would have to make their way as best they could, and she must concentrate on her own life. Brantridge Street might still be there, but it should not rule her.

The shadow of Edwin Dry should not rule her.

⁓⚜⁓

Lottie Chambers adored, though did not always understand, poetry. Catherine understood much of it after a couple of readings, but gained little joy from doing so. Schemes of rhyme irritated her as being forced; the language used was maudlin, or excessively, ridiculously romantic. Often both.

Having grown bored of Robert Louis Stevenson, Lottie was currently enamoured of the blind poet Philip Bourke Marston, who she saw as a suitably tragic figure. His death in February had set his sad star in her heavens, and Lottie gave meandering recitations of Marston's work on a regular basis.

"You are *such* a Philistine, Katerina," she said, when Catherine asked that she be spared—at least until the following week.

For Madame Rostov was Katerina now in Lottie's company, almost a friend and certainly a mysterious figure to be trotted out when Lottie wished to make her mark.

They were usually two rather than four now. Lady Seldon was much involved in her husband's work, and in the Irish Question, she and his Lordship being in favour of Home Rule. Amelia Baring-Smith announced her engagement to a Major in the Guards, not long after Christmas, and flitted back and forth between the capital and the country.

"I must go, Charlotte. Besides, your mother will return soon."

Mrs Chambers considered séances and spiritualism—any adventure of a supposedly psychic nature—to be too racy. Her own tastes lay in Sunday worship amongst good, stolid Anglicans.

"True. I shall read to Jemmy instead, this evening."

Feeling sympathy for Lottie's little sister, Catherine broke free of literature and stepped out, relieved, into a brisk April morning.

It was a difficult truth that her adoption by Miss Chambers, and by a few of Miss Chambers's friends, did not buy coal. Most assumed that she had some independent means, and that the spirits somehow paid her bills, much as parents or husbands paid theirs…

"Watch yerself, there!"

She felt the brush of air and horse-sweat as the brewer's dray clattered past, mere inches away, and realised that her eyes had been half-closed, her thoughts on other than the streets around her.

Money, once more.

THIRTY-THREE

On Good Friday, April 8, 1887, Mary Jane watched a couple of men playing Mumblety-peg at Spitalfields Market. One of the two clearly had more skill in the game. She'd never seen anyone so comfortable and capable with a knife. He noticed her watching. She smiled for him. While his opponent mumbled the peg, he introduced himself to Mary Jane as Seph Barnett. A licensed fish porter at Billingsgate Market, he'd come to Spitalfields to make a delivery to a fishmonger, the fellow still trying to pull the peg from the ground with his teeth.

Mary Jane and Seph had drinks at the Britannia pub, also known as the Ringers, and later had a dinner together at the Golden Heart, a tavern in Commercial Street with tall windows and numerous skylights. They got along well. She saw him again the next day, and he asked her to take up with him. She surprised herself when she accepted his invitation. Or had that been Miss Laudanum's choice? Mary Jane told herself that the nagging feeling that she needed protections had not driven her into his arms. Still, having a man on hand who was good with a knife couldn't hurt.

A slim, dark-haired, blue-eyed fellow, she found him appealing enough, though he frequently smelled of fish market. She called him simply Barnett. He had a funny habit of repeating the last word anyone said.

Mary Jane removed from Cooley's to Barnett's lodgings in George Street, a miserable little cell at the back of an old wooden house. Because he didn't wash his clothes right after work each day, the place smelled of the fish market.

Her dislike of the lodgings must have shown. Barnett said, "I'll begin the search for a better room tomorrow."

To reach the chamber, they passed through a hallway rented as lodgings to an old woman, Mrs Hollis, who slept on a narrow straw mattress on the floor. Her few possessions were neatly stacked against the wall so Barnett and Mary Jane didn't tread upon them. By day, Mrs Hollis begged beside Christ Church wearing a placard that told of the loss of her son, a midshipman aboard HMS Penelope. Something about the story seemed familiar to Mary Jane, but she didn't know why.

The room had rotten floorboards, a coal grate that didn't quite fit the large old-fashioned fireplace, and one small window that gave a view across a paved yard to the backside of Satchell's Lodging House. Barnett pointed out the soft spots in the floor so she could avoid them. He enclosed the firebox with stacked bricks until the flue drew better and the air they breathed while heating the room improved. Nothing could be done for the view.

To improve the smell in the room, Mary Jane insisted that his work apron should hang outside the window, and that his work clothes would remain in a barrel with a tightly fitting lid if he wasn't wearing them.

Barnett could be sweet when sober, angry or maudlin if drunk. He didn't mind the laudanum, probably because she hid the drug from him most of the time. He wasn't pleased with her soliciting.

"One day," he said, "you'll give it up for me."

Mary Jane had no intention of abandoning her means of independence just for him. She kept that to herself.

Quite different from the affection she'd had for Fleming when she'd taken up with him, she knew she'd never love Barnett.

Will be easy to leave him when I'm ready.

He was a man of few words unless in his cups. They quarrelled then, and he struck her a few times.

Although she hadn't decided she deserved that sort of treatment or the wretched living conditions, she supposed she believed it all the same. The laudanum helped make it all tolerable.

THIRTY-FOUR

April 10, a warm Sunday, Catherine went to Brantridge Street with a handful of coins, suggesting they might be used to buy something for the children. The amount was less than usual, part of Catherine's new determination.

Clarissa took the offering with curt thanks, but no smile.

"And is Jennie well?" asked Catherine.

Clarissa shrugged. "We see little of her, excepting that she helps carry the mending back and forth to the laundries some days. These people for whom she cleans and skivvies seems to work her most nights."

It seemed an odd arrangement, but Catherine supposed the family must take whatever work was on offer.

She thought little more of the matter until, after another brief visit a few days later, she spotted Jennie on a street corner by the Mile End Road, laughing with a red-faced soldier. Her cousin wore a bright yellow bonnet with artificial flowers, one that Catherine did not recall seeing before. It was late afternoon, and people scurried down lanes and alleys, returning from one job or heading out for another. Children shrieked on doorsteps, and more than one drunk had already collapsed across the cobbles of the side streets, slurring imprecations to passersby.

She turned in Jennie's direction, intending to go over and ask after her cousin's health, but as she did so, she observed something in the man's stance, the shifting of hands and shoulders, which puzzled her. As she might read clients at a sitting, she saw not a courting couple but two people in the process of a transaction. She slowed, letting other pedestrians shield her as she went near.

The soldier was jangling coins in his hand, and leaning close, too close, into her cousin's face, an expression on his own face which seemed more like hunger than affection. An omnibus clattered by on the edge of the pavement, raising a string of curses from a flower-girl as its wheels spattered her with mud. The man glanced round at the noise, and saw Catherine looking at him.

He grinned.

"If a shillin' ain't enough for one dolly, maybe another'd be less fussy. What say you, eh?" He winked at Catherine. "Fancy a soldier-boy, stiffened with good mutton and the Queen's brandy?"

"Sheep carry disease, I hear," said Catherine, meeting his look with a cold stare.

Jennie paled at seeing her, and pushed the man away. "Later, Johnny—if at all."

His language was coarser than the flower-girl's, but he edged away from the two women, grumbling to himself. He was none too steady on his feet, and Catherine judged him to be no great threat. She took Jennie's arm.

"Come, cousin," she said, sharp and loud, "Let us walk awhile and catch up."

They left the soldier behind, Catherine marching Jennie down the road. She wasn't yet sure if she was angry or concerned at what she had witnessed.

Next to a saddlemaker's, an enterprising grocer had his awning up and was offering refreshments in a makeshift parlour open to the street. Catherine steered a silent Jennie to one of the three rickety tables, and ordered tea. A sign declared that samples of various blends were available "for the discerning customer."

"We have our own speciality, miss, blended here," said the grocer's assistant. "Or there are some pleasant Indian—"

"It's tea." Catherine passed the young man a handful of change. "Two cups."

She sighed, and took Jennie's hand.

"What were you doing, cousin?"

"You know what I was doing." Jennie's normally pleasant, easy face held a certain defiance. "I was earning."

"But—"

"I do not sew well, unlike Clarissa, and hereabouts are only the most menial, back-breaking jobs. I have used my imagination, Catherine, and done well enough."

Catherine's upbringing had hardly been sheltered. There were many prostitutes in Keighley, even on Fell Lane where they first lived, and there must be thousands more in London. They were part of the background on so many streets, especially in the East End. Nor was shame an issue that concerned Catherine. It was the risk—beatings and other ill-use; infection and impregnation...

Jennie must have seen some of this in her cousin's expression.

"Some of the men are nice enough, and most pay fair. I have had advice…"

"From whom?"

"I have a friend, Ginger—she was most kind when she saw I was set on this."

"She encouraged you?"

A blush of red high on Jennie's cheeks.

"She did not. She worried that I was too inexperienced and ill-prepared; she made known the pitfalls, and ways to tell a safe client from an unsafe one—all manner of issues a 'dolly-mop' must consider. The best protections to use, as well."

"Oh. Better that way, I suppose." Catherine knew she still sounded grudging, almost censorious. But who was she to dictate another's life?

"Exactly," said Jennie. "I bring money into the house, and am at no one's constant beck and call. And Ginger watches out for me."

The grocer's assistant, obviously unable to determine quite what class of customer he had—and whether his superior would want them or not—placed a tray of tea things on the table and backed away. Cheap china, but clean.

"So I have been careful—and cared for—as well as any could hope—"

"In the circumstances." Catherine felt weary. "Jennie, dear, if I could find a little more money—"

"I would do as I do now." There was no doubting her cousin's resolve. "We must all make choices, not be constantly looking to others." Her expression softened. "Cathy, you have been more generous to our family than Clarissa wishes to acknowledge, I know that. And I know that you do it in remembrance of Charles. The children are the better for it. But we are not your burden." Jennie finished her cup, and rose. "Do look after yourself, Cathy dear."

Catherine watched a patched dress and a linen shawl slip down Mile End Road, only the bright bonnet standing out from those around her. The woman beneath the bonnet had surprised her and worried her. Was this another milestone on the Weatherhead road to a sad and worthless end?

We are not your burden.

Perhaps.

She spent the remainder of that day shopping. In an anonymous coat which had seen better times, she visited various modest milliners and haberdashers who had kept their shutters open in the hope of a few late sales. By evening she had everything she needed.

Mrs Bessovitch was in the parlour, ready to assist.

"You see," said Catherine, "The look is everything. I cannot wear the same outfit all the time, yet I cannot afford high London fashion, or whatever it is fine Russian ladies might wear at the moment…"

"I understand." Mrs Bessovitch held up some pale muslin. "A veil, yes?"

"I think so."

The two women pinned and stitched, exchanging only the occasional word. An old green jacket, slightly the worse for wear, received military frogging and braid; a broad-brimmed hat was steamed over the landlady's kettle and reshaped, acquiring a short grey veil and a rakish feather along the way.

"Madame Rostov will catch the eye," said Mrs Bessovitch.

"Just as Miss Weatherhead must not."

"I understand. Is clever, this you do."

Catherine refilled the kettle, this time for a cup of tea.

"These people don't want an ironmonger's daughter from Keighley pronouncing on the living and the dead. They want to sit with mystery."

"Sometimes is comfort only they want, nyet?"

"Yes, well, that too."

THIRTY-FIVE

In mid-April, Barnett and Mary Jane heard about a larger room that would become available in a house in Little Paternoster Row, Dorset Street at the end of the month.

The week before, she had written to Jennie, giving her the George Street address. She had been about to write again to give her the future address, when, on April 29, Jennie turned up on the doorstep in George Street.

"May I come in to talk?" she asked.

"No, my room is not suitable." Mary Jane said.

She took her friend to the Ringers and they sat down together with glasses of bitter.

"He seemed a friendly gentleman," Jennie said, seeming out of sorts. "Please forgive me!" She covered her face with her hands.

"Who?"

"That man! The red-haired one."

"Stuart Brevard, the one after me?"

"Yes. He showed me a drawing of you with the name, Andriette. I took it to be one of your assumed names and thought little about it. He said he was an old friend of yours visiting London for a short time, and asked me how to find you. Though he might know you by that name, I wasn't going to inform him otherwise. I said simply that the picture looked like a friend of mine that lived at the crossing of Globe Road and Green Street, since I remembered you saying that once. Only afterward, almost a month, did I remember him from the attack on Bale Street. He must not have recognised me."

So, Gabby had not chased me, had not led Stuart Brevard to me in Globe Road.

"You did not give him the name Ginger or Mary Jane?"

"No," Jennie said. "I most humbly beg your pardon. I am not used to the ways of the streets. I am *not* clever. Forgive me, please."

"There's nothing to forgive," Mary Jane said

"What do I do should I see him again?"

"Say you have not seen me. Do you know who might have put him on to you?"

"No."

Jennie took on a worried look. "You look as if you're not feeling well."

"I have not," Mary Jane lied, "though I am getting better now."

She knew the unhealthy look came from too much laudanum.

"I am currently lodged with a man named Seph Barnett," Mary Jane said. "We are about to remove to a room in Little Paternoster Row, also here in Spitalfields. I wanted you to have the address."

"I should think you might not want to give it to me after—"

"Nonsense."

"We must find other, less expensive lodgings," Jennie said, "Clarissa, my niece, nephew, and I. What do you pay in George Street?"

"Four bob per week, but the crib is a wretched hole."

"Less than what we ought to pay in a doss house." She paused, became thoughtful. "Yes, the cost is a good bit less than what we pay now, and, being here, I might lose Brevard. Would you ask your landlord if he'd consider us?"

Mary Jane could see the advantage, and nodded. "Yes, if it would help."

Leaving the Ringers that day, the two women chanced upon Mary Jane's neighbour, Mrs Hollis. She stood on the footway beside Christ Church with her placard, begging.

"Mrs Hollis," Jennie said.

The old woman seemed surprised.

"It's me, Jennie Weatherhead."

Mrs Hollis dropped the imploring look she gave passersby.

"Oh, Miss Weatherhead," she said, "What a delight."

"You two are acquainted?" Mary Jane asked. "Mrs Hollis is our neighbour, perhaps soon to be your neighbour."

"I've known Mrs Hollis for some time," Jennie said. "She and her family joined ours in the civil suit against the man, Caille."

The name sounded familiar to Mary Jane.

Mrs Hollis had a nearly toothless smile. "My son, John, were a midshipman aboard HMS Penelope with Jennie's brother, Lieutenant Weatherhead, a fine officer."

Mary Jane remembered that her friend's brother had died, poisoned somehow.

As Mrs Hollis's smile disappeared, Jennie took the old woman's hands into her own.

"My poor John," Mrs Hollis said, "two other midshipman, and the Lieutenant died at sea. Were bad victuals supplied by Frederick Caille's company what killed them."

Caille, the victualing yard! Mary Jane almost said the words aloud, but thought better of it.

"Caille was murdered not long ago," Jennie said.

Mrs Hollis's jaundiced eyes grew large. "Good!" she said with surprising force.

So, Jennie knows!

The two women hugged for a time. Mary Jane stood, uncertain what to do with herself.

Finally, Mrs Hollis and Jennie separated, and discussed the possibility that they might become neighbours.

"That would be most welcome," the old woman said.

Jennie smiled and seemed to remember that Mrs Hollis had been begging. With a look of embarrassment, she gave Mrs Hollis a ha'penny, then looked to Mary Jane expectantly. She gave the old woman tuppence.

"God bless you both," the old woman said.

Jennie and Mary Jane walked south along Commercial Street, the noise of traffic and the many people using the footway oddly giving a sense of privacy.

"What do you know about the murder of that man, Caille?" she asked.

"Only what I read," Jennie said. "He got what he deserved after his fraud against the Royal Navy cost the lives of my brother and the others."

"Did you also come to Spitalfields to find a room?" Mary Jane asked.

"No. I'm glad I did, though. I came to warn you and to see how you're faring."

"How *I* am?"

"Yes," Jennie said with a look of surprise. "You're not the only one who can look out for others. With your help, I've settled into a routine that earns a small income. I can bring that to Spitalfields. I don't like what I do, but I am grateful for your help, and I've *missed* you."

To hear that warmed Mary Jane's heart.

"I haven't yet built up my weave of friends here," she said. "I'm working on that at the Ringers. I miss the dressing screens. Have you been taking clients to Dresser's so the girls can look them over?"

As Jennie nodded her head, Mary Jane caught a glimpse of another cut, a deeper one under her chin. She stopped walking. When the older woman stopped and turned toward her, Mary Jane gestured toward the cut. "Nick Shears again?" she asked with some outrage, thinking Jennie didn't take paying the protection money seriously enough.

She nodded sheepishly, then said with clear defiance, "I was late paying."

Mary Jane saw that Jennie pridefully thought she'd got away with something. Perhaps she hadn't heard what failing to pay had got other ladybirds, the gruesome mutilations they suffered. Mary Jane knew that some had been killed. She took Jennie by the shoulders and shook her. "You must not make light of the matter!" Mary Jane said angrily.

The older woman shrugged her off, retreated toward the wall of a building, a frightened look in her eyes. Jennie glanced around, probably to see if they were watched. No one passing on that street cared what the two women did.

"He is a terrible leach!" she cried. "Someone must stand up to him. At least I made him wait. And hopefully I'll leave him behind, should I remove to Spitalfields."

"No," Mary Jane said, trying to pull herself together. "He and the Gully Bleeders work the whole of the East End. There's no escaping him. He drew blood again. The cut is a further warning. He shan't always warn. Should you be unable to pay, come to me. In the future, he will—"

"*You weren't there!*" Jennie said, loudly interrupting, "and *I* didn't have the funds. I am *trying* to help support Clarissa and her two children."

With the older woman's angry tears, Mary Jane had to tell herself that she wasn't obliged to protect her friend. The thought did little to change the sense of duty she had. "Promise me that won't happen again."

"I promise."

The look of hurt in Jennie's eyes pained Mary Jane.

"Will you speak to your landlord?"

"Yes," Mary Jane said coldly. "But should you come to Spitalfields you must still pay your protection money. I will not have your blood on my hands."

She took Jennie's right hand and tried to put two shillings into it.

"I don't mean to frighten you," the older woman said with a look of hurt.

Mary Jane could not help showing her fear and anger. "You do."

Jennie turned away quickly, and walked back the way they had come.

Finding that the two shillings remained in her hand, Mary Jane nearly went after her friend, then decided not to bother—she was too proud to take the money.

THIRTY-SIX

Mid-April held more bookings than usual, and Catherine was nervous. Tuesday and Wednesday sessions, held in dull suburban drawing rooms, went smoothly, and a collection was held at the end of each, netting her almost three pounds in total.

To Catherine this seemed only modest recompense for long hours of reassuring words on the nature of mortality, and hints as to the fate of a missing cat, respectively. The furtive look on the husband's face, and the recent scratch marks half-hidden under his shirt-cuffs, made her sure that the truth would come out after she had left.

On the Thursday, she sat for a young woman whose baby had died of the croup, and her ability to perform deserted her. Her own youngest brother had died at much the same age.

"There is no spirit to mourn, or soul to wander," said Catherine, holding the client's hands. "Your child was taken back, innocent, untouched by the world."

This may or may not have been true, but it would have to suffice.

She took the half crown offered and left quickly, made uncomfortable by the mother's gratitude.

The crowning event of the week would be Saturday. A group of regular sitters from West Hampstead had asked if Madame Rostov would join them, though they did not ask for her to perform. She had considered the names cited—these were not the usual dowdy worriers or dilettantes looking for diversion. They were professional people, including a doctor, a town clerk, and the chairwoman of a number of charitable foundations.

Was she being assessed? She thought so. It was possible that at least one of the circle might be a journalist, or have connections to the Society for Psychical Research.

The first concerned her somewhat—most journalists preferred to uncover fraud, which made good copy. There would be no room for trickery—either she would be able to perform, or she must be honest and admit that her abilities were intermittent. Better to be written up as inconsistent than as a confidence trickster.

As for the second possibility, what little she read suggested that men and women joined the Society because they wanted the world of psychic phenomena to be real, not because they wanted to disprove it.

She could have pleaded other engagements, but it was the second time they had invited her. She was not going to appear as if she had something to hide—that was how rumours started.

Mrs Bessovitch helped her assemble a muted outfit, and the cheaper rings went in a drawer. Catherine was to take the train to West Hampstead, where she would be met. The night was cold, and it spattered with rain, but the train was well-lit and comfortable. She made herself inconspicuous in a corner seat, her head cowled, and let the rattle of the journey soothe her. Late workers came and went at each stop, mostly clerks and office juniors by the cut of their clothes. One of them dropped his evening paper, and she caught sight of a headline.

Caille.

She swallowed, and read on. A banquet hosted by the Lord Mayor; a grand gathering of luminaries—by which they seemed to mean men of industry and money. The headline was less relevant than she had feared, the article itself only remarking on the fact that Frederick Caille, who had been a regular speaker, would be absent for the first time in ten years. True enough, unless they dug him up.

A man and a woman signalled her as she stood at the station in West Hampstead. They were middle-aged, quietly dressed.

"Madame Rostov? I am George Conners, and this is my friend, Mrs Bless."

"I am pleased to meet you." Catherine dipped her head to both. "Do we have far to go?"

"Only around the corner to Lowfield Road, a mere stroll."

She pulled her cowl tighter around her, and followed them to a recent terrace, a stretch of red and ochre brick frontages pierced with arched windows, lit against the night.

Conners ushered her into the front room of Number Eighteen. Introductions, and a cheaper sherry than that at Lady Seldon's, followed.

"Most mediums abstain," said Conners, as Catherine fortified herself.

"They do," she agreed. "I am not of their kind."

She could not interpret his slight smile.

"So good of you to come, Madame Rostov," said a thin, overdressed woman, Mrs Treach. She would be the woman of "good works," as someone had described her. Her husband, equally scrawny, nodded at her shoulder. He would be the town clerk. A Dr Mercier, a Mr Gayle and another man whose name she did not catch, completed the group. An unusual number of men for such sittings.

Conners seemed to be the master of ceremonies.

"Let us welcome Madame Rostov to our small circle of friends. Lady Seldon speaks highly of her abilities."

Which might be true, but did this come from general talk, or had they enquired directly? Did Lucy Seldon know these people?

"Am I to display my abilities for you tonight, ladies and gentlemen?" Catherine allowed a touch of practised Russian haughtiness to play around the words.

Conners coughed. "Only if the conditions are suitable for you, Madame. If you feel it would not be appropriate…"

"No doubt it will become apparent," she answered. She would have to tread carefully.

She was shown through into a large dining room, where a suitable table awaited them. They were observing her; she was observing the house. Despite the presence of appropriate furniture, of antimacassars on armchairs and fresh flowers in the hall, the place was too clean, unscuffed. The lack of certain little touches spoke to her…

"Is there a reason why this house is unoccupied, though it is made to seem otherwise?" She stared directly at Conners.

"Ha! Got you fair and square with that one, old man." The doctor laughed.

"Indeed," admitted Conners. "You are perceptive, Madame Rostov. We only use this place for sittings."

"And before each session, you check anew for wires and trickery, trumpets in cupboards and children hidden up chimneys."

Mrs Treach looked interested.

"Have you yourself been subject to investigation, Madame?"

"No. But I am used to doubt. Is that what the company brings to the table tonight?"

Conners stiffened. "Hope would be a more accurate word. We have come across what we would describe as the most striking psychical experiences, and yes, we have also been played. But our interest is genuine. It would be our pleasure to confirm Madame Rostov as a bona fide talent."

Catherine saw that she could melt and confess to her limited talent, or she could continue the front that Madame Rostov would normally present.

"Do I need such confirmation?" she said, chin raised. And she broke the moment with a broad smile.

"We are all friends here, I am sure."

She was sure that they were not. George Conners was, for some reason, observing her. As for the round-faced Mrs Bless, who had not yet spoken, there was something about her...a sketch Catherine had seen in the Illustrated News. The woman was a medium in her own right.

"You have the gift," said Catherine, one hand to her forehead, pretending that she had divined this fact from the Aether.

Mrs Bless smiled and templed her fingers before her.

"Shall we be seated?"

⚜

The harmonium droned; six voices of varying ability raised an opening hymn, whilst Madame Rostov sat stiff-backed and silent.

"Behold a Stranger at the door!

"He gently knocks, has knocked before,

"Has waited long, is waiting still;

"You treat no other friend so ill.

"But will He prove a friend indeed?

"He will; the very Friend you need;

"The Friend of sinners—yes 'tis He,

"With garments dyed on Calvary."

Conners looked at her when they had finished and the harmonium was quiet.

"You do not approve of English hymns, Madame?"

"I have no voice for them."

"I find the vibrations most helpful in clearing the air for others to come through," said Mrs Bless. She had mousy hair, pinned tightly back, and a mole below her left nostril, the very vision of a strict but kindly aunt. "Such sounds alert them to congenial and receptive souls below."

"Perhaps Madame Rostov is receptive but not congenial?" That was the doctor, Charles Mercier, with a smile. His high forehead and neat beard gave him a studious appearance, as did the notebook in his hand, pencil ready.

"Are we a case study for your practice, doctor?" asked Mrs Treach. It was a cautious, prim enquiry.

"Mercier's an alienist," whispered the young man next to Catherine, the one called Gayle.

"I am a student here." Mercier put down his notebook. "Nothing more."

Conners lowered the gas, taking his place next to Mrs Bless. Faces and shoulders could be seen; most else was in deep shadow. The seven seated around the bare table were instructed to join hands, lightly, and Mrs Bless threw back her head.

"If there are strangers at the door, be welcome. We seek only enlightenment."

Conners raised both hands. "And if there are those who need guidance, who wish to move on, let them come."

Gayle, who seemed to have appointed himself Catherine's interpreter, leaned closer. "Sometimes there are troubled souls, stuck on this side of the Veil. Mrs Bless can assist them to be quit of earthly concerns."

Catherine's presentiments had been correct. These people were from the serious regiments of the spiritualist world, not the volunteers or yeomanry. She could expect any manner of attempts at physical manifestation, apportation or pronouncements from those higher Planes in which she barely believed. She doubted any of it would be genuine.

"For the benefit of the less experienced, Mrs Bless will now see if one of her guides will honour us," said Conners.

The traffic outside had stilled, the polite evening of the suburbs slipping into place. Maids might take an evening stroll, and men might straggle behind their dogs, but little else would be seen or heard. A sombre atmosphere filled the room. Mr Treach appeared to have a throat infection, and coughed occasionally, apologising each time. Gayle, to Catherine's left, smelled of alcohol and shaving lotion; the doctor to her right presented only a whiff of carbolic.

"There is a presence…" said Mrs Bless. "Lucy, is that you?"

A rap on the table then three more. Mrs Treach looked delighted. "Sad Lucy is one of dear Mrs Bless's controls."

The guiding medium shuddered, smiled.

"Sad Lucy says that there are strangers here. One…one of them has a great gift…"

A few heads turned in the gloom to Catherine.

"They have seen sorrows, oh, such sorrows. We must pity them. What is that, Lucy?" Mrs Bless put her hand to her ear. "You see domes, and spires, all layered with snow, and narrow streets below— it is so cold…and the people, their tongue is strange."

"That would be Russia." Mr Gayle's comment was almost inaudible.

Catherine thought she should be helpful, until she understood what was happening.

"Moy staryy, staryy dom," she said, one of the phrases she had learned to parrot from her landlady. *My old, old home.* "Where I lived once."

The Treachers clapped. "How wonderful."

Had Mrs Bless been a horse, Catherine would have not have backed her on what she'd seen so far. The table trick she knew herself; and a pretended vision of a Russian city was safe ground when you had a Madame Rostov present.

More raps, imperative.

"Sad Lucy says that this night is one of importance." Mrs Bless put her hand to her ear again. "She senses…"

The act went on. Someone had suffered a loss in the family. Another was destined to find what they sought, and a third should no longer worry about his mother.

"Why is Lucy sad?" Mercier had his notebook and pencil under the table, barely visible even to Catherine.

"Because…" Mrs Bless hesitated. "Because there are so many whose spirits cannot escape this earth, this anchoring Plane. They burden themselves with their failures and misdeeds, not seeing that above them, all is Light."

"I see. Then all controlling spirits must be sad."

"In part." Mrs Bless did not sound entirely pleased. "But our friends above have joy, as well, for as they guide us, they see us shed our mortal concerns, and many do ascend. Especially those who understand." She placed quite a lot of emphasis on the last word.

In the hour and a half of her performance, Mrs Bless spoke for Sad Lucy, then another "friend" who was a long-dead American chief called Black Eagle, and finally a small girl whose spirit was somehow trapped. The small girl was guided into Sad Lucy's hands, and all was well. The table spoke from time to time, and the curtains rustled wildly at one point, though the windows were shut.

Catherine tried to gain the measure of those around her. The Treaches seemed complete believers, and so did the young man whose name she had missed. He was hardly more than a boy, but listened attentively to every word.

Conners she did not understand, because he seemed to accept even Mrs Bless's weakest moments as sound, yet his eye was on Madame Rostov at many points. The doctor was politely curious; Gayle was politely dubious.

The question was—did Mrs Bless have some psychic gift, augmented by trickery just as Catherine might do, or was she a complete fraud? There was no point in her trying to expose any fraud in public, as it might rebound on her. On the other hand, she hardly wished to be connected professionally with the Mrs Blesses of the city—she wanted only their clients.

It seemed that proceedings were coming to an end. Mrs Bless nodded to Conners, who opened his mouth to speak…

"There are hands at her throat!"

Heads turned to the young man next to Mrs Treach; Mrs Bless looked confused.

"What is that, Mr Hough?" Mrs Treach's eyes were wide.

"There…there are hands at her throat. Oh God—thick, brutal hands…"

The air thrummed, burned in Catherine's nostrils, and she gasped for breath.

Fever, the bare plaster of the attic.

She pushed away from the table. The young man called Hough was on his feet, dancing—no, he was jerking and turning, as if he could not control himself…

As if someone had him by the throat, lifting him up…

A fourteen year old girl cried out, using Catherine's lungs to vent her horror at what she saw.

"I believe he's having a fit," said Mercier, rising to take hold of Hough's arm. The young man sank to his knees, only spared the floor because the doctor had a grip on him, and a child-like voice sang out from lips flecked with spittle.

"No, Uncle Jack, no..."

One of the gas mantles flared and shattered, the bare flame casting a blue, flickering light across the company; Hough slumped and was silent, his chin on his chest.

The men carried him into the adjoining room and eased him onto a couch, one of them turning the lights up. Mercier took off his jacket, rolled up his sleeves and examined Hough for some minutes. Straightening up, he looked to where he had put his cufflinks.

"Chap's asleep. Perfectly normal sleep, as far as I can tell."

"An errant spirit," said Mrs Bless, clearly trying to control the situation. "Nothing to be alarmed about, friends."

"It alarmed me, I don't mind saying." Gayle had been examining the gas mantle, disintegrated in its holder. He stood in the doorway, white powder on his fingers. "Pretty old, that fitting. They get damned fragile after a while."

Conners had found another bottle of sherry from somewhere, and was pouring it into small glasses. Only the Treaches did not indulge this time.

"It can happen, when the conduits, the channels to other Planes are opened," he said. "We had not...Mrs Bless had not yet closed the session, or led us in our final hymn, you see. If there are troubled spirits who see the opening, well, there you go. It can happen," he repeated, unconvincingly. He looked pale.

Catherine stood back from the group, trying not to show how much she was trembling. Cold sweat ran beneath her undergarments. The boy had seen what she had seen, and it had taken hold of him. How was this possible? He could only have read it from her mind, surely? She wanted to run from Lowfield Road, to leave that very moment, but she knew that Madame Rostov would do no such thing.

"I say," said Mr Gayle. "Did I hear you call out, Madame?"

"I was...taken by surprise. Nothing more."

"Weren't we all? Damn queer business." He winked. "That wasn't part of the act, now, was it?"

Hough awoke moments later.

"Why am I in here?"

Mercier recounted what had happened; the young man shook his head, looking puzzled.

"Don't remember any of that, doctor. Not a jot of it."

"No history of epilepsy or fits?" asked Mercier.

"Certainly not. Nor in the family, neither."

Catherine stepped forward, her hands behind her back. She could feel her fingernails cutting into the palms. It was difficult to keep her voice steady, portraying herself as an interested observer and no more.

"You spoke...you mentioned a name." She made herself say it. "Uncle Jack. Does that name have some significance to you?"

"Can't say it does, Madame," he said, polite but awkward. "I mean, it's common enough, but I don't have an Uncle Jack—or even John, for that matter."

Against her better judgement, she joined Conners at the sideboard.

"This young man..."

"Reggie? Nephew of mine, always interested in spiritualism. Fancied a go, and I said he could attend tonight, if he kept his mouth closed and acted respectable. Never known him to have the gift, though. His mother will be furious with me."

Mercier strolled over.

"Quite a show, Conners."

"All genuine, all quite genuine."

Catherine glanced at the doctor. "You are not a believer, sir?"

He smiled. "If I did not believe, it would be most rude of me to say with Madame Rostov before me. A doctor, if he struggles hard enough, can be a gentlemen. I have, however, treated patients in a delusional state, caused by nervous exhaustion or neurological damage. The manifestations are much the same." He spoke in an amiable, everyday tone. "I practice at the Flower House private asylum, by the way, Madame. In Catford."

She would have said he was in his thirties, certainly under forty. Old enough to have some experience—possibly not old enough to become hidebound and inflexible. As Conners moved away, she thought of asking Mercier more, but Gayle, cheerful in his rounds between the others, paused by them. "Old Conners is Mrs Bless's commercial agent, you know? He wants to ascertain if you're a professional threat."

"And what did you come here to ascertain, Mr Gayle?"

"Oh, I'm a reporter. Didn't anyone say? Here to separate bombast and bluster from the real thing, don't you know? If there is a 'real thing'"

And he was off across the room, slipping into a conversation between Conners and the Treaches.

Catherine made her goodbyes, hardly noticed in the continuing chatter over the evening's events, and walked out onto Lowfield Road alone, despite the doctor's offer to see her to the station.

She did not trust herself to conversation, not yet.

THIRTY-SEVEN

Jennie and her family removed to the George Street address in early May, once Barnett and Mary Jane had gone to the new lodgings in Little Paternoster Row.

Mary Jane concentrated on efforts to rebuild her savings. She located cribs in the area that rented by the hour and saw as many clients as she could. To help insure her safety, she did her best to organise the ladybirds of Spitalfields, using the Ringers much like she had Dresser's in Stepney.

THIRTY-EIGHT

The weeks that followed were tainted by Ctherine's experience at Lowfield Road. Madame Rostov continued her usual work, adding one or two "regulars" every so often. When at last she found the courage, Catherine enquired after the young man, Hough.

The Treaches informed her that he had quit such events. Apparently he had no recollection of what had happened that night, and showed no other signs of unusual behaviour or sensitivity. The letter from Mrs Treach suggested that the circle was rather disappointed with his departure. They made no mention of the episode having any connection to Madame Rostov.

Catherine had to assume that the boy was what she had been at his age—no more than an unwitting recipient of images from others, without rhyme or reason.

She hoped that it never happened to him again.

THIRTY-NINE

Infested with insects and rodents, the new room in Little Paternoster Row, though larger, was worse than the last. Mary Jane and Barnett took lodgings in Brick Lane in July, 1887.

FORTY

The matter of Uncle Jack and what he had done on Fell Lane was not quite finished, though. By chance or grand design, she received a letter from her brother Josiah in July, saying that Jack Witten was dead, of jaundice and a sudden apoplexy. His liver was found to be swollen and purulent; his heart laced with fat and disease. Their father had gone to the funeral, but it was poorly attended. Jack's second wife, Josiah wrote, had run away to the coast that spring, to set up home with a Flamborough fisherman. No one blamed the woman; some wondered she had waited so long.

Josiah's words conveyed no sorrow at the news.

In September, Catherine was asked to sit as medium for the same West Hampstead group. It was an invitation she accepted with great reluctance, and only after mention of "expenses" and an assurance that young Hough would not be present.

Neither Gayle nor Doctor Mercier were there either, their places occupied by two elderly sisters who had doubts about moving to Chelmsford and wanted to consult their late mother. Feeling rash, and aware of Mrs Bless watching her, Catherine indicated that their dear departed had passed too long ago, and was now far higher above than would allow for mundane communication. However, teasing out a little of the "dear Mamma's" nature as the evening progressed, she suggested that the move would be appropriate. It was obvious that they wanted to do it anyway, and this went down well.

"How marvellous you are, Madame," said one.

Mr Conners exchanged glances with Mrs Bless.

After the session he eased Catherine to one side.

"Madame Rostov—I wonder, would you consider joining in some modest explorations of the spiritual world before larger audiences. Mrs Bless has been asked to tour a number of Temperance Halls and spiritualist meeting places around our fair capital, and I confess that it will be much for her to endure alone."

"It is kind of you to ask," said Catherine. "But I am a quiet woman. I wish you much success, of course." She offered him a winning smile. "I doubt I shall aspire to such public affairs."

And that was what the other wished to hear. That Madame Rostov, if not to join his stable, was not competition for his existing protégée, Mrs Bless. Conners, underneath his professed beliefs, was obviously no more than a theatrical manager seeking to ride the spiritualist tide and line his pockets. Catherine imagined that he sought out rivals and possible accomplices—the Hampstead sittings were used to gather intelligence and occasionally for recruitment. Why not have journalists and sceptics present? They would help weed out the weak.

Catherine still had occasional ambitions, but not with Mr Conners.

That autumn the *Illustrated News* published a series of lengthy articles by Mr Philip Gayle, exposing some of the tricks of the "spirit trade." He questioned the bona fides of some mediums, and doubted many of the phenomena they produced, but he did not the attack the honest beliefs of most spiritualists themselves. His unfavourable references in one piece to a Mrs B were veiled enough that no one could be sure he meant Mrs Bless, though to Catherine it seemed obvious.

His final article came out at the start of November. Gayle had saved certain reflections for last.

'But there are some figures, such as Mme R—v and those like her in conduct, who should intrigue the genuine investigator. They stand apart in some way, with hints of true talent. They disdain the tilting table and floating face, the trumpet and the tambourine. As to whether they represent the future of spiritualism, few can say at this stage. We remain cautious but open…'

Catherine wanted to feel pleased at this assessment. She was at least surviving; Fredrick Caille and Jack Witten were dead, and she was largely free of her family. Yet she could not help but notice the date of the article's publication.

A year ago to the day, almost to the hour, she had sat down with a man called Edwin Dry and stared at the clean, neatly manicured hands of an assassin…

FORTY-ONE

Mary Jane and Barnett lost the room in Brick Lane because he, while drunk, had an argument with the landlord. She contacted Mrs Carthy and asked if her husband, John McCarthy had anything. He offered a room in Miller's Court, number 13, another Spitalfields address. Mary Jane and Barnett settled into the room in February, 1888. All the places in which the couple had lived being within easy walking distance of the George Street address, Mary Jane had the claustrophobic feeling that her world had shrunk.

To her utter dismay, she spent little time with Jennie. Though many months had passed since their harsh words about Nick Shears and the importance of paying protection money to the Gully Bleeders, their friendship had never recovered. Even so, as Mary Jane developed her weave of friends and associates, she drew Jennie into the work and introduced her to all the women who took part.

On a gloomy day in late March, 1888, alone in the room in Miller's Court, Mary Jane closed the curtains over the windows and retrieved the Chinese tea tin that she kept in an inner pocket of a jacket she rarely wore. From the tin, she extracted her savings, and set it out on the table. She stacked the coins and folded the soft together as she counted the funds.

Seventy pounds—just what I had when I left Joseph Fleming and the children robbed me. Took about a year to recover that. By summer, I'll have a hundred pounds. Then I'll leave Barnett and London behind.

The goal of one hundred pounds seemed arbitrary.

I would be more comfortable if I made it one hundred and fifty pounds. Then I might stay a little longer.

Mary Jane had yet to decide where she would go to live. Unfortunately, she couldn't think of anywhere she'd rather be than London. She hadn't liked Paris. The idea of traveling to America frightened her. Even staying in Spitalfields was preferable to returning to Cardiff. She could find arguments against any city she considered.

Mary Jane returned her savings to their hiding place. As she'd done before many times, she put the decision off.

FORTY-TWO

Southwark, March 1888

He holds the blade, the exquisite blade. A perfect design, with razor edge and needle point, with subtle and balanced weight. It will kill, but it does not need to kill to be what it is, to be admired.

Alone in manufactured gloom, he places his jacket just so over the back of a chair, smoothing the lapels. His starched shirt collar is already on the chair seat, a white C against dark hessian.

He moves, his will extending from the pommel of the knife to its glinting tip. Here, and gone; there and up, to the side before his heart can take a second beat. The blade flies free of his hand and is regained, this time pointing down to pin, to trap...

And he is somewhere else, six paces further back, low and ready. There and not there. Flexing on the balls of his feet, angled like a Limehouse drunk but with complete control. The bullet that would have caught his shoulder is a wasted shot; the fist aimed for his head swings wild. The discipline of not being struck is as important as the one of striking true.

After an hour, a light sweat gathers in the small of his back, and the scent of it tells him that he has done enough for this night. Tomorrow he must attend to his wrists. They are the steely anchor chains for his hands, and must never be neglected.

He did not learn to move this way. It came with bone and sinew, muscle and ligament, a gift that only needed recognising, using to its full potential.

You take that which is given, and you hone it, like a blade.
You make it exquisite.

The arrival of spring, even a London spring, was welcome. The rain which fell on Southwark streets was warmer and less frequent, the air less fugged with hearth-smoke, though Catherine missed the broad, empty skies of her native Yorkshire.

Her client group had grown, but not as much as she had hoped—the occasional contact suggested by Lottie, but for the most part quiet people, solidly middle-class. Such folk donated towards her time in a manner commensurate with their lives—carefully and without excessive generosity—and had to be nurtured over months to be worthwhile. She heard of fortune tellers and minor psychics being taken under the Vagrancy Act, as a result of charging for their services, and was always careful to protest that no reward was required. Unfortunately, some took her at her word.

This would have to change. She needed to improve her game in some way. More than once she had seen a medium being ushered out of a house even as another was ushered in—there was competition in bringing "comfort" to the widespread congregation of believers.

Her visions of the bowler-hatted man, and the killings at the Victualling Yard, had dulled her spiritualist ambitions throughout the previous year, constrained her to the safest of practices. Much of her expected progress had failed to materialise, and she knew that it was her own fault. The plans she had made in her Keighley attic, the ideas which sprang from her early sittings in London—these must be re-examined in order to decide her future. Where she made ten shillings from a session the year before, she must make fifteen now; a two-guinea consultation must become a three-guinea one. Preferable four.

Attempting to become better informed, she enquired into telepathy, a term which was gaining ground over older concepts of "thought transference," and into apportation. She dismissed the latter, the movement of solid objects, as simple trickery, but she explored the other common practices of mediums with her more experienced sitters, never letting it be seen that she might know less than they did.

She came to no definite conclusion. She could not rely on her gift, whatever it should be called, nor could she focus it, it appeared. It was in vogue to believe that some control or guiding spirit assisted the psychic. She had never sensed any such thing, and had good reason to believe that these controls were fabrications—or self-delusion.

She saw no conceivable reason why a "Mrs Peewit" or a "Running Bear" would hover over a medium, unreliably channelling fragments from another Plane. If these spirits had perfect knowledge, why share imperfect knowledge, imperfectly, to the earth-bound?

The wise Mongolian "Temur" was never summoned again as part of her performance.

She met Dr Mercier a second time at a séance, quite by accident. A group's regular medium had been taken ill (the rumour was drink), and Catherine accepted an invitation to take the man's place.

Mercier remembered her, and was polite, almost gracious, in his silence for most of the sitting. A twitch of his eyebrows here and there marked his doubts, and she took the unusual route of talking to him afterwards. She had a feeling that Mercier was one to be headed off before he dreamed of deeper enquiry.

"You did not challenge my comment on Miss Wright's sister," she said.

They stood on the pavement outside the terraced house where the session had been held, nodding as the other sitters passed them, dispersing into the cool evening.

"It was a reasonable assumption, Madame."

"Or word from the Aether, channelled through my admittedly limited abilities."

"That too is conceivable." His expression amiable as ever.

"But less likely, in an alienist's view." Catherine laughed, pulling her fur collar closer.

Mercier pulled out his half-hunter. "Unfortunate that I have a patient in an hour's time. I would have enjoyed discussing these matters with you, Madame."

"And exposing my little tricks?"

"I dislike false logic, poorly tested theories, and errant fraud. I have no firm opinion on Madame Rostov. I might almost say that she promises less than most of her kind, and delivers more."

He bowed, and hailed a passing hansom, which clattered to a halt by them.

"You have a means of conveyance?" he enquired, one foot on the running board.

"I shall be borne aloft by the spirits, doctor."

Or, thought Catherine as she watched the cab pull away, she would save a few pence and walk home…

Mrs Bessovitch asked why Katerina did not have a young man. Was she, as the landlady put with her usual turn of phrase, "more happy with the other ladies?" In truth, Catherine had avoided the issue most of her life. She had to go back to her grandparents, the Two Gentlemen, to find anything of promise within her own family, any example of genuine love and affection.

A kiss on the cheek from Lottie Chambers was more appealing than the looks of most men she met. They so often seemed that they might wish to acquire her, like a fine and unusual piece of furniture. Or a sculpture, which if they polished it enough would be suitable to show to their acquaintances.

The fad for spiritualist enquiry had largely passed from Charlotte Chambers's circles. This was to be expected, but by some strange quirk, she and Lottie still saw each other. Catherine remained Katerina Rostov, the interesting "older" woman, and they continued to read to each other three or four times each month, with the occasional afternoon entertaining Lottie's younger sister, Jemmy. The planchette and board came out for idle moments; nothing of consequence was revealed.

"I had word from Evelyn Caille," said Lottie one dull afternoon at Cheyne Gardens. "She is to take Beresford abroad for a few months, after so many months of trying to sort through Caille's business affairs." She scowled. "He left such questionable dealings behind as may yet raise more court cases."

"Is she well, in herself?"

"Better than I have seen her for years." Lottie plucked at her hair. "She asks to be remembered to you."

Evelyn Caille's remembrance came in the form of a small velvet-covered box, which contained an assortment of rings, some of which appeared quite valuable.

"She admired your old-fashioned rings, apparently. In clearing out Grove House, she found these, and begs that you should take them as a small token."

"You think I should?"

"Katerina, she would be offended if she heard that you refused them."

Catherine sighed. Taking out the smallest, a simple gold band, she placed it by Lottie's side.

"Give this to Jemmy when you see fit. Then this underserved profit is not mine alone."

"If you insist. Evelyn also asks that you forgive her for not contacting you this last year. She could not think of the words to say."

"Why would that concern her?"

Her friend's smile was hesitant.

"Did you not know? She believes that Madame Rostov was her salvation. It was following your visit that she began to gather her own courage—and then, so soon after, there was the affair at Deptford. It was as if you were a…what is the word, a harbinger of her freedom."

Catherine made sure to look at her book, at the wainscoting, anything but Lottie's face.

"I did nothing," she said, almost a whisper.

I killed four men.

～✦～

It was after this meeting that she began to receive regular images of Edwin Dry once more. Having hoped that the bloody events in the Victualling Yard had been the climax of her visions, it was a bitter blow. The episodes came when she was deeply tired, or trying to sleep but failing; only rarely did they occur during séances, and by now she had learned to suffer this, to complete the sitting without panic.

Her only comfort was that much of the intensity had gone. She saw neither murder nor blood, but brief flashes—fireflies in the night, brightening and dimming, sometimes not even truly remembered when she woke. A snow-specked street with empty windows; his progress across the river on a waterman's launch; the looming chimney of an anonymous factory. Once she saw him moving through great crowds, untouched and unnoticed, as if he were an inexorable force as yet undocumented by this scientific age. He was out there, though his activities no longer seemed to have relevance to her, for which she was grateful.

Yet she read the papers each day, and shivered if she saw any report of a suspicious death…

～✦～

More promising change arrived by accident, the result of a call to visit a young woman in Vauxhall, Mrs Ameley, the widow of a borough finance officer. She was some vague relation to Miss Bournelle's neighbour, and was distraught—her husband had committed suicide.

They sat across from each other in Mrs Amely's large parlour, tea-cups perched on their knees. The house was well-appointed but appeared in disorder, and there was no sign of a maid. Mrs Ameley had draped black crepe on every conceivable object, from the mirrors to the plaster figurines crowded on the mantelpiece; black window blinds were pulled almost down, shutting out the world.

"He could not bear his thoughts, Madame Rostov."

"Thoughts?"

"It was the same with his father. Deep moments of undeserved gloom, without rational source. I found him…" Mrs Ameley stirred her tea, adding a third spoonful of sugar. "I found him weeping one night, and all he could say was that the sky pressed upon him; the earth awaited him. He was not a lunatic." Said with sudden force. "Melancholy gripped him from youth."

"You cared for each other?" Catherine had known a woman in Keighley who had been that way. Close to vagrant, without relatives, she was committed to a public asylum and never seen again.

"We did. He worked hard at his job, and I hoped…I hoped that it would pass, with time. But this last winter brought him low, and whilst on borough business in Folkestone, he…he threw himself from the nearby cliffs. That was three days ago."

"I am so sorry."

Mrs Ameley's hazel eyes were filmed with tears. "Is he at peace, Madame Rostov? Has his torment passed? I feel I must know…"

Had this recommendation not come through the reliable Miss Bournelle, Catherine would have left, pleading that "the spirits will not settle today." What real comfort could she bring with genuine sorrow abroad in the house? A departed uncle, or an annoying mother—she could weave words around them easily enough. She could tell people that their faithful greyhound was at rest, or that their cousins felt no pain. A twopenny priest could have done the same. Mrs Ameley's grief was raw and recent, quite specific.

"I will seek," she said. "But I may not find. There is no map for the Aether, and I use no contrivances."

Mrs Ameley put a fourth sugar in her tea, sipped it and grimaced, pushing the cup aside. "I have a table ready in the dining room, which is suitably dark and quiet. There should be a hymn as well, should there not, or music? I have read—"

"I am Madame Rostov." Catherine raised a hand heavy with rings from Mrs Bessovitch and Evelyn Caille, stemming the flow. "The visions will come, or they will not. Clear your mind, and think of your husband. Tell me of him."

Haltingly at first, but gaining confidence, the young woman spoke of Edward Ameley. Catherine listened, opening her mind, searching for those rare impressions which could come to her during such sessions. Mrs Ameley's voice became a litany, a life recited from a distance, as Catherine sought to find the essence of what the dead man had been.

Other minds, she was convinced, roamed the Aether—perhaps all were living, and there were no lingering dead, no disincarnate souls...

She gripped the arms of the chair, caught suddenly by other eyes...

The line is too heavy. The feathered hooks are fat with mackerel, but it is still too heavy. He hauls on the winch and wonders. Once they took a shark, a rasp-skinned streak of grey which had drowned on the tackle. Drowned, aye, that a fish could do so—suffocate was the word, said old Doctor Johns, who often saw the small boats in...

There is no shark with a pallid, lifeless hand, nor one which wears torn cloth above the wrist.

"We have a man!" he cries to his brother at the tiller. "We have a man!"

The body comes slowly, and though it has been roughly served by the sea, the face is unmarked—a short moustache above full lips, leached of colour, and large grey eyes, never to close. The expression is of pale serenity...

Catherine choked, imagined saltwater in her lungs, and was back in Vauxhall. A parlour, a fallen cup, a broken saucer. The woman across from her looked shocked.

"Madame Rostov, are you well?"

"They did not find your husband's body."

"No, the police suggested it...it may return with the tides."

For a moment she matched what the young woman had said about her husband—his appearance, his bearing. This was not coincidence.

"He has been found. The fishermen will bring him in."

"Oh dear God!" Mrs Ameley pressed her hands to her mouth, took them away, placed them there again. She seemed as if she did not trust herself to speak.

"His pain has fled," said Madame Rostov. "His pain has fled, and now he sleeps. Grieve no more for him."

What else could be said?

The kitchen at the lodgings smelled of fresh bread and caraway seed; coffee and something else which lingered. Fish, of the oily variety. She hoped that it wasn't mackerel. Mrs Bessovitch laboured and cursed in the small back garden, calling down divine punishment on the cats which scratched up her herbs.

Catherine had found—in a manner of speaking—a missing man. It had not been intentional, but it sparked a thought. She had read a headline in Mrs B's paper a few weeks ago—"Medium assists police in baffling case." She had dismissed the article beneath—her view was that most results were either predictable or meaningless. When predictable, the self-proclaimed psychic had put snippets of fact together, as she might "read" a client, and come to a logical conclusion a half day before the police would have done so themselves. When meaningless, they had supplied such nonsense as could apply to a hundred cases, and thus lost little face in the process.

Her Vauxhall experience was different. There was nothing vague about what she had seen. A new possibility for a headline appealed to her as she buttered a piece of warm, crusty rye-bread.

'Madame Rostov solves Southwark Mystery; Police Commissioner expresses gratitude.'

Perhaps this was one route by which her name might spread, and by which fatter purses might join her client group?

FORTY-THREE

Wednesday April 6, on Whitechapel Road near Saint Mary's Church, Mary Jane paused to look at the selection offered by a hawker of books, Eliza Cooper.

"You've heard about the woman murdered," Eliza asked, "Emma Elizabeth Smith? Lived at Bewley's Common Lodging, I believe."

"No!" Mary Jane said, more a rejection than an answer. She nearly dropped the copy of *A Crystal Age* by W. H. Hudson she'd picked up. To hear the name gave her a heart-thumping fright, it being close to the one Jennie Weatherhead had assumed for use on the street.

Eliza looked at Mary Jane with sympathy. "You knew her?"

"No," she said again, because the name wasn't exactly the same.

"Two nights ago she were attacked," Miss Cooper said. "She died in hospital yesterday."

Jennie keeps a room at Bewley's!

"Elizabeth or *Lizabeth*?" Mary Jane asked.

"Don't know her," Eliza said. "I'd *heard* Elizabeth."

Distressed, Mary Jane set down the book, and left the hawker, crossing Whitechapel Road and moving north. She intended to go to the Weatherhead family lodgings in George Street, to see what she might find out. The building was but a few doors away from the passage that led to Bewley's.

Unless she'd done so unknowingly, perhaps on the street, Mary Jane had never met Jennie's family—her sister-in-law, Clarissa, nephew, Benjamin, and niece, Maisie—and didn't know what she might say to them if her friend were not home.

Instead of going to the Weatherhead family lodgings, Mary Jane decided to go to Bewley's Common Lodging. Jennie did her soliciting late at night and took her clients to Bewley's so her family would not know about her activities. At times, she did not return home for a day or more. She'd given Clarissa to believe that she worked nights as a housemaid for a Jewish family in Poplar. To explain away her periodic overnight absences, she said she stayed with the Jewish family to help out when they entertained their many friends from abroad.

Bewley's Common Lodging consisted of an ugly set of wooden

structures that squatted in the interior of the block of buildings that faced George Street to the west, Thrawl Street to the north, Brick Lane to the east, and Wentworth Street to the south. A through-passage into the paved yard before the entrance to Bewley's ran beneath the second floor of an old, stone building facing George Street several doors north of the one in which the Weatherhead family lived. Confident that her family would not see, Jennie could enter even in daylight if she chose the moment with care.

In Osborn Street, Mary Jane saw an acquaintance, a prostitute named Francis Booth, walking the opposite direction. She didn't participate in the weave of associates at the Ringers.

"Do you know anything about the woman murdered?" Mary Jane asked.

"Emma Smith," Francis said. "I've met her, but that's all. Wouldn't know her to see her."

"Emma *Elizabeth* or Emma *Lizabeth*?"

"I don't know." Francis pointed out a trail of dried brown drops that continued along the footway running into the distance northward. "That's her blood," she said. "I heard she removed her shawl as she struggled along the lane, were holding it against the flow from between her—uh, well…you can imagine, I suppose. She wouldn't let anyone help her. The blood continues on Wentworth Street."

"Thank you." Mary Jane said, and hurried on.

How can she do the work and not be able to speak of that part of the body? She realised her feeling of disgust toward Francis was an effort to distract herself from thinking the worst had happened to Jennie.

Just before she got to Wentworth Street, a greater stain appeared, what had clearly been puddles and spatters. Mary Jane could tell that much of the violence had occurred there. She hoped the victim had gone south from that point, and that she'd already seen the extent of the blood.

But, no, the trail turned the corner toward the west and George Street. Her imagination sent tears welling up in her eyes. She wiped them away, and took a deep breath, nearly tasting the odour that came from the chocolate and mustard mill, Taylor Brothers Limited, on the corner.

Nearing the crossing of George and Wentworth Streets, she saw that the blood trail continued north toward both of the rooms Jennie rented.

Fresh tears obscuring her view, she had to pause and collect herself before entering the busy crossing to make the turn into George Street.

Once across, she felt some relief to see that the trail did not enter the building where Jennie's family lodged. Further on, she saw that the stains did enter the passage that led to the yard before Bewley's. Still, she followed the blood, holding in sobs that tried desperately to escape.

The lodging house has lots of tenants. Any one of them might have done the bleeding.

Mary Jane entered Bewley's and found the deputy in her office, a middle-aged woman with hollow cheeks, and oily hair pulled too tightly into a bun to be attractive. Sitting, having tea and biscuits, the woman glanced up quickly, then returned her eyes to her food and drink.

Mary Jane stood beside a chair facing the desk, trying to gather herself together enough to speak. She knew she presented a red face and pained eyes. "My name is Ginger," she said, voice unsteady. "I am a friend of Emma *Lizabeth* Smith. I've heard that Emma *Elizabeth* Smith were murdered. Both may be lodgers here."

"Mrs Mary Russell," the woman said flatly, not rising from her seat. She aimlessly pushed papers around on her desk in a manner clearly meant to give an impression that her work shouldn't be interrupted.

"I mean to find out with certainty that the woman killed were Elizabeth, not Lizabeth." Mary Jane said forcefully, her voice rough and cracking. She feared that her tone gave an impression of anger and that the woman might become unwilling to answer. She took deep breaths. "Can you give me assurance of that?"

Still looking at the papers on her desk, Mrs Russell said, "Yes." She had a troubled look, though, one that Mary Jane might not have noticed had she not had such a clutching need for answers.

"Are you being honest with me?" Mary Jane asked, the words somewhat garbled as they caught in her throat. "Please look at me."

The deputy lifted her gaze. In her eyes, the lie could be seen clearly.

Mary Jane collapsed in the chair opposite her, weeping. "Tell me," she cried.

Mrs Russell stared at her in horror, then with resignation, a deep sadness troubling her eyes and the left corner of her mouth.

Waiting for the woman to speak, Mary Jane began to shake. She struggled to regain control of herself. Mrs Russell pushed her plate of biscuits across the table.

Mary Jane shook her head, more a product of her quaking than anything else. Deciding that having something to do with her hands and mouth might calm her, she took a biscuit anyway.

"Miss Emma Lizabeth Smith came in very early Tuesday morning," Mrs Russell said carefully, "about four o'clock. She were bleeding heavily, had her woollen wrap—"

Mary Jane cried out, her pent up sobs suddenly released with great force. She knew what it was to be violently abused and considered herself hardened to such experiences. Not Jennie, though. Mary Jane's awareness of the room fell away as she pictured her friend, deeply wounded and struggling along the street, frightened and in severe pain.

Finding her fancy too agonising, she pushed the vision aside, found herself back in the deputy's office, staring downward from her seat at the deputy's worn boots beneath the desk.

Mrs Russell got up, and closed the door of her office. She leaned against the edge of the desk, and laid her hand warmly on Mary Jane's cheek.

They both wept.

Mrs Russell pulled a bottle of scotch whiskey from a drawer, poured a generous amount of the drink into each of two glasses on the desk. One she handed to Mary Jane, the other she lifted to her mouth and quaffed all at once. Mary Jane did the same.

Some time elapsed before she located her voice. "Please tell me what happened," she said.

Mrs Russell had an apologetic look as she began. "She returned here about four in the morning on Tuesday. She were bleeding heavily, said she'd been attacked on Osborn Street. I couldn't imagine her walking so far in that state."

Mary Jane hid her face in her hands until she realised that the darkness allowed her imagination to visualize Jennie's suffering all the better.

Mrs Russell poured more whiskey in each glass.

"I found my boy, Harold, had him fetch his barrow, and with the help of Annie Lee, we prepared to haul Emma in it to the London Hospital." She shook her head. "'I don't want to go there,' Emma said. 'I don't want my family to find out. I'll just go to my room and rest.'" Mrs Russell wiped the tears from her eyes. "We took her there all the same. On the way she told me what happened—said she were returning from the docks when a scarred man come for her with sheep shears. She seen him in the corner of her eye, and wanted him to get close because she had a knife. He were faster than she expected. Clipped her right ear nearly off."

Nick Shears, Mary Jane thought.

"She turned quickly and gave him a cut across the face. They fled in opposite directions, and she thought she'd got to safety. Then some young men appeared, and began following her near Saint Mary's."

Trying to hear the words, yet not wanting to further imagine Jennie's suffering, Mary Jane concentrated on things within her immediate experience: the faint residue of peat smoke from the scotch on her tongue, Mrs Russell's slight lisp, the varying shapes and sizes of triangles formed by the overlapping pieces of paper on the woman's desk, the occasional rumble of footsteps coming from movement on the floor above.

"They set upon her across the street from the chocolate factory."

Mary Jane remembered the larger area of bloodstains where Osborn Street became Brick Lane at Wentworth Street. She winced and her eyes filled again with tears.

"I suffer a deep sadness for her loss," Mrs Russell said in a manner Mary Jane took to be a conclusion of the tale.

"No," she said, "You must tell me all of it."

The woman breathed deeply for a time. She wiped her tears away again before continuing. "They beat her. They raped her, then jabbed an iron bar—" She covered her mouth, struggled to swallow. "I cannot say—"

Mary Jane could readily put the story together, yet kept her personal vision of the incident at arm's length. Though she'd been irritated with Francis Booth's inability to speak of such matters, she found herself grateful that Mrs Russell could not say the words.

"I understand," Mary Jane said.

"No, not until I'm done, you don't." Mrs Russell had a look of frustration. "You must help me keep her secret."

Confused, Mary Jane sat up, focused more intently on the woman.

"She asked me not to tell anyone for fear that the truth would harm her family." Mrs Russell looked down, rubbed her brow, and shook her head. "Once, I were one who judged. Since taking this position, I have learned what many spinsters and widows must do to get on. I judge no longer."

She poured more scotch into both glasses, raised hers and drank it down. "Her face were terribly battered. I would not have recognised her. Until she spoke, I had mistaken her for Emma *Elizabeth* Smith, who lodged here until Sunday when she absconded, owing a week's rent. She were a dishonest person, always looking for advantage over others. I regret allowing her to stay without paying, but now saw I could put her absence to good purpose. On the way to the London Hospital, I told Emma Lizabeth Smith that she ought to say to those who asked that she were Emma *Elizabeth* Smith. I said that I'd do the same, and explained to her that the woman had gone away. Lizabeth said that was good, that her family would think she were staying at the place she worked, a Jewish family, and she'd clear it all up after she got better."

Mary Jane knew that the Weatherheads did not know Jennie's assumed name. "When my friend doesn't return home," Mary Jane said, "the reason for her loss being unknown will torment her family."

"Better that," Mrs Russell said, "than knowing the truth, don't you think?"

Mary Jane thought about that for a time, found that she agreed, and nodded.

Again, they sat in silence for a while.

"I stayed with her in hospital as long as they permitted," Mrs Russell said. "There came a time I think she knew her end was nigh. She said Ginger would look for her, and that I ought not to tell you. 'If she gets the truth out of you,' she said, 'tell her that I love her, and that I know she'd done her best for me.'"

Mary Jane had lost her mother again. Even as an adult, she'd failed to protect her.

"Thank you," she said, weeping anew. She rose unsteadily from her seat, stumbled out of Bewley's, through the yard and passage to the street. Dusk had settled with deep shadows that helped her avoid seeing the blood trail. Mary Jane turned north, intent on returning to the wretched hole she and Barnett currently called home in Miller's Court.

Alone with her thoughts, she ignored the many others using the footways at the end of their work day. Instead of the ever-deepening sadness she'd experienced with Mum's death, an anger welled up inside her. Recognising her inability to protect Jennie, she knew a disdain for herself, but she also saw a larger picture of the conspiracy to destroy her loved one. Mary Jane had been an unwilling part of the scheme, insisting that the protection money must be paid to those who committed the crime.

Too weak to take on Nick Shears and his bullies, she wondered who else supported them. Possibly, she might find someone to harm who was key to the conspiracy, yet still vulnerable to her limited power.

As she turned into Dorset Street and made her way west, something tugged at the edges of Mary Jane's memory, suggesting she did indeed know of such a person. With time, perhaps she would remember.

Resentfully, she thought that Emma Elizabeth Smith had got away with a crime, small though the offence seemed, because Jennie's corpse provided an alibi of sorts.

She walked through the Miller's Court passage, and entered her room.

Thankfully, Barnett had not yet returned home from Billingsgate Market.

Intent on escaping into sleep, Mary Jane took thirty-five drops of laudanum.

⚓

Despite the large dose of narcotic, Mary Jane could not find insensibility. She left the room at seven o'clock in the evening, stumbled through the Miller's Court passage, then east into Dorset Street toward the Ringers through a heavy downpour of rain. Slow and awkward with so much intoxicant in her, she felt as if she moved through water up to her neck.

The gutters along the street flowed with heavy runoff. Thinking of Mum in the River Towy, she entered the Ringers, and ordered violets to toss into the water outside.

"We don't have violets," the barmaid said impatiently.

"Irish whiskey, then," Mary Jane said.

She would later recall that women she knew greeted her and asked her to sit with them, but would not recollect their names or faces. After drinking her whiskey, she had a row with someone and struck that person in the face, yet she would not remember anything about what had started the fight or who the person might have been. The publican, Matilda Ringer, had Mary Jane put out in the street.

She awoke near dawn the next morning in her bed, lying next to Barnett. He stank of the fish market so badly, her gorge began to rise. She got out of bed, lit a lamp, and went out to the privy. Head aching and gut churning, she vomited into the privy vault. Her stomach calmed somewhat and she sat. Too backed up from the laudanum, she succeeded only in passing water.

Mary Jane noted that her right hand hurt and had bruised knuckles. The few memories of the night before brought a distant feeling of embarrassment for the way she'd acted at the Ringers, one eclipsed, though, by her grief over the loss of Jennie.

Mary Jane returned to her room.

Barnett gave her a look. He rose to begin his day as she got into the bed.

Trying to return to sleep, something of memory kept suggesting that Joseph Fleming had helped her home the night before. A mere fancy perhaps, she still found the idea comforting, in spite of her desire to stay away from him.

Barnett moved about the room, washing with a flannel at the basin, preparing a cup of coffee, packing and lighting his pipe. Eventually he took a seat at the table beside the largest of the two windows.

Unable to sleep, Mary Jane made some decisions. *I shall wean myself from laudanum.* Should she somehow find a way to avenge Jennie, she'd need a clear head.

"I'm giving up soliciting," she decided aloud.

"Soliciting," Barnett repeated, blowing smoke from his mouth and nose. She knew he was trying to wake up before heading out to the market to begin the day's labour. She didn't usually rise early enough to see that. With the curtain pulled back, he sat looking out into the court. The view offered little of interest; the wooden privy stall, the rusted pump with its peeling blue paint, and the whitewashed brick of the facing building. He looked toward the left, beyond the bend in the court beside their room.

Why does he bother? Mary Jane had to wonder. *The view gives merely more brick. We live in a sad, little hole.*

She remained in Miller's Court because she felt somewhat safer hidden in its shadowy depths from the likes of Brevard. The only entrance to the court's thin, L-shaped paved yard was from Dorset Street by way of a three-foot-wide, twenty-foot-long through-passage under the second floor of the building that held their landlord's chandler's shop.

"That's good you're giving it up," Barnett said after a time.

As usual, he'd had much to drink the night before and had little desire for conversation.

"I shan't be contributing much to the household accounts until I find a position."

"Position…" he said. "That's fine for now. I can work longer hours at market."

He knocked the ash out of his pipe into a tin on the table.

Mary Jane had decided to give up soliciting because of what had happened to Jennie. She could not escape the fact that helping her friend learn to work the streets, she'd contributed to her death. Mary Jane had insisted that Jennie pay the protection money the Gully Bleeders demanded, as if that were all that was needed to keep her safe.

I might have seen that she could not afford to pay. I should have persuaded her to give up soliciting and find a position.

Somehow, she found that her mood fit with Barnett's silent contemplation of bricks—a mute acceptance of a grim world. That didn't please her.

The grief is too hard. To bear up, I ought to take action.

Someone had to pay for what had been done to Jennie. Mary Jane knew that to become the instrument of the revenge she sought, she'd have to be secretive because of her limited strength.

She would spend time gathering information from the ladybirds of Whitechapel and other districts within the East End.

My savings will allow me to move freely, at least for a while.

She would watch the Gully Bleeders and look for an opportunity to strike out at them. Though she had given up soliciting, she would pay her protection money so those she watched would be none the wiser.

Barnett finished his coffee, and put his pipe in his pocket. He donned his hat and jacket, took up his apron, and headed toward the door.

"This evening, then," he said.

"I'll be gone much of the time, looking for work." Mary Jane said. "I'll look for night shifts too, so I might not be home till late."

"Good luck," he said, and left.

FORTY-FOUR

Superintendent Denis Neylan of M Division believed in the Living God, the Rule of Law, and that he and his men were serving both when they walked the streets of Southwark. He made this plain to Catherine at their first meeting in April.

"If you..." He pointed a stubby finger at Madame Rostov. "If you, Madame, are privy to the Voices of those who cannot find their way to the Lord, then you are Blessed. There may be purpose for you, even here in the Bastion of His Justice."

Neylan spoke with the use of many obvious Capital Letters. He would be a lay preacher, she imagined, a tee-totaller, making love (she wondered if he called it copulation?) to his wife at exactly half past nine every Monday evening. Probably after a prayer. Madame Rostov's approach would have to be adapted.

"I am a fallible instrument, Superintendent." This brought an approving nod, one which also betrayed the fact that the portly officer wore a hair-piece. All is vanity, Saith the Preacher. "Sometimes I can uncover truths and bring comfort, sometimes not. I do not dissemble when there is nothing I can do."

"Good. Ability must always listen to Humility." He paced in front of his office window, one eye on the street. "I dismissed a fortune-teller who came to me last year. I believed that by coming to me, he sought to place himself at the hem of Justice, and thus evade it. I had him followed, and not long after, I gave him a month for Vagrancy. He gulled coin from decent folk, claiming that he could predict the years ahead."

"The Future is closed to mortals," said Catherine, her own language becoming more portentous to match Neylan's.

"It is. The Past and Present are our rightful domains, as He grants. I shall consider your offer of assistance to the Southwark Constabulary, Madame. Should a suitable case arise, you will be notified. Leave your details with Inspector Mallick."

Anonymous again on the busy Borough High Street, Catherine tried to weigh what she was undertaking. She knew from the newspapers that members of the public swamped the police when wicked deeds were done. Some claimed to be witnesses, hoping for reward, and were not averse to naming their neighbours out of spite.

Others might be better served by Dr Mercier and his fellow alienists, confessing to crimes they had not committed. A few were "morally outraged," a phrase which amused her.

And then there were the spiritualists, offering assistance...

If she could be considered first, be the woman who the police came to, rather than leaving her to join the throng at the police station desk, she would have the advantage. It was hard to tell if the forthright character of Superintendent Neylan would be help or hindrance.

She walked south, diverting through an empty alley in order to come out at the other end as Catherine Weatherhead. With hair tied down, rings gone, and wearing a dowdy hat and plain coat, there was no hint of the Russian psychic apart from the same cracked leather bag, which she draped with a woollen shawl to make it less obvious. She was an actress now, and the two parts she played must never be apprehended by the same audience.

Madame Rostov was the star. Every time Catherine loosed her hair and put on the many rings, she was reminded that no one in London cared a fig about the ironmonger's daughter, or about Mardy Cath, the "odd" girl once of Fell Lane, Keighley. Excepting Mrs Bessovitch, of course.

Madame Rostov was also an intimate performance, one maintained best in private parlours. Catherine had lost confidence that she could put on the shows of which she had dreamed in her Fell Lane attic. The more she heard of Mrs Bless and her adherents, the less she wanted to be known as part of such a movement. Bluff and obfuscation she could contemplate, if not overdone, but the grand show was too much.

Perhaps another, slightly less astute Lady Seldon would come along, and be her patron? For whilst Lady Seldon believed Madame Rostov had a gift, she was immune to showmanship and quite able to spot outright fraud.

In the meantime, she would hold her modest séances, and try routes such as the police, possibly even the newspapers. Tomorrow she would adjust arrangements so that communications for Madame Rostov went to a post office elsewhere, in order to muddy the trail. Holborn might suit—a relatively easy walk, and an easier cab ride, from Blackfriars Bridge. An agent would have made more sense, but agents, she understood, took a percentage.

Remembering that there was occasionally correspondence for Miss Weatherhead, rather than Mme Rostov, Catherine enquired at the usual Southwark post office, and found there a letter from Clarissa dated March 25. It thanked her for "going out of her way and being so generous" when marking Maisie's eleventh birthday. It was polite, but managed to be snide and begrudging at the same time—appropriate, perhaps, for Catherine had come close to resenting the postal order she had sent.

Clarissa wrote that George Street would never be to their taste, but that they were making do. According to the letter, Jennie was still engaged as a part-time maid for a Jewish family outside the area; they saw less of her, but the extra income helped.

So the pretence was still intact. Clarissa knew nothing of her sister-in-law's true activities. Catherine did not visit her cousins any more—had not been to George Street, wherever that was. Somewhere in Spitalfields, apparently, which did not add to its attractions. Levinia's death had almost severed the ties between them. Under other circumstance she might have spent a little time with Jennie, but even she was at least fifteen years Catherine's senior. What they might have shared was difficult to see. Stories of Charles, and the Weatherheads at Harwich, of times lost.

Lost was lost.

The concept of becoming a respected consulting psychic had more and more appeal.

⁂

A fortnight after her visit to the police station, Madame Rostov returned to Borough High Street to enquire if anything had been done about a recent case of a factory foreman who had failed to come home after work. With his wife and colleagues being mystified at his disappearance, it seemed a good opportunity to test herself. When she explained her situation and the possible use of her talents, an ageing sergeant politely told her the matter was in hand, and they needed no "public hinterference."

The foreman's body was eventually found on the mudflats of the south bank, with a fatal fracture of the skull, probably caused by falling against a bollard by the river path. She attended the inquest, which recorded the incident as "misadventure." No one seemed very bothered, not even the wife.

Feeling discouraged, Catherine undertook a series of small sittings. A few shillings from one session; a guinea from another. She had cab fees to bear, to appear respectable, and still she needed new boots. London was hard on the feet. She frequented certain tearooms, where the "Russian medium" began to be recognised, and that was more expense. Madame Rostov could not ask if there were any stale buns left over from the previous day.

Her dreams were absent, or dark.

He understands the dead.

He is a student of what makes them so.

The subtle difference between the tainted froth of poison on the lips, and the slack saliva which comes from a natural fit or illness, for example. Not that venoms and toxins are fit tools for a journeyman, except under duress. They are the recourse of serpents, of thwarted and disappointed lovers.

The proper angle of a thrusting blow to heart or kidney, and the quarter inch, often less, which would give an opponent long enough to make a last blow in return.

The foolishness of assumptions, of believing that a single shot is enough.

The drum of a choking man's heels on polished floors.

The slow pressure of a pillow across the face.

The smell of disease.

As a carpenter knows timber, so Edwin Dry knows flesh.

At the end of April, Catherine received a note from Inspector Eden Mallick, of M Division. She was requested to call on him, should she be free to do so, the following day. With nervous fingers, she penned a brief reply that she would be there at ten in the morning.

Mallick was a tall, lugubrious man whose right eyelid had a disconcerting twitch. He showed her through to a cramped office.

"I am not Mr Neylan," he said, with gloom. "Matters of spirit and soul, would that I had time for them. Days plodding the Southwark streets, followed by a dried-up steak and kidney pie…"

"You do not hold with mediums, or with séances, inspector?"

"Don't hold with them? Know nothing of them, Madame. And care less, but the Superintendent will have his foibles. A case vexes him, and he says we shall explore all routes—'The Lord will shine His Light on the correct one.'" This in a passable imitation of Neylan's voice.

Catherine smiled.

"The Superintendent believes I may be of use?"

"He's a rare bird. Anything that sounds right and Christian goes in his armoury." The eyelid twitched and shook. "You must have had the proper cant when you met with him."

"I am no fraud, inspector," Madame Rostov was sliding into her own. "The gift comes; the gift goes. At least I will not deceive you."

"So you say, so you do say." Twitch. "Well, Madame, we have a gang of lads—the Compass Rose Bravos, they call themselves—who parade around South Street and the Compass Rose public house. Mostly machine and factory boys. They drink overmuch, and offend the Superintendent with that and their language."

"Not a fertile ground for spiritualism."

The corners of Mallick's mouth turned further down.

"There was a shooting, two days past. A girl from the Union Boys, a rival gang, was wounded in the leg, and a Union fellow lost the sight in one eye. All were at fault, I expect. The gun has been found, you see, but we have no proof of who fired it. Neither side will speak; Mr Neylan will have one or more of them go down, as an example." The inspector gave her a sideways glance. "Mrs Neylan, a most righteous woman," He extended the "righteous" to stretch across the table between them, "Is on the Holy Trinity Ladies' Virtue Committee. She will be pressing him…"

Catherine's thoughts flickered, as unpredictable as the inspector's eyelid.

"If no one is killed, or wishes to speak to their late mother…ah. Perhaps I have it. Mr Neylan wishes me to guide him to the one who used the gun?"

"Aye."

She could express her regrets, say this was not her line of work. But they had come to her…

"An unusual request. Let me meet with such suspects as you have, Inspector Mallick. And if there is nothing, I will tell you so, plain."

"We have them remanded for disorder, in the cells. They will get a fine only, if that, unless we have better proof."

He led her to the cells below, where carbolic and stale alcohol vied with each other in the narrow corridors; one small cell contained only a pool of bloody sick.

"Not a place for a lady," said Mallick, noticing the vomit. "Maybe I should have them brought up to the interview room."

"It is no matter."

"Aye, well. Here are the likely boys from the Compass Rose Bravos. Not so bravo now."

The end cell held five youngsters of sixteen or seventeen years, clothed in cheap suits and sullen looks. They were the spit of boys who had plagued her around the backs of the factories at home—the half-poor, which meant they wanted more but could not quite grasp it. They had wages, but not good ones. Decent enough boots waited too long for new soles; collars had to be turned again and again. Boredom was washed down with drink, and tempers to follow.

The taunting gangs, following her through the muddy streets; Ellie, who had rickets at twelve and yet threw handfuls of dirt at Mardy Cath. The men who swore and urinated—and looked at her as they did so—at the back of the Cavendish Hotel. Slow Charlie, wondering why she would never touch him "down there" again…

There was always a weak one. He would be her way in. These boys were certainly not ready for the bone-china cups, almond biscuits and harmonium of a séance.

"Inspector, I will require a separate room, the weapon that was used, and…that boy on the left." The one who would not meet her eye, whose back was turned slightly from his comrades.

She stepped closer to the cell bars.

"I am Madame Rostov. Mr Neylan, the Superintendent of this place, would know which one of you fired on other children." She used the last word with scorn. "His men have better things to do than slap your faces, and so he calls on my gift."

"What gift's that, then, lady?" a sly-faced lad called out. "Summink under yer skirts?"

Someone snickered and she swivelled on one heel, surprising them with a cold stare.

"I am a psychic of some ability. I have dealt with death before, and worse miscreants than you. Do not toy with me."

Uncertain, they went quiet.

The available interview room was small and airless. The constable who had charge of the boy, whose name was apparently Ally Parfit, pushed him down onto a creaking chair and took up position behind it.

"It is Alastair?" She took her own place at the table, where lay the unloaded revolver. It was mud-spattered, and looked in poor repair, but the inspector assured her it had managed to fire twice.

The boy said nothing, and the constable cuffed him across the back of the head.

"Yes, miss," muttered the suspect.

"Madame. Madame Rostov." She took up the gun and stroked it, making a show of running her fingertips over its length. "Ah yes, this weapon has killed," she said, as if to herself.

"We didn't kill no one."

Cuff. "When you're spoken to, lad."

It was hard to tell if the constable was zealous, brutal, or both.

She asked for Mallick to be brought in, and achieved a reluctant agreement from him that she could sit alone with the boy.

She had one chance to impress.

When the policemen had gone, she lowered her head, and placed both hands on the revolver. For a long moment she was still, and then she gave a theatrical shudder. Watching Mrs Bless's performances had been good for that, at least.

"I turns me 'ead," she said, aping the talk she heard on Southwark streets. "I turns me 'ead, and I sees 'im; 'e has that barker up, pointed at me cannister. 'Fire,' says Parfit. Fire and—'"

"Raggy said that!" The boy protested, slapping the palms of his hands against the table. "It were 'im as found the barker, an' gave it to Ned—I never seen it 'til then."

"Easy to lie when one boy has an eye missing and a girl may not walk properly again."

"I'm not lyin'—you're lyin.' That 'Says Parfit' game, you made that up. You're some Ikey's wife they paid to nark on me..."

He subsided, confused and close to tears. Catherine put the revolver down.

"Violence confuses the Aether, makes many voices speak across each other. Is it so, then, that a boy called Ned had the barker—the gun—and he took the shots?"

He was quick to grab the lifeline. "He did, yes. I done nothing."

"Nothing?"

"Didn't 'ave no barker, never," he said more carefully, avoiding the question of any other role he might have played in the Compass Rose Bravos.

"Wait here."

She went outside and found Mallick trying to light his pipe in the corridor.

"Is one of boys you hold called Ned?"

"Ned Ginny, a butcher's apprentice, though not a good one. He's the big red-head in the cells. Why?"

"He fired the shots. The revolver came from a boy called Raggy. I don't know if Parfit will speak openly against them, but I assume you can work with the information?"

Mallick gave up on his pipe.

"The spirits told you all that, did they, Madame Rostov?" Twitch. Twitch.

"You do not believe, inspector, and so my explanation would mean nothing to you." She said it with a smile. There was no need to antagonise him, not if further work might come her way. "After all, if you get Ned Ginny to talk, you will have pleased your Superintendent—and Mrs Neylan as well."

He squinted at her, stilling his twitch for a moment.

"Aye, there's that. And Raggy? Hmm. That's probably the printer's boy. We let him alone, but I know where to find him. I'll not say I catch your game, Madame Rostov, but still…I'm obliged to you."

"Pleased to assist the constabulary, inspector."

He showed her back to the front desk, where a short-dark-haired man was screeching at a sergeant about missing spoons.

"She's gorn and taken them all, the bitch!" he yelled, until the sergeant gestured a constable over, and the man quieted.

"Eden Mallick—any news, laddie?" Someone called from across the busy room, and Catherine halted. She knew that voice. It was the policeman who had come to Brantridge Street, asking about Caille's murder.

"Aye," said Mallick, loud enough to carry. "We'll have the right lad lagged and in prison linen soon enough, Donald. But I fear there's nothing more to it. A petty enough falling out, no great game underway."

"Pity, pity." Donald Swanson pushed through a group of quarrelling women. "And this lady, did they trouble her too?" He looked at Catherine, a look which turned quizzical. "Ha' we met afore, lass? I thought for a minute I kenned yuir face."

A long time had passed since their meeting in the damp, cluttered front room in Stepney, and under such different circumstances. He would not, could not, recognise Catherine Weatherhead.

"We have not, inspector."

"Chief Inspector," said Mallick. "Chief Inspector Swanson here is with the Criminal Investigation Department. He has an interest in the gangs of our fine city, and wished to know if the Compass Rose Bravos might become a problem worth his notice. Donald, this is Madame Rostov. She is…" He faltered.

"A psychic, Chief Inspector. A medium, of a sort. Mr Mallick is shy of the word, and shy of the path I tread."

"Ha. Eden Mallick tapping on tables, there's a wee change. That'll be old Neylan's doing, I'll guess."

The inspector's usual mournful look returned.

"He tasks us sorely, right enough." Which was not said so loud that any of the other officers round the front desk could hear. "But better we fear God than dance a Highland tune."

She could see that the two men, much of an age, were well known to each other.

"Madame Rostov, eh." Swanson tipped his head to her. "Be welcome, Madame. The Force needs all it can muster some days."

"You approve of my profession, Chief Inspector?"

"Not greatly, Madame. Shysters and charades, for the most part, begging yuir pardon. But if Mallick here has found ye of value, then we must ay learn new tricks, ye ken."

"We are in agreement on that, sir."

And she made her exit. What Donald Swanson might learn if he gazed upon her face for too long was not to her liking.

FORTY-FIVE

Making the rounds, talking with her ladybirds and trying to make new friends and widen her territory, Mary Jane saw Gabriella Gorse at the Black Eagle Pub in Brick Lane. The prostitute spoke to a young, thin, dark-haired woman.

Again, Gabby talks to the green tail. She saw that the younger woman had the gaunt consumptive appearance. *She ought to do well. Plenty of fools attracted to that helpless, hopeless look.*

She had presumed Gabby lodged in Stepney, but didn't remember anyone ever saying where she lived.

Seeing her over the following weeks at other pubs in different parts of the East End—the Bricklayers Arms in Poplar, the Black Dog in Shoreditch, and Bunch of Grapes in Limehouse—Mary Jane grew curious. In the ensuing summer months, she followed the woman whenever she turned up.

While following Gabby, Mary Jane had a stalker as well. She first noticed the shadowy figure following her along Market Street in Poplar, then again among the foot traffic at several other locations in the East End. The stalker stayed in the distance, keeping well enough to the shadows that she could not make out any definite features. She saw the silhouette clearly a couple of times framed against a brighter background, and became certain the figure was male. The shape did not have the thicker build of Stuart Brevard. Fancy told her he might show himself more clearly any time. She feared he might be one of the Gully Bleeders. Were they somehow on to her desire to harm them?

Ridiculous.

Numerous men had stalked Mary Jane in her short life. She didn't let fear of them stop her.

Gabby visited streets where Judies plied their trade. She went from pub to pub, and a couple of taverns that had back rooms with entertainment. Everywhere she went, Mary Jane saw her approach and try to talk to the green tail.

Since Gabby rarely took a cab anywhere she might walk, she remained easy to follow. Her eyes seemed to fail her with much distance. Not seeking clients, Mary Jane did not dress as a ladybird. She wore a bonnet and sensible clothing. The one time Gabby noticed Mary Jane, they were at the Horn of Plenty pub in Poplar.

The sound of the coarse saw dust crunching beneath her tread took away from the graceful approach Miss Gorse attempted. She asked, "What are you doing here?"

"I needn't be surprised to find I'm here for the same reason you are," Mary Jane said. She glanced around the half-empty establishment as if looking for someone. The rainclouds outside brought heavy shadows inside among the age-darkened wood furnishings. The men at nearby tables stared at the two women.

Gabby looked Mary Jane up and down. "You're not dressed the part."

"I'm dressed for the client what hired me."

With a contemptuous curl of the lip, Gabby turned away.

Mary Jane wasted no time moving beyond the woman's range of vision.

Because Gabriella Gorse, another fallen toffer, reminded Mary Jane of her own failure, she'd always considered her dislike of the woman unfair.

No, there's more to the feeling, something wicked *about her. I just don't know what that is.*

Mary Jane remembered the words of the prostitute, Sally Fourth, whom she'd met in Deptford: "I haven't seen you try to earn a single farthing." In Deptford to help Joseph Fleming with his criminal scheme, Mary Jane hadn't been soliciting, but wanted to appear to be. The prostitute had caught her out.

Mary Jane thought she was on to something like that. She'd never seen Gabriella Gorse take a man up on an offer; never seen her "disappear" with a man, as ladybirds were wont to do.

At the King of Prussia in Shadwell, while watching Gabby talk to an older woman, Mary Jane got an odd feeling that raised the small hairs on her neck and gave her a chill. She couldn't say whether that feeling had something to do with Gabby's appearance or what she did. Still, intuition seemed to be trying to tell Mary Jane something.

The ladybirds of Stepney had given Gabriella Gorse her nickname for talking so much, particularly to the new girls. They joked that she acted like a mother hen, taking poor young chicks under her wing. They thought that foolish, but kind. Somehow, Mary Jane had always known that was a sham.

She suspected the woman had got herself into something sinister, having seen her in conversations with Nick Shears.

The Gully Bleeders bled prostitutes a little at a time; not so much that women would balk after learning something of the consequences, and not enough that the gang's efforts were worth the trouble for the take from just one. Yet taking a little from all the women engaged in soliciting in the East End each week amounted to a fortune. And that fortune grew with each new woman who turned to working the streets as a means of making ends meet, something that happened more and more as the growing ranks of the unemployed competed for positions, day labour, and piece work, driving wages down. Earning a living by legal means had become more and more difficult. Still, prostitution being a secretive pursuit, a woman entering the trade would not take it upon herself to inform the Gully Bleeders of what she did for a living. No, she wouldn't want to. And one woman engaged in prostitution without paying the protection money could inspire others to do the same. A spy was needed to collect the names of those just joining the ranks of the East End ladybirds, one that looked like a ladybird herself.

Once Mary Jane had reasoned out the lay, Gabby's betrayal seemed obvious enough. She knew the business. She could recognise all the signs of fresh, budding tail. Who better than that for the Gully Bleeders to have as an informant?

Those ideas about Gabriella Gorse solidify but slowly over the summer of 1888. Even though Mary Jane had always disliked the woman, she'd believed the kind face the prostitute showed the new Judies to be pure cokum, Gabby's way of looking for opportunity and advantage, nothing more.

Perhaps she'd been scornful toward Mary Jane to keep her at arm's-length. Gabby would know that Mary Jane could do the same job for the Gully Bleeders. With that ability, she might also easily discern what Miss Gorse was up to.

Almost two years earlier, Mary Jane had seen her in the East London Cemetery with Nick Shears and some of his bludgers. She'd watched Gabby counting out something on her hand. On that day, had she counted off the women she'd told the gang about that week? Did she get paid a little of the take from each new Judy?

Not long before sighting the woman in the cemetery, Mary Jane had seen Gabby nodding her head toward Jennie's table at the Angel and Trumpet to direct Nick Shear's attention. He must have seen Jennie. Shortly thereafter, he'd come to her for protection money.

Mary Jane felt foolish for taking so long to fit the pieces together. Gabriella Gorse was a blower for the Gully Bleeders. She put the gang onto Jennie. If Mary Jane could not take on Nick Shears, harming Gabby was a more manageable goal.

Standing there in the King of Prussia, watching Miss Gorse laugh with the older woman, the pitch of Mary Jane's anger rose. She fancied murdering Gabby and trembled at the thought.

Should I not go after the one who directed his gang to kill Jennie?

Nick Shears was always a threat, an obvious one. Gabriella Gorse knew the cruelty of his gang's methods. She pretended friendship among innocent and needy casuals, and then betrayed them to the Gully Bleeders.

She *must be the target of my wrath.*

Not seeing clients, traveling about the East End, frequently in cabs, purchasing meals while on the move, Mary Jane's funds had diminished over the summer. What in the spring had been about seventy pounds, had become forty-five.

At present, she didn't care about growing her savings. She realised that her goal of leaving London had been replaced with one of exacting her revenge. Her anger over the death of Jennie had pushed aside her fear of Stuart Brevard.

Before I leave London, I shall see Gabby pay for what she's done.

FORTY-SIX

Three welcome gratuities from the Southwark police in less than three months. With the fees passed to Catherine through Inspector Mallick, and the donations from her sittings, she met the arrears on her bed and board in July, though Mrs Bessovitch always waved the matter aside as not pressing. The extra money would also help with the hansom cabs needed to maintain Madame Rostov's reputation and distance. A medium who turned up late, limping in worn boots and soaked with rain did not command respect.

From what fund the police paid her, she did not know. Monies set aside for informants? Unclaimed rewards? True to the law, she never claimed openly to any at the station that she could succeed. She never asked for recompense. That was the necessary game.

The money had no taint when she spent it at the milliners, purchasing Madame Rostov a sombre, wide-brimmed hat, or when she settled her own account with the butcher—she could not expect Mrs B to buy every mutton cutlet that was cooked for her lodger.

In mid-July she was called back to Borough High Street for a minor "case" that she suspected had more to do with Mrs Neylan, the police superintendent's wife, than any wished to say. That woman's occasional appearances at the station were viewed with dismay, involving as they did more perfectly straight collars and brightly polished boots than even her husband demanded.

"Boadicea would have surrendered to that 'un," the desk sergeant confided to Catherine the week before.

She sat alone in the same small room where she had questioned Ally Parfit, a missing persons report in her one hand, and a distinctive child's hair bow in another. According to Mallick, the police had no suspicion of foul play, only that the child, Ellie Smith, was an active and generally disobedient eleven year old of good family. She had wandered off the previous evening, in a huff over a meal, and might be at large anywhere in the borough. Nothing had come back from officers on the beat, or from the general public. The father had offered a reward.

The report described her as well-dressed in a new cotton smock, long of limb, and with short curly brown hair. The red velvet bow, far larger than was considered stylish, was included with the file as being identical to the one the girl was wearing when she disappeared, and had been shown to each constable as he went out on his rounds.

This time the images came easily, free of violent taint or the horror that had once attended many of her visions. A lonely place seen through blurry eyes, but a skyline which Catherine knew, not far from the Walworth Road coal depot. It could not be mistaken, for the factory chimney there was in perilous condition and had a number of bricks missing near the top.

They found Ellie Smith exactly where Madame Rostov said, not abducted but a victim only of venturing into unsafe territories. Even now the authorities were preparing to harry the owners of the old factory, demanding that they seal the premises against further accidental intrusions. A fractured arm for Ellie, after her fall, and tears of relief for her parents.

The matter was concluded smoothly the same day. Granted, her involvement would not reach the newspapers—Superintendent Neylan would have none of that—but she held Inspector Mallicks's most recent speech close to her breast. "A tidy enough job," he'd said with a double twitch of the eyelid. "We'll no doubt see you again." None of the usual scepticism.

Eden Mallick was not an imaginative man, which made her success all the more satisfying. He was methodical, and she could work with that, as long as she only went along with him when she was sure she had a genuine insight. There was no point in treating him as she did her usual clients, playing on their need or their gullibility.

There was, though, a slightly unpleasant taste to the incident when she thought it over. The Smiths, respectable and vocal, were such that the police bothered mightily with their concerns when their daughter went missing. Catherine had no doubt that other children met death by accident every week, sought by few and mourned by even fewer. Were Benjamin or Maisie to wander off, she doubted the police would even note it, unless there was a general outcry from Spitalfields.

But this success was currency of another sort for her, to be used in her sittings. Hints as to her status.

"I do, occasionally, assist the constabulary," she would say, and make it sound as if she did so at her own discretion, not only when she managed to get the police to take her seriously.

All in all, she should have been elated, but what was it that still held her in its grip, this cloud of doubt? She never made any declaration that the Future was open to her, not even at her most extravagant sessions. Madame Rostov was no Nostradamus, to be able to predict such things; she had no more known what was coming for her than she knew the results of next week's races. That last would have been a welcome gift.

Late in the month she undertook a lengthy morning sitting in Bermondsey, which went adequately, but provided only seventeen shillings. More disturbing, the hansom took her there by Blue Anchor Lane, where a canning factory sat in gloom. Not so far from here to Deptford, the face of the factory said to her. Not so far to the world of the late, unlamented Frederick Caille.

Business concluded, she saw no sign of a cabman, and thought she might go to the Old Kent Road, where there would be hansoms in number. Her early life around Fell Lane and the poorer parts of Keighley had left her with little fear of walking alone—she knew how to run, how to kick, and how to place a boot between a man's legs, where his pride was easily bruised.

The streets were crowded, and tiresome. Bermondsey was not an area she knew well; better to be back in Southwark proper and on territory she understood, for all its failings.

"My apologies," she said absently as she bumped into a woman on the pavement in front of her. The woman turned, and Catherine recoiled. That face…

"Do you support us, ma'am?"

The words were slurred, issuing from lips dragged to one side by a swollen lower jaw, the tissue grey and unhealthy.

"What?"

"The strike, ma'am."

Catherine steadied herself, seeing that the stranger was a girl, really, no more than sixteen or seventeen. Above the disfigurement, the eyes were brown and gentle.

"Lil has phossy-jaw," said another, older woman in a heavy shawl, coming up at her side. "On account of what they do make us work with."

"Phossy-jaw?" Catherine tried to look at the girl, Lil, without showing her feelings. There had been something…"Oh, phosphorus."

"That's right."

She had seen the news. The match-girls' strike.

"This is what it does, the damned stuff," said the older woman.

"I'm so sorry." Catherine reached for her purse, but the woman stayed her arm.

"It ain't brass we ask for, but that you do talk of us, and tell others. We only ask fair pay and fair conditions. Bryant and May, they do profit as we suffer."

Catherine took a smudged leaflet from the younger one, stammering agreement that she would indeed spread the word. The girl's face disturbed her more than she expected, and she found herself rushing away without decorum, possessed by guilt and horror in equal measure.

Her second sitting of the day, near Blackfriars, went badly, perhaps as a result of her disturbed mood. Whatever talent or gift she possessed was elusive, silent. Mrs Ledworth was a demanding client, who would only sit between four and five pm, would not suffer others to be present, and cavilled at minor discrepancies. Catherine had paid the woman's daily to pass on snippets of information, but the daily was often drunk by the time she disclosed anything, and was unreliable.

Worse, Catherine kept imagining Mrs Ledworth, who was pale and patrician, with the sort of terrible affliction that affected the match-girl, Lil. In the gloom of the Ledworth's parlour, her mind took a grip on that cold, flawless face and distorted it, causing the lower jaw to crumble and bulge, the lips to part with discoloured spittle…

"Madame Rostov? I think I pay handsomely for your attention, do I not?"

Catherine blinked. The woman was fool enough to talk of pay, as if Madame Rostov were a tradeswoman, to be bought. That was how the fraudulent were taken, charging for nonsense.

"It is a troubled time, Mrs Ledworth," she said. "The Aether swirls, shifts. Do you think we can order such things?"

Her client was clearly dissatisfied, fussing at the lace around her shoulders.

"There are others mediums who might be more suited to my

needs, of course—"

"There are." Catherine straightened in her chair, let her wild black hair frame a direct stare at the other woman. She knew it could be effective. "But they are not Rostov."

Mrs Ledworth hesitated.

"If—"

"I have recently been with the police, a matter of a doomed girl, foully treated, whose soul was almost lost…"

Catherine extemporised a tale of tragedy, of black deeds, embellishing Ellie's Smith's accident in the disused factory into a story of such villainy that Mrs Ledworth was captivated. Hints were given that the matter would not be widely reported because of the girl's connections. Ellie's parents were transformed from prosperous drapers to some echelon of high society, and the play was complete.

Mrs Ledworth was duly impressed, and insisted on providing a donation for the session after all. Catherine had no doubt that a further distortion of what she had said would soon be winging its way around the Ledworth's social circle. She left with relief, and this time she did take a cab, all the way back to Mrs Bessovitch's.

Her landlady was solicitous, seeing the weariness in Catherine's eyes.

"Come, I bring steak and dumplings, is good for young woman," she said, ushering her into the kitchen. "You sit."

"I ought to rest—"

"Rest after," said Mrs Bessovitch. "You are big girl, you need feeding."

Catherine smiled. Her landlady was a little shorter than her and twice the weight. It was said she once laid out a truculent boarder with one blow of her fist.

They ate together, and talked of their day. Only to Mrs Bessovitch did Catherine tell the truth of her activities, or admit how mercurial was her link to the psychic world, augmented of necessity by a keen eye and a lot of gossip.

"This is why you do not sit for me." The old woman smiled. "There is no gossip of Gilda Bessovitch—no one would dare."

"Very true." The steak was tender, a cheap cut but simmered for hours, with great floury dumplings, heavily-peppered, floating in the broth. She cleaned her bowl.

"I will sleep, for a while, I think."

"No crazy widows tonight, heh?"

Catherine gave her a look of reproof. "Or grieving parents, distraught sisters."

"I know, I know. Some of them is sad, true. Go rest."

The bed had been made, the room tidied. Mrs Bessovitch, whilst the best of landladies, had an inquiring mind, and Catherine was careful to keep any private papers well out of sight.

She unlaced her boots and lay on the bed, wanting only a dreamless rest. Instead, there came what might have been more use at the Ledworth's—a murmuration of voices, the disorganised fringe of other places. Tired and vulnerable, she pushed away the whispering, but found that the face of the young match-girl haunted her still.

Catherine jerked in half-sleep. There had been a smell, too, on the girl's breath—disease, the rotting of the flesh…

He raises his head, draws in the air, and knows his surroundings. A flash-house on the corner, ripe with drunks and counterfeiters; an abattoir close by, dogs fighting in the gutter over discarded innards. There is a pig-yard a quarter mile beyond, where beasts are brought for a final week of fattening; his fine nose is not needed to detect that. He stands on the edge of Bermondsey, and a walk which will consume half of the evening. Mr Dry does not take undue exertions, but his is a demanding trade. The walk will stretch sinews and strengthen muscles, prepare him for a commission later in the week.

He is, in general, satisfied. Many things are known to him, from many sources, and like the modest clerk which he appears to be, he files each fact according to its value. The Member of Parliament for a certain borough has a mistress, and his visits to her leave him open, away from his friends and servants. The director of Kimmet's Light Engineering is beholden to a money-lender who grows ever more demanding, and there may be work to be done.…

And on the streets, ah, it's there the plague is spread, through the veins and arteries of the city, carried by Judies and dippers, fine dandies and stiff-collared baronets. Distrust, greed, and betrayal. All are carriers, and all may have need of him.

If they can meet his price.

By the abattoir, one dog triumphs, dragging ruined meat into the shadows; the other, thwarted, sniffs and scuffles at a gate in the alley.

At leisure, and not immune to curiosity, Dry goes over. The value of knowledge, in even the smallest things, should not be discounted. He may need to pass this way again, one day.

He leans down and touches the hound's back, gently. It looks to him, whines, and slinks away. If he had a morsel on him, he would be generous. The dog, as a species, is not given to such vice as humans hoard.

The gate is fixed by a latch which yields easily. There is a whiff of putrefaction in the alley, not strong but enough for hounds and Mr Dry.

The yard beyond, no more than four strides across, contains stacks of staved-in barrels. They once held vinegar, he suspects, but have been abandoned for years. They are not the source of what he can smell. He slips between the barrels, towards the rough brickwork of the far wall.

The body is that of a pig, one of moderate size. A sow. It lies with its back against the wall, not quite prone. There is no blood. The throat has been slashed, the result of several assaults with a long blade, with only one cut deep enough to reach the vertebrae.

Dry examines these, reconstructing each blow. From the left and from the right. Violent, but inefficient. One accurate cut would have sufficed. No experienced slaughterman would waste his energy so.

Lower down the pig's body, there are mutilations. The abdomen has been opened, and some of the internal organs are visible.

He stands in thought for a moment, and then leaves, securing the gate again.

Someone has been playing. But to what ultimate purpose?

FORTY-SEVEN

In late July, 1888, Barnett lost his fish porter's license at Billingsgate Market. He'd been stealing fish for Mary Jane to cook at their lodgings.

"Don't worry," he said, "I'll look for work."

She gave fifteen pounds of her savings to Barnett to help with household expenses. He looked at her with surprise. "You finally found work?"

"No," she said, "'tis from my time soliciting. I haven't been able to find anything that pays nearly as well. That should see us through for a time, but I could always return to—"

"No," he said quickly, "I don't want that."

Barnett seemed to have accepted her explanation for the source of the funds. Thankfully, he didn't ask if Mary Jane had any more.

She would not return to earning until money became tight.

Continuing to follow Gabby, Mary Jane looked for opportunities for revenge. She had a notion to push her in front of a moving vehicle or throw her from a height. She tried to think of ways to destroy the woman's reputation and possibly sabotage her efforts with the Gully Bleeders so they might turn on her. Nothing she imagined seemed remotely possible for her to pull off. The more times she pictured the woman's demise, the more sympathy she seemed to gain for the horrible creature. She remembered that Gabby had once taken a beating meant for Mary Jane. Her heart wanted the woman to suffer, but her conscience told her that intentionally harming others was wrong and would scar her own spirit.

Frustrated, she watched Gabby climb into a cab, an old-fashioned cabriolet, and ride off down Whitechapel Road.

"You have lost your quarry," came a voice from beside her.

She looked at the man, took a step back away from him.

How does he know?

Though his presence seemed nonthreatening, she felt uneasy. Mary Jane wanted to think of him as a gentleman. His voice, his bearing, his fine dark grey suit, black shoes, and black felt hat, all suggested a proper gent, yet something about him forbid such a term. She found herself unwilling to look him squarely in the eyes.

Feigning confusion, she said, "Sir?"

"I have certain requirements," he said.

"Of what do we speak, sir?"

A woman walking past accidentally bumped against Mary Jane's shoulder. She moved toward the nearest building, a tobacconist's shop, to get out of the busy walkway.

Unfortunately, the man followed. "You appear to be familiar with the streets. Am I correct?"

A policeman, a private investigator? Mary Jane wondered.

Somehow, she didn't think he was the one she'd seen following her on and off throughout the summer.

Perhaps he was a potential client who saw through her disguise, recognising her as a ladybird.

"What gives you that impression?" she asked.

"Not what you'd think."

Not a potential client—good! Something about him did not sit right.

Mary Jane said cautiously, "I know something of the goings-on hereabouts. What are you looking for?"

"Anything out of the ordinary," he said. "Things that don't sit well with you."

Like you? she wondered.

His eyes narrowed slightly, and she had the oddest notion he'd heard her thought.

"What tells you I know about such things?"

"What I see, or think, are none of your concern. I require a sense of changes, disturbances—the gutter-talk, the huddled conversations. Rumour."

With the coldness of his tone, Mary Jane felt threatened. Sensing that he was indeed a dangerous man, she had an impulse to run, yet knew better than to show her fear. She pushed the feeling down and leveled her gaze at the man's black eyes. They were not black after all, merely gave that impression. They appeared a light blue or grey.

"Are you a policeman?"

He didn't answer.

"You need a blower?"

"I need an informant, yes."

Did he have something to do with Brevard? Her heartbeat quickened, and she struggled to conceal her fear again. "Do you work for someone?"

"If you do not want coin for such services, there are others who no doubt shall, such as the woman you follow." He turned away and began walking in the direction Gabriella Gorse had taken.

No, he might tell Gabby I follow her.

"Please," Mary Jane said. "I mean only to know something of the terms of our communication."

He stopped and turned back. "Communication is my business. I will find you when I need to. On each encounter, I will provide a guinea, assuming you provide, in return, such snippets as interest me. Do you have anything for me now? You speak to me as you might to a priest. Consider me a servant of God."

He gave a faint, cold smile, the first time his features had given anything away. Mary Jane knew that he was not a servant of God and that he had contempt for such ideas.

She thought of what she knew about Jennie's death, and decided that might be worth a guinea. "The woman attacked on Osborn Street on April 3, and died two days later, she wasn't Emma Elizabeth Smith as reported. She were Miss Jennifer Weatherhead."

The man held out his hand. She extended one of her own, dismayed to see it shaking. He dropped a coin into her hand. The golden relief of the Queen's likeness flashed briefly at her. Excited to see a gold sovereign, an 1888 Victoria Jubilee minting no less, Mary Jane slipped the coin into a concealed pocket of her bodice.

The man turned and seemed to instantly disappear among the foot traffic.

She didn't know what to make of the encounter, but knew with a dread certainty that she'd see the man again. Unexpectedly.

～❦～

Mary Jane sat in the Ringers pub, having a glass of bitter with ladybirds, Madeline Grissette, and Merrilee Sweeney. A tatterdemalion woman, possibly sixty years of age, approached them.

"May I sit?" she asked. "I am Mrs Glory Sagebart." A bit mushy, her words came so quietly that Mary Jane barely heard them over the hubbub of conversations among the patrons of the busy pub. "Mrs Maria Harvey said I'd do well to talk to you, should I want to take up soliciting."

Mary Jane didn't like the uncharitable look of scorn Merrilee gave Mrs Sagebart.

The publican, Mrs Matilda Ringer, appeared. "You are not in a condition to be in here," she said to Glory. "You must leave."

Mary Jane gave Matilda a look.

"She reeks," The publican said flatly.

Glory kept her head down. The weary, hungry look about her suggested she didn't eat well. With the way her lined face collapsed when she shut her mouth, her lips folding inward to create a thin seam, she probably had few teeth, limiting what she might eat. She wore several layers of clothing; a couple of chemises beneath a ragged wool jacket, three skirts, two thin cotton bonnets, one inside the other, both rotting from exposure to hair oil, and brown boots split at the toes between the uppers and the soles so that her darned black wool socks peaked out.

Mary Jane had spent her money freely on herself and others in the Ringers lately. "Do you want *me* to leave?" she asked Matilda.

The publican hesitated, then shook her head and went back to the taps.

"Of course you may sit with us," Mary Jane said. She pushed the chair beside her out and the raggedy woman sat.

The Maria Harvey of whom Glory spoke, a woman of about forty-five years of age with dark hair and brown eyes, had left her eight children with her brother in Shoreditch and come into Spitalfields to earn through soliciting.

"Foolishly, I thought the police could make my husband stop beating me," Maria told Mary Jane the day they met. "Instead they sent him to prison. His wages gone, we have nothing. Should I miss those beatings?"

Mary Jane had spent a little money helping the woman because she saw something of Jennie in her. She justified her charity in part with the notion that she currently had extra funds that came from little effort. Twice in two weeks, she'd seen the odd man who asked her to be his informant. She'd given him information about the streets on both occasions, earning a gold sovereign each time. She thought of him as the black-eyed man. Mary Jane did not tell Barnett about the income because she truly didn't know what to say about her new client, and she wanted control of the funds for her own purposes.

She would contribute more to the household as the need arose.

The experience of losing Jennie also drove Mary Jane to persuade Mrs Harvey not to take up soliciting. She had allowed Maria to sleep in the room in Miller's Court while Barnett worked at the market. Then, after he'd lost his fish porter license, Mary Jane had shared her bed with the woman on the nights when Barnett was away looking for work in other districts. She had felt good about helping Maria.

Casting the need for justification aside, Mary Jane had then helped Julia Venteney, another middle-aged woman who had recently considered soliciting. Julia was rawboned and freckled all over, had pale eyes and greying ginger hair. With Mary Jane's help, providing funds for meals and occasionally paying their doss at Cooley's Lodging House, both Maria and Julia had been able to find work at White's Laundry. The work was daily, and irregular because they weren't always needed. Nights, they repaired damaged clothing for the laundry, sewing buttons back on and stitching torn seams.

If Miss Harvey had told Glory Sagebart to talk to Mary Jane about soliciting, that no doubt meant that Maria didn't want the older woman to become a prostitute.

In such poor condition, Glory could not earn the going rate of a casual: Four pence. Her aspirations of earning as a prostitute were hopeless. Mary Jane hoped to persuade the woman of that.

"May I get you a cup of soup?" she asked. "They have a lovely fish and potato."

Glory's eyes brightened. "Yes, thank you." Saliva drooled down her chin. She wiped the spittle away with her hand.

Mary Jane signalled to a barmaid, who came and took the order. "Can you write?"

"Yes," Glory said. "I taught at Saint Mary Magdalen National School."

"Oh, my," Mary Jane said, surprised. "How did you—" She had intended to ask how the woman ended up in such a state, but stopped herself.

"My husband, Roderick, gambled," Glory said, seemingly unashamed, "had a large debt, and decided to remedy that with a robbery. Something went wrong. A policeman caught him in the act. Roderick struck him in the head and accidentally killed him. He was among the last to get *the boat.* "

"The boat?" Mary Jane asked.

"Transportation to a penal colony in Australia," Merrilee said.

"Twenty-one years ago, that was," Glory said. "I lived with family until they could no longer help."

So many ways women end up on the streets, Mary Jane thought.

She remembered what the black-eyed man had asked for: "I require a sense of changes, disturbances—the gutter-talk, the huddled conversations. Rumour." He'd also said, "Anything that doesn't sit well with you," and had been interested in her revelation that Emma Elizabeth Smith was Jennie Weatherhead. If he were somehow involved in law enforcement and could do something about the bad apples among the Ladybirds' clientele, assembling a list of such would be helpful.

"Do you think you could help me begin a record," Mary Jane asked.

"I could if I had pen and paper." Glory said. "I used Pitman shorthand as a secretary for a time. Really quite fast."

"I'll get those for you."

The next time Mary Jane saw the black-eyed man, she had just exited the Whitechapel Public Baths. He wore spectacles that looked at if the glass were coated with a thin layer of lamp black. In the warm summer air, with the disturbing man approaching along the hot granite footway at midday, she began to sweat in her fresh clothes.

My feeling of being clean were too brief.

Even so, she eagerly handed over what she'd prepared for him. Without a word of greeting, he briefly looked at the pages she'd offered, then gave her a gold sovereign. For his payment, he'd received a list of violent ladybird clients Mary Jane had put together with Glory Sagebart's help. With utmost secrecy, and assuring confidentiality, they had interviewed as many of the ladybirds of Spitalfields as they could find, and recorded what names and description the women could remember. Mary Jane had made certain that Stuart Brevard's name was at the top of the list.

In return for the woman's help, Mary Jane had paid Glory's doss at a common lodging and kept her fed for the week.

Rubbing the gold sovereign between her fingers, Mary Jane

wondered if the black-eyed man might help her in some other way. "And should I need more than the coin?" she asked.

"Then you should find a more remunerative trade," he said while glancing at the pages.

Undiscouraged, Mary Jane pressed on. "I might need a bit of muscle instead."

She tried to look him in the eyes, though that made her uncomfortable. He remained busy, his eyes scanning Glory's fine script.

"*Please,*" she said.

Her last word had no evident effect.

He seemed to think nothing of her concerns. If her interests did not promote his, he would probably not consider them.

"I shall gladly help without coin," she said, "should you consider payment of another sort."

"What would that be, this other currency?" he asked, still considering the pages.

"Doing something about the woman you saw me follow."

Finally he looked up. "I am not unreasonable." He held up the pages she'd given him. "More of this. I want a greater part of the East End."

"Yes," Mary Jane said, "I can do that."

He turned around and walked away.

I shall take Glory with me to Stepney.

They would go to Dresser's coffee shop and interview the women there. Mary Jane would dress conservatively, a disguise of sorts to throw off Brevard, should he still be rooting around those parts for her. If that went well, they could work on interviews in other parts of the East End.

Something about the black-eyed man's manner suggested he didn't value the lives of others. From his reaction to Mary Jane's words, he did not seem opposed to doing something about Gabriella Gorse, yet he had not truly said as much.

Nonetheless, Mary Jane's fancy had him harming and even killing Gabby.

Then it occurred to her that she might also employ him to kill Stuart Brevard…and Nick Shears, as well.

FORTY-EIGHT

So Dry had truly returned.

Not in passing images, which she could for the most part dismiss, but with the same stark immediacy as at Deptford, and there was a clarity to the experience which once again was close to pain. Catherine could almost smell what he smelled, feel the movement of each individual finger. His thoughts were ice, even though she barely skimmed them. Not evil, as she understood it, but ice—cold and crystalline in their reflection of the world around him.

The image of the mutilated pig haunted her.

Edwin Dry haunted her.

She cried off the few bookings she had arranged for early August, staying close to her lodgings. Somehow it was no surprise when on the August 8, she read of a brutal slaying across the river.

The late editions of the newspapers dwelled on Martha Tabram's position as a prostitute and a drinker; they dwelled on the terrible nature of her injuries. The woman had been discovered at five in the morning on the stairs of a tenement building in Spitalfields. Numerous stab wounds had brought her life to an end at the age of forty. Surely not his work? Catherine could not believe that Dry would have used such violent excess—unless…

She put down the paper, and held firm to the kitchen table, steadying herself.

Robert Louis Stevenson. The first novel Charlotte Chambers had persuaded her to read, so long ago. Was it possible for the bowler-hatted man to be two killers in one—the careful, precise assassin, and the maniac, letting loose his frustrations? A dark Jekyll; an even darker Hyde, emerging when the ice cracked.

No, it was too much to entertain. For all that Catherine knew, Tabram was the victim of in-fighting between prostitutes, a chance robbery which ended in violence, anything. A meeting with a client gone wrong—common enough from what she read. The squalor of the streets and those who must live on them. Doctor Mercier had said after one séance that there were many in his asylum he thought safer company than those who roamed free. She would say a prayer for Jennie that night.

Mrs Bessovitch bustled into the kitchen, headed for the kettle.

She noticed the paper.

"Everyone talks. Was Southwark girl, her."

"Martha Tabram?"

"Da. She drink much, move to Whitechapel. Commercial Road, last I hear."

Catherine took the tea things from the shelves behind her, cradling Mrs B's old gilt-painted teapot in her hands.

"A dreadful end."

"Is over. That is what 'end' means. She will have peace."

A spoonful each and one for the pot. Decent tea, not dust and shavings. The Southwark police had paid for it, which gave it extra savour.

"Was your land in north so different?" Mrs Bessovtich sniffed the milk.

"Less people, less murder. Otherwise, I suppose not. Keighley has its slums and degradation—in part of Leeds and Bradford, only the doughtiest constable walks his beat alone."

"I was in Kiev once."

Catherine wasn't sure where Kiev was. Part of the Russian Empire, certainly.

"And conditions were bad there?"

"Maybe. But I was young girl. We go to grand affair—many rich merchants, fine house with many rooms. Do you know what happen?"

"No. I hardly could."

"True. Well, we have good time, enjoy ourselves. Then we go back to small hotel. Next day, is news. Fine house was too near new railway cutting. Rain, heavy rain, in night, and back of house slide into big hole. Many rich merchants now dead in ruin."

She squeezed half a lemon into her lodger's cup.

It was, once more, one of Mrs B's strange parables.

"I suppose you mean to say that no matter how lucky you may seem, how rich you are, the end can come without warning? We are all mortal."

The landlady raised her eyebrows. "Nyet. I say, do not go to Kiev. They are not good builders."

~⚜~

That evening Catherine retired early, ostensibly to read something that Lottie had lent her. It appeared to be a book of children's stories by a man called Wilde, former editor of *The Woman's World* magazine. As the titles included happy princes and nightingales, she put it to one side. There were no princes, happy or otherwise, in the Spitalfields tenements where Martha Tabram was found. She closed her eyes, breathing in the musty but not unpleasant scent of the bedding and the old clothes in the wardrobe, listening to the late omnibuses passing outside…

As she drifted, Dry touched her mind—the brush of a crow's wing and the first snow, then the uncomfortable opening of a vista, something scratching at her nerves. He did not know of their connection, she was sure of that by now.

So where was he?

Chimney stacks and roof-peaks; high attics and a cross upon one peak. He knows the building, though he doubts the value of purpose. That rich and poor might live in Christian harmony—which is to say, that the rich tolerate the poor and the poor do not rise up. He rarely entertains politics—it is not his trade.

Commercial Street and George Yard. That is where she was taken, in George Yard Buildings. He has the pocketbook of a sergeant who attended, and the whispers of journalists from all around. He has word from the street.

This is the first.

Or the second practice run, if that is a more appropriate term. Too many blows, too little sense or purpose. That may be refined, as the killer progresses on his path.

Dry cannot name him, describe him, or predict exactly what will happen as a result of this deed. But there will be others. It has started with a sow and then a street woman, a prostitute. The sex of the victim is important. The next one taken will also be a woman, and the work done will be animalistic, brutal.

Unnecessary.

The journeyman is economical in his work, at one with his tools, and respectful of his materials. The unnecessary should never occur.

More, Dry senses that there is emotion at play. Lust or anger, much the same. This man is gratified not by the precision of ending a life for a genuine purpose, but by the protracted act, the involvement. He kills like the sullen, angry boy, who kicks a dead beast long after life has gone.

It is distasteful.

Those who take pleasure in such things—they are not journeymen. They are amateurs and lunatics. They besmirch his careful trade.

And this is only the first.

He will need more information, if he is to understand what is to come.

Catherine gasped, knocked over the water carafe with a flailing arm. Half-conscious, she became tangled in the linen and she panicked, forgetting where she lay. She was unable to escape a tiny attic, unable to unsee dear Uncle Jack, alcoholic malice on his red face as he strangled his wife...

No, she was in Southwark, not in Keighley. She lay there for a moment, her heart pounding.

The double image had given her a glimmer of understanding. That had been the moment, had it not?

She took a half bottle of brandy from the back of the wardrobe and sat on the bed, letting a hot mouthful burn her throat.

What she had seen, what she had sensed that night in Fell Lane when she was fourteen—brutal murder, only yards away from where she slept—had been the start. The first real wound in a young girl's mind. Otherwise she might have gone through life receiving flashes of nonsense and dismissing them.

Perhaps it would have healed and been forgotten, but the repetition of circumstances at the Islington séance had stripped her of the possibility. It had allowed a quite different killer into her head, one who unlike Jack Witten had murder as his trade.

She was a psychic, yes, but one who knew nothing of departed souls or ethereal spirits. The dead were gone, as far as she could tell, leaving a maelstrom of impressions in other people's minds. She knew Miss Bournelle's late aunt because she could sense—on occasion— what Miss Bournelle and others had retained, the memories and impressions.

That talent, however unusual, might have served and caused little distress, but it was not alone inside her.

Her real knowledge was not of the dead, but of that which made them so.

The violence of the living.

She had a weakness, a wound inside her. If at times she could twist her abilities enough to be of use, such as with Mrs Ameley's drowned husband, or the missing child, it was a matter of luck and circumstance. A small consolation for the greater burden.

Catherine Weatherhead was damaged.

She plucked up the courage to write to Charles Mercier. She had questions of a spiritual and possibly medical nature, she wrote, and she hoped he would oblige.

Dr Mercier replied to her letter immediately, saying that he would be most pleased to meet with Madame Rostov. Not far from Flower House private asylum were tea-rooms which he described as "popular with the quality"—she was welcome to join him there an hour after noon on the seventeenth.

There was no direct train, but by changing twice, she made Catford well in time, and found the Prince Albert Tea-rooms, which occupied the ground-floor of a Gothic building which must once have been a school or workhouse.

A tall, prim-looking woman intercepted her in the doorway, and asked what "Madame's preference might be." Unwelcoming eyes had noted Catherine's worn furs and dress.

"I am at this establishment," said Catherine, with a more extravagant touch of the mock-Russian than usual, "To meet with my colleague, Doctor Charles Mercier."

The prim woman had lost the high ground, even more so when Mercier himself rose two tables away and tipped his head to her.

"Madame Rostov! How charming that you could attend."

This display brought two maids at once to take their order.

"The manageress is a talented snob," murmured the doctor. "Remain in 'court' fashion, and you'll have her begging you to patronise the Prince Albert again."

Initial conversation was easy. They talked of Mrs Bless's touring performances, and shared their mutual doubts about the woman. Mercier was tolerant and good-humoured as ever. He brushed his fair hair back with his hand on a regular basis, trying to tame it, and kept one eye on the other customers.

"I have a curiosity about people," he admitted when she pointed this out. "You still have my full attention, Madame."

"The cake here is over-iced, and over-sweet."

"It is."

They both laughed.

"You had matters you wished to discuss, though. I do not believe they involved patisserie."

He rested his bearded chin on his hands, the picture of an attentive doctor.

She spoke of a client she had encountered, and the client's concerns. Of visions which this invented figure had. The woman, said Catherine, was distraught, unsure as to her next steps.

Mercier listened, nodded, listened again.

"Are we talking of the 'departed,' intruding upon her thoughts? Of the souls of the dead?" he interrupted at one point.

"No." Catherine.

"Good, good."

What did he, as a psychologist, an alienist, think of someone who had visions which appeared to show actual events, violent ones—not predictions, but genuine occurrences, as they happened or perhaps a short time later? Yet the individual was not there, could not know of these matters. Was this a mental disorder she was describing?

"Not necessarily." He looked more serious. "I understand—I believe I understand—your predicament. You say that you yourself do not belief this lady to be partaking of matters 'beyond the Veil?'"

"Dr Mercier, I will try to be honest, and say that which I would not say at a sitting. Nor must it leave these rooms, I beg you. You see, I have no great conviction that there is life, conscious existence, after death."

"Aha!" he clapped his hands together, drawing looks from others in the tea-rooms. "I knew that you were cut from different cloth, Madame Rostov. No tambourines, rickety tables or halting 'spirit guides' who cannot finish sentences. You are, then, a follower of thought transference, or as some now prefer, telepathy."

"If I am a follower of anything," she said, cautious. "I have read a little on the theme."

"At least it is a potential discipline, not a re-enactment of witchcraft and such mummery under a different name. It may be nonsense, of course, but no black cats or monkey skulls are required."

Catherine paused, working out how to take his comment. He seemed to mean no offence by it.

"We may differ on some points, doctor. But I have never had a cat."

"So, you wonder if your client is either a telepathist, or mentally unstable and confused. Such things can be explored through experimentation, but most experiments connected to so-called psychic phenomena are, well, phenomenally flawed." His smile faded. "I cannot, naturally, say much more without your client becoming mine. Barring misfortune, I suspect that will not happen.

"Let me propose that if it is not the transference of thought, then it pertains to my own studies of the interactions between mentality and physicality, between the mind and the mechanisms by which we feed it information."

She pushed her cup to one side, then back, trying to grasp what he said. She had read so much that at times it confused her. Bluff had grown far more informed over nearly two years, but she was unschooled in the formal talk of medical men.

"More simply?"

"Your client is receiving quite normal stimuli, but is not processing them well. Permit me a demonstration, Madame. Put your hand forward, on the table."

She did so. Mercier unclasped his tie-pin, and without great force, pressed the point of the pin into the back of her hand, enough to cause mild hurt. She felt pleased that she did not flinch.

"Where is the pain?" he asked.

"In my hand."

"No. Your hand does not understand pain, not a bit. The pain is in your mind, your brain. Your hand recognised intrusion and disruption of the dermal layer. It was telling you that you have been breached, and should be aware. Your mind, however, translated this and called it pain."

"Yes…I think I comprehend."

"I expected that you would, from what I know of you. And so, this client has encountered stimuli, akin to my pin. These stimuli may be a melange of visual and auditory ones, olfactory and tactile. She may not have noticed them consciously—take, for example, a murmur of words overheard on a train or glimpsed in another's newspaper for only a split-second. When they reach her brain, it does not know what to do with them. With the added confusion of memory, it seeks to form a narrative, much as a dream constructed of random images might appear coherent at the time."

She watched the ebb and flow of customers in the tea-rooms, the thousand interactions of each minute.

"You are suggesting that such visions are the mind's attempts to make sense of…to organise these things? Things we are learning without realising?"

"You should have been a student of psychology, madame. I would say Bravo, but I would not want to appear condescending."

"A medium must be a student of psychology, doctor."

"As must every salesman of snake oil." He smiled with genuine amusement, and she smiled back.

"I'm sure that is true."

They took more cake, and had the pot freshened.

"But I may not have helped, Madame Rostov. Our beliefs intersect, possibly, at points, but do not meet. Still, it has been fascinating to have an open debate for once. Alienists and neurologists can be as inflexible as spiritualists."

"You have given me much to ponder, doctor, for which I thank you."

Their meeting ended with lighter conversation and few comments on his work, after which he rose, and they shook hands.

"Flower House demands me."

"And I have clients of my own for which I must prepare—though I shall say nothing of stimuli or physicalities. Good day, doctor."

Catherine did not know what she thought on the journey back from Catford, and by the time she reached her lodgings, she was too tired to sort out the tangle of her mind.

She slept free of visions or nightmares for once, and was thankful.

FORTY-NINE

On Friday, August 17, Mary Jane took her last dose of laudanum. Over the past three months, she'd systematically weaned herself from the intoxicant with smaller and smaller doses, rigorously measured by droplet and taken at regular intervals. Feeling confident that she was free of the habit for good, she entertained thoughts of seeing Joseph Fleming, then decided that would be a terrible mistake.

Mary Jane's appetite, uncertain in recent days, had returned. About ten o'clock that morning, she sought something to eat at Spitalfields Market. Allowing her nose to lead her, avoiding the eyes of the hawkers and duffers, a chapmen, a badger and his plant, she made her way between the rows of vendors through the many browsing the market. The odour of cooking meat caught her. Within moments she found herself watching German sausages sizzling in a pan on a small stove.

As she stood considering a purchase from the old, grey woman preparing the food, the black-eyed man approached. Mary Jane quickly turned away from the food, thoughts of delivering the information, and all the emotion surrounding her dealings with the odd man, having replaced the drive of hunger.

The folded leaves of paper she had for him barely fit in a pocket beneath her top skirt. She extracted them and kept them folded small. Watching to make certain no one saw, and that the quickest of thieves, little nippers, were not nearby, she made the exchange. He received Glory's written record of information gathered in Spitalfields about the tragic Martha Tabram, a woman stabbed thirty-nine times ten days earlier, a quarter of a mile away in George Yard. Also included in the pages was the fifth list of dangerous clients the two women had assembled, and whatever additional information they had thought unusual or disturbing in their interviews. They had even included flights of fancy people had conveyed that might hold a grain of truth.

Without looking at the pages, he gave Mary Jane another gold sovereign. Perhaps he'd come to find her dependable.

Concerning Martha Tabram, no doubt most of the information he might have got for himself from the press or the police, had he tried. But the interviews the two women had conducted with the ladybirds of Spitalfields had turned up traces of the woman and her circumstances that the interviewees might not have willingly given up to those bodies.

With work at the laundry less regular, Maria and Julia had found time to help with the Spitalfields interviews, while Glory and Mary Jane had gone into several other neighbourhoods. Within a short time, they had secretly covered a large part of the East End in their quest for information. Then Julia landed work as a charwoman, and took up with a lumper named Harold Owen in Miller's Court. They occupied the room nearest the one where Mary Jane and Barnett lodged. With her new charring position, Julia couldn't help with the interviews as much, yet Mary Jane and her "girls," as she liked to call them, still did well because they had got better at the work.

Though his manner was difficult to fathom and he hadn't said a word, Mary Jane had the impression the black-eyed man got from her what he wanted. After they parted ways, she turned back to the sausages. They no longer looked tasty. None of the smells of the many foods available seemed appealing.

Dodging a patterer trying to sell some trifle to make embroidering easier, and a mountebank offering a bottle of what he called "liver cleaner," she made her way through the many browsers to exit the market at Commercial Street, and from there to the Ringers.

Mary Jane felt at home sitting in the pub with her girls. Within a short time, they had coffee and warm food in their bellies.

"Were quite a row between your Barnett and that man, Fleming," Maria Harvey said. "I wanted to slip out, but they blocked the doorway."

Maria had stayed the night in their room. Barnett didn't want her there. To make matters worse, Joseph Fleming knocked on the door in the early morning, rousing everyone from sleep.

"I need to talk to Mary Jane," he said.

"Mary Jane," Barnett said, shoving her aside and standing in the doorway. He looked Joseph up and down, must have seen the plaster on his clothing. "Are you Fleming?"

"Yes."

Barnett had turned surly on the few occasions she had spoken of Joseph, so she'd ceased to say anything about him.

"She wants nothing to do with you."

"She might speak for herself," Fleming said.

"Herself," Barnett said.

Mary Jane pushed past the two men on her way out to the privy.

Fleming tried to take her hand. Barnett grabbed his right arm. Fleming swung his left fist. Barnett ducked under it, caught Fleming's other arm, twisted the limb up behind his back, and escorted him through the passage to Dorset Street.

As angry as he'd been about losing his job, Mary Jane thought Barnett showed restraint not striking Fleming while he had the advantage. Instead, he shoved him away, said, "Don't come back. I've a knife what's gutted better fish than you."

After the privy, Mary Jane returned to the room, discovered that Maria had left.

Barnett said, "I don't like sharing the bed. 'Tis small enough you don't keep putting bunters in it."

"You mustn't talk about my friend that way," she said. "She hasn't been soliciting for over a month now."

"Now," he had grumbled, but added nothing else.

"Barnett said Fleming were cruel," Maria said, "that he'd been in the habit of hitting you."

"Told me that too," Julia said.

Why Barnett had lied, Mary Jane didn't know. *Probably to turn them against Fleming, should he show up again.* She wasn't interested in defending Joseph and kept silent.

Thomas Morganstone approached their table. Mary Jane's surprise and delight left her speechless. He had dressed down for the coarser neighbourhood. His checked black and red wool coat with holes at the elbows and his bent brown felt hat reminded her of the times when, as a young man in Carmarthen, he'd worn old clothing to visit the worksites where he learned about construction. With his handsome, clean-shaven face and the curling locks that fell from beneath his hat, Mary Jane again knew her girlish crush on him had not gone away.

She finally found her voice, and introduced Thomas to Maria Harvey, Julia Venteney, and Glory Sagebart. "Please sit," she said. "How did you find me?"

"That's not for me to say," he said. "Indeed, I ought to speak with you privately."

The other woman excused themselves quickly, got up, and left the table, taking their coffee cups with them.

Thomas looked surprised. "They didn't—" he began.

"They left us for me," she said, "not for you. We are in the habit of seeking privacy in certain communications. They're following a discipline we've imposed upon ourselves."

"Perhaps the need has something to do with what I've come to say. I hope I'm not too late. I let the matter go too long."

"How mysterious," Mary Jane said. "Too late for what?"

Thomas craned his neck, looking around the Ringers. A Friday afternoon, the place had few seats not taken and many people standing, drinks in hand, milling about and talking, the ten-day-old news of the Martha Tabram murder still the most discussed topic. Mary Jane had arrived early enough to take a corner table. Tobacco smoke hung in the air like fog, and the murmur of many voices created sufficient confusion of sound that conversations remained intimate with little effort.

Matilda Ringer approached the table. "Good afternoon, sir," she said, taking a good look at Thomas. She nodded her approval to Mary Jane. Apparently the publican could see through his disguise. Mrs Ringer didn't seem to like the company Mary Jane kept lately; older women with no money. Not that the matter was any of Matilda's business. She stepped to the wall and yanked a bell-pull. A barmaid perked up and headed toward the table as Mrs Ringer went back to the taps.

"What'll you have?" the barmaid asked.

"Your inkiest porter, Thomas said.

"More coffee," Mary Jane said.

The barmaid nodded and went away.

"I'm afraid I may have got you mixed up in something dangerous with that Deptford job," Thomas said.

"More than just the murder?" Mary Jane asked. She laughed to give him the impression that she wasn't concerned, that she didn't blame him for her exposure to risk. She had given that role to Joseph Fleming, however unfairly.

Thomas had a troubled look. "Should the situation have ended with that, and we heard no more, no. The one who hired me to map the victualing yard, and asked for the distraction that you and Joseph pulled off, he came to see me, and asked about you."

"Did you ask about the murder?"

"No!" Thomas said, his eyes briefly wide-open, "of course not."

"What did he want?"

"I'm not entirely certain. When I told him I didn't know anything about you, he went away."

"What is his name?"

The barmaid returned with a pint glass of porter and a pot of coffee. She placed the glass on the table, poured coffee into Mary Jane's cup, and left.

"I don't know that either." Thomas looked embarrassed. "I never did. Sometimes I get paid to do a task for people who never reveal anything about themselves." He shook his head. "I'm not proud of that sort of thing, and I hate to think you might be hurt because of it."

Mary Jane shook her head, denying the possibility that he might bring her harm. "What does this man look like?"

"That's difficult to say. He's a rather ordinary-looking fellow."

Mary Jane remembered Joseph Fleming telling her of a man talking to Thomas about the extra work at the victualing yard.

"He doesn't *look* dangerous," Thomas said.

"Yes, I remember Joseph saying he was an ordinary cove."

"That's right. I let that impression settle my fears when I knew I should not have done. To deal with him, though, one gets the impression that he *is* dangerous. I ought to have found you and told you about his query immediately. I've allowed a couple of months to pass. Finally, my conscience would not let me sleep until I located you."

Thomas had the most distressing look of shame.

Mary Jane reached across the table and clasped his hands. "You believe he is the one who killed the man, Caille, in Deptford," she said. "Am I right?"

"Yes."

Mary Jane shrugged. "No one has tried to harm me, but I suppose I ought to know who to look out for."

"Not much about him stands out. In truth, the feature of his that most comes to mind is one that seems to withdraw rather than stand out—his eyes seem…I'm not certain how to say it. They are rather—"

"Black?"

"*Yes,*" Thomas said with a look of surprise. "Have you seen him?"

He is the one who murdered Caille. The ordinary cove and the black-eyed man are one and the same!

Mary Jane held back her surprise. "Yes. The blackness is only an impression. He has blue eyes. When he's not looking you in the eye, he's just an ordinary cove."

Fear had returned to Thomas's expression.

"He's not a threat," Mary Jane said quickly, squeezing his hands. "I've spoken to him."

Thomas seemed to relax, and finally took some of his drink. "Hmm—that's good porter."

"She gave you the good stuff. Most of their mild drink is watered."

"You're right about his eyes," Thomas said. "Something of his character is reflected in his gaze and gives the impression. Somehow, he knew of your involvement at Deptford and wanted to know where he might find Fair Rose. I told him you had moved away and that I didn't know any more about you."

For some reason, Mary Jane didn't want to say much about her encounter with the black-eyed man, possibly because of her desire to have him harm Gabriella Gorse. "He offered me funds in exchange for information from the rumour mill. I don't think he's a danger to me."

"Well, that's a relief." Thomas, said. Then he became thoughtful for a moment. "Later that day, at a job site, I saw him talking with Joseph Fleming."

Mary Jane wanted to ask after Fleming, but didn't want him to find out about her interest. Although she'd wanted to learn something of his wellbeing when he came to her room that morning, she had done her best to ignore him for the same reason.

"In truth, I suppose that is what troubled me. The man had walked away once I'd said I knew nothing about you."

"What do you mean?"

Thomas had a sad smile. "Poor Fleming has gone to pieces since you left. I believe he truly loves you. Watching Joseph talk to the man, I saw a spark of hope in his eyes not seen for a long while.

I grew fearful that he'd somehow help this fellow find you. And perhaps he did."

"I have a feeling the man in question is resourceful. Joseph would do nothing to betray me."

"I quite agree, at least not intentionally. He's been queer lately, though, disappearing for days on end. I didn't want any of this to come as a surprise to you."

"Thank you for finding me. I'm happy to learn that someone is looking out for me."

"Joseph would too, should you let him."

Mary Jane merely smiled in response. She didn't want to explain herself.

"Would you allow me to take you for a fine meal?" Thomas asked.

"No, thank you. I've cast my lot with these women for now, and feel the need to stay close to them for a time."

"Well, come and visit when you can," Thomas said. "I miss you."

Mary Jane nodded.

He left the Ringers.

Anticipating the return of her girls, she drew the remainder of his porter, most of the glass, to her side of the table.

Though Julia, Maria, and Glory, helped her put together information for the ordinary cove, they knew nothing of the source of the money that Mary Jane spent on them. If she gave the funds to the women, Maria would drink rather than eat, and Julia's part would end up in Harry Owen's pocket. Thinking of her past need for laudanum, Mary Jane chose not to judge Maria. All three seemed to trust Mary Jane. She'd bought them new clothes and fed them. She had also provided them with shelter, including Julia before the woman had taken up with Owen. They had all expressed their gratitude, and seemed quite willing to follow her advice for keeping their efforts secret.

Mary Jane's intuition had been correct. The ordinary cove with the dark gaze most certainly was *not* a policeman, nor a private investigator.

Of all the millions of people in London, I was unwittingly involved in the black-eyed man's scheme to murder the man, Caille, the one Jennie believed responsible for the death of her brother. What a rum coincidence.

Jennie and Mrs Hollis thought the murder of Caille a good thing.

Did Mary Jane's gathering of information for him somehow serve the side of decency and good? Most likely not, but she wanted to think he could perform further good services for her.

Either the ordinary cove had something against Caille or someone had hired him to kill the man. Certainly, that had not been Jennie, although she might have done, if she'd had the price.

The black-eyed man had somehow known of my involvement in his scheme.

How?

And does he see me as a lose end, a possible threat should the police somehow place me at the scene of the crime and question me?

Again, she worried about the hatred of Sally Fourth.

Mary Jane told herself that if he considered her a threat, he might have got rid of her any time within the past couple of months.

She preferred to look to the future she hoped to see.

She had been saving back some of the funds received from the black-eyed man for the coming time when her payment from him might instead be retribution for Gabriella Gorse. Though she knew that in her conversations with the man she had never fully discussed the matter, somehow Mary Jane believed he had not forgot.

While she didn't like him, strangely, she did trust him in their business arrangement. He was dependable as clockwork, showing up lately on Mondays and Fridays. She gave him whatever information she had and he paid her.

Mary Jane intended to earn the ordinary cove's good will, if that were possible.

Once he's got enough from me, she told herself, *he will consider further what I want done to Gabriella Gorse—perhaps he'll help with Nick Shears and Stuart Brevard too.*

He *did* know what she wanted regarding Gorse. Of that, Mary Jane remained confident. She'd needed a killer, and found one, yet she couldn't seem to bring herself to speak directly to him about the matter. Perhaps that suited him.

FIFTY

Mercier must have known, Catherine was sure, that she was speaking of herself in the tea-rooms, speaking of Madame Rostov. And he had tried to assist her, to present an alienist's, or a neurologist's, explanation, one which would not alarm her.

That he was wholly wrong on certain key points brought clarity to her own thoughts. Not with Maggie Witten, nor with Philip Tether, the man outside the Crown and Sceptre, the priest...not with any of these could she possibly have gained the detail of information that had been in her visions. She had no disorder, no confusion of the senses or the way in which her brain organised the stimuli it received; she knew that she was not mad—she and Mrs Bessovitch had seen the newspaper columns which matched her visions so precisely. Her gift or affliction was real, and her mind was doing its best with what came to it.

Which was all she could ask. Damaged but sane.

Strangely cheered, she replaced a button on one of her boots. She bought blue paint, refreshing her night-stand with it, and read a fatuous adventure story borrowed from Lottie Chambers. As the month simmered around her, she went to the local park and listened to the brass bands. She even smiled at a strolling singer—a pretty lass with a freckled, up-tilted nose—who expressed her admiration of Catherine's raven hair.

She tried to be a young woman.

As a young woman with rent to pay, food to buy and undergarments which needed replacing, she returned to the dim parlours and expectant tables of the medium's world. A friend of Lottie's engaged her for an after-dinner entertainment, which netted her more than ten guineas. The guests were somewhat pompous and irritating, but the coin was true.

Police work raised its head occasionally. She failed to find an absconded and violent debtor for Eden Mallick, but did discover, through an accidental blur in the mind of a boot-black, the whereabouts of a hammer which had been used to club down a local tobacconist.

And in unguarded moments, she saw the Deptford Assassin as he prowled…

In Spitalfields there are few places, so very few places, where eyes do not look and ears do not listen. Even in abandoned courtyards and alleys which go nowhere, a window is open above, or a beggar lurks close by. He sifts fact from malice; truth from wishful thinking.

The woman before him—Mary Jane Kelly—picks at her lace sleeves and tries not to meet his gaze. She has already been more useful than most, and he remembers her from Deptford, though she never saw him that night. She knows what he did there, and what he is capable of. She has many encumbrances—fears, small enemies and desperation—but is bright enough. Prostitutes can be excellent listeners.

He takes the folded sheets of paper from her.

"On Friday, again, as usual?" she asks. She wants the money, but there is more than that. Dry wonders when she will speak of it openly— the matter is clear enough to him. She wants him to kill a rival of hers, a woman called Gorse, but she cannot yet bring herself to say it. He can wait.

Gorse, who also knows the streets, might have suited him, but he has observed her. She is duplicitous, and beholden to the worst of the local gangs. He has no doubt that she would try to play him. She would fail, of course, but he is not inclined to waste the time.

Mary Jane Kelly will do. That she fears his abilities and yet wants to employ them puts her firmly in his grasp.

His stock of information grows, and serves many purposes. Not all is accurate; not all is precise. Those who gather it do not know what it is he seeks—which is as it should be. As he has put word out among certain prostitutes and alley girls, so does he make quiet enquiry concerning the rough hands from Smithfield and the slaughterhouses.

He makes progress.

Catherine received not only fragments of Dry's search, but also other intrusions which confirmed the Deptford Assassin was still about his usual work. In mid-month she contracted an infection of the throat, which laid her up for a couple of days and carried with it a slight fever. Her room was thick with the smell of endless hearty soups brought up by Mrs Bessovitch, and the sharpness of the chamberpot. At the height of her croaking discomfort, she dreamed without sleep...

The history of Father Emmanuel Groves, and his "tendencies" is long and sordid. Mr Dry finds himself irritated by the protestations and weak rationalisations which the man makes as he realises his likely fate. On his knees, the priest has sudden remorse for dreadful acts. That such acts have been committed upon children does not help his case with Edwin Dry.

"I do not believe in the confessional," says Dry. "Neither does the mother of young John Berrowes. And so I have her coin in my pocket."

The priest dies quickly, the wire sufficient, and the commission is complete. He cleans the garrotte on a discarded surplice from the vestry, and wonders as he does so at the dirt around the groove it has left in the man's thick neck—do priests not wash?

He has time yet before dawn, time to spend in those narrow places which snake out from around the church—the alleys, lanes and cul-de-sacs littered with hopeless lives. He will walk a while. London, his city, is of a considerable size, and even he cannot be everywhere, but he needs the feel, the smell of the streets.

There will be another death soon.

Not by his hands, but by the one who still practices.

Following her recovery a day or so later, she searched through the newspapers, and found grim confirmation of what she had seen. A Fr Emmanuel Groves, of St Luke's Presbytery, Hoxton, had been discovered murdered in the vestry of his church, on the evening of August 27—a garrotte had been applied until death occurred. The Hoxton Courier of the following morning had much more on the subject.

'On apprehension of Mr Geo Clegg, the husband of the Presbytery cook, the constables in question were subject to a litany of astonishing accusations against the deceased, including certain appetites of the flesh which plagued the priest. Inspector Taylor, presiding over the investigation, informed us that he could not provide more detail, nor would we wish to print it, lest we overwhelm our readers' sensibilities. Clegg is not considered a suspect, and we learn that he and his wife have been offered alternative positions by the Church authorities, who would also not comment to this journal.

'One Mrs Grace Berrowes, a widow and seamstress resident in the parish, remarked to our reporter that God did indeed understand justice, but she would not elaborate. Readers may remember that the body of Mrs Berrowes's youngest son, was sadly found last year in the Regent's Canal.'

Catherine had seen and heard enough in her visions from Dry to understand the nature of the late priest's deeds, and his way with the children who were supposed to trust his position. She would not weep for Father Groves.

Yet she thought back to the solicitor Philip Tether, who had not seemed to be involved in anything of great mischief. The bowler-hatted man took the guilty and the innocent. For every Frederick Caille or Father Groves, was there also a victim merely of someone else's ill will—deaths commissioned out of jealousy and spite? Rivals in love or business; inconvenient relatives and inconstant friends. She thought this likely.

Edwin Dry was not justice, even if he sometimes served it.

He simply killed people.

The erratic nature of her abilities still vexed her. She could not "read" the thoughts of others as a discipline. She could not shut Dry out, or filter what came to her. Her learned talent to interpret the expressions and general demeanour of clients was more reliable. Could she learn control over what she possessed?

She took many of Mercier's comments seriously, reading up on the subject of telepathy once more and even recruiting her landlady to help. Late one night they sat in the front room and experimented. Mrs Bessovitch drew a number of figures or words on pieces of stiff paper cut into squares, and the two women sat apart, facing each other.

"What is on card?" Mrs B asked, making sure that she was not near the front room mirror. The landlady could see what was on the card; the side held up to Catherine was blank. As was her mind. After two or three minutes, she shook her head.

"A fish...a sea creature?"

"Tch." The landlady turned the card around, to show a crude drawing of a dog.

"It is an animal," Catherine said, knowing how feeble she sounded.

The next card was the word "Kettle," to which Catherine had suggested she saw the image of a horse. And so it went for another dozen cards.

The landlady laughed.

"Katerina, is all trick. In theatre, there is other man who can see card, makes signal with fingers. This is not you."

"Perhaps I wish it was."

Alone in her room, and smarting from her failure with the cards, her mind swirled with doubts about everything, from lemon tea to the suicide of Mrs Ameley's husband.

She had one certainty, which stayed with her throughout days of seeking to earn her living, with her on omnibuses and in hansoms, whether she stood on spit-covered cobbles or the plush carpets of a respectable household.

The Deptford Assassin was moving, probing.

⁂

A woman was slaughtered on August 31. Another prostitute, as the newspapers were quick to add. Mary Ann Nichols—a cut throat and several savage wounds to the abdomen. Her body was found slumped by a wall on Buck's Row. Not far from the London Hospital, which had sent a doctor to Levinia Weatherhead and pronounced that there was no hope.

Some papers mentioned the earlier death of Martha Tabram; some did not. One even raised the case of a murder from the preceding April, a death of which Catherine had not heard—an Emma Smith, killed in Spitalfields. She should probably look that up at some point—Mallick would know of it.

Catherine was taken by the shakes for a moment, and had to push the paper away.

Edwin Dry had expected this death.

Was there something she could have done? She had no idea who was doing the killings, where they would happen or when. No details at all. The thought of going to Superintendent Neylan and predicting that there would be violent death in London, and amongst the Whitechapel slums of all places…it was ludicrous.

Despite her visions, she had nothing of substance to share.

Closer.

Many possibilities have been explored, discounted, but London is a swamp of lustful, intemperate men from every station of life. Not that he considers the female of the species immune to such things.

A mile from Brick Lane he finds a man crouched over the body of a woman, a few yards from the noisome sprawl of a brewery. The man's hands are thrust up under the woman's ragged skirts, and he looks up as he realises that they are not alone.

"The kind of cove who likes to watch, eh?" The man laughs. "They don't charge when they're this drunk."

Dry moves closer, sees the steady rise and fall of the woman's chest.

There is no sign of either knife or any intent beyond base passions, and he leaves them to sink deeper into their own vices.

Such vices are not his business, this or any night.

FIFTY-ONE

Mary Ann Nichols was murdered in Buck's Row in the dark hours of early Friday morning, August 31, 1888. Polly, they called her. She'd been about the age of Martha Tabram and Jennie Weatherhead. Talk of the killing everywhere, Mary Jane and her girls did their best to collect it.

Some women they spoke to saw a pattern that fit with the murders of Martha Tabram and Emma Elizabeth Smith, as they knew her, one that suggested the Gully Bleeders had decided to come down harder on the women of the streets. Yet the gang did nothing to encourage the belief. Since their business turned on fear, they missed an opportunity if indeed they'd done the Nichols murder. From what Mary Jane and her girls gathered, she did not believe the Tabram or Nichols killings were warnings to prostitutes from the Gully Bleeders.

⚜

Friday September 7, while in Spitalfields Market, Mary Jane saw Stuart Brevard at a distance talking with two men, a tall one in a blue and black striped suit and bowler, and a stouter one in a brown and tan checked jacket, black trousers, and pale straw hat. As if giving commands to the men, Brevard gestured, first north, then south. One man went in the first direction the other the second. Though he had not seen her, Mr Brevard headed eastward, in her direction, looking all about.

Did he hire punishers or private investigators to help him?

Mary Jane exited the market into Commercial Street and headed south toward the Ten Bells pub at the crossing with Fournier Street. She thought to lose herself among the patrons of the public house, then decided against entering for fear of becoming trapped.

The ordinary cove approached her at the corner, turned his black eyes on her.

"I must keep moving," she said, walking swiftly eastward into Fournier Street. "I have something for you, but there are men following me."

"They are of no consequence," he said. The black-eyed man did not move with urgency. The distance between them grew.

"They are to me. One has been after me for almost two years." With the noise around them in the street, she wasn't certain he'd hear her. Still, she had to get away.

"Yes, Stuart Brevard," he said, his voice quiet, yet somehow focused well enough to reach her.

Mary Jane turned to look back at him. He'd stopped some twenty feet away.

Glancing around, looking out for Mr Brevard and his men, she approached the ordinary cove. Strangely, she feared her pursuers less while she stood in his shadow.

"Who hired you to kill the man, Caille, at the victualing yard?" Her boldness surprised her.

"You have something for me," he said.

Mary Jane recognised one of Brevard's men, the taller one in the black and blue striped suit and black bowler, moving toward them on the footway.

"He will not see you," the ordinary cove said, "if I become the brother you haven't seen in a month."

Mary Jane thought of Jack, gone to Australia so long ago, and imagined meeting him on the streets unexpectedly. "I thought I'd never see you again," she said, as if surprise and delight were equally caught in her throat. She thought to catch the black-eyed man's hands up in her own, to hug him toward her, but couldn't seem to bring herself to do that, nor did she believe he'd tolerate such intimacy. "Have you returned to stay? Does Mum know?"

The ordinary cove turned, and Mary Jane with him as Brevard's man walked past. She glanced at the fellow's back. He kept moving eastward.

How had he known the man approached?

In a rush, Mary Jane extracted the pages of information she and her girls had put together about Polly Nichols and her circumstances. Again, they had included in the record whatever other strange goings-on they came across while interviewing people.

"Do not hurry," he said.

She took a calming breath, said, "Stuart Brevard will kill me if he catches me. Can you do something about him?"

He provided no answer.

Mary Jane handed over the folded pages.

He palmed to her another gold sovereign.

"Your friend, Jennifer Weatherhead's, cousin," he said.

Mary Jane was confused. Then she remembered the question she'd asked him: *Who hired you to kill the man, Caille, at the victualing yard?* He'd provided an answer to her question!

Dumbfounded, she stood for a moment, lost in thought and memory.

Jennie had talked about a cousin, Catherine Weatherhead. Mary Jane pictured a tall, dark-haired woman, and recalled that she'd met Catherine briefly a couple of years ago. They were about the same age. Jennie had said that her cousin helped her family with funds from time to time.

When her full awareness returned to the street around her, the ordinary cove was gone. In a panic to disappear before her enemies spotted her, she dashed into the road, passed between carriages and a car loaded with bushels of potatoes, and got across Fournier Street with little dung caked to her boots.

Taking to the footway and glancing back, she nearly bowled over Mrs Hollis. She stood, as usual, beside Christ Church with her beggar's placard. Mary Jane held the startled old woman by the shoulders to steady her. She had seen Mrs Hollis there many times, but had avoided speaking to her since Jennie's death out of shame and a desire to avoid the painful thoughts of loss.

"Forgive me," Mary Jane said. "I didn't mean to frighten."

"N-not at all, uh...Ginger. I-I—"

Face to face with Mrs Hollis, Mary Jane suddenly knew that she had questions for her.

"Please walk with me for a time and answer my questions, and I'll give you a shilling."

The old woman nodded her approval, and the two walked to the crossing, then south on Commercial Street.

"Do you know a cousin of Jennifer Weatherhead's named Catherine?" Mary Jane asked.

"Yes," Mrs Hollis said.

"And has she private means, a good position?" Mary Jane recalled something about the young woman being a widow's companion. That would not pay very well, she presumed.

Mrs Hollis had an awkward look. "There are rumours that she

is a spiritualist or fortune teller of some sort, though the family does not know this."

"Oh?"

"Is what I've heard," Mrs Hollis said. "I last saw her at the funeral of Jennifer's mother, Levinia."

Mary Jane had no notion as to what earnings came from such pursuits. She didn't know what she believed about spiritualists. Many people considered them swindlers. She wondered if she ought to be suspicious of any information that came from Catherine Weatherhead.

"I want to know if she hired someone to kill Frederick Caille at the Deptford Victualing Yard, and, if so, what she knows about him."

Mrs Hollis's eyes became large. Her near-toothless mouth gaped.

"I believe I have become acquainted with him," Mary Jane said. She described the black-eyed man to Mrs Hollis.

"I will write to her and ask. She may not be willing to say. I don't know how long it will take to get an answer."

"Thank you." Mary Jane gave Mrs Hollis a shilling and they parted company.

FIFTY-TWO

Only a week of September had passed when Catherine encountered two pieces of news which troubled her, for very different reasons.

The first was the murder of Annie Chapman. Mutilated, and in Whitechapel, on September 8. It seemed impossible that it had happened again, so soon after the killing of Mary Ann Nichols. The streets were now ablaze with talk of the deaths in Whitechapel. Rich men walked the streets at night, some said, seeking out fallen woman to carve; others talked of Jews, taking out their twisted frustrations on gentile women—or even workers seeking to raise sentiments against the Jews. There was a single madman; there was a gang. A doctor had gone insane; a slaughterhouse man had been cheated and now took his revenge.

Southwark may have been south of the river, but it was still not so very far from Whitechapel and Spitalfields. The dolly-mops and professional prostitutes began to walk in pairs, or find meagre wages from other activities for a while. Superintendent Neylan commented that "offences of the flesh" were down, and Inspector Mallick, tasteless as he could often be, opined quietly that Mr Neylan would make a good suspect—righteous in his condemnation of the prostitute's trade, and in thrall to an overbearing woman.

"I'm sure I did not say that, Madame," he added. His eyelid flickered with unaccustomed vigour, and he grinned.

They stood by a cab-man's shelter, cradling mugs of tea in their hands. It was a convenient way of avoiding the bustle of the police station. She had met the inspector as a courtesy, concerning a woman the Superintendent wished to charge with duplicity. The woman had asked a half-sovereign a time to tell the future, working from a basement near the Compass Rose, and a disappointed customer had reported her. Mallick wanted to know if Catherine had anything to add, or knew anything of the woman. She did not.

Their business concluded, talk of the murders had been inevitable.

"Scotland Yard seems to have no ideas, if the press are to be believed," she said. "But they must surely be gathering intelligence on such a horror?"

"Aye, Donald's awash with reports from every eager watchman, constable, and sergeant from Cripplegate to Limehouse—and numerous letters from the public. Names are made or lost on cases like these."

"Donald? Do you refer to your Chief Inspector Swanson?"

"They gave him oversight last week—he must sift the lot, and find a diamond in ten thousand pebbles. Poor fellow, I don't envy him."

"A thankless task, I imagine."

What might Madame Rostov report to Swanson? That she knew a second killer strode through Whitechapel, sniffing after the first and watching?

She would be ejected from his office within the minute.

Her second piece of news, received later that same day, cut deeper for being so personal. It was a letter from her younger brother Josiah, and came to the lodging house, which puzzled her until she remembered that she had sent Clarissa her true address weeks ago. So few wished to contact Catherine Weatherhead that it had seemed pointless to keep up the rigmarole of going to the post office if her cousins needed her. Josiah must have had it from them, meaning no harm.

The letter was short.

> *Dearest Cath. Father has read of the dire murders*
> *which afflict the capital. Be warned, he comes for you,*
> *and will have you back in Keighley. In haste, Yr Josiah.*

She had made one simple mistake. She had assumed—absently, foolishly—that Clarissa and Jennie would keep Mrs Bessovitch's address to themselves.

And they had failed her.

Cloud came with Joshua Weatherhead; cloud and a mean rain which dampened but did not wash the city. The sky matched the ache at Catherine's temples, the same sensation that she had when the barometer swung wild. Pressure within; pressure without.

He arrived before ten in the morning, a single rap on the front door of the small Southwark Terrace. Isaac Green, a snot-ridden seven year old, had been paid to watch for a large stranger heading in the direction of the lodgings, and had been given a description. The child did his duty, and they were forewarned.

"You still have choice," said Mrs Bessovitch. "You keep out of way—I say I do not know where you are gone. Or…I do not let him in. Is my house."

"I will face him." Catherine tugged savagely at her hair, bound it back with an elasticated band. "It would have happened—this year, another. Let it be done, and done with."

"You really do not know why he comes?"

"Josiah said that my father wants me back up north, but not the true reason. I doubt that it is to do with my own welfare. That Josiah should even warn me is a surprise. My brother is not…brave."

Mrs Bessovitch spat a boiled sweet out into her palm, stared at it and then put it back in her mouth.

"Katerina is brave."

"No, I'm not. I ran before. I will not run today."

The landlady shrugged, and trudged down the hall to let the man in. Catherine heard short words between them, and then he was there in the kitchen doorway.

"I am in parlour, Katerina," said Mrs B. "I wait, if you need."

There was more grey than she remembered in his long black hair, and in the meagre beard which clung to a chin grown corpulent in its own right. His waistcoat bulged, pulling on the buttons of mother-of-pearl, and his trousers were of fine material but an inch too short. He was only half of his father, sharing the late Joseph Weatherhead's large frame but not the old man's angular lines and strength of feature, which had gone to Catherine.

"Meet all your guests here, do you?" said Joshua, glancing around the cluttered kitchen without enthusiasm.

Catherine, standing by the small range, wished that she had one of the fire irons to hand.

"You're not a guest, Father. You brought yourself—I did not ask for you."

"True. But now I'm here. You look different, lass."

Joshua's smile owed nothing to that of his father or his daughter. It was pinned to thin lips, a merchant's smile without meaning. Buy from me. Nothing had changed in almost three years.

"I'm fed well, cared for." Catherine pointed to a chair at the table. "Best tell me what you want, now you're here."

They sat opposite each other, chess-players without a board. He would have his pieces to hand, no doubt.

She made herself look at his face. His eyes, a muddy grey and crouched beneath heavy eyebrows, were raised to hers.

"Your mother's not well," he said. "She could do with you near, Catherine."

"You travelled more than two hundred miles to tell me that? You could have written."

He flexed his fingers, placed his hands on his knees. "Mebbe I came to make it clear. You never listened to owt unless it were said twice, and then more."

"She has Josiah."

"The good he is. Counting doesn't make caring. She's your mother too."

"And your wife."

The pressure around her forehead was getting worse. She stood up and fetched Mrs B's brandy, two glasses. She needed drink to prop her up against his presence, even at this hour of the day and in her own home.

"Tea's more than enough for a man," he said.

"Tea, then." She glared, poured herself a glass of spirits, and set the kettle on the hob. Sitting down again, she took a mouthful of brandy because he would not, because he did not want her to.

Joshua's expression shifted, much as when a customer moved from one rack of goods to another, undecided.

"I can read, you know, lass. The stories we're seeing from London—such bloody murders. God must weep at these women being cut down. Another only a few days ago, they say."

"God should do something about it, then."

"You'll not use His name like that!" He reddened. "It's man's evil as walks the streets here. Even if they were…women of a certain nature, they might have been saved for His mercy."

"You have money, Father. You should endow a mission."

"I do enough at home. Temperance and prayer, there's many look to me in Keighley."

She eyed the brandy, managed not to refill her glass.

"What do you want of me? Just have it out."

338

"I told you, your mother needs you."

"Get her help—another maid, a nurse."

"She needs a dutiful daughter." He turned away from her hard look. "Besides, lass—what's happening down here, wouldn't you be safer back home? With your family. We worry about you."

There was an undercurrent—what had Josiah said of her circumstances?

"You think I'm a prostitute, perhaps? Risking myself for a few shillings down the back alleys, like these other women?"

"I had a letter from Clarissa, saying you came and went with shillings—not that she's seen you for months. You've no civil tongue, and could never mend nor sew proper. You're no companion."

"And so you think I let men up my skirts?"

He looked awkward for once, perhaps sensing he'd been wrong on this estimate, if nothing else.

"Mebbe I worried, like a father does. A girl in this place, this Godless den of thieves…"

Back to the almost reasonable appeal, which he did so well when he had a mind to. She filled the teapot, and pushed it towards him across the table. A cup and saucer from the dresser; milk from the shelf above the sink. Teaspoon and strainer clattered on to the polished wooden surface, and she frowned, thinking over his earlier words.

"And why did cousin Clarissa write to you at all?"

"Money. They only write, any of them, for money. Said I owed Levinia, that I'd wrung the best from both sides of the family." His eyes narrowed. "I worked. I worked, and made what we have. Thomas, he had no need to go south, marry Levinia. He could have had a share in the business."

Tom Weatherhead had died before she was born. A respectable travelling man, father of Charles and Jennie, dead with his heart at an early age. Levinia had ruled since then, until her end.

"You could spare it. You could make them a gift, for the sake of family. I have done my part, despite you."

"And what would I leave you and Josiah? The Lord does not reward the profligate, but the frugal and careful."

She could see his blunt thoughts. He would arrive in London, the dutiful and caring father, and sweep her up, put her back in her place by the hearth and the range—until he could trade her in marriage and add to his empire. There would be some merchant somewhere in West Yorkshire with useful assets and a dolt of a son. He was only here because he had a scheme laid out—or because his own wife was becoming more of a burden than an asset. He had never had time for the weak and the sickly.

"How many shops now?" she asked, sudden and direct.

"Five, and one more in Leeds to come." He looked pleased at her question. "Wholesale as well. And the coal trade brings in a fair rate."

"Then go back and look after them. Leave me be, Father. I'll not return."

"You will." His broad, fleshy face was dark again. "I came this far, and you'll do your duty. You're an unnatural child, Catherine Weatherhead, to leave your mother without a daughter's love, to abandon good family for...for this!" He waved a contemptuous hand at the room in which they sat. "Never a thought for what is proper, for the needs of others. For—"

"What do you know of anything but your own greed and comfort?" She swept her arm across the table, dashing the tea things to the floor. "Oh, you sanctimonious bastard! If I could—"

Pain. The ache which had been clinging to her temples, gathering behind her eyes, released itself in one needle of memory, one vision...

She saw him.

Joshua Weatherhead, more than ten years younger, and the houses on Fell Lane, from the Union Infirmary to the terraces, neat enough. The Weatherheads, and next door, the Wittens. Joshua and Jack, always close and often in drink together, before Joshua took the pledge.

She saw her father.

He belches, rises from his bed, restless. Damn, he's left his watch in the back room, where Jack is sleeping off the drink. He stumbles down in stockinged feet.

Jack isn't there. The back door is open. Joshua rubs at his eyes and looks out onto the small yards, left and right. The door to the Witten's is open as well.

He should go back to bed, but he wonders. Padding from his yard to the next, he looks into the house next door, the moon holding up a lantern for him.

The act is almost done, the woman sinking to the floor, lifeless. Joshua gasps, and Jack looks round. No surprise, no penitence.

"I did for her, Josh. No bairn from her in ten years, and only harping about the drink, the cards, the rent—never a rest for a man."

"You'll hang."

Jack smiles, steps over the body and comes closer, almost outside.

"Will I? For a thief what came in the night, while yet I slept at my old mate's house. A thief what was taking his due, and being surprised in the act, rode the life out of the one who saw him. Would you give me to the law, Josh, or help me?"

Broken sleep, a belly of dark ale, and a man Joshua had known all his life. Laughing Jack—Uncle Jack to his own children. And Maggie Witten, she'd not been so bad, but she was gone now. A lumpen shape on the carpet before them. Nothing he could do about that.

They pull out the cupboard drawers, and scatter spoons, letters, fragments of lies across the floor. Joshua picks two decrepit silver candlesticks.

"He'd not leave these. There's good metal to them."

"Hide 'em, then. They'll go to Bradford when all's quiet, fetch a crate or two and still change for us."

Uncle Jack takes a screwdriver, quiet, to the back door latch, scratching all around.

"That's how he came on her," he says.

Joshua hesitates. He hears a plan in his friend's voice, one which surely did not spring newborn from this ugly night...

Maggie Witten never liked Joshua anyway.

He turns over a chair, tucks the candlesticks under his arm.

"We slept through it," he says. "They'll find her soon enough in the morning, and wake us."

"Oh, to lose my poor dear darling wife so," says Jack Witten, and the moon sees a narrow smile on the man's face...

Catherine managed to stand. She managed to stand because she had Madame Rostov, who knew how to be in control, to be imperious. To walk the Aether, and bear the sight of murder.

"What is it, lass?" Her father looked puzzled.

Had this been in her these many years? Buried thoughts, the

341

other half of young Cath's vision. A knowledge of her own father's complicity, of his lies, that she had pushed aside in desperation. Or had she read it from him here and now, in a moment of anger across a kitchen table?

She had known. It had coloured her life in Yorkshire, and played its part in driving her to London.

"Did it trouble you?" she asked.

She held on to performance, to Madame Rostov with eyes of grey ice and wild, unmanaged black hair, the heavy rings glinting on her fingers. She imagined the rings, even though they lay boxed upstairs in her room.

"What are you talking about?"

"Did it trouble you, seeing Aunt Maggie lying there, stripped of breath, of life? Did you wonder, as you ransacked a cupboard and grabbed at the candlesticks, if you should have checked? Or perhaps you had light enough to see her mottled face and know that she was gone. Did you?"

Her belly was hard, her blood rushing to strengthen her. Her father's hands were veined claws, gripping his thighs as if he could not release them; his face was soured milk, pale and poisoned by her words.

And the words would not stop.

"You took the belt to me for lies and slander, for having thoughts which came from the Devil and his sendings. You marked me, and you let others mark me. 'Touched,' they said, and you let them say it. Chapel every Sunday, where Cath sat slumped and sullen, whilst her father, the industrious Joshua Weatherhead, sang out—upright, decent.

"Here I am, father. The 'unnatural child' you helped make. Is this what you want back at your hearth, to order and to use? To break, like you did my mother?"

"You can't speak to me like this, you—"

"Can't speak to you? Oh, I can, and more." She advanced on him, laid her shadow over him. "Maybe there are other secrets? Shall I look deeper, and lay out your finest moments for you?"

This lifted him from his seat, a hand raised as if he might strike out at her.

"I'm your father, you ungrateful whore! You'll show respect—"

"I could have you killed." Said soft, but clear.

"What?" He halted.

Philip Tether, the man of bluster at Clerkenwell, the priest at St Luke's—she had seen them slaughtered. She was tainted, and knew the trade of death. And always Frederick Caille. A man of business, proud of his status. Like her father.

"This isn't Fell Lane; not your coal-yard or your little empire. This is London. You came for someone who no longer exists. Here, I could have you killed, and they would never find you. Not like Aunt Maggie—you remember? You would be ended and unmourned."

"You're insane. I should—"

"Leave my house," said Mrs Bessovitch from the doorway. "You upset my Katerina."

He looked from one woman to the other.

"Two candlesticks," said Catherine. "Two battered silver candlesticks. Did they ever go to Bradford, to the pawn shops, or a publican who asked no questions? You and 'Uncle' Jack must have drunk deep when they were safe away."

"I...you don't..." Unmanned, uncomprehending—or beginning to comprehend something with which he could not cope. He edged towards the doorway, and Mrs Bessovitch stepped aside.

"You will not come here, to my house," she said. "You understand this?"

He was gone, the front door creaking behind him, the thin rain at his back.

The landlady set the brandy glasses upright, tutted at the broken cup on the floor.

"You are not good for my crockery, Katerina. Maybe I add this to your rent."

She poured out spirits for both of them. Catherine could not speak. She took her glass and drained it.

The clouds grew thicker, and darkened the street outside.

✦

That night she talked of her mother, and Mrs Bessovitch listened. She talked of a poor marriage, founded on the money which her mother brought with her, and the slow loss of will. Of a weak woman, easily swayed and ordered, who had clung to her two surviving children as if they were little dolls with which to toy—until they grew too old for the game.

"Did you not love her?"

"Love did not live with us." Catherine and her landlady were close to drunk, down to gin from around the corner. Catherine hated the taste of gin. "Josiah played longer than I, knew how to say the right words to keep in favour. And he dwells under it still, caught between pathetic need and harsh command. Poor Josiah. I should have loved her, yes, like any proper daughter. I am unnatural."

"Is true," said Mrs B, and they laughed until the gin ran from Catherine's nose.

Later, she was very sick.

FIFTY-THREE

On Saturday, September 8 in the early hours of the morning, the body of Annie Chapman turned up behind a house in Hanbury Street. She'd been murdered and mutilated. Mary Jane and her girls continued their interviews in an effort to gain information about the murder.

Although she worried they might catch up to her anytime, Mary Jane did not see Stuart Brevard or his two men Saturday or Sunday. Even so, she carried a sick feeling in her gut. Suddenly her past had caught up with her again. The need to escape London and start over elsewhere had returned, while unfinished business with the ordinary cove and Gabriella Gorse remained.

Until the previous Friday when she'd seen him, Mary Jane's fear of Mr Brevard had diminished consistently throughout the year and a half she'd not seen him. With a renewed sense of the threat he posed, she again thought about how to fund a relocation. Still not seeing clients, and having spent much of the money she'd earned on her girls and their interviewing efforts, she had little savings left, about ten pounds. Her thoughts circled back to ideas of recovering the necklace from the Phoenix gay house, though that seemed hopeless. Surely by now, someone had discovered the hidden jewellery.

On Monday, September 10, she and her girls had just concluded an interview with a friend of Annie Chapman's, a woman named Amelia Palmer, when the black-eyed man appeared in the Ten Bells pub. He approached their table as Mrs Palmer got up and left. Mary Jane's girls excused themselves and left without explanation. She would later learn that the man had so unnerved Maria, Glory, and Julia, that they could not stay.

He sat across from Mary Jane.

"I must finish my work here and make a fresh start somewhere I am not known," she said to him, "unless you can do something about Stuart Brevard."

He made no response.

"Shall I have any hope that you will deal with Gabriella Gorse?" she asked.

"I am paid in coin for my services," he said.

Most of her funds were hidden away in her lodgings. She had

little in her pocket. "How much do you require?"

"Whatever token amount is to hand."

"You make a jest of my need?"

Again, the ordinary cove did not respond.

Holding back a desire to show her disgust, Mary Jane slipped the hidden pocket out from beneath the waist band of her top skirt. She raised the pouch to the table, and turned it out to display the two shillings and one tanner within. "A token amount," she said as flatly as possible. He deserved no better than he gave.

"That would be sufficient," he said.

Mary Jane sat back a bit hard, her seat rocking.

He didn't make any sense!

She put her hand to her mouth for fear that she might say something rude to him.

His black gaze remained unwavering. Mary Jane turned away from the terrible sight.

Had she gained his trust?

In some ways, perhaps. More likely he'd gained leverage over *her*. She still knew almost nothing about him.

She'd trusted him enough to do business with him. So what had changed?

His suggestion that a life was worth no more than two and a tanner. Yet Gabby's life is worth less than that to me.

He does not make a jest. The truth is there in his eyes.

Again, she turned away, looked down. "Then allow me to pay you for Stuart Brevard instead."

"As I told you, he is of no consequence."

Is he afraid of Brevard?

No.

Mary Jane stared at the dented wood grain of the table top, unable to think of a winning way to press her need. The black-eyed man didn't respond to her charms as other men did.

He stood as if to leave.

"No, please," she said quickly. "The woman, then."

He sat.

Mary Jane carefully plucked the three coins from her pocket, hearing her decision to have Gabriella Gorse killed in the metal on metal sound of each coin touching its neighbour. She slid them across the table to the ordinary cove. They stayed in a small puddle of spilled coffee for a time before he picked them up and wiped them carefully with a handkerchief.

"When shall you do the job?" she asked.

"When I am ready."

She wanted to ask why he would kill for so little, but knew the answer, or lack of one, would trouble her more, and she'd have to live with the knowledge for possibly many years. Better that she didn't know.

The proper question is, does Gabriella Gorse deserve to die for what she's done?

Yes.

After the ordinary cove had gone, she realised she had not given him any of the information she and her girls had gathered about Annie Chapman and her circumstances. All they had so far were Glory's shorthand notes, not yet transcribed into a legible document.

He shall reappear on Friday.

Having paid him to commit the monstrous act, Mary Jane already knew the shame she would experience every time she had to look at the man, whether he committed the crime that day, the next, or never.

Still, she would suffer that shame for Jennie.

FIFTY-FOUR

Three have now fallen to the unknown knife.

Tabram. Nicholls. Chapman.

The authorities prevaricate and bicker. They debate who was cut down by whom, how many murderers there are. A gang of low-lives, working in concerted effort? A single madman loose upon the streets, or a conspiracy?

Their debates are pointless. The three deaths have the same sense, the same feel—this is the professional assessment of the journeyman, deep in his craft.

And he is able to make another assessment.

He himself can take life in a hundred different ways. He can deem a commission to be of no value one week, interesting the next. He can wait for a month, or for a year, before he acts. He can improvise. A door creaks and a child's hoop lies across the cobbles in Clerkenwell; as a result, a man who has walked the same way home for ten years decides to go another way and take the omnibus...

Each plan is the right one until it is not.

He understands change. It is the essence of his world. The ability to consider, and to change. Without this, he could not do what he does.

The newcomer is likely to be deficient in this field. Dry sees stubborn pattern, not flexibility. Emotion, not intellect. The bloody acts may develop in intensity and focus, but they are steeped in specific needs, wreathed in warped and personal judgement.

There will be a story, of course, behind the one they call the Whitechapel Murderer. It will be a maudlin, confused one. The same story is available in every public house, heard from drunken Lascar seamen and penniless students; bitter apprentices and thwarted accounts clerks. Each tale is some terrible indictment of humanity. Jealousy, betrayal, brutality.

And each is, in the end, quite dull.

Ten thirty-seven in the evening, and Whitechapel is ripe with life, despite the killings. The prostitutes cling closer to the street-lights and the tavern doors, but trade must continue. Bellies are still empty—throats rasp for ale and spirits. One mouthful of a man's spend, spat out when he's away down the street, and then a welcome gargle of gin.

Dry slips from one dank alley to another, noting crumbling bricks which would offer a toehold, a broken window where the frame could be cracked without undue noise. These observations are stored away. As ever, he times the constables as he goes. Colchester Street to the Jews' Cemetery. East and south, quartering Stepney without haste. Each nest of streets has a smell, a prevalent wind of poverty or ambition.

The night is a circle, carrying him back to the pale, dawn-touched bulk of Christ Church in Spitalfields. He admires architecture which is of use. What use this is, he does not know—he has no interest in religion or spirituality.

A ragged shawl and missing teeth reach out to him on Dorset Street. When the owner of shawl and teeth sees his eyes, she huddles back into shadow.

Mary Jane Kelly lives close by. His gatherer of intelligence on the comings and goings of men who cannot restrain their manhoods. Are some of their clients more violent, more frantic or sly than most? Do any have a penchant for the knife, even in play? Something will betray the newcomer.

To be alone and pure in his craft, to work without the need for others—that would please him. There may come a day. For the moment, for such a sprawl of streets, he makes reluctant use of those he must.

The police double their patrols and scatter inspectors, down to the dullest placeholders from idle stations, across the breadth of the East End. Scotland Yard is unhappily alert. Reporters and vigilantes creep through the streets, followed close by the mission faithful, seeing this as chance to hoard souls. All in all, too many eyes are open for his liking.

But the sun lifts behind Christ Church, a coral tint to the chimney smoke, a soft glow which will be beaten away within the hour.

Even Dry must sleep.

A day with a blinding headache, after a night where the Deptford Assassin flickered in and out of her dreams, showing her places she had never been, would never go. Catherine took salts and a tonic, made one trip only, to buy chocolates and violet water for Mrs B.

These she presented, her head still throbbing.

"I am sorry to bring this to your door," said Catherine. "Yesterday, I mean."

"Tch. I have seen worse than your father. Go bathe, Katerina. Sleep some more. And do not disturb me. I have much chocolates to eat."

The newcomer has no clear scent. A minor problem, for which adjustments must be made. That is to say, he is so close to the streets and the filth that there is nothing which marks him in a crowd. If he is a man of note, he has walked among the beasts for many nights; if a beast, he is as yet indistinguishable.

Method and persistence. It may not be the third, or even the thirtieth. There are many men in London.

On a sultry Stepney night, a thick-shouldered seaman looms over a woman, pressing her against the Board School wall. Metal glints, but the blade which clatters to the ground is a pen-knife, the tip broken away. The woman who is being serviced has a shallow cut to her cheek, the mark of a drunken bully.

Dry moves on.

Off Anthony Street he watches a thin girl being beaten by a Greek or Levantine; a half mile east he sees two men puking into the gutters whilst a third watches. He waits, but when they have done emptying their guts, they join their companion and kiss.

Nothing of importance.

As he pads away, Dry holds a question tight to himself, unanswered. It is a question he does not like. There is no commission in play here.

When he identifies the Whitechapel Murderer, when he truly knows the man and his nature, has assessed the potential there and has the measure of how far the killer might go…what next?

Catherine woke cleaner and clear-headed. There was something she needed to do. An afternoon session with the miserable, priggish Mrs Ledworth, which would net her ten shillings if she was lucky, and then a private matter.

At four in the afternoon she took an omnibus, all trace of Madame Rostov abandoned, and made her way to Spitalfields. She would have words with her cousins, for giving her address to the family in Yorkshire. And there would be, should be, the inevitable coins to be left, a token for Benjamin and Maisie, despite her irritation with Clarissa. She hadn't seen any of them since they left Brantridge Street.

Quite where the George Street lodgings were, she was unsure, but there were maps in her mind, shadowy ones that had not come from her own experience. The bowler-hatted man had passed down these streets, many times, and recently.

There was Christ Church, as clear as she had seen it in her visions. Box-like, surmounted by the tall Gothic steeple—and all around it the alleys and lanes which Edwin Dry walked. This seemed no better place than Brantridge Street, and she wondered how low Clarissa and her family had fallen.

Martha Tabram. Catherine shuddered. She had paused by the Christ Church graveyard, now more a public green, and the thought had come—the connection she had never made. Tabram had been found in George Yard Buildings. Her cousins must live close by the site of that brutal murder, yet it was never mentioned in Clarissa's infrequent letters. To avoid her pity at their circumstances? She thought of Jennie—how safe was her cousin in such surroundings?

"Miss Weatherhead? Miss Catherine Weatherhead?"

Catherine looked around. By the churchyard wall, an old woman in shawl and clogs was beckoning to her. A scrawled placard, which Catherine could not read, was propped against the stone wall.

She went over. The woman seemed familiar from somewhere. A jaundiced, toothless face, the hair grey and straggling.

"I am Catherine Weatherhead, yes."

"Mrs Hollis. I was at poor Levinia's funeral."

"Oh. I...I hope you are keeping well." It seemed doubtful, looking at her. Memory ground slow like a mill-wheel, and she tried to smile. "Yes, Mrs Hollis. I apologise—I did not recognise you for a moment. Your son—John?—was on the Penelope, with my cousin Charles."

"Served with that good man; died with him," said the old woman. Spittle gathered at the corner of her mouth. "But my dear, I was so sorry about poor Jennie."

"Jennie? Is she ill? I heard nothing from Clarissa."

Mrs Hollis's eyes widened, faded colours against the yellow-grey that tinged her cheeks.

"I only meant…it's no matter."

"Something has happened." Catherine focused her attention on the bent woman. There was terrible news underneath the torn lace shawl.

"It's not my place—"

"Tell me, please."

Mrs Hollis glanced around, a rabbit pinned in lantern light. "I could so do with a wet, my dear. Anything…"

The King George public house was shabby and mostly occupied by working men, taking an early dinner from the bottle. Their dull eyes marked Catherine as she pushed past them, but there were alcoves at the far end where a few women sat. Some were entertaining, clutched by costermongers and barrow-boys; others hunched over half-empty glasses, showing no interest in anyone.

The barman provided two glasses of pale ale, eyeing Catherine as he did so. She was not in the mood.

"Is there aught you want to say?" she snapped. He scowled, and turned to another customer.

Pressed into a corner, with the smell of Mrs Hollis thick in her nostrils, Catherine sipped the weak, sour ale.

"What has happened to Jennie?"

The old woman tried to drink, some of the ale spilling from the corner of her mouth.

"We spared Clarissa," she said, a plea for understanding. "We all did spare her, for the loss she'd taken."

It was a bleak tale that unfolded. Mrs Hollis knew that Jennie Weatherhead had never served as a maid—that it was entirely a fiction for Clarissa and the children—and that life on the streets had been hard.

"She admitted it to me last year," said Catherine, remembering her fears at that time about the path on which her cousin had stepped.

"It were Jennie's choice, dear," said Mrs Hollis. "Girls around here, they do make best."

The woman continued in a rambling tale of rivalry, the gangs who drew tithe from the street women—and the violence of the men they served. A toothless saga which took Catherine into places she wished not to visit. She did not want to see her gentle cousin in that story, but choice was denied her. The old woman's words had only truth in them, however mixed and mumbled.

"Emma Smith," said Mrs Hollis. "The name she took, see. But she were not made for that trade, poor soul. And in the end they had her, fist and stick. Oh blessed Lord, they had her, and put an end to her."

Catherine knew the name. Emma Smith. She remembered the comment by Eden Mallick. She had heard of her own cousin's death, and put it to one side, ignorant, considering it the sad fate of a stranger.

"Then Jennie is dead," said Catherine. Flat, drained of feeling.

Mrs Hollis wept. Catherine could not. At last the old woman looked up.

"We kept it from the family, like I says. And Easter hardly passed. With poor Charles and my Johnnie gone, then Levinia—what could we say? Better to say that Jennie had left, maybe found something better, than to talk of such a day. I laid a few flowers, such as I could get."

Mrs Hollis stared into her empty glass.

"White roses, mostly. They weren't the best…"

"Are…are Clarissa and the children well?" It was all she could think to ask.

"As they can be. The air is not good on George Street, but they have a roof, and Clarissa has her mending."

She could not see them. She could not go there and lie, now she knew of Jennie's fate. She found a half crown from her purse, laid it on the table.

"For your troubles."

"I would have done it anyway." A flash of dignity from the old woman.

"Take it. Have another beer in Jennie's memory."

The half crown slipped under the shawl.

"I think I were supposed to ask you something." Mrs Hollis frowned. "About what happened a while back…"

"Write to me." Catherine wanted to hear no more. "The world has my address these days."

It was unbearable.

She rose and tried to push her way to the tavern door.

"You looks worth a shillin' or two, girl," slurred a corpulent man with tattoos down his forearms, blocking her way. He grabbed at her shoulder, his dirty fingers digging into her flesh. "I knows a room nearby…"

To have faced her father down and buried a murder from long ago, only to find another death had come close to her.

The instincts of Keighley alleys, and the certainty of Edwin Dry, wrapped her fingers around the neck of a beer bottle on the nearby table. She swung, shattering the bottle across the man's skull and sending him reeling back, blood in his hair. A few men growled, but most laughed. They did not stop her leaving.

Her hair wild, her thoughts as dark and unmanaged, she fled for Southwark.

He has no sentimentality as to the slaughter of women—parson's wives or prostitutes. They are human beings, and can sin, can cheat and lie. And they can achieve through those approaches, or through virtue and bold works, if they choose. They are no different from men. He sees no reason why they should not vote and hold high office, be mistresses of banks and great industries.

That the stranger has chosen women—and street women—as his victims is merely a mark of the man's own weaknesses. Another sign of sullen, twisted prejudice.

Edwin Dry does not entertain prejudice in his work. Deptford came from a woman; not a month after, he took ten pounds from the towering black first mate of the merchantman Bewcastle, a man whose captain had swindled him of his due. The captain's permanent retirement came quickly.

All are equal when there is a commission.

All are equal before the blade.

FIFTY-FIVE

In the afternoon of Friday, September 14, having just emerged from a urinal on Booth Street, Mary Jane saw the black-eyed man standing in a doorway along the lane to the east. She approached, gave him the record she and her girls had assembled of the Annie Chapman murder, and received another sovereign, all without looking directly at him.

Annie Chapman had been an acquaintance of Mary Jane's, someone she had seen at the Ringers on occasion. The woman had been one of countless casuals, an unfortunate with a kind though wary smile.

Mrs Chapman and Mrs Nichols had had their throats cut and their guts laid open. They were left in open view, in positions that suggested that the murderer found a certain sexual delight in the cruelty. One such killing had little power to hold the public's imagination for long, but two similar murders indicated that someone hunted in the East End with a mysterious and depraved motive.

With the ensuing confusion, fear, and panic in the streets, the information Mary Jane and her girls gathered became widely varied and more difficult to parse. Some saw Mary Jane and her girls as possibly in league with the killer. Others could not talk enough about the matter, turning to fancy when the facts ran out—stories of demons, murderous immigrants, slumming nobles, and political factions trying to start riots or foment rebellion.

The whole of the East End seemed to go mad in September of 1888. People called the fiend the Whitechapel Murderer. Bloodstains on the streets, a common enough sight ignored before, turned into evidence of his further crimes. Rumours of new murders or suspects arrested drew crowds this way and that within the East End, blocking traffic and stirring the growing fear. The Whitechapel Vigilance Committee made noise in the streets and in the press, spurring anger that the killer had not been caught swiftly. A reward offered for the capture of the murderer further fed the frenzy.

In their interviews, Mary Jane and her girls had met numerous people who described Jewish men as somehow more capable of inhuman violence. Some said they took part in hounding Jews through the streets.

A man with a knife attacked a woman in the open, and she suffered several wounds. The angry crowd that formed around the violence insisted on lynching him. The police arrived in time to save the victim and her attacker.

Someone cried out about a theft, and a young man ran from the scene. In little time, a large crowd formed, even in the midst of giving chase. But for the constable who caught the thief, the fearsome horde might have run the young man to ground and torn him apart.

A Jewish man called Leather Apron, thought to be the killer of Polly Nichols, was said to be loose in Whitechapel, terrorising prostitutes. The descriptions of him that appeared in the East London Observer terrorised more than the man himself. Captured, questioned by the police, and found to have an alibi for the night of the murder, he'd been released. A boot closer, he used the leather apron in his work. Other arrests of suspects for each murder occurred, yet all turned out to be innocent.

The city first heard the name Jack the Ripper from a letter that appeared in the newspapers, one taunting the police and signed with that moniker.

FIFTY-SIX

She asked.

Catherine sat at the Borough High Street police station in Southwark, and she asked Mallick what he knew. Was the death of Emma Elizabeth Smith, on the night of April 4, 1888, considered to be the work of the madman now loose in Whitechapel?

Not knowing why she asked, he reeled off the broad case—as he had it—without concern. Where Emma Smith had been attacked, and how she died two days later in the infirmary. It was painful to hear, but she tried to show no great emotion.

"Unlucky, that's all," he said. "Maybe she crossed one of the gangs. They take a cut, see, and if you're late in paying...well, they get rough. If you look like you're going to stand up to them, they get rougher. Set an example, like."

It was not Jennie's world. She would have been ill-equipped for such men, however much—as Mrs Hollis said—other women had tried to help her.

"Unlucky." Catherine thought of how much could be said with such a short word. "And so many like her."

The inspector shrugged. "There are men who'll pay, always men who'll pay." His eyelid twitched more rapidly, a distracting sight. "It's not as if I like it, Madame. I've a daughter, going on twelve years old. Not as if I like it, and not as if there's much we can do."

"You're married?"

She had never thought to find out anything of Eden Mallick's circumstances. He was somewhat shabby, as a rule, with a creased collar and a waistcoat button missing at that very moment, the sort of things he hid from Mr Neylan when he could.

"Fifteen years, and contented enough."

There was little else to say about Emma Smith, who had once been Jennie Weatherhead. No point in telling Mallick the dead woman's true identity or circumstances.

Oh Jennie, to end up so! Catherine was angry, and...she was trying to avoid what else she knew she felt.

Guilt.

Would a few extra shillings have turned Jennie in another direction, and kept her off the streets? Joshua Weatherhead could have paid his dues to family, and acted on those Christian virtues which moved his lips but not his wallet. Or Catherine might have managed to help more, with care—even if she had to force the money on them. Extra sittings in the early days, a chance that she could bluff her way through to more substantial donations. For that matter, she might have found a way to beg Lady Seldon and the others for a small remuneration.

Though Jennie was gone, Clarissa and the children had to survive. Perhaps there was a favour of a different kind she could beg, a last gesture in the memory of Charles Weatherhead, and poor Jennie.

Family.

⁂

Madame Rostov presented her card in Chelsea, and was welcomed in. Charlotte and "Katerina" kissed, followed by the ordering of cakes and tea with lemon. Lottie had become enamoured of the drink since she had seen Madame Rostov liked it so—Catherine still did not—and now it was always tea with lemon.

"I did not entirely understand Mr Rider Haggard's piece," said Catherine, passing the book back to her friend. "This Ayesha ruling over her black subjects—an odd choice. Is it meant to be clever, a satire on the Queen?"

Lottie giggled. "Is it? Goodness, I must read it again. I never thought of that. Anyway, your timing is excellent. Lucy is coming in half an hour."

A cat yowled in the hall, and Jemmy ran in, breathless.

"Tiddy doesn't like the new game," she said, and mocked a curtsey. "Good day, Madame. Do psychic ladies have cats to attend them?"

"They may," said Catherine. "But it is not required."

The girl grabbed a piece of iced sponge from the cake stand and ran off again.

If Lady Seldon was soon to be there, then Catherine's request—her purpose in coming—should wait until then. She talked hats and books with Lottie, and made light fiction of a recent sitting, where the old man who was hosting almost passed away in the middle of it.

"A heart tremor—nothing serious in the end, said the doctor. Such was the man's panic that he near died of fear."

Lottie wondered aloud that if the man had died in mid-session, his spirit might have spoken there and then through Madame Rostov. They debated the technical issues as if it were a game.

"Speaking of the psychic world, dear Katerina, I met a fascinating young man on the Embankment, a Mr Thomas Carnacki. He has recently taken a place on Cheyne Walk, and would you believe—he is a student of what he calls 'astarral vibrations,' which apparently—"

At the moment Lady Seldon was announced, whereupon a maid brought extra tea things, and fresh scones.

Other lives.

Two weeks ago Catherine Weatherhead stood below Christchurch, to be accosted by a ragged old woman, and to break a beer bottle over a man's head. Two weeks ago she heard of her cousin Jennie's brutal wounding and subsequent death. And here she sat in comfort, attended by servants, nodding her head in greeting to the slim, capable Lady Seldon—whose cream silk dress and lace trimmings would probably have paid a year's rent for some.

"You do not care for the style, Madame Rostov?" The other woman noticed Catherine's gaze.

"The dress is most pleasant, Lady Seldon. You will have to forgive me—I recently undertook a small task which has given me thought. I am distracted."

"Do tell. I have little enough distraction from committees and Harry's work. This escape to Lottie's is one of the few I will have this week."

Lady Seldon could not be played, not easily. Catherine would serve up fragments of the truth, well-larded for present company, and see what might come of it.

"I had cause to visit Spitalfields," she said. "You know that I occasionally assist the police, when there is reason to think that the Aether holds answers that the streets do not."

"With some success," said Lottie, smiling.

"It is unpredictable, I fear. Still, I had to sit with some there, poor souls. And I came across a well-spoken woman who was so down on her fortunes that I wonder she can manage another winter. The widow of a naval officer, left with two children and only a half pension, if that arrives at all."

"She should apply to the nearest Mission, or the Widowed

Women's Charitable Board, perhaps?" Lottie looked to Lady Seldon, who waited on Catherine.

"Her husband has gone, and she clings to pride. She was a seamstress once, and takes in mending. But imagine, from her own little house to a hovel in three years, and in Whitechapel, with murder all around at this very moment..."

The older woman put her plate down, her scone half-finished.

"I doubt you tell us this for instruction, Madame. A seamstress? Was the woman—is the woman—skilled with needle and thread, with materials?"

"Undoubtedly. I have seen her work."

"Would you vouch for her character?"

Catherine thought of Clarissa, and all that she knew of her cousin.

"Yes. Hard working, and steadfastly honest. She would rather her fingers bled than that she took charity. Even though she has suffered from childhood with her breathing, as well."

Lady Seldon nodded.

"We have never acknowledged," she said slowly, "The considerable amount of time that Madame Rostov has spent, indulging our curiosity concerning the spirit world. Or the inconvenience this must sometimes have caused. You might say that we are in your debt, Madame."

You might well say that, thought Catherine. But then again, this elevated circle had also offered social advantages to Madame Rostov, and to Catherine. She should not complain.

"There is no debt." She met Lady Seldon's eyes. "I do not ask for favour. I mention, only, a matter which has bothered me."

Lottie touched Lady Seldon's arm. "Lucy, you might—"

"I might. And I imagine that Madame Rostov thinks I might, as well. She is no fool." She smiled at both of them. "We are all politicians. I shall enquire, and write to you. There may be a place for a hard working seamstress in such straits—possibly somewhere that might be more conducive to the raising of children than the stews of Whitechapel. Is that satisfactory?"

"It would be a mercy for those concerned."

"Good. Your penance for raising a serious matter, Madame, will be to hear of Harry's latest row with Salisbury, and the uproar at Horse Guards. It will be instructive for you both—and it will allow me to say what I really feel, instead of nodding politely at every Godforsaken dinner table in London..."

The field narrows yet again.

There is initial promise in a medical man, who flits between a fine town-house off Finsbury Square and the byways of Spitalfields, bag in hand. Dry watches the comings and goings of women who visit a ground-floor room behind the Brick Lane brewery. The reasons for the man's furtive passage become obvious. The doctor removes the threat of new, unwanted life from women's bellies—for a price, no doubt. Nothing suggests that he conducts more extreme surgery in the Whitechapel alleys.

A lanky, square-jawed Jew prowls late past Christ Church, but only to meet a woman—married, Dry suspects—of his own religion beneath leafless trees. A student from Lincoln Inn stares at women as he skulks his way past—Dry follows him as well, but it seems that he is here in the East End to see his family, perhaps preferring that his classmates know nothing of his origins.

He pays little interest to public rumour. Jews, Poles, and Germans; actors, surgeons, and occultists. Any or none of these groups and individuals could display the behaviour he seeks. Edwin Dry is an educated man. A poor Jew in the East End is more likely to be knifed than to wield the blade.

For some, this work would be tedious; for him, these nights provide information which may be of use at some other time. He knows his city all the more because of them.

His routine shifts as he sees fit. Human behaviour interests him.

As long as they do not insist on talking.

She knew what the Deptford Assassin was doing. Whether her mind drifted on an omnibus, or she woke from night-sweats, it was the same. The bowler-hatted man was quartering the East End, observing, and his observations haunted her. She took strong drink late at night; it did not help. She immersed herself in sessions for the middle-classes, but even then she was not free.

In Vauxhall she was supposed to speak of a brother lost in war, and instead received images of huddled men, drinking in a Spitalfields tavern. She quit that sitting, with apologies, saying that malevolent spirits were on the Aether. Which they were.

One desperate evening she asked Mrs Bessovitch to stay with her in the parlour a while.

"I want to see if there is another mind there to be touched," she said. "The Whitechapel Murderer."

"Is big thing to do. And I am not psychic woman. What use am I?"

"To watch over me."

"Da. That I do, willingly. You want trumpet, maybe? Fancy board with letters?"

Catherine struggled to smile. She squeezed Mrs B's hand.

"Your company will be enough. I plan no tricks."

They sat with the gas-lights turned low, comfortable in loose clothing and the two over-stuffed parlour chairs. Mrs Bessovitch's knitting needles clicked and clacked, a reassuring rhythm.

Catherine sat back and closed her eyes. She had no set ritual, but sometimes there was a way to empty her own mind, to leave space for whatever might come.

At first she drifted through idle thoughts, from sad memories of Jennie to wondering if she had left a missing ear-ring under her correspondence. Should she buy lamb cutlets again; had Josiah suffered for writing to her…

Gradually she pushed these aside, trying to look into those wicked London nights where a killer roamed.

She is fear and the weight of the ceiling and the hand raised the heavy hand which has a stick but it does not this night and no there are tears and she has tried and this is his doing that she thought was his wish but it does not work it does not work she is lies and she is fear…

Catherine gasped, shifted, but dared not open her eyes. What was the grey face above, the red snarl filled with white teeth? Conners. Mr Conners from Hampstead, his wrath engaged with Mrs Bless…

She is lies and she told him so but she did not know she could not know and the soldier the soldier who cried out who shouted and the audience which hissed and booed and she had done had done her best oh so very much to please...

She tore away from images she did not want to see, and from the idea that Mrs Bless might deserve sympathy. Why those images had come she had no idea. What Conners did, what Bless pretended— these were not her concerns. Only...in the process, she felt pity, because she could sense that Mrs Bless might have a genuine gift, a slight one, and had squandered it, seduced by Conners's grand schemes and tours.

Her search. That was what mattered.

There were minds and a maelstrom of thoughts out there...

Fruitless.

It was half-expected. She had not sensed Jennie's death, after all, nor Martha Tabram's, nor those murders which followed after. She received only vague flashes of other lives, insights she could not use, and a muddle of unconnected images.

"I cannot sense him," she admitted at last. "It is as if he does not exist."

"Yet you see this other man." The needles clacked, and paused. "The man who wears the hat, who kills so neat."

"Edwin Dry, yes." She opened her eyes, breathed in the calm and quiet parlour. "Perhaps...is it possible that I cannot see both? That the presence of one masks the other?"

"Or is your own daemon, this Dry," said Mrs B. "So is not room for second daemon."

"I suppose that is possible." She felt dejected. "And there must be accidents, without any purpose. Minds meet and blur upon the Aether, and once in a hundred thousand times, they stay, bound and burdened. Unlooked for. My burden appears to be Mr Dry."

"Is Sud'ba, they say in St Petersburg. Fate."

"Are you really Russian, Mrs B?"

"Russian, Pole, Czech. I am many things." The landlady smiled. "I am Jew, most holy Orthodox, and so on. Even good Catholic once. I have travelled. It is best —on surface—to be whatever is useful, whatever does not bring more problem. Is why I understand there is Miss Weatherhead and Madame Rostov. Useful."

"Is why we are such friends," said Catherine, mimicking her

landlady's accent.

But her brief humour soured in the depth of night. At this moment, to be rid of Dry and to "see" the Whitechapel Murderer would have brought her some satisfaction, however savage his deeds. Then she might have been of use.

⚛

A letter from Doctor Mercier, arriving unexpected, included a pamphlet on the work of Washington Bishop, an American mentalist.

> *Though I place no great faith in so-called psychic disciplines, you may find this of interest, considering our occasional discussions on the matter. Mr Bishop states that his performances are based not on spiritual insights, but on close reading of the psychology and physiology of his subjects.*

A touch of the truth, thought Catherine. After so long a period of observation, she was closer to being able to place her fellow "psychics" in firm categories, fit for cardboard folders in any records office.

There were the open, sometimes even brash, mentalists, who claimed no powers beyond concentration and practice in legerdemain—they mystified and entertained by trickery, but did not mislead. She had nothing against them.

Then came the frauds, who flew the false flags of spiritual learning and ab-natural insight to cover their mentalist tricks. Their nonsense was drawn from the betrayals of the sitters' words and faces, common sense and such other information as could be easily gathered beforehand. Their sin, if that was the term, was that they did not admit it.

Next, if there were to be a stated hierarchy, came the Rostovs of the world, where inexplicable gifts came and went, requiring either periods of admitted failure or the employment of techniques used by the fraudulent. She believed that there were others of her kind, walking that thin line.

And above them…the truly sensitive, perhaps. Those whose talents had no explanation, who might well be able to seek out and converse with spirits, even the disincarnate souls of the dead. She had heard gossip of, but never met, one of this tier. She imagined that at the very least, they might have what she possessed, but be able to tune and turn the gift at will.

It struck her that there must be others who had attempted to do what she had, to sense this new killer. Curious, she brought out a selection of the various spiritualist magazines she received, all of which lay under her bed, by the chamber pot. She had not read any of them for weeks.

It did not take long to identify the prevailing wind. Spiritualists were imploring the authorities to listen to their disparate and often contradictory voices. They clamoured at police stations, and wrote to the newspapers, and yet nothing they provided appeared to be of any use.

The *Medium and Daybreak* journal carried a typical report, from a séance held in early September at a house on Kentish Town Road.

> The medium, Mrs C. Spring, was controlled, and appeared in great pain all over her body, as if suffering from severe wounds in the body; also went through the action as if cutting her throat. One of the sitters (being impressed) asked the control if it was the spirit of Mrs Nicholls, the woman who had been murdered at Whitechapel a short time ago, and the spirit answered: "Yes." It seemed that Mrs Spring, genuine or not, had stayed on safe ground, as the medium continued, "The fiend! The fiend! I am not the only victim; there will be others yet. More, more, before long, and of a more brutal kind. The police are asleep; in fact, it requires soldiers to keep watch. There is a gang of them. 'Tis a secret society."

The further Catherine read, the less faith she had in her profession.

By Upper Swandam Lane he kills a man, a Chinese standing watch by the Wheel of Fate, one of the opium dens near the wharves. Kelly's reports noted a client prone to lashing out, who rarely managed to perform. He was described as middle-class—a clerk or overseer in a cutlery firm—fair-haired, with a light beard and a temper, often to be seen in both Whitechapel and Limehouse.

The den's sentinel against police raids does not want to let Mr Dry into the Wheel of Fate, and presses the issue with a long, curved Eastern knife.

"You do not come to smoke," says the man. "I see your eyes."

Mr Dry is not a soldier or street brawler. Fighting is not his profession, and he avoids casual violence, but the Chinese man is insistent.

When it is over, Dry steps across the body and down crumbling steps which lead to an unmarked side-door.

The sentinel has died for nothing. It takes mere minutes to discover that the cutler's poor sexual performance is due to his persistent ingestion of opium, and that the man lacks the strength or co-ordination to be the Whitechapel Murderer.

Another name has gone from the list.

The last day of September 1888 was a Sunday. A few minutes after eleven in the morning, Mrs Bessovitch returned to the house with a newspaper. She placed the paper on the kitchen table next to Catherine's plate of toast, without comment. The headline said what was necessary.

Two more women had been murdered in Whitechapel.

FIFTY-SEVEN

The night of September 30 brought the worst night of murders in the East End, if only because two killings occurred within the span of an hour. Elizabeth Stride, who had come to London from Sweden when much younger, had her throat cut. Catherine Eddowes's throat had been cut, her face mutilated, and she'd been disemboweled.

Mary Jane briefly wondered if Stuart Brevard were the one doing the killing.

No, he is bold in his attacks, not secretive.

Reason kept telling her to leave London before Mr Brevard found her. Her heart insisted on staying to see Gabby's demise.

On Monday, October 1, Mary Jane had little more to offer the ordinary cove about the new murders. Even so, she gave him what she could from the rumour mill.

October 2, the trunk of a woman with no head or limbs was discovered within a structure on a construction site in Whitehall.

More rewards were offered for the capture of the murderer. The feeling of severe unease in the streets continued into October. As if suffering symptoms of a new contagion, the people Mary Jane saw walking the footways hurried when walking alone and clustered more tightly when in groups. They more frequently whispered their words, and cast suspicious glances in all directions.

With such horror common in the streets, Mary Jane thought her crime of hiring a killer ought to trouble her less. Though her heart had won the argument, her conscience would not let the matter rest.

She told herself that the black-eyed man was not the killer terrorising Whitechapel. He made little show of his work, while the one known as Jack the Ripper left his victims in the open, placed proudly on display.

FIFTY-EIGHT

They speak of "Jack the Ripper." There is a letter from the killer, signed thus but with no certain provenance. A ludicrous title, which may even be the creation of a minor journalist, eager to progress in his trade. Dry sighs and tuts. There is a stranger, a murderer in Whitechapel, yes, but such vainglorious names are for the credulous. A cheap affect, to give prominence to those who are commonplace. Any cat's meat man with a grudge could have done what has been done thus far.

More Jews are assaulted. They might as well mob Limehouse and find a random Chinaman or Lascar to adorn a lamp-post.

Dry pads the daytime streets, listening, sniffing the air. He is close to knowing this slaughterman who stirs the police, the newspapers and the mob so. As he surmised, there will be nothing about the killer that matters, excepting that he does what other weak men have only entertained in their cups. There will be deep-seated hatred for a mother, a wife, a girl who slighted him—and inadequacy.

This will not be a creature of his kind.

The authorities make no progress. Is Edwin Dry alone in understanding what might need to be done?

At times he wonders if he himself is the first journeyman or the last.

Catherine was allowed one shred of good news to set against her concerns. A letter came to say that Lady Seldon had spoken to a friend of her uncle, the friend being a Royal Navy captain who had retired due to injury. Unhappy that a fellow naval officer's family should be brought so low, he had an offer. The old lodge house by his house in Kent was empty—tiny and in poor repair, admittedly, but serviceable.

Subject to his housekeeper meeting Clarissa and approving, he would be willing to relocate Clarissa and the children there. Duties would include linen repairs, mending of the servants' clothes and such similar, minor tasks as were needed.

Catherine went to see her cousin, knowing that this could not be done through a note. The meeting was not easy. The family's place on George Street was a slum, if a clean one. It was worse than Brantridge Street, and even though Catherine knew that larger families lived in worse conditions, it was hard to bear. She showed Clarissa the offer from Captain Meredith.

"You have done this?" asked Clarissa.

Catherine steadied herself for the lecture on charity and interference. It did not come. Her cousin sat down by her mending, and twisted her hands together.

"I have hated you, Catherine—for your father's wealth; for your youth, and for your kindnesses. With Jennie gone, no doubt to tread her own path, away from my complaints, the children's needs and this dire place..."

Catherine could neither bear to speak the truth concerning Jennie, nor conceive of any coherent lie.

"No doubt Jennie...had her reasons. Or a sudden opportunity, we might hope."

"No doubt. I do not blame her."

It seemed awkward and unnatural, but Catherine knelt at her cousin's side.

"See, Clarissa, take this opportunity—for Benjamin and Maisie, at least. Be free of this place, and let them breathe the Kent air, not the London smog. Charles would have wanted it."

A remark which would have brought bitter words once, but Clarissa nodded.

"You are right." She eyed Catherine with sudden worry. "This is... genuine, to be trusted?"

"It is. The woman who arranged it is a chance acquaintance, above our station, much vexed by social conditions. She would not toy with me, I assure you."

She took an envelope out of her bag.

"Five pound notes are in there, Clarissa. If you will not take them, I shall find Benjamin and give them to him. Or if I must, to Maisie. Dates have been offered, and the money will see you to Captain Meredith's residence in good order."

"The housekeeper will not want me, sour and wheezing as I am."

Catherine stood up.

"Buy linctus, and sew a fixed smile to your lips."

Clarissa's cheeks were flushed. "I do not know what I should say to you—"

"Say nothing. Do what is needed." Catherine picked up her bag, pausing at the door. "I shall write to you, cousin—in Kent."

"And I shall reply," said Clarissa, seeming close to tears. "I shall reply."

⚜

Clarissa and the children would have a future. This change in their fortunes left Catherine with a sense of satisfaction. The nagging obligation she had felt to Charles's memory and to his family was discharged at last; better, she had frustrated her father in an issue of loyalty and responsibility to kin. She had stepped up where he would not. The act confirmed not her own selfless virtue, for she had no pretences to such, but Joshua Weatherhead's selfish vice. She took malicious pleasure from the thought, and was unashamed.

The news from Whitechapel had not improved, though.

Eden Mallick managed to get Catherine into the first day of the inquest on Catherine Eddowes. Rows of grave faces inside, an uneasy crowd without. They had stood at the back long enough to hear the City Solicitor, a Mr Crawford, questioning Frederick Brown, surgeon for the police. At least five minutes to make the wounds and cut out an organ, said Dr Brown. A kidney was missing. Death first, from a slashed throat, and then mutilation. She felt herself strangely detached from the reports; the violence of her visions was surely burrowing into her, becoming a part of what she knew.

Only later, as she and Mallick were heading back to the police station, did she lean against some railings and try to keep her breakfast down. It was not horror of the deeds described that turned her stomach, but the fact that the people who thronged the street immediately outside the inquest had shown such eagerness for gore. She saw no sign of care for the dead woman, only an almost savage curiosity as to the bloody details of the case.

More distressing was a shadow from the past that returned a few days later, a shadow which came in the form of a badly-written piece of correspondence from the old woman she had met at Christ Church, Mrs Hollis. Catherine had forgotten that the woman had something to ask of her.

The letter was a jumble of mismatched words which took time to decipher, but in the end held only one central question.

Mrs Hollis wished to know if Catherine Weatherhead had been the one who hired the killer at the Victualling Yard, the man who murdered Frederick Caille. If she were, wrote Hollis, then God bless her and keep her, for she had done a fine thing.

The question alone was a shock; that Hollis then explained that she was asking on behalf of a woman named Ginger made matters no better. How had that idea ever entered their heads? Catherine recoiled at the thought that another woman, a stranger, might know something of her involvement in that affair.

She wanted to tear up the letter and forget it, but a half-formed recollection troubled her. The woman Catherine had encountered with Jennie on Brantridge Street, the prostitute, had been introduced as Ginger.

Worse, Hollis wrote that her acquaintance enquired because she had fallen in with a certain man, a most unusual one, who was asking questions in Whitechapel. Ginger believed that this man was the Deptford Assassin. There was a description as well, enough to make Catherine sure that it was Edwin Dry.

Was it not enough that he was in her visions? Now he trailed blood through her correspondence.

Catherine lay on her bed that evening, reading and re-reading the letter. There was something she could not quite catch, a truth which eluded her until she woke from sleep with a start, around four in the morning. The room was cold, as cold as her tight belly.

No coincidence, no idle chance.

The Deptford Victualling Yard is sizeable, and has many shadows. He blends, dances in darkness, noting small details as he leaves. On Windmill Lane he sights a female figure clutching her shawl as she hastens to be elsewhere. She would be the one assigned to distract the night rounders...

First at Deptford, and then in Stepney...

The woman before him—Mary Jane Kelly—picks at her lace sleeves and tries not to meet his gaze. She has already been more useful than most, and he remembers her from Deptford, though she never saw him that night.

That face from outside Jennie's home, and the one in the vision— they blended so easily into each other now she had the link.

'Ginger' and Kelly were the same person.

And for two years Mary Jane Kelly and Catherine Weatherhead had circled the slender blade of Edwin Dry, knowing nothing of each other...

She plucked at her pillow, held it tight to her as if she were a child again.

All was connected, from her vision of Dry as he murdered a man in Islington, to the height of the Deptford Assassin's hunt through the squalor of Whitechapel; from the moment she first stepped into the house in Brantridge Street, perhaps, and became entangled in an affair of vengeance which should have been long forgotten.

She was a pawn in a great mechanism she could never hope to understand.

Later that morning she sat with Mrs Bessovitch and let her landlady read the letter from Mrs Hollis.

"It is too much," said Catherine. "What should I do? Should I write back—deny any knowledge of this?"

Mrs B brewed coffee, fortified with a spirit whose taste Catherine did not recognise—a fruit brandy of some type.

"Is hard," said Mrs Bessovitch eventually. "Here is old lady who hurts, and other woman who is not in good place. Somewhere is your bowler-hatted man, always watching."

"I know that." Catherine felt peevish. "Should I admit—in writing—what I have done? Is that not a dreadful risk?"

The landlady squinted at her. "Maybe I write with your words, and you do not put name. Then hand is different, and no one can prove it is you who says this or that."

It was a bearable compromise. She would go to Christ Church that week or next, speak as briefly as possible to Mrs Hollis and, if satisfied, hand over a reply which she had neither penned nor signed.

What "Ginger" made of it would be out of her hands.

The cab-man's hut by Borough High Street again—mugs of scalding tea, too much sugar and the milk on the turn. The occasional odd look from a hansom driver as the tall Russian woman spoke earnestly to the police inspector.

"Will you do it?" asked Catherine, for the third time.

Eden Mallick twitched and frowned, his face a map of indecision.

"He's mobbed, you know? Scrawny women holding up drawings of the Whitechapel Murderer, wives demanding their husbands be taken into custody. Bully boys who have nabbed a Jewish costermonger who once gave them the wrong change for a bag of oranges; letter after letter of useless information. Never seems to end."

For she had asked if he would assist her in seeing Chief Inspector Donald Swanson.

"It is a matter of great importance," she pressed.

"Not seen the murderer in one of your rum sessions, have you?" Mallick spat out a lump of milk, apologised. "Like half the table-knockers in London—and a few beyond."

"No. I have nothing to offer on the nature of the killer. But I do have something which may be of use to your friend."

"If you could tell me at least a little of what you intend..."

But she could not. She had seen Mrs Hollis, and satisfied herself that it was safe to leave the letter for Ginger with her. She had stayed through most of two sittings of the Eddowes inquest, and she had grown uneasy listening to the exchanges of men—some worried, some complacent.

As she heard yet another officer of the law admit that the investigation had made no progress, she became angry. She was not constrained by the thick, leather-bound books of medical and legal nonsense at the coroner's side, or by the tight collars of clerks, solicitors and officers of the law.

If Catherine Weatherhead was to be caught up in this dark game, whatever she chose, she would not be a pawn, she would be a queen. She would try, at least, to take a hand in what was to come, instead of waiting to be assailed by visions and hear of yet more terrible things beyond her ability to change.

A queen could order that dark things must be done, for the good of others.

"I beg that you trust me," she said to the inspector.

Mallick hummed and hawed, twitched, and gave in.

"I'll speak to him, if he has time."

"Thank you. I...I would appreciate it if you do not mention the matter to anyone else."

The inspector gave a sharp laugh. "Who would I tell, Madame? Hard enough that I must work with you, on rare occasion; harder if the lads at the station did say that I was all for tambourines and floating faces. Spirits should only come from bottles."

"It might be easier for us if that were so."

Mallick looked upon her thoughtfully, his eyelid stilled for once.

By Smithfield market, faced with Dry in the flesh, she had been consumed by fear and doubt. She had seen no option but to have her presence misunderstood, to commission him for murder before he grew wary of her, and left her bleeding in those alleys. In one sense, Frederick Caille died because at the height of her meeting with the assassin, Catherine Weatherhead wished to live.

Dry was the key. He was surely more lethal than any Whitechapel Murderer, meticulous, and, to the best of her knowledge, unstoppable. Not a vicious amateur with a hatred of street women, but one who was perhaps a master of his terrible trade.

A man who understood what was happening in Whitechapel; a man who might interest Chief Inspector Swanson greatly...

⁕

The summons to Scotland Yard came, at last.

At precisely eleven o'clock on Wednesday, October 17, Madame Rostov was ushered into an office inside the maze of the Central Police buildings. She walked from stark corridors into a room which was a monument to the investigation. Great maps of the east side of London were pinned to the walls, along with newspaper cuttings and handbills. Shelves bent under the weight of gazetteers and ledgers, propped against cardboard evidence boxes, and by the windows stood a large oak desk on which lay a single piece of blank paper.

Donald Swanson, the man behind the desk, rose to his feet. He had a long, heavy face with a prominent nose and a thick, drooping moustache. The eyes were sad, pre-occupied.

"Madame Rostov." He gestured that her uniformed guide could leave, and the door was closed on them. "I'll see ye for Eden Mallick's sake—the laddie and I go well back. We've shared a case or twa. But yuir pardon, Madame, I have nae time for fancy theories and spirit talk. A dozen letters from women claiming the Sight this day already, ay, all saying they know our Whitechapel man—"

"Deptford Victualling Yard," said Catherine, standing before the desk. "November 1886. A fire deliberately set in the rail sidings nearby, and four men dead."

He stroked his moustache.

"Sit ye down," he said, and took his own place as she did.

"A single man killed Mr Frederick Caille and his thugs. A single man who left no trace. Scotland Yard has no more idea now of that man's identity than they did almost two years ago."

"Ay, many have said the same. What do ye bring to me that's so new?" He squinted at her. "Is it yuir thought that the Deptford Assassin is this so-called 'Jack'?"

"Quite the opposite, Chief Inspector. My belief is that the Deptford Assassin may be your only chance of halting the Whitechapel Murderer."

"He has something useful tae me, this mystery man?"

"Yes."

They stared at each other.

"Ye're no a Russian," he said.

"You're not an Englishman. Does it matter? I can ask you, sir— do you seek an end to what is happening in the East End?"

He eased his large frame back onto the chair. "Frederick Caille is long gone, and scarcely mourned. Does this fellow of yuirs—if he exists—ken the name of the Whitechapel killer, and where he abides, for example?"

Catherine took a deep breath, clutched her bag across her lap.

"No. But he will, soon."

"Yuir spirits tell ye this?"

She stared. "Ask Eden Mallick again if I'm given to wild and vague statements. The Deptford Assassin is…I find it hard to explain. He is Death, when he wants to be. When he is paid to be, and he likes the coin."

Swanson tilted his head, his eyes narrowing. She was surprised, despite her bravado, that he had let her get this far.

"What is the blank piece of paper that you have on your desk, Mr Swanson?"

He looked puzzled.

"Not that it's yuir business, but it is from Sir Charles Warren. I am tae write tae him upon it when the Whitechapel Murderer is taken. A reminder of my duty."

"The man of whom I speak knows the streets as well as this 'Jack', and I do not believe he has ever failed to see a commission through."

He spread his fingers out on the desk top, almost touching the sheet of paper, and drew them together again.

"I have yuir general drift. Ye would set a hound on a hound, that's what ye're saying. But I dinna ken why ye're here before me with the tale, what Madame Rostov has to do wi' it. Last I heard, ye'd found a missing lassie in Southwark. Quite a step tae this."

It was. An insane, ludicrous step. But if it were taken, if the bowler-hatted man were all he seemed, then there would be no more women like Jennie killed, at least at the hands of the man sought by the police.

"Nor do I ken what you're bringing me that changes anything. I could offer bounty, as they say, but there are rewards on the air already. I'll wait, shall I, until yuir man decides if he's interested? Tell Inspectors Abberline, Reid and the rest tae wait a while?"

She was losing Swanson. She could see it. He was beginning to place her amongst the wild schemers and dreamers with just another fancy plan, people wanting to show that the authorities lacked skill and imagination. And the Deptford affair had been described again and again in newspapers and journals. Anyone could know if it.

She could walk away...

"You cannot wait." she said. "There are...rules. He needs his commission, and his coin. He needs to be asked."

A cough, a laugh, troubled Swanson for a moment.

"And ye'll be the one tae ask him?"

"I have done it before."

A definite laugh this time, deep in the policeman's throat.

"Lassie, I think we're done—"

"Deptford. Police Constable Retton was shot in the middle of the chest, with a bullet from Frederick Caille's gun. He fell next to Caille's desk. There was little blood there, because Retton was already dead. A long slender dagger had been thrust up under his jaw and into his brain."

Swanson bulked forward, his elbows on the desk.

"We didnae—"

"A single strike, and I saw it done. You did not publish all the details. If you wish, I can describe each move that was taken, each angle of thrust and fire. I can tell you which of the men in the outer office died first. These things are burned into my sight."

"How is that so?"

"It is so because whilst I work as Madame Rostov, I am also Catherine Weatherhead. I am the one who paid a man, a terrible man, to remove Caille from this earth, for what he had done to my family, for what he did to all those he touched. You will never prove it, Chief Inspector, because the man I hired does not make mistakes. He does not leave evidence. He has no personal interest in, or connection to, any that he has killed."

It was more than she had meant to say. It was more than she should have said.

His eyes widened in recognition.

"I did see ye afore, yes! I knew it. In Stepney, by God, where the Weatherheads lived, ay, when we sought motive for Deptford. You came to the door. I kenned there was something about yuir face when I met ye with Mallick, but could not settle on it."

"I told you. I am Catherine Weatherhead. I had good reason, very good reason, to do what I did, and you yourself know that is true. Not that anything said in this office could convict me—words from a hysterical young woman, the courts would say."

"I dinna..." He trailed away, his gaze drawn to the blank sheet on his desk. Catherine took her chance.

"I can help you lift your pen, Mr Swanson, and write upon that paper there. I can set the Deptford Assassin upon the Whitechapel Murderer."

An hour passed, with many turned away from Swanson's office. The two of them argued, and she managed to return as good as the Scotsman gave. She came close to being taken in charge, and close to being ejected from Scotland Yard as a hysteric who wasted police time. But he could not shake her—and he could not let go of what she brought to him.

Ye would set a hound on a hound.

Oh, she would, if she could manage it. Dry was almost there—a specific request and a decent purse would surely net him.

And he would net the killer of women.

She left Whitehall with more threats than promises behind her. But not only threats. Swanson and his colleagues were under intense pressure since the deaths of Catherine Eddowes and Elizabeth Stride.

He could not hide the fact. He did not consider it impossible that he might petition for a 'fighting fund', to be used as it must be, without the usual accounting.

Most unsettling for her, most unsettling of everything which happened in his office that morning, Swanson mistrusted Madame Rostov—but was close to believing Catherine Weatherhead.

⚬⚫⚬

Four descriptions left, four men who appear to have the qualities and habits he seeks. A changeable way with women, from callousness to wheedling compliance; moments of brutal action or obvious intent; long hours spent in the East End where they cannot be located, and glimpses of a knife close to hand. The killer will likely cover inadequacy with arrogance. Other matters of physique and manner will be evident.

One of these men will fit the bill.

Mary Jane Kelly has done her work with commendable efficiency. So many incidents of violence, gathered from the women of the streets— incidents from the petty to the almost murderous. Almost. Someone has stepped across that thinnest of lines, and has not stepped back.

Dry will soon understand.

And there is the Gorse woman. He has agreed to remove her, to settle his informant's fears. Business is business, however small the coin. The woman who must die has no apparent value; had it mattered to him, he would have described Gabriella Gorse as an unpleasant individual. But then, so are a number of his clients. Morality is rarely relevant when craft is required.

The journeyman who works only for the virtuous has few customers.

⚬⚫⚬

October tore at Catherine, pushed her from one imposture to another. Revealed to Swanson by her own hand, she feared the consequences. She spent as little time as possible at the Southwark police station, wondering if Swanson would tell what he knew to Eden Mallick. And there had been snide comments from some of the officers at the station. If she were so good a psychic, why had she not yet identified the Whitechapel Murderer? They too had seen the newspaper reports of everyone and their spirit guide coming forward with wild theories.

Superintendent Neylan was less perturbed.

378

"The Lord will guide us, Madame Rostov," he said. "Only He can provide us with the Instrument we need."

The Instrument we need. Much the sentiment she had used with Chief Inspector Swanson, although she doubted that the bowler-hatted man came from the Lord.

As Catherine Weatherhead she brooded, steeling herself for what she must attempt; as Madame Rostov, she kept such appointments as would meet her living costs, nothing more. Her sittings were turbulent, broken in on by impressions of the East End, meaningless flares of dirt-floored rooms and filthy alleys, unexplained passage through rookeries, as if Dry were shedding images as he went, and only she were there to pick them up.

The nights were worse, for she was more open and vulnerable in sleep. Her fortune was that most of these fever-dreams were forgotten on awakening—most, but not all…

One man speaks to another, a joke which does not please. This is hardly a public house, more a ground-floor room with the back wall knocked through, a couple of casks raised on a broken table. The drink is cheap, taken illicitly from a brewer's dray between deliveries.

The men separate in ill temper, and Dry follows the one who did not laugh. A circuit of Flower and Dean Street, Thrawl Street and Angel Alley, then up towards Christ Church, and east.

His quarry has the look, the way of moving. It may be him. Eyes hooded, noticing each woman on the streets, a minute pause when a prostitute stands alone beneath a gas-lamp. Tall enough, strong enough. It would fit those copies of the autopsy reports which were so easy bought. Such a frame could have managed the tasks easily. Long, flexible fingers. The stranger has clothes that any man might wear at night around here, too anonymous to place his profession, neither so fine as to catch attention nor rags to elicit pity.

The description also fits well with that of an unknown client who could not stiffen his wand or spill his seed during two separate encounters with Kelly's prostitutes, back in June. Both women had been kicked in crotch and belly afterwards, though not fatally.

Most telling of all, Dry loses him. Somewhere in the maze by the Hanbury Street baths, his man is gone. Not because the stranger knew he was being observed—no one has yet seen Edwin Dry if he was truly not willing to be seen—but because it is a habit, a way of being. This man, this beast, slinks quiet and cunning by nature. He does not want his passing to be noted, even if there is no one to note it.

It is sufficient. Now Dry has a true feel of the man.

A note for Madame Rostov waited at the Holborn post office, unsigned:

Anderson has returned, but he has nothing. The hound from Deptford may be needed. By any means necessary, one far above me says, such is the pressure upon us. There are funds.

Chief Inspector Swanson had come to a decision, then. More, he had written to Madame Rostov. He had not named Catherine, which implied he might keep her deception between them.

It was to happen. Should she have the ability to find Dry, the courage to face him…and should he be able to isolate the Whitechapel Murderer. Her nights, her unwished-for moments in other places—these suggested that he was close to doing so.

He knew nothing of her mind, of that she remained sure, but she knew something of his. She also knew that he had places of business, not often used but always available.

At six o'clock on a Tuesday morning she was settled in an alcove off the main room of the Crown and Sceptre, not far from Smithfield Market. A repetition of the time when she had, almost by accident, commissioned the murder of Frederick Caille.

She read the papers, and sipped at a chipped mug full of tea— the latter provided unwillingly by the landlord. She drew attention, a respectable-looking woman alone in a working men's haven, and she drew visitors. Each visitor to her table, from the awkward young apprentice butchers to the lurching porters with a glint in their eyes, received the same response. She would lift up an unread newspaper, and expose the barrel of a small revolver which lay beneath. A loan from Mrs B.

"Is from Belgium," her landlady said. "Has six shots, only three bullets."

"I hope to use none of them," Catherine reassured her.

The sight of the pocket revolver, and her hard stare, kept her from molestation. It also protected the fifty pounds that Swanson had sent her, a token of his seriousness.

When the patrons accepted that she had no intention of being chaperoned or providing them with entertainment, her presence brought talk, most of it on the edge of her hearing, and that was satisfactory. Necessary, in fact, for her purposes. Two hours later she folded up her newspapers, slipped the gun into her purse and departed.

She did the same the next day, with no result except braver chatter around her, gossip as to who she might be.

On the third morning, he was there when she arrived, his bowler hat placed in the very centre of the small table. This time he had round, tinted glasses and a short moustache. His suit was dark blue, with a narrow navy stripe in the trousers, and his boots gleamed.

"You wanted to speak to me," said Edwin Dry, and he rose slightly from his seat.

She sat down opposite him.

He was silent, motionless; she tapped her fingers nervously against her leg, an echo of Evelyn Caille. Catherine tried to look at him properly, struck by the lack of anything extraordinary, threatening or even interesting about his appearance. A bank teller, an accountant's clerk, secretary to a solicitor. A man of no importance in the greater schemes of those who thought they mattered. He smelled of… nothing. No cologne, no hair oil or other preparation.

She began to understand why he slipped so easily unnoticed, un-witnessed, across the capital. He was no one's concept of anything except a modest, quiet middle-aged man. Nor was he even middle-aged. Under thirty, she would have said now she was paying attention, but easily passing for almost fifty if he wanted.

"The moustache was not there before." It was an inane thing to say.

"It did not exist yesterday; it may not exist tomorrow. You require something of me."

She started to turn her head, to look around the tavern and he flicked one finger against the beaten copper of the table top. She stopped at the sound of his fingernail against the metal.

"The cautious, sidelong glance," he said. "The habit of those who feel vulnerable, feel they might be observed. It is one of the ways that others realise you *are* vulnerable."

"Yes, I…I suppose so."

"Preparation is key. I have already looked, already seen. The others in here are noted, filed for reference. None will interfere." He examined the finger he had flicked against the table, seemed to find it to his satisfaction.

"If you do not require my services again, then you have information for me. There is a matter which presses, that you feel you must bring to my attention."

"No, I have…I do have another commission." She had to haul that out, to make her lips form the words. That she could say "another" seemed ridiculous at that moment, however determined she had been when she planned this.

Pale eyes regarded her. Irises that were a watery, washed-out blue, with wide pupils. Wide black pupils, like the eye-sockets of the dead. Beneath those smoothly shaven cheeks were bones, hard white bones. He wears a skull, she thought. And he lets me see it.

"I am somewhat engaged at this moment. You have encountered another Frederick Caille?" The enquiry seemed perfunctory, without great interest. "I may be available, later in the year."

She felt over-heated; she perspired, and her hands were helpless things, fluttering from her wrists, unsure what to do with themselves. She must be more Madame Rostov, less Catherine. She had managed it with Swanson. Everything that came to mind was away from the point.

"Do many…do many clients come back to you, a second time?"

"No."

"Why not?"

"Because seeing me reminds them of what they have done, and their own vulnerability." The left corner of his mouth lifted, almost unnoticeable. "I am not owned, indentured or beholden to anyone. Thus anyone may purchase my services. This makes them uncomfortable. As it should."

"I do not fear you." Which was almost true, to her surprise. She feared the situation, the madness of what she had conceived, and she feared failure in her endeavours. What she felt about Dry himself she could not grasp.

"That is why I am still here. You interest me. To a point."

To a point. Her belly strained against her undergarments; her collar was choking her, and her throat was so dry. In the background, men laughed and sank their pints of dark ale, jostled and argued. Lived.

Say it. Say it. Strike to the heart of it.

"There is a murderer, in Whitechapel," she said, nearly a gasp. "You must know this. He has slaughtered four women at least."

"You assume that it is a man behind the recent killings."

"I..." Catherine laced her fingers before her. It was no assumption—it was taken from her visions, a matter she must not let slip. "Yes. I mean, surely—"

"Women should not be underestimated in these times."

Was this his humour, at her expense?

"But it is a man?"

"It is," agreed Dry. "A flawed one, but persistent. Weak, as far as temperament goes. He will continue, in a fruitless attempt to avoid his own failures."

"You know this already?"

"I do. He will not stop, because he can not."

"Unless the Deptford Assassin tracks him down and kills him."

His pupils widened slightly, a black stare that pinned her, examined her. As with their previous meeting in Clerkenwell, he was silent for some time, and then she saw that single, studied blink of his eyelids.

"That is your commission?"

"It is." There, she had said it. "I have access to funds from... certain authorities. I should say no more than that. If you need some proof, I may be able to bring clearer details of—"

"That will not be necessary."

"But do you not wish—"

"I take my clients at their word. If their word turns out to be false, then I remind them of their mistake."

You kill them. She wet her lips. "I would not deceive you. But I must know, can you stop him? The police would have him taken, and face justice."

"The police would have many things, but will receive few of them. I can put an end to him. That is my trade. You should know that better than most, after Deptford."

She had expected that response, even though she knew that Swanson would prefer the Whitechapel Murderer alive, in chains.

"You are sure that you can do this?" A remark she regretted immediately, for fear he would take offence.

He did not seem bothered. He took off his glasses and wiped the lenses with a small white linen handkerchief. "You speak of the constabulary—the source of your funds, I imagine. They are well-advised to have used you so. It caught my attention. And no doubt you have some personal stake in the matter."

"I want him dead."

She had not expected to speak with such vehemence. Yes, she wanted it, and for so many reasons that she could not sort them for herself. Sense did not apply. Because her brother Josiah would be waking now, and wondering at the cramps in his fingers from last night's book-keeping. Because Uncle Jack had taken so long to die of the rot within him. Because she had never been to Jennie's common grave…

Because Mrs Bessovitch was out of cocoa, and Catherine had forgotten to fetch more.

She drew a leather purse from her bag and placed in on the table.

"An advance for your efforts, a token, but better than a single sovereign this time"

He pocketed the purse with an economy of movement, slipping it inside his jacket.

"There will be one more death," he said. "Someone who is inconvenient, who is no loss."

And there is the Gorse woman. He has agreed to remove her, to settle his informant's fears. Business is business, however small the coin.

She remembered that, from her dreams. Something to do with the prostitute called Mary Jane Kelly. Again, Catherine was not supposed to know of such things.

"Surely that can be avoided?"

"No. She will die, whatever you say next. This way she will die and might be of use. An end to 'Jack,' and all well again in London Town." He turned the hat before him, first to the left, then to the right, until it was exactly where it been. "Tell me, I am interested. We sit here in polite discourse, early on a fine—if brisk—morning. You are a young woman who tells her clients she can converse with the dead. I, on the other hand, tell my clients the truth."

"I do not understand your point."

"But you do. You wrestle and agonise over morality, ethics. I imagine that you have deceived parents, friends, acquaintances. You have done what was necessary. I make no judgement, but it is clear that you do. You judge me, and you judge yourself. Are such exercises a good use of your time?"

"You kill people!" she protested.

"Everyone does." He smiled, and took up his hat. "Good day, Miss Weatherhead. I have work to do."

She did not look up to watch him leave the tavern.

She merely sat, and wondered what she had done. *Good day, Miss Weatherhead.* She realised he had told her, without any particular emphasis, that he was aware of both of her identities.

He knew all that she was.

"Your tea," said the landlord, setting the mug down on the table and spilling some of it. He eyed the open door, then Catherine, almost crouched in her corner. "The gentleman paid. Yesterday."

FIFTY-NINE

Maria Harvey continued to spend nights with Mary Jane on the occasions Barnett went away seeking work in nearby districts. That saved funds that would have gone to paying doss. Barnett came home early from one of those searches drunk and angry that he'd had no luck. He and Mary Jane had a row about Maria being in his bed, and he threw her out. Mary Jane went with her to Julia's room across the court. The man she'd taken up with, Harold Owen, had been away for several days, and she was glad for the company.

Mary Jane had spoken with Mrs Hollis each week since she'd said she would write to Catherine Weatherhead. On Friday, October 26, beside Christ Church, Mrs Hollis handed Mary Jane an envelope addressed simply to "G." Inside, she found a hand-written letter. She did not pull the letter out completely. Instead, she tucked the envelope into her bodice, turned to the old woman and said, "Allow me to take you for a meal."

They moved south along Commercial Street to the Golden Heart tavern. On such a gloomy day, the tall windows and skylights of the establishment provided a welcomed brightness. From the side service, they chose cold chops, pea's soup, buttered bread, and hot tea. Since Mrs Hollis had few teeth, Mary Jane helped cut the chops into small pieces.

"What can you tell me about Jennie's brother, Lieutenant Charles Weatherhead?" Mary Jane asked.

"I didn't know him, and can tell you only what I've heard." Mrs Hollis told all that she knew about the life of the man, her few words on the matter easily fitting between the mostly gummed mouthfuls of her meal. Mary Jane wished she had taken more interest in Jennie's family.

"Can you tell me about what happened to your son and the Lieutenant?" Mary Jane asked, hoping the request did not stir the woman to further grief.

Mrs Hollis took a deep breath, wiped her eyes, and said as if reciting, "On the last day of October, 1885, my son, John Hollis, were among three midshipman and an officer killed by bad victuals aboard the HMS Penelope, God bless their souls, while the ship was on coastal guard duty out of Harwich." She paused for a moment, wiped away tears.

Mary Jane imagined that Mrs Hollis, having offered the tale many times while begging, had unknowingly acquired the sound of recitation in her delivery of the words. Also that way of speaking of the events perhaps helped the woman keep her distance from them.

"Lieutenant Charles Weatherhead were invited to dine with the midshipmen," she continued, more at ease. "Frederick Caille, committing fraud against the government, supplied those deadly victuals. When we took the case to court, he bested us, and we all lost everything we had."

They stayed quiet for a time eating, until Mrs Hollis broke the silence, an embarrassed look on her face. "I have become uncomfortably full, and after you purchased so much."

"Not to worry," Mary Jane said with a smile.

Poor woman, her stomach has shrunk away from lack of good food.

She helped Mrs Hollis load the remainder of the chops and buttered bread into handkerchiefs and sent her on her way.

Alone, Mary Jane moved south toward the River Thames, eager, yet strangely unwilling to read the letter. Somehow, the communication seemed a message from Jennie—her last—and Mary Jane wasn't certain she wanted to know what it said.

She got the feeling someone followed. Glancing behind her quickly a couple of times, she saw a figure at a distance among the foot traffic, one that aroused her suspicion. Each time she caught sight of him, he seemed to hide, once behind a stack of barrels at the opening to a back lane, and then into a building entrance the next. She had the impression that the ordinary cove wouldn't do anything as undignified as duck out of sight. Remembering Stuart Brevard's previous attack, and his willingness to rattle locked doors and enter buildings in Globe Road, Mary Jane didn't think he would merely stalk her. No, he wanted to get his hands on her.

Could be one of Brevard's hired toughs—not the tall one, though. Wrong shape.

A member of the Gully Bleeders might have been sent to keep an eye on me. Did they discover that she had kept Julia, Maria, and Glory off the streets? That didn't seem to represent a loss of income sufficient to anger them. Might they have somehow caught wind of her efforts at information-gathering? Would they care about that?

Mary Jane realised the stalker could be Barnett. Though she thought he'd be looking for work, he had the free time and clearly wanted to keep her from talking to Fleming.

And that left Joseph Fleming. Thinking briefly that he might be the stalker, she had a desire for him to catch up, but knew better than to wait and find out.

Glancing back, she saw the figure once more, across the street. He ducked out of sight, just as a red haired gentleman, moving swiftly, turned into the street at a crossing directly behind Mary Jane.

Stuart Brevard!

His eyes locked on hers. His straining features showed that he clearly recognised her. He rushed toward Mary Jane, closing the distance between them to a few yards.

Without looking first, she entered the road. A passing carriage clipped her and she spun around, but kept her feet. She dodged her way across, and didn't look back until she'd gained the footway on the other side. Hearing an angry cry, and the complaint of a horse, she turned.

A hansom had stopped, its driver climbing down. Stuart Brevard lay just beyond, his head stove in against the granite kerb. Blood pooled beneath his head quickly.

Mary Jane froze. The man was gone. He would never rise, would never trouble her again. She could see that he was indeed dead.

The Black-eyed man's confident words came back to her, "He is of no consequence." *Did he know Brevard would end this way? Did he have something to do with it?*

As pedestrians gathered around to gawk at the tragedy, Mary Jane stumbled away, her heady feeling of relief a confusion while her heart still pounded and her trembling continued.

At the next crossing, she looked back at the knot of stalled traffic around the calamity, and saw the stalking figure once more.

Mary Jane turned away, took deep breaths to calm her racing heart.

Pure fear and fancy. I have nothing to fear anymore!

No longer must I leave London!

I shall remain in Miller's Court long enough to see that Gabriella Gorse pays. Then, I'll leave Barnett, find lodgings of my own, and improve my situation. Once I have the chink, I might remove to the West End and reestablish myself there.

SIXTY

By chance, Dry sees one of his informant's enemies die—an unimportant, red-headed thug by the name of Brevard, who had been following her. Kelly had clearly hoped that the Deptford Assassin might step in to rid her of the man. He might have; he might not. It would have depended on how useful she was—otherwise, it was her own affair.

In the end, there is no need for blade, gun or garotte. The day is overcast, and Brevard steps out into the road too quickly, without looking. He is taken by the hooves and wheels of a hansom cab; those or the cobbles beneath make swift work of him. The man's eye had been on Kelly crossing the street, and for that he died.

Appropriate, perhaps.

Dry is watching over his interests, as always. He slips between the gawking and trilling pedestrians. He murmurs the single word "Doctor," and makes a quick examination of the body. The head is crushed. As the cab driver protests his innocence, two drunks try to unhitch the horse, and further arguments ensue, drawing in the onlookers. In the moment afforded by this, Dry retrieves a wallet and a sheaf of small posters. They appear to be a duplicated drawing of Kelly, a sketched portrait that Brevard must have distributed as he tried to track her down. It is a reasonable, though not perfect likeness. "Andriette" is the name below the picture—one name amongst the several that his informant has used.

He pockets one of these, already seeing a use for it, and he is gone, before any can question his actions or his true profession. This incident has done no harm.

No harm at all.

SIXTY-ONE

Within a half-hour's walk from the site of Stuart Brevard's death, she found herself at the river. She suffered a puzzling melancholy in the midst of elation over the death of her tormentor.

Though she felt that luck had served her, and that Mr Brevard had got what he deserved, after seeing such a chance death she felt small and fragile within an uncaring world.

The feeling will pass, and my life will get better.

Standing on the east Customs House stairs that led down to the muddy bank, she heard the drone and grumble of the city behind her, across the river, and in the water below. Above, the grey, overcast sky threatened rain. She watched the living water roll unconcerned beneath the bustling activity on the Thames. Ships moved slowly, ponderously through the current, some manoeuvring into position for mooring, while smaller boats moved more swiftly around them. Many inactive vessels lined the banks, moored to docks or dolphins.

A wonder they don't jam up the waterway.

A bell drew her gaze to a crane in motion at a dockyard to the east. She watched the machine pluck cargo out of the belly of a steamship. *Like a red kite enjoying a meal*, she thought. A steam-powered signal horn sounded at the construction site of Tower Bridge less than a half mile further downriver. Though they were indeed building and not dismantling, the men and equipment on and around the bridge's black skeleton put Mary Jane in mind of carrion-eaters going after a carcass.

The breeze brought her the unpleasant stench of rotting fish and other river life atop an ever-present, but light odour of night soil. She caught a smell of something burnt, probably a remnant of the docks fire that had occurred the night of Polly Nichols's murder.

Thoughts of death and destruction—I must banish them.

Mary Jane finally pulled the envelope from her bodice, unfolded the letter from within, and read:

> *I know not how to address you because I do not know your true name. Perhaps that is for the best. Although our poor J defended you as a true friend and I only know what she told me, I had misgivings about her involvement with you.*

I have trouble deciding whether to love you for befriending and helping her or hate you for teaching her the business that killed her. I would like to include you among those I blame for her death, but know that her situation was complicated by her own grief, anger, and pride. I might just as well include myself for being single-minded in pursuing elusive notoriety in a dodgy business of my own, while I should have helped her more than I did.

I know from speaking with the woman who delivered this message to you that you seek answers only I can provide. Should you have questions about our shared tragedy, she can answer them.

Yes, I hired a man to dispatch the one responsible for our family loss. From the descriptions conveyed to me, it seems that you know him. I was drawn into using him after hearing J's mother, my aunt, request such a resolution on her deathbed. I know almost nothing about him, and suspect that I will never know more.

I do not anticipate consequences from the hire, beyond the torments of my own conscience. Of that, I warn you, should you find yourself considering business with him.

Perhaps we shall meet one day. I remain uncertain how I might feel about that.

All the same, I wish you good fortune,

So much did Mary Jane share the misgivings conveyed in the letter, she could have written the message to herself.

Self pity!

She wiped away her tears.

The message didn't seem like words that might come from a swindler.

Mary Jane realised that she was relieved to find little new information about the ordinary cove. Now that she'd paid him to kill, she had some fear to learn more about him.

Though hard to resist, better not to pick at that scab.

"You have something for me," came his voice from directly

behind Mary Jane.

Startled, she let go of the letter. A breeze sent the paper sailing up and northward, past the ordinary cove, who stood three steps above her. To her relief, he made no move to catch it.

She watched the letter go, not wanting to turn and face his black gaze for fear that he might read from her eyes or expression Catherine Weatherhead's message.

An unreasonable fear, yet he might well see that I hide some new knowledge of him.

"Yes," she said following an uncomfortably long silence. Out of the larger pocket Maria Harvey had sewn for her, Mary Jane pulled the pages that she and her girls had assembled concerning the lives and murders of Elizabeth Stride and Catherine Eddowes. The number of pages had grown because of all the increased fear and fancy they had recorded, not just involving the two murders, but all sorts of tales of crimes and oddities from the Whitechapel rumour mill. Increasingly, Mary Jane and her girls could not decide what held a kernel of truth and what was mere chaff.

The black-eyed man had killed at least one murderer: Caille. Perhaps Mary Jane's efforts with her girls would help him kill more of them. She handed the pages over with a glance in his direction, then quickly returned her gaze to the activity on the water.

With that short glimpse of his eyes came the notion that he *had* somehow read Catherine Weatherhead's message before Mary Jane did and that he didn't care what it said. She didn't know why she thought that, and she wasn't going to bring the matter up with him.

"Someone follows you," he said.

"Brevard?" she said without thinking.

The ordinary cove didn't respond.

Not just fear and fancy, then—I did see another man.

Again, she wondered who else might be after her. She didn't think Barnett dangerous. If Fleming stalked, he did so with amorous intentions. That left innumerable members of the Gully Bleeders, including Nick Shears, and possibly unknown persons. Fear began to well up inside her again.

"What can be done to stop him?" Mary Jane asked, hoping he might offer to remedy the problem.

He merely extended his right hand toward her.

She looked at him, concerned that if she took his money, he might not deal with Gabriella Gorse.

"I will deal with the woman," he said.

Oddly, his evident lack of concern calmed her fears somewhat.

He wouldn't bother paying me if he thought my life was in danger, she thought.

Mary Jane held her hand under his and received another gold sovereign. The Saint George and the Dragon image on the coin's tail flashed dully at her, bringing with it a sense of danger.

"The Whitechapel Murderer...," the black-eyed man said.

Is that the man following? Mary Jane's heart took a rapid turn in her chest. She held her hands out for balance. The air cooled on her exposed flesh.

"...as part of my plan for the woman, Gorse," he said, "he will be on to you."

"No!" Mary Jane cried. Her vision shifted dizzyingly—trying to take in everything at once—and a wave of nausea took her to her knees.

The ordinary cove remained impassive.

"Is he now?" she asked, words barely a whisper.

He didn't answer. Perhaps he did not hear.

"Is he!"

Again, nothing from the man standing above her.

In her horror, Mary Jane dropped the sovereign and folded in the middle. She hugged the stair, the chill granite all the world offered in that moment that felt certain and solid. Her life had come undone and seemed to fly apart with the sound of the golden coin rolling and bouncing against the stone stairs in its increasingly mad dash to the muddy bank below.

I cannot continue!

"Should you want to live...," he began.

She barely heard him for the thoughts churning in her head of the recent murders; what she'd learned of the cruelty of the killer, and the mutilations of the victims.

"...if you don't want to end up like those women..."

Those words came to her clearly, and she listened.

"... you will do as I say and ask no questions. Stay close to home and people you know until I instruct you otherwise. You must go on as if nothing is amiss. I will be watching."

He still needed her for something, but what? She knew he wouldn't answer if she asked.

What had Thomas said on the day Mary Jane discovered him in London? "Misery loves company. Criminals need coconspirators, and they'll get them by hook or by crook. Once you've worked for them, they'll hold it over you or find some other way to make you do it again."

Mary Jane had had a strange confidence in the ordinary cove before. Without something of that again in that moment, she might have thrown herself in the Thames. Finally, she gained the courage to ask him to remove the threat stalking her. She glanced up, only to discover that he had gone.

Mary Jane remained, clutching at the stone stair.

Did he trick me? Did he want me dead all along? Does he have any reason for that?

He'd said he'd deal with Gabriella Gorse, and somehow Mary Jane still believed him. Why fulfill his contract with her if she would soon be dead? He said he'd be watching. Would that be to protect her, or for pleasure in seeing the cruelty that might unfold?

She found no answers to the questions.

The coming of the dark got her moving.

Mary Jane abandoned the gold sovereign. Some lucky mudlark would find the coin.

She had to get home to Miller's Court before nightfall.

Mary Jane did not sleep that night. The next day, she wanted to return to laudanum. Instead of resuming her old habit, she drank heavily in the following days.

The black-eyed man had said, "As part of my plan for the woman, Gorse, the Whitechapel Murderer will be on to you."

Because he had not responded when she asked if Jack the Ripper were the one following her, Mary Jane tried unsuccessfully to persuade herself that the Whitechapel Murderer was not indeed after her.

I could pack up and run out, catch a train, and start over somewhere else with nothing.

If he wasn't then after me, he may be now. She realised that fleeing the city might give him a chance at her in a place with fewer potential witnesses. *Better remain where I might have the help of those I know.*

She would have spoken of her fears, yet to do so she would have had to speak of the ordinary cove. Considering that, she wondered what might be said that anyone would believe. He seemed a figment, indescribable. She didn't even know his name. Even though her girls had helped her, she'd never told them who had charged her with the task of gathering rumour. They knew nothing about him.

Above all, Mary Jane knew that he would not want her to speak of him. She would do as he'd instructed because, oddly, she feared the black-eyed man more than she did the Whitechapel Murderer.

With her distress and disquiet over the looming threat, Mary Jane took out her frustration on the one who might have protected her. She started drunken rows with Barnett over nothing. She chided him for knocking over and breaking her only wine glass. She could not let go of her outrage over the burn spots in the bedclothes, a consequence of his drinking too much and falling asleep in bed while smoking his pipe. An affront to a woman who "ought to be seen with a handsome man," Mary Jane could not abide the length of his moustache ends not matching. She laughed at him for what she saw as his need to always repeat the last word anyone said.

Repeating *his* last words, she mocked him on and off, until the early evening of October 30, when he'd had enough and gave her a shove. Mary Jane fell back, putting an elbow through a glass pane and cracking another in the smallest of the room's two windows. Her sleeves protected her. She stormed out angrily to have more drink at the Ringers. Worried about the Whitechapel Murderer stalking her, she fairly ran all the way to the pub, a distance of about twenty-five yards.

The next day, Barnett's side of their bed felt cold. He had gone, taking some of his things with him.

Mary Jane never dreamed he'd leave her.

I used and abused him, but he is not the fool I am!

Trying to remember how she'd got home the night before, she found either fancy or hazy recollection of Joseph Fleming coming to her aid. Had he seen her home, tried to pay her for services, and

kissed her while standing at her door?

Fancy, she decided. *Wishful thinking! A desire for a protector, though I had one and drove him away!*

The next day, November 1, Barnett came to Miller's court. Upon answering the door to his knock, Mary Jane thought hopefully that he was returning.

"I've come for the rest of my belongings," he said. "I've taken a room at Buller's boarding house." He moved about the tiny room, stuffing clothing and a few items in a sack.

Disappointed, she stood in the doorway, hoping to keep him there. She could not feel good about her motives—she did not want the man himself, just the protection he might provide.

"Please forgive my horrid treatment of you and come back," she said.

"Back" Barnett said. He offered her two shillings. "Please take this. Won big on the dogs for once."

"No," she said, "you'll need the funds."

He approached the door to leave.

"Won't you reconsider and stay?" she asked, still blocking the threshold.

"Reconsider," he said. "I've paid for a week at Buller's. Perhaps when that's done."

That may well be too late.

The look in his eyes suggested he could not be persuaded. Mary Jane stepped aside, and he left.

SIXTY-TWO

Dry has been commissioned, which means there is no longer need to ponder or make judgments on what he should do concerning the Whitechapel Murderer.

The decision has been made.

He watches, hat pulled low, overcoat tightly buttoned to the neck. High on the roof of an abandoned tenement, inches from a chimney stack of prodigious height and dubious integrity, the soles of his boots flat and firm against the few reliable tiles. Good boots make all the difference in his line of work. Double-stitching and supple leather; support for the ankle and enough iron in the toecap to disable with one kick. Laces which, if needs be, can be threaded free and twisted around a vulnerable throat.

Of late, he makes his own footwear.

Perched there, four stories above the streets, the sad world of human endeavour is spread out before him. He has often marked how rarely people look upwards.

A sly rain falls on Spitalfields, finding its way under every door, through every crack in every window. People talk of weather as a gift or curse, which should dictate their habits and their moods; they are close to obsessed with how it drives them.

To him it is merely one factor amidst a hundred others.

He faces an interesting challenge. The man is quick and handy with the knife, a beast as cunning as the rain—and fast. He has the measure of the area, and is watchful for interference—no one has yet been able to say they have seen him at his bloody work. Near every description Dry has seen contains a fragment of the man's appearance, but none are correct.

Are you sure you can do this?

That is what she said, the woman with ice grey eyes, her hair disordered, her jaw jutting out to hide her own doubts.

How would he be Edwin Dry if he was not sure?

As with Deptford, this will be a demonstration piece, the work of a journeyman who advances in his trade. Once again this curious woman, Catherine Weatherhead, brings him something of interest, something which offers to extend his abilities.

And there is the issue of his informant—Kelly—who wants her rival dead. Some matter of street gangs and prostitution which scarcely interests him, but she has been useful. The police and Weatherhead require this "Jack" removed; Kelly requires Gabriella Gorse removed. He sees no need to separate the two commissions.

He will conceive a single plan.

An elegant plan.

Eden Mallick was shot on November 1, not far from the Compass Rose. It was a wet Thursday evening. Around the same time that East End dockers broke into the house of a Polish family in Stepney and said they would haul the husband away as Jack the Ripper. The man had "looked queer" as he passed down Flower and Dean Street, on his way back from work as a cobbler. Cobblers used knives, said the dockers.

In Stepney, two constables managed to restore order. Called out to the uproar, one Inspector Reid of H Division swiftly concluded that the Pole had no part in the Whitechapel murders, and lost his temper with the crowd. On the arrival of more constables, five men were arrested for affray and disorder.

In Southwark, no one witnessed Inspector Mallick fall. He dragged himself to the door of the Compass Rose, and a doctor was called. The inspector would live, but there were doubts if he would regain the use of his left arm. The bullet had shattered the shoulder.

Superintendent Neylan had the entirety of the Compass Rose Bravos gang arrested. None would admit to having fired the shot. More distraught than she had expected at the news, Catherine visited Mallick in the infirmary the next day. He was conscious, his twelve year-old daughter out of school, presumably, to sit at his side. The girl had the same mournful look as her father habitually wore, but she had justification at the moment,

"This is Madame Rostov, Sally." He patted his daughter's knee with his free hand. The surgeon had told Catherine that they could not yet decide if amputation of the damaged arm would be required. When they were sure that he had escaped serious infection, more fragments of bone might have to be removed to see the state of the shoulder joint.

Unsure, the girl bowed. "Madame."

"You have heard me speak of her, Sal. She is the lady who sees things."

His face seemed more drawn than ever, his cheekbones prominent and his brow discoloured, pale. The surgeons said the policeman was in considerable pain. He was receiving morphine, but the doctors here were of a modern mind. They did not want to induce addiction to the drug, and were sparing in its use.

His eyelid had stopped twitching.

"We will find them, Mallick," said Catherine.

"We?" He managed a hoarse chuckle. "Have they given you rank now?"

She tried to smile.

"Sal," he said, "Fetch Papa a fresh jug of water, there's a girl."

When his daughter left, Mallick gestured Catherine closer.

"What did you say to Donald Swanson?"

She frowned. "Don't concern yourself, Inspector. You need to rest, recover."

Mallick's feverish gaze searched the small side-room, came back to her.

"He contacted me…Swanson. Said he might be about to make a grievous error, and was…was troubled in himself. Whitechapel. What did I think of you, he asked, and pressed me."

"What did you say?"

"That I had questions about the nature of your abilities, and much besides. That you are a strong-minded woman who could easily cause problems, and your solutions might not be much better."

"I—"

"And I told Donald that your word is as good as mine, if it's trust that worries him. He should listen to you. If you have gone this far and dared the heart of Scotland Yard, there will be sense there somewhere." He managed to smile. "I'm not deep, Madame, nor one for God and religion such as Mr Neylan is. But there are fellow officers who've not called on me, nor on the wife, yet here you are, and not that much of a surprise to me that you came. That says something, also."

"Get better," said Catherine. Mallick's daughter was in the doorway with a jug of water, watching them. "Try to keep both arms, and get better, Inspector. Good day to you, Miss Sally."

She swept out before anything else could pass between the three of them, before a tear came to her eye, and she had to work out what it meant.

SIXTY-THREE

Mary Jane remained near home. If out, she'd stay close to friends and acquaintances. She kept a wary eye out for her stalker, and wondered when the ordinary cove might come to her with further instructions.

He did not appear on Friday, November 2 to gather the information Mary Jane and her girls had collected. He had what he needed, she supposed.

Barnett visited the room that day, and repeated his offer of shillings. She didn't take them, and he seemed troubled. Again, she asked him to come back to her, and he declined. On the third day of the month, he found her at the Ringers. When she refused his funds again, he turned frightfully insistent, drawing concerned looks from those with her, Madeline Grissette and Sarah Lewis. He appeared so distraught, Mary Jane felt relief once he'd gone.

The next time she saw him, November 4, he acted worse still. She had accompanied Maria Harvey, who was on her way to look at possible new lodgings in New Court, another thin avenue off the north side of Dorset Street accessed by a tight through-passage. Barnett saw them as they emerged from Miller's Court. Maria, perhaps not wanting to further upset him, had continued on toward their goal.

"I don't want you going back on the street," he said, grabbing Mary Jane by the shoulders.

Passing nearby, a man paused to watch with a scowl. Barnett showed him a fist, and the fellow moved on.

"I'm afraid of what might happen to you with that fiend loose," he said, a queer, feverish look in his eyes. "I don't know what I'd be willing to do to stop you. You *take* these shillings!"

"Should you be willing to come back," Mary Jane said, "I would have no need of them."

He did not respond to her statement. The look on his face frightened her. To calm Barnett and quiet his fears, Mary Jane took his money.

Having presumed that the information gathering for the ordinary cove had concluded, she could use the funds to keep from dipping further into her savings.

She watched Barnett walk away.

He wants me safe, and knows he's better off without me. He knows I were merely using him. Still he cares. I don't deserve it.

I did the same to Joseph Fleming, even though I love him. Admitting her feelings for the man to herself in no uncertain terms brought a pang of loss. *He, too, is better off without me.*

Mary Jane caught up with Maria. Her friend decided to take the room they visited when it became ready.

On November 5, Maria, Julia, Glory, and Mary Jane sat together again at the Ringers.

"We are done with our efforts to gather from the rumour mill," she told them.

"Why?" Julia asked.

"The need for the information has passed, and we shan't be paid for more."

From the start, they had all seemed to think it best not to question the source of the income Mary Jane shared. The present, apparently, was no different.

Clever Glory wondered aloud, "Possibly the newspapers would be interested in our work."

Maria and Julia showed interest, and seemed confused by Mary Jane's silence. Still, they let the matter go.

"Will you stay with me until your new lodgings are ready?" Mary Jane asked Maria.

"Yes. The room shan't be ready until Wednesday."

SIXTY-FOUR

Dry came to Catherine that night, when she sat alone in the front room of her lodgings, half-awake over a book on the travel of spirits through the Aether. She had warning this time, a pulse at her temples, but now she could only bear it and hope…

He approaches the Whitechapel Murderer in a nondescript tavern off Brick Lane. Stands next to him, breathes in the faint camphor of the jacket, the polish recently applied, shoddily, on the boots. And he speaks to him, soft-voiced.

"There is one who knows what you are. What burdens you."

The other man does not turn his head. "Are you some canting preacher, about to tell me of where my soul is bound?"

"Hardly. I bear a message which you should hear. Do you know of the Deptford Assassin?"

This time the neck—muscle and sinew—twists. The man's eyes are dull, a muddied brown. Dry knows what they see. They see an unimportant figure of barely middling height; round glasses of the type cheaply had from any maker of spectacles or travelling man. A Derby hat and a clean collar. A nonentity.

"Yes. I know the name," says the other. "A fine fellow, I hear. Happy to carve, but always gone by meal's end."

Dry can tell by the man's tone that, as intended, he has been dismissed as posing no immediate danger.

"He is interested in the way you take your birds, and slice them for the plate," Dry says.

"I would not—"

"He knows who you are—do not play. Do you think he has not marked your progress?"

The brown eyes swivel, looking to every exit from the drinking den, measuring distance and the nature of the other patrons. He may yet run, thinks Dry. Will he take such directness as a compliment? Another touch must be added.

"He knows of some pretty ducks for you, if you have a hunger."

The man hesitates. "Meet me behind this place, in five minutes."

The alley is little more than a trail of mud between pitted brick walls. Night-soil and a large dead rat are its only decoration. Dry allows the sudden punch to his abdomen, and the thick-haired arm which pins him to the wall. They would have been easy to evade.

"What is this talk, then?" says the man. "Talk of business that does not concern others."

"It concerns him. You may have talent."

"Threatened, is he?" The forearm lies hard across Dry's chest.

"Interested, I said. Else why would I have been sent here?"

The pressure eases. "An errand boy. Well, speak on."

"He has been watching for some time, the one of whom I speak. Did you think to work his fields and not be noticed?"

The man's lip curls, relaxes. He appears unsure of what response he should make.

"Your master wants something of me, does he?" Truculent, guarded. "A piece of those I cut, maybe? These sluts can spare a kidney or two. Get to your point."

"Not now. The Deptford Assassin will not be rushed—he had to be sure he had the right man. I will be here Wednesday, in this very place, by ten."

The other man smiles.

"So might I be, errand boy. So might I."

Catherine awoke, cramped in the armchair, but could not trust herself to move. The book had fallen to the floor; her heart was pounding. She had seen the face of the Whitechapel Murderer. Seen it, and pushed it away, out of her thoughts. She would forget that sight. There was nothing that she, the police or the vigilante mobs could do, now that Edwin Dry was in play.

Nothing that he could not do better than any and all of them.

SIXTY-FIVE

In the overcast afternoon of November 7, Maria Harvey removed to her new lodgings.

Alone in her room following Maria's departure, Mary Jane saw the ordinary cove enter Miller's Court. The moustache he wore had to be theatrical, because he hadn't had time to grow one since last she'd seen him. The spectacles he wore did not have darkened lenses. She decided they were probably theatrical as well, since she'd seen him more without glasses than with them. He carried a paper-wrapped parcel tied with string.

Watching the man through the small window, she began to shake with a fear of having to face him again. Mary Jane had decided that Jack the Ripper fit into the black-eyed man's plans, yet she could not fathom how. While she wanted further instructions to aid her survival, she didn't want to know more about the murder of Gabriella Gorse.

He walked the "L" of the court, looking all about the damp, mouldy brick, then came to her door. Mary Jane reigned in her fear, steadied herself, and answered his knock. Without a word, he entered and looked at the room.

She had left the door open so she might have an escape.

Indian Harry, the man who worked for John McCarthy, the landlord, walked by and looked in briefly. Once he'd gone past, the ordinary cove shut the door.

"Regarding the plan for the woman, Gorse," he said, "you shall give me the key to this room."

No! was her answer, but she held her tongue. What a frightening thought, that the black-eyed man would be able to enter her lodgings. Even so, Mary Jane decided to say nothing, and handed over the only key she had. Following that, to use the lock on the door, she'd have to slip an arm through the broken window to reach the mechanism.

"She will have to be christened," he said. "You know the term from thieves' cant."

Mary Jane believed that the expression meant to remove identifying marks from something stolen—an inscription perhaps from a ring or watch, an owner's mark from a firearm, a name stitched into a garment—to reduce the possibility that the item might become a damning piece of evidence.

How does one do that to a human being?

"If you have had a change of heart..." he said.

With a murderer pursuing her that she did not know, Mary Jane found herself afraid to cease her dealings with the one who'd shown a willingness to kill for her.

"No," she answered quickly.

"You will learn little of my plan," he said. "Tomorrow night, you must resume soliciting, be seen to see clients until after midnight. Since your man has left you, no one will be surprised. If you are in the room late at night and do not have a client, keep a candle lit, and make what sound you can to remind others who live in the court that you are here. You shall keep this up until half past one o'clock in the morning. At that time, you must be prepared to vacate your lodgings immediately and quietly, never to return. You will leave London and take a new name. Before leaving, you must put on these clothes. Fold the clothing you've removed and place them on a chair. Take nothing else with you." He handed Mary Jane the paper-wrapped parcel.

If not for the continuing mystery of his plan, she'd have been relieved to hear him speak with such confidence about her escape from London. She remembered him saying while they had stood on the stairs at the river, "Should you want to live, you will do as I say and ask no questions."

Mary Jane closed her mouth, and nodded her head to show she understood.

Exiting her room without another word, he made one more circuit of the court, walking slowly, flipping a coin and catching it several times. The man's black eyes that were truly blue, seemed to look past the tumbling gold disk, another sovereign, as if absorbing all the details of the yard.

She took a deep breath of relief when he left the court.

⌒⌒❖⌒⌒

Unable to sleep, Mary Jane spent most of Wednesday night in nearby pubs. Wanting to confuse her trail some, she decided to go to the Blue Coat Boy instead of the Ringers. The entrance to the pub was on Dorset Street, six doors west of the passage to Miller's Court on the same side of the street. She had little fear since she wasn't out in the night for long.

In the pub, she sat with Pearly Poll Conolly and Frederick Simons, and drank watered bitter. That cost little, and provided something to do. Once Pearly Poll, who had been with Martha Tabram the night of her murder, began talking about the killing, Mary Jane excused herself and went to the Ringers. Even with the drink in her, she felt a rising panic on the way to the pub, though the establishment sat even closer to the entrance to Miller's Court than the Blue Coat Boy. Mary Jane decided she ought not to stay out late or there would be few people in the street when she wanted to go home.

Once at the ringers, she sat with Eliza Cooper, Alice Lacroix, and Madeline Grissette. They sang songs, and she had more bitter and a couple quarterns of gin. Mary Jane knew she would not sleep even if she returned to her bed, and stayed much later than intended.

SIXTY-SIX

At the police station the next day Catherine saw the Compass Rose Bravos in their cells, but she had little to offer. Some of the young men were bloody-cheeked and bruised, as was one of the girls also swept up by the local force. Either they had not come easy, or the constables had vented their displeasure as they pushed the youths into police wagons.

"It will get worse," she said to one of the oldest boys as he pressed forward to the cell bars and tried to complain to her. "You have given a grievous wound to a good man."

"The Lord knows that they have grown up in a rough nest, with few kindnesses," said Mr Neylan, pacing behind her. He was more agitated than usual. She suspected that Christian charity and the near-murder of one of his inspectors were at war within him. Her own charity was close to breaking point.

"Then let them go back to shooting their own." She could sense nothing from the sullen crowd incarcerated before her. These days her gift brought her little more than Whitechapel.

"Madame!" Neylan spoke in awkward reproach. "We must trust in His Justice prevailing."

"Yes, Superintendent." Said hollow, and signalling her retreat. Alienating Neylan would serve no purpose.

"Is the inspector mending, Madame Rostov?" asked the elderly desk sergeant, a man who had once sniffed at her presence at the station.

"We must hope so, Cubbins. The surgeons are positive as to his life, and possibly his arm."

Assuming they did not lose him if they had to operate.

Alone on Borough High Street, uncertain where to go next, this was her small hell. She could not help Eden Mallick, nor conjure any sudden evidence to identify his assailant. And for the second time in two years she had sat with Edwin Dry and set death in motion—that was out of her hands, as it had been with Deptford.

Back at her lodgings, she cursed instead of weeping. Mrs

408

Bessovitch baked and watched her, saying little at first. She had heard the tale of Inspector Mallick.

"I will ask." The landlady eased a large meat pie from the oven, and set the golden pastry, pooled in its own gravy, down by the sink.

"Ask?"

"Henrik Kaars, he knows men who know men. And women who know women. He is fence, moves things that may not be his. Lotte Kaars is friend of mine."

Catherine ran one fingernail along the grain of kitchen table.

"What would you ask him?"

"Southwark is not so big. I ask where is gun from? Where is gun now? Who had gun that shoots your police friend?"

"And he would be able to find out? I can't imagine him wanting to get involved in police business."

"Is not police business. Is Katerina business. And so is mine. Henrik does not speak to police, no. He speak to Lotte, and Lotte speak to fat old Mrs Bessovitch."

They face each other, in the alley where they stood before. The Whitechapel Murderer looms, his coat open. Dry knows where the other's knife is—slid into the belt at the back. One of the man's hands is always close to his hip, ready to reach behind him and slip it free.

It is tempting to end matters here, but Dry has purpose. The greater satisfaction would come from seeing this through to a more subtle conclusion than a mere back-street stabbing.

The other man is waiting. Dry begins.

"A woman—a cheap whore—has been gathering word from others of her kind. They talk of you, and would name you to the police if they could be sure. Jack, she says, I think I may know Bloody Jack."

"They have all been wrong, the poxed birds. She does not know me." *The other man pulls his arm back, steps left and then right, watching the alley ends.*

"This one is closer than you believe." Dry reaches slowly inside his jacket, so as not to alarm, and pulls out a handbill with the picture of a woman printed upon it. The man takes it.

"I am not sure I recognise that face," he says.

"The one who sends me knows it well. She has had many names—Andriette is one. She spreads her legs cheaply."

Catherine turned in troubled sleep, her memories and visions blurring, confused. She needed to urinate, but could not seem to rise, to pull away from what invaded her night...

The Whitechapel Murderer spits. "And she has wind of me, you say? This is your master's warning?"

Dry is satisfied to see the first trace of agitation.

"A courtesy, between two who know the value of a sharp knife. And an opportunity."

The man's face betrays his need for acclaim. A compliment, passed on from the Deptford Assassin. Respect, recognition, for his actions. He is close to being hooked.

A fox or cat shrieks some streets away. Men stumble and laugh as they pass the alley, not looking in.

"It is true I have not carved for some time," says the man. "Not since the two who offered themselves up in one night."

"The woman will be alone this Friday morning, between three and five of the clock. It has been carefully arranged. Before that time, her legs will be spread, and you would be seen by whatever man that uses her; after five of the clock, the world awakes and there are no guarantees."

"Little more than a day away. Why?"

"To determine if you are one who merits attention. Besides, if it is to be done, better now than when the woman squeals at the nearest police station. She is a cunning vixen, and may soon be sure enough to risk it, perhaps next week."

"And if I ignore your master's word? What if I leave this whore to her fleas and fluxes, or slice her when I please—tonight, or in a week's time?"

"Then you are not Jack," says Dry. "The Deptford Assassin has seen such as you come and go, cocksure in their prowess and dedication at first. They do not last. They relent, repent; they blunder. Or they are given up by mothers, sisters, wives and Andriettes, betrayed to dance the hangman's jig."

Dry feels that last touch appropriate. The man wears prejudice on his arm.

"A test, and one not on my terms," mutters the other.

"Each kill is a test. You know that better than most."

A grunt of assent. "Alone, you said. Where?"

"At her room. Thirteen Miller's Court, off Dorset Street. I have seen it—a dismal, quiet place, not visible from the street. Though if you are afraid…"

The other man kicks out at the dead rat, almost splitting it with his boot. A flare of anger in the gloom of the alley.

"Afraid? What need have I of fear? That's what I give them, before I open their bellies. But if I find this Miller's Court lined with bluejackets and pistols…"

"You do not have to fear the police," says Dry. "That I guarantee."

On the Thursday morning, two days after she visited the inspector in the infirmary, Catherine was handed a name and an address, scrawled on the back of a butcher's account slip. From a cousin of a woman who once worked with a friend of Henrik Kaars's daughter, said the landlady.

"No one knows where name is from," said Mrs Bessovitch, and gave a slow, solemn wink. "Is mystery."

The details, rewritten neatly on a sheet of notepaper, was in Superintendent Neylan's hands within the half hour. He peered at it, turned it over a few times.

"This comes from your Sight, Madame Rostov?"

"A Guardian Spirit heard me, superintendent."

He nodded, smiling faintly. "Mrs Neylan…often wishes she had the Gift."

"It is a burden, also. Not to be asked for lightly, or used lightly either. I do not think that she would welcome the troubles it would bring."

Stronger nods, of approval this time.

"Indeed, indeed. I do feel the same. I am, as ever, pleased to note that you understand these matters, Madame. I shall have the men out instantly, and to this place. Let us pray for Justice."

Being Neylan, he meant that quite literally, and Catherine had to stand with him in the corridor for a long minute, head lowered.

"Good," he said at last. "Sergeant Cubbins, rouse a patrol. Two inspectors, and six of our most experienced constables."

"Should I perhaps—" Catherine began.

"Your part is done, Madame. Now we men must do the Lords' work."

The Superintendent was not someone with whom you argued, however dubious his statements. Though to his credit, she thought, he was actually going to lead the raid on the address in question. For the injury done to Eden Mallick, or for the principle of the matter, she did not know.

This time she kept her nerve and waited. She had one of Charlotte Chambers's more lurid novels in her bag, started the previous week, and she read it without seeing the words—at the end, she could not have given a single clue as to the plot, or the names of the major characters. Excepting that too many of the men in it were called George.

One hour, then a half hour more, and another quarter...

Superintendent Neylan strode into the station, his jacket askew and a rip in his right sleeve.

"Taken, Madame Rostov!" It was the most cheerful she had seen him. "Taken, praise the Lord, and the crime confessed, before all."

It would not have done to shake his hand, but she would have liked to. The officers who followed him were of equal good cheer, muted only by their superintendent's presence. One had his arm in a makeshift sling, another a bruised eye.

"The brothers of Ned Ginny, the butcher's apprentice," said Neylan, restoring some order to his uniform. "Hard, powerful men. We were Davids to their Goliaths, but we had Right on our side."

"Ginny? The boy who fired on that other gang near the Compass Rose tavern, months past?"

"The very same. His older brothers have apparently held grievance against Inspector Mallick ever since Ned Ginny went down for his crimes. Another gun came into their hands; a sudden opportunity taken, the cowards."

One of the other inspectors, Jentry, could not restrain a chuckle. "We took them in their lair, three of them, with the weapon and a fair few other goods which weren't rightfully theirs as well. And Mr Neylan was at them, bless me, he was."

Justice, at least, for Eden Mallick. If she could trust the surgeons, then one small corner of her world might yet be in order. She must go and see Mallick again, take him fruit. It was admitting that he was practically a friend, but she had few enough of those. There would be a reason for that, but what it was she did not know.

She had a slow, strange walk home, her head filled with so many thoughts. Exhausted and footsore, Catherine stretched out on her bed.

Turning on her mattress, she hoped she would not dream. And she doubted that her wish would be granted. Friday morning was only hours away.

Today was the eighth day of November, 1888.

SIXTY-SEVEN

Mary Jane set out for her room about four o'clock in the morning. The streets were nearly empty. She had less than twenty-five yards to walk. Even so, time passed too slowly, giving the Whitechapel Murderer too much opportunity to strike.

Despite the gaslight in the court, she had shadows at her back. Mary Jane could barely quiet her trembling enough to slip her hand through the broken window and unlock the door. In the room, she got in bed with her clothing on in case she had to get up and flee into the night to get away from an intruder.

As she'd feared, Mary Jane failed to find sleep. She became lost in dreadful thoughts, running over possibly unanswerable questions. She wondered what would happen to Gabriella Gorse at the hands of the black-eyed man. He'd asked for the key to the room while talking about Gorse, so Mary Jane supposed he would somehow bring her there.

Did his plans for Gabby have anything to do with the Whitechapel Murderer?

Why would the ordinary cove take it upon himself to find out who were Jack the Ripper?

Having made that determination did not mean the killer would be easy to find or catch.

Cokum—he's too wary and clever to be caught easily.

Yet the black-eyed man has his own cokum.

Is he *the Whitechapel Murderer?* Considering what she knew of the killings on the street, she discounted the notion. *He does not show his work proudly, and he might have killed me anytime.*

Mary Jane's thoughts shifted to examining what she knew about the ordinary cove, a frustrating exercise at first.

I know next to nothing about him. I suspect he's in the business of killing, an assassin of sorts. I know he has killed at least once.

Thinking back over her experiences with the man, a few of his traits occurred to her. He was exacting in a strangely compelling way, and seemed always in control. His ability to find her, as he'd done, and his awareness and knowledge of Stuart Brevard and his toughs—how did he acquire such information? Did he have other teams of information gatherers, like Mary Jane and her girls, or did he have access to police files?

That would explain a lot, but certainly his manner held something of the uncanny. Thinking of Catherine Weatherhead's business as a spiritualist, Mary Jane couldn't help wondering if the woman had allies that were more than human. From which side of the veil did the black-eyed man hail? Was he indeed an agent of the supernatural?

The intelligent command of situation and circumstance that he demonstrated appeared to be otherworldly, yet that didn't make it so.

No, he's too much of the grit and grime of the cruel world I know. He belongs here.

Cokum, he has. The ordinary cove has uncanny cokum, that's all.

He wanted her to make a show of herself Thursday night. He wanted her soliciting to be obvious to those living in the court as well as her presence in her room in the late hours.

To what purpose? Is he trying to lure Jack the Ripper here? Am I his bait?

Does he have a deal with someone to kill the Whitechapel Murderer? If so, what does Gabby have to do with that?

What if Barnett had not left her? When did the black-eyed man come up with the plan?

Mary Jane got the strange notion that he had given her a role in a drama, one that he deftly directed without having given the full script to any of the actors. Had he told her that Jack the Ripper would be after her so that, in her distress, she'd drive Barnett away? Was he that good at reading character?

Again, no answers presented themselves.

Her thoughts fixed on Gabriella Gorse.

My killing. Though he will commit the act, I shall own it.

With no ability to control her fancy, she had little success turning away from countless visions of the woman being strangled, knifed, bludgeoned to death.

My killing, she thought again, but instead of her thoughts of owning the act, Mary Jane found herself wondering if the Whitechapel Murderer would catch up to her before half past one o'clock Friday morning, or even as she tried to make her escape at the appointed time.

So listless that she had insufficient will to rise, and still vulnerable to unwanted fancy, thoughts about the promised killing intertwined with the one she imagined happening to her. She *was* Gorse. The terrible visions commenced again, a jumble in which she and Gabby, combined, endured innumerable, horrifying deaths.

When she began to feel a kinship with the woman in their shared suffering, she could stand the visions no longer. She rolled to the edge of the bed and allowed herself to fall to the floor. A jolt of pain from her left knee striking the hard wood brought her to full wakeful awareness of herself within her room.

SIXTY-EIGHT

The second act is easier than the first. He has sent a note that day to the prostitute Gabriella Gorse, writ in a fair copy of his informant's weak hand, easy done.

> I must speak to you urgent. There is something you do not know about the gang with which you run, a threat. Though we are not friends, we are both women who must trust the street, and you are at risk. Come to Thirteen Miller's Court between two and three in the morning, when I pledge none will see. Ginger.

This to set his other target in motion.

Show them what they desire, what they fear. They do not understand the craft, will not sit and wait as he will. They will rush to heed the call. Gorse will go to Miller's Court either to learn, or to punish Mary Jane Kelly. Nor is the Whitechapel Murderer likely to resist his role in the intrigue.

And if, by some unlikely stroke, neither arrives and none of this can come about, then there are a dozen other ways to achieve the end he requires, all waiting to be played upon the stage.

They do not understand how Time is their servant, not their master.

They are not Edwin Dry.

Catherine woke, relieved herself in the pot. Her head held lightning from temple to temple, and she could tell that it would not matter if she slept that night. From the house next door to the lodgings came the strains of Mr and Mrs Gowing, the retired couple once more at their hymns. They sang late each night in their parlour, accompanied, Mrs Bessovitch said, by a small glass of whisky to end the day.

"Doubts are abroad: make Thou these doubts to cease;

"Fears are within: set Thou these fears at rest!

"Strife is among us: melt that strife to peace!

"Change marches onward: may all change be blest!"

She put a shawl around her shoulders, and brought out the last of the brandy from the wardrobe. It was Deptford again, and the night would unfurl inside her head regardless.

Edwin Dry haunted her, possessed her.

Strife is among us.

SIXTY-NINE

Daylight had come at last.

Mary Jane stood awkwardly and backed away from her bed toward the larger window.

The half-light coming through the closed grey curtains illuminated the bedclothes in a manner she found disturbing, though she could not have said why. She didn't want to look at the dilapidated piece of furniture, yet couldn't quite turn away. Something about the sweat-stained, rumpled linens on the lumpy mattress, the scarred wood of the frame, and the crooked headboard, gave her an unaccountable dread that if she ever used the bed again, her greatest agony would find her.

The ordinary cove had given her too little to do and she was going mad!

A knocking came from her door.

Mary Jane cautiously approached. "Who's there?" she asked.

"'Tis Maria, what's brought you breakfast."

Mary Jane opened the door immediately, relieved to have a smiling ally on her doorstep. She hid away her fears. "Come in."

"I brought stirabout for us to share." Holding a pot wrapped in a towel, along with a couple of mugs, Maria entered and set it all on the table by the large window. She opened the curtains.

Mary Jane shut the door.

Maria glanced around the room, her nose wrinkling. "Odd smell. Shall we air out your room a bit?" She stepped over and opened the door.

Mary Jane moved to close it.

Before she succeeded, Julia Veneteney walked past, glancing in. "Good morning," she said.

"Join us for breakfast," Mary Jane called out.

"Thank you, but I'm expected—" Entering the passage, apparently in a hurry, her words grew unintelligible.

Maria had cleared a spot on the table by the window, and spooned some of the milky corn from the pot into the mugs. She pulled another spoon from her pocket, handed that and one of the cups to Mary Jane, and sat.

"Thank you."

They ate in silence for a time.

"Are you out most of the day?" Maria asked.

"No, I'll be staying in."

"Shall I bring my mending to work on in your room this afternoon?"

"Yes, yes," Mary Jane said. "I'll help. I'd like that very much, indeed!"

Maria chuckled. "Look at your grin. I have never seen such eagerness for dull toil."

Mary Jane's smile wilted as her friend took up the remains of their meal and left.

Mary Jane hoped that the mending work would distract her from her worst thoughts. Maria arrived with a bundle of clothing from White's laundry in need of repair: shirts, a black overcoat, a black bonnet, and a girl's white petticoat.

They talked for a time, her friend rattling on, but Mary Jane found herself slipping into silence. The work took too little concentration, and her dark mood returned. She could not escape the feeling that leaving her room, her life, in the middle of the coming night, taking nothing with her, represented death of a sort. With the sense that despite whatever the ordinary cove had planned, doom awaited her at the hands of a murderer, she had difficulty looking forward to anything. Mary Jane had an urgent desire to put her affairs in order before the end.

Time gets away from me, while much is left undone.

Even with the desire, she had to wonder what there was to do? The ship of her life had no crew and no anchor as the vessel entered dangerous waters. She had no heirs and nothing of worth to pass on. No one who loved her would remain, save perhaps the Morganstones, and they didn't truly know her and what she'd become. Fleming might suffer for a short time, then move on with his life. Surely, she would be forgotten.

"No!" she said aloud in an effort to banish self pity, and accidentally poked herself with the needle she used.

"Don't stain your work," Maria said.

Mary Jane set the petticoat aside. She watched a small red droplet form before wiping the blood away.

Again, she thought of catching a train, and starting over somewhere else with nothing.

No, my heart would not let me live with that. For Jennie and the countless other women Gabby betrays, I must stay and play my part to make certain she pays.

"Thank you for your help," Maria said when they'd finished their work.

Mary Jane lit a candle and drew the curtains closed over the large window after her friend left.

The dark came too early.

Barnett arrived with fried fish and potatoes. He placed the food on the table and sat. Wanting to take the other seat, Mary Jane noticed that Maria had left the clothes they had mended on the chair, all except for the coat which she'd also forgot after hanging the garment on the frame of the small window.

Mary Jane set the clothing on the chair aside and she and Barnett ate in silence, sitting at the table before the large window.

Lizzie Albrook knocked upon the door, and came in.

"Good evening, Lizzie," Barnett said. "You been a good girl?"

"Why, yes."

Mary Jane gave him a look. She'd confided in him that the young woman had asked her advice about solicitation.

Lizzie also lived in Miller's Court. She was a slavey at Crossingham's Common Lodging, four doors west of the passage to the court. A flaxen-haired saucebox, all of twenty years old, she'd treated Mary Jane with undue deference since they'd met over a year earlier, and had asked numerous questions about soliciting. Lizzie would have been a delight if not for her adoring fascination for Mary Jane. She found herself unsettled to see in the girl so much of what she'd been at eighteen in Cardiff: naive, yet hard-bitten and willing to risk for a little adventure.

Working as a maid of all work at a common lodging house, Lizzie would be accustomed to long hours of exhausting, at times disgusting, even degrading toil. The work would wear her down over time, expose her to vermin and disease.

At first, she'd no doubt felt lucky to find the position at Crossingham's. No secret that stable employment in London had become a rare beast, especially in the East End. While true enough for men, that was ever more so for women. Most jobs offered back-breaking day labour of little variety that could not be done for long without harm to one part of the body or another, depending on the task. If Lizzie didn't know that from watching members of her own family go through the experience, then she'd seen the effect in the lives of others.

With the notion of soliciting, just like Mary Jane had done when young, Lizzie probably saw past the unpleasant task of sex with a stranger to the coin at the end. Knowing she'd start out at the rate of a casual or little better, she possibly saw beyond the low pay to a time in which she might gain a reputation that brought her more.

Seeing her take a seat on the edge of the bed gave Mary Jane more of the foreboding she'd felt earlier, but she said nothing.

"I seen a possible earlier today," Lizzie said brightly. She had an excited look about her that Mary Jane didn't like to see.

In the past, when they had talked about soliciting, Mary Jane had done her best to discourage her. She had told Lizzie that if she must engage in the practice, to always walk her possible clients through the Ringers so the other ladybirds might provide warnings about the bad ones. Mary Jane had introduced her around.

"He made eyes at me at the crossing with Commercial Street. I says, 'Take a drink with me at the Ringers.' He must have had a change of heart, 'cause he walked on. But he almost decided in my favour."

In that time and place, the young woman's hope broke Mary Jane's heart.

"Favour," Barnett said, turning to her and frowning. "You're teaching the young ones how it's done, are you? While I'm trying to keep *you* off the streets, and there's a madman loose?"

"No, I would not have her start," Mary Jane said, "yet circumstance may put her there whatever I say. She has a desire, and should she follow it, I want her prepared."

"Prepared," he said. "She's just a girl, what ought to find a beau to buy her a tussie mussie. You needn't talk to her about the streets at all, unless to frighten her notions away telling the dangers." He threw his hands in the air in disgust. "*Jack the Ripper!*"

"I know," Lizzie said, "I'm not a *child*."

Barnett looked down, shook his head, mumbled "Child."

"Yes," Mary Jane said, "the murderer is out there…hunting up casuals…cutting their throats, and, well…*worse*." She said the words slowly, hoping they might lodge uncomfortably in Lizzie's mind.

"Odds of meeting him are slim," the young woman said. She acted brave because she needed to persuade herself as much as anyone else. That backbone would serve her well, if it didn't get her killed. She had little else in life.

Mary Jane shuddered, thinking of Lizzie alone on the street at night.

"Barmy girl is what you are," Barnett said. "You don't know what you're about."

Lizzie hung her head.

"Don't pretend you know what it's like," Mary Jane told Barnett, turning a fierce gaze on him. "You don't know much about the choices women have to make."

He did not look her in the eye. He grumbled, huffed, and said no more.

She knew plenty of women willing to take the risk, and so did Lizzie. If the madness of the East End, the ceaseless talk of the Whitechapel Murderer hadn't changed her mind, Mary Jane would not succeed in dissuading her with fears.

She gripped the edge of the table to steady her shaking hands. A tear of frustration rose to her eye. She wiped it away before they saw, turned to Lizzie. "You don't want to turn out as I did. I am a poor, wretched creature by my own estimation. *I have nothing.*"

"Nothing," Barnett said. He gave Mary Jane a look that said he'd found insult in her words. He gathered the remains of their meal, made his goodbyes, and left. When he had gone, Mary Jane discovered two shillings he'd left on the table. Despite her poor treatment of him, he would still provide what he could for her.

He deserves much better than he got from me.

Lizzie smiled sadly. "I *shall* take care."

"*Please* do," Mary Jane said, holding down a rising anger. Her ire was not for Lizzie. Mary Jane was disgusted with herself, and angry about the state of affairs in London's East End, an order of things that left many women, young and old, with so few expectations that prostitution became appealing.

Again, she thought of Barnett's generosity. *What did he expect, taking up with a whore?*

Perhaps sensing the older woman's mood, Lizzie grew uncomfortable, and soon made her goodbyes. Once she'd gone, Mary Jane's anger faded and the dread returned.

Weary from too little sleep and considering a nap, she looked at the bed.

Don't you ever get in that bed again! she told herself. Once more, she could not have said why.

Instead, Mary Jane did as she hoped the younger woman would not do, and went out to find a client, all the while knowing full well that Jack the Ripper was indeed after her.

～✦～

Remembering that the only candle in her room was reduced to a short nub, Mary Jane stopped at McCarthy's Chandler shop and bought a new one from Indian Harry. Leaving the shop, she walked East on Dorset Street to Commercial Street, then north to the crossing with Fournier Street, to spend time out front of the Ten Bells pub. The lighted clock on Christ Church said five minutes past nine o'clock. Rain had come and gone, leaving a dampness in the cold night air. Feeling fairly safe, standing near the entrance to the busy pub with people coming and going, she bundled into her plum-coloured woollen shawl to keep warm, and looked for a client.

Mary Jane tried something ladybirds had taken up in recent days; asking for the loan of a tanner as a way to indicate the price they were willing to take. The scheme had its problems. Should a man misunderstand the true message, and offered a tanner, one had to decide whether to keep the money, or give it back right away. If kept…well, the dangers in that were easily imagined.

Deciding that she could always drop her price, Mary Jane asked for a shilling.

The rain came on again. She gave up and went into the Ten Bells for a glass of bitter. She sat with Elizabeth Foster, a friendly face from the neighbourhood.

"Any luck?" The woman asked.

"Can't say I deserve any," Mary Jane said, shivering.

"Let me get you a whiskey," Elizabeth said. "Irish?"

"Yes, thank you."

Miss Foster had the same. When they'd finished, Mary Jane bought another round. Others joined them; Louisa McGregor, Maggy Evans, and Faye Holmsford. Along with more drinks, they had songs together. Then Mary Jane found herself singing for her companions. The song "Myfanwy," by Joseph Parry, with lyrics by the Welsh poet, Richard Davies, told of the sadness of a man confused that his beloved, Myfanwy, had lost her feelings for him. The lyrics asked, "Where has your love for me gone? Why do you give me dark looks? What have I done?" The song concluded with the message, "I only wish you well."

Though they no doubt did not understand the Welsh lyrics, they praised Mary Jane's singing.

She became subdued, thinking of how she'd treated Joseph Fleming. He might just as well have written the beautiful, sad song about her.

Remembering that she ought to be soliciting, she excused herself, and decided to leave the pub altogether during a lull in the rain. She walked south, used the urinal beside the churchyard, then looked up at the clock on Christ Church again. Ten till eleven o'clock, it said.

Mary Jane felt safer than she had the previous night. A moment passed before she understood the reason: She was doing what the ordinary cove had told her to do, and, though she did not see him, she believed he watched her.

Mary Jane crossed Commercial Street, and entered the Ringers. After fetching a glass of bitter, she looked for a place to sit. She shied away from the few people she recognised, and felt lucky to find a small table against the eastern wall vacated by a couple headed for the exit.

The damp air, much warmer inside the establishment, brought out the worst smells of the place, even with the heavy tobacco smoke. Sodden with wet foot traffic, the saw dust on the floor gave off odours of mould and mildew. As always, the furnishings reeked of whatever food and drink wasn't entirely cleaned off of them, and from contact with countless human beings, their often unwashed clothing, and bodily fluids. A long brown spatter on the floor nearby suggested that an American was present in the pub or had been recently. Matilda Ringer kept spittoons beneath the bar for the Americans and the few locals with the disgusting habit, but they frequently went unused.

The odours got in Mary Jane's head and moved her gut uncomfortably.

I shall not miss Dorset Street, she thought, drawing a hand over her surprisingly moist face, and hoping she would not lose her fish and potatoes. *Indeed, I shan't miss the whole of London's filthy East End.* The thought, while not entirely true, told her that she had reconciled herself with the black-eyed man's plan for her departure in the early morning hours. *What choice do I have?*

Removing her hand from her face, she found Joseph Fleming standing across the table from her. He'd grown a moustache, and dressed in a manner perhaps meant to impress her.

Mary Jane stood to leave. She could not abide her feelings for the man.

"Please, talk to me, Mary Jane," he said, his earnest expression clearly meant to appeal to her.

She got up, made her way between the tables and patrons, and left the Ringers.

Fleming followed her outside, caught up and said quietly, "I'll be at the Horn of Plenty." He walked away toward the west along Dorset Street. The pub he mentioned stood at the other end of the short lane.

At least she'd know how to avoid him.

Mary Jane returned to the Ringers and resumed her search for a client.

The glowing clock on Christ Church read half past eleven as Mary Jane stepped out of the Ringers having landed a client, something of a whale. She'd become drunk in an effort to suppress thoughts of what would happen to Gabriella Gorse that evening. Despite her intoxication, pride would not allow her to take less than a shilling, and that left her with few choices. Finally she'd settled for the heavy man of thirty years and more. He wore a long, ratty top coat and a billycock. His round red face held ginger side whiskers, a moustache, and numerous blebs. He'd been too drunk to care about her price. She'd made him show that he had the coin before they left the pub.

Neither of them walked with any confidence. Hanging onto her as they both staggered along, he spilled splashes of bitter from the pail he'd taken away from the pub. They made their way west on Dorset and into Miller's Court. He wanted to stop in the darkness of the passage and kiss her, but she would have none of that until he paid.

At the door of Mary Jane's lodgings, Mary Ann Cox surprised her, coming through the corridor and pushing past. "Goodnight," she said.

"Goodnight to you, Mary Ann," Mary Jane said, banging awkwardly into her door. Her hand searched the pocket under her top skirt. She couldn't find her key.

Ah…gave it to the ordinary cove.

She remembered that he wanted her to make noise—at least, that was how her drunken mind remembered his instructions.

"I'm going to sing," she called out to Mary Ann, who had reached her door, the last on the left, in the darkest corner of the court.

Ah, the window.

Mary Jane began to sing "A Violet from Mothers Grave."

Her client turned away to urinate on the wall of the passage.

Mary Jane moved around the corner to the small window, reached carefully through the hole in the glass. She pushed aside a sleeve of the coat Maria had left hanging like a curtain, and unlocked the door. She was glad her client had been occupied with his toilet so he didn't see her method of opening the door.

She got him inside, and left the door open. "Sit on the bed, sir," Mary Jane said.

He sat, then lay back.

By the light of the gas lamp on the wall of the court outside, she pulled out the candle she'd bought, and lit it. Mary Jane shut the door, and set the candle in the wine glass Barnett had broken. Turning to the man in her bed, she found him asleep and snoring.

Good.

Mary Jane took the near-empty pail from his right hand and set the container on the floor. She sat in a chair and resumed her singing:

> Scenes of my childhood arise before my gaze,
> Bringing recollections of bygone happy days,
> When down in the meadow in childhood I would
> roam;

No one's left to cheer me now within that good old
home.
Father and mother they have passed away.
Sister and brother now lay beneath the clay;
But while life does remain, to cheer me I'll retain
This small violet I plucked from mother's grave

Only a violet I plucked when but a boy,
And oft' times when I'm sad at heart, this flow'r has
given me joy,
But while life does remain, in memoriam I'll retain
This small violet I plucked from mother's grave.

Well I remember my dear old mother's smile,
As she used to greet me when I returned from toil;
Always knitting in the old arm chair,
Father used to sit and read for all us children there.
But now all is silent around the good old home,
They all have left me in sorrow here to roam;
But while life does remain, in memoriam I'll retain
This small violet I plucked from mother's grave.

Mary Jane heard the church bells ring midnight. An hour and a half would have to pass before the time of her departure. Having had little sleep, she struggled to stay awake.

Mary Jane hoped the man in her bed didn't wake up until close to half past one o'clock, and that when he did she'd be able to get him out in time and quietly.

She sang the song twice, sang other songs, then "A Violet from Mothers Grave" once again. With the song, she wept for Mum, for Jennie, for Lizzie Albrook, for herself, and Gabby too. After all, the woman had once taken a beating meant for Mary Jane.

With time, she rose and undressed, folding her clothing neatly and setting them on a chair. She placed her boots before the fireplace. She gathered the clothes Maria had left behind and set them beside her boots. Reaching under the bed to retrieve the package of clothes the ordinary cove had given her, she disturbed her client's sleep. He awoke with a start. Mary Jane backed away, still naked.

"I'd just got you dressed, sir," she said, thinking on the fly. "I didn't mean to wake you. You were so weary after your proud performance."

He blinked, mumbled a few words, and finally said, "I did?"

How well he possessed his own mind and memory in that moment, she did not know. Mary Jane could only hope he wouldn't see through her flam.

"I have rarely got a wapping like that." She took a few light, dancing steps. "Such a pleasant, *long* swyve. And at the end...oh, what a great flood of bliss." She giggled, as with delight. "Took some time to clean up your warm gush, it did." Mary Jane gestured to her naked madge.

He smiled with a look of pride, despite his drunken state.

She unwrapped the package and dressed.

He remained seated, gathering himself together.

The clothing would not stand out; grey skirt, petticoat, pale-blue chemise, black stockings, black boots, a grey woollen shawl, and a black felt hat.

The bed groaned as he rocked unsteadily, and she feared the crooked head board would release the side rails and the whole kife would come crashing down on the wash tub stored beneath.

"Now, I must go out to attend a sick niece," Mary Jane said. She picked up the pail, handed it to him, and gestured toward the door. "If you'd be so kind..."

She held the way open for him. He got up and stumbled out of the room, then paused and turned to her.

"Your pay," he said with concern.

"You paid when we arrived," she said.

Hoping he would not make much noise, Mary Jane watched him move away through the passage, searching his pockets. She worried that he counted his money, would remember at last, and come back for what they'd bargained.

A great relief came once he'd turned east into Dorset Street, and she no longer saw him. She shut the door.

In an overwrought state, Mary Jane sat in the empty chair, her breath coming in short, shallow gasps.

She heard the chime for the one o'clock hour. Knowing she must wait longer still, she sang again.

SEVENTY

Midnight has long gone, and the deep dark of the small hours clings to the streets around Miller's Court. Dry attends to those streets, keeps them under his eye from the heights.

Two figures move through the thin fog.

The woman called Gorse has not come alone, which is no surprise to Dry. She heads for Dorset Street with a man trailing her at a distance, a member of the local gang she serves. She and Kelly are near enough alike to the eye for his purposes, but her escort must be removed. This is not a time for complications.

When Gorse is about to turn off Bell Lane, Dry moves, slipping down from his vantage point. A hand goes over the man's mouth and a slender blade pierces one kidney, then the other. Less bloody than the throat. He slides the body into shadows to be dealt with later, whips free the man's long coat and puts it over his own shoulders, purloining the battered, wide-brimmed felt hat as well. A moment later, the woman's supposed protector is on the corner of the street, half-obscured by brickwork.

"I 'as to check a matter," says Dry, a low whisper which could come from any man. "I'll be behind yer."

The woman hesitates, but heads down Dorset Street all the same, to enter Miller's Court.

This is not a coat suited for what is to come—it constricts his shoulders and flaps at his thighs. He bundles it into a doorway near the body, retrieving his own hat as well.

Gorse will find the room in Miller's Court—Mary Jane Kelly's room—open and empty. A low fire burns. There are papers on the bed, copies of the information which Kelly collected on difficult and dangerous clients, on men who held some peculiarity in their stance or in their eyes. The route to the Whitechapel Murderer, when placed next to Dry's own observations. The woman will pry, will look at these papers, pondering their significance. Her attention will be distracted...

She will bear a different name by the time the night is done, and Kelly herself will achieve that other goal, to flee this place, supposed dead—free of debts, enemies and history. The small fears which have plagued her for so long.

Mr Edwin Dry is a fair man, and keeps all fair bargains.

SEVENTY-ONE

"Quietly," he'd said. Mary Jane thought of that as she stumbled in the passage and nearly fell on the way out to Dorset Street. The black-eyed man told her to leave with nothing but the clothing she wore. She didn't believe he'd meant that she should take no push. Mary Jane had several pounds worth in her pocket. She'd padded the coins so they would not jingle.

Her drunkenness had gone. She decided to make her way to Aldgate High Street and find a cab. Cabmen waited there near Goulston Street during the early morning hours for two reasons: People getting off the rail lines in the area looked for cabs, and there were public urinals on an island in the road. She would go to Stepney and knock on Thomas Morganstone's door. Thomas would allow her to stay while she made plans to leave London.

Mary Jane stepped into Dorset Street suspecting that Jack the Ripper had somehow been lured to the area by her efforts that night.

Can he see me now? Is the ordinary cove still watching?

No, I cannot think of those things. She had to put trust in a plan she knew little about.

He had left the route of her escape to Mary Jane. She put one foot in front of the other, moving east. Although west on Dorset Street would have been the fastest route, Joseph Fleming said he'd be at the Horn of Plenty, and she wanted to avoid him.

Moving south on Commercial Street, Mary Jane kept a wary eye out, assessing the potential danger of each person she encountered. She turned west into White's Row.

Many of the people up and walking the footways at that hour had far to go to get to a work shift that began near dawn. Mary Jane noted fewer sleepy-eyed ones than usual, especially among the women, no doubt a response to the news of the murderer loose in the streets.

At the western end of White's Row, she turned southward into Bell Lane, which would become Goulston after it crossed Wentworth Street. Once that happened, she told herself, she might run the rest of the way to escape an assailant. A murderer would not want to draw attention to himself in Aldgate High Street.

She increased her pace, knowing that she truly could not outrun most people.

A glance behind revealed the silhouette of a man following. His pace showed no urgency. Still, unlike most others using the footway, he carried nothing. Those on their way to work often carried a meal, or items necessary for their labour.

Mary Jane increased her pace again, glancing back to gauge the response, if any, from the silhouette.

The figure had picked up speed!

Mary Jane wanted to call out, drawing attention to herself, and her possible assailant, yet didn't want to feel foolish if the fellow was merely in a hurry to make a rail connection.

She considered moving west into the passage to Cox's Square. Then she might continue south on Short Street. The darkness of the passage discouraged her.

A glance behind showed the figure having closed some of the distance between them.

Her breath caught in her throat. The light drizzle of rain blurred her vision for a moment, and Mary Jane felt a rising panic. She quickly turned west into Montague Street, and immediately regretted the decision because the much thinner lane had fewer gaslights and much less foot traffic.

She heard rapid foot steps behind her.

Mary Jane ducked into the recessed entrance of a tenement.

Ready to scream, she held her breath as the footstep drew nearer.

"Mary Jane," came a familiar voice.

She exhaled and gasped for a breath, feeling lightheaded, her heart pounding in her chest.

Joseph Fleming came into view. Mary Jane leaned back against the brick wall behind her, held her head in her hands. "You frightened me nearly to death!" she croaked.

"My apologies," he said, approaching slowly. "You needn't be out in the night alone."

"That is my business," she said, realising that she meant that in two ways.

His resigned look and the nod of his head said he understood both meanings.

"A mutual acquaintance told me to keep an eye on you."

"Who would that be?"

"I can't say."

The black-eyed man! Joseph worked for him in Deptford. Just because he said he didn't know about the killing of Caille, doesn't mean that's true. The assassin is using me as bait for Jack the Ripper, and Fleming is involved!

If he has Joseph watching me, are the ordinary cove's black eyes focused elsewhere?

Mary Jane pushed past Joseph and moved toward Goulston. He followed her into the street.

"Please, Mary Jane," he said. "What have I done to get such black-eyed looks?"

"I'm not your Myfanwy!"

"I don't understand."

She hurried on toward Aldgate High Street.

Fleming followed without further conversation.

Mary Jane felt safer with him at her back, despite not wanting him around. He'd be useful right up until the moment she climbed into a cab.

She could see the gaslights of Aldgate High Street ahead, and with the sight came renewed hope of escape. Mary Jane sprinted forward through the increasing rain, noting oddly that the boots the ordinary cove had given her fit perfectly. The pair she'd left in the room had a cracked sole that became a nuisance in rainy weather. So far, the ones on her feet had let in no water.

Approaching her goal, she looked back and saw that Fleming still followed.

Reaching Aldgate Station East, where Goulston Street ended, she was tempted to enter one of a couple of pubs attached to the station and have a drink. Seeing a hansom standing idle at the corner, the driver huddled into a pile of blankets with his hat pulled down low, she forgot about the drink. She ran toward the carriage, fearing someone else might call out first. She had no need to signal the driver. The cabby's head lifted and he moved the hansom forward to anticipate her arrival.

"The Stepney Gasworks," she said, stepping up into the carriage. Avoiding the reins, she turned and sat.

Joseph Fleming, closer than she'd expected, lifted himself on the driver's step-up to talk to the man. She could not hear what he said.

"Drive," Mary Jane said. She knocked on the trap door to offer her money. Ignored, she had decided to get out and find another cab when Fleming pushed in with her. The driver shut the doors and she felt trapped.

As the cab pulled into the road, Mary Jane opened her mouth to cry out in complaint. Joseph clapped his right hand over her mouth, while his left hand gripped the back of her neck. She struggled and he wrestled with her, shoving her down in the seat and wrapping his left arm all the way around her neck, the elbow beneath her chin. She wanted to tell him she'd give in, but she couldn't get her words past his hand. She felt his hot breath on her right ear. Though she could still breathe through her nose, Mary Jane grew lightheaded.

He *is the Ripper!*

Darkness crept into her vision, and took away thought.

SEVENTY-TWO

Through the passage Gorse goes, under the damp brick arch. A candle burns in Number Thirteen, a single shabby room with a broken window-pane, directly off the courtyard. The door is half open, and she goes inside.

He waits a minute, and follows.

In, and across the room to where she stands by the table, her back to him. His hand goes over her mouth; his blade comes round from behind and pierces her heart in a single thrust, stilling it forever. This is his act of mercy. If the woman must die—and she must—he will not leave her alive to satisfy the perversions of the one who comes.

He props the body on the bed, face to the wall, as if asleep. It will do, and he must be away, to a perch already prepared. If "Jack" comes to Miller's Court, all will fall into place.

The houses clustered around the court are of mixed substance, crumbling in parts. Dry has been here twice recently, testing for loose tiles and stonework too weak to bear much weight. He has rope ready, to ascend and descend, and the drainpipe by Number Thirteen is just sufficient to bear him up and to the side. Only just—the brackets set into the wall give slightly as he climbs.

Crouched by a chimney stack, he lets the night hold him quiet.

SEVENTY-THREE

Mary Jane awoke lying in a bed. She saw Joseph sitting in a chair to her left in the darkness.

Alarmed to find him so close, confused to see him inactive with eyes drooping, she noted that he didn't seem to be looking at her. Perhaps he was half-asleep.

She looked for the way out of the tiny room. The chamber appeared no more than eight feet square. A door stood closed to her left. A small coal grate occupied the same wall. Little light from the night without came through the sooty pane of the room's single window. Through the glass, she saw the back sides of a couple of brick buildings, and smoke rising lazily from chimney pots.

Joseph must have seen her glancing about. "My room in Brick Lane."

Mary Jane realised that he must have been in Spitalfields for some time if he had lodgings.

He rubbed his forehead, peered down at her in a curious way. "I beg your forgiveness. I didn't want to frighten you. You were drawing attention to yourself while I was trying to get you out of London."

And the horror of her flight to Aldgate High Street, the assault in the cab, fearing that death had found her, all came back in a rush. She struggled to maintain an appearance of calm.

The fact that her stalker had been someone she knew and he'd not actually murdered her had meant nothing. She had feared for her life in a manner she would wish on no one, yet Gabby would suffer something quite like it, and much worse. Mary Jane gasped with the realisation.

I called for that.

Swinging her legs off the bed, she sat up slowly, not wanting to alarm Joseph again. Her boots, hat, and shawl had been removed. Otherwise, she remained clothed.

Mary Jane saw a poker jutting out of a bucket of coal by the grate.

A weapon.

"Should people see you after they learn of the one in your room," he said, "you might be charged with a crime." Joseph got up and stood by the window, looking out at the brickwork and the dirty sky above.

He means Gabby. Has she been killed or is that yet to come?

"You're *helping* him," she said in accusation.

She made little sound getting to her feet.

"Thomas too," he said.

No, not Thomas.

"We didn't have any choice. I don't know his name, but I know he's a dangerous man."

Yes, Mary Jane thought, *the black-eyed man is a criminal who shall kill us all in the end.*

"He knows something of our past crimes," Joseph said, "and though a freelance assassin, he's working under a police commission. I know little of the particulars."

She made for the poker, slowly, hoping he would not hear. The floor boards squeaked, and she froze, holding her breath.

He turned toward her briefly.

As if struggling to awaken, she kept her head down, pretended to busy herself arranging her hair.

"The cove told me what to do," he said, his voice sad and weary. He turned back to the view outside. "For now, he's guv'nor,"

Perhaps Joseph believed that the feelings she had for him left her harmless.

"You'll stay here today, and we'll leave after dark."

Imagining Joseph hearing the rasping sound of iron against coal, and turning quickly, Mary Jane knew she'd have to anticipate his movement and be swift. She pulled the poker from the bucket and immediately made a back-handed swing for his head, struck him above his right ear as he turned.

Joseph toppled to the floor.

She examined him, felt his head. Finding wetness, but no deep hole, she was thankful the hook at the end of the tool had faced away from him. He appeared to be out cold.

Mary Jane discovered her boots under the bed, her hat and shawl on a chair, and donned them. She felt for her pocket and the money within, reassuring herself that her funds hadn't been taken.

The door opened easily. She slipped out and exited the building.

SEVENTY-FOUR

By Dry's pocket watch it is twenty minutes until four when another shadow falls in the passage. A figure slides along by the brickwork, glances around the empty courtyard and is presumably satisfied. The single gas-lamp on the wall below is enough to show Dry that this is no passing stranger or drunken seeker of a woman's pleasures. It is the one.

No doubt the killer has already quartered the area, assuring himself that the constabulary do not lurk in wait. Satisfied, his vanity has led him to the heart of the affair. It is as Dry expected.

The candle is guttering as the man enters Number Thirteen. Gorse's body will still be warm. Unless the Whitechapel Murderer suspects intrigue against him, he will follow his pattern and slice the woman's throat first, thinking he guarantees silence. If he realises that he deals with a corpse, he may run.

Or he may still carve, believing that an offering has been left for him.

There is no sudden exit, but a scuffle of activity inside. Dry can smell the opening of the body, even from where he is. He remains motionless for almost ten minutes, knowing that butchery is underway, and then his rope, slender but strong, goes over the edge of the wall. He slides down it to the paving stones, blade in hand. It would not do to fire a shot this night.

He approaches Kelly's room, the door still slightly ajar. Through the dirty window next to it he can make out the killer standing over the bed. Carving. If the man thought the woman dead, unconscious from drink, or deep in the grip of laudanum, it did not make him pause. The huffing of excited breath as he cuts is distasteful.

SEVENTY-FIVE

The cold bit into Mary Jane's face and hands, while the clothing the ordinary cove had provided kept her body warm.

To determine her location, she fled along Brick Lane toward the closest crossing.

Where shall I go?

I can't go to Thomas—he's working for the black-eyed man.

To Liverpool Street Station, and away by rail—anywhere!

Mary Jane's black thoughts, like the murmuring motion of a flock of starlings in flight, flew this way and that, broke off at odd tangents, trying to avoid a firm, frightening centre wherein the happenings at 13 Miller's Court might be imagined. She did not want to think about Gabriella Gorse, yet thoughts of her continued—what *had* happened, or what might *be* happening, even then, to the woman.

Her feet carried her forward while she remained lost in thought. In her mind's eye, she and Gabby had merged as one. Mary Jane had the unwanted feeling that she would suffer whatever her nemesis suffered. Their experience in life having been so similar, one might stand in for the other easily. Hadn't Gabby once suffered a beating meant for Mary Jane?

She may not know that the Gully Bleeders murdered Jennie.

Gabby's crime against Jennie truly amounted to the extortion of one tanner per week.

I have discovered as much and more lying on the pavement several times, dropped by careless pedestrians.

No one could have known that Jennie would so enrage Nick Shear that he'd have her killed. She'd cut his face!

I should have given his name to the black-eyed man instead.

Gabby is no more wicked than many I've known, and some that I've loved.

No telling what sort of criminal I'd had in Joseph Fleming. No matter what he'd told me, he were involved with a murderer.

He strangled *me!*

Had he indeed wanted to kill her? Had he resisted the urge all those nights when she lived and slept with him?

Damn my feelings for him!

People walking by on the footway stared after her.

I must have a hysterical look.

438

Carter Street—have to keep going.

No, that's the Black Eagle Brewery on the left. I have to turn back, move south.

Mary Jane turned around and hurried forward in the good boots, past Pelham and Hanbury Streets.

I must avoid Dorset, take Fournier and Brushfield.

Jennie were courageous, much braver than I.

If she had not taken the risk of swinging a laundry sack at Stuart Brevard, what might have become of me?

I'd be maimed or dead.

Impatient to move westward, she took a turn into Princelet Street.

I don't know the time!

Has Gabby met her death yet, or is there still a chance to save her?

Left into Wilkes Street.

No! I mustn't think of it.

Oh, give me a church bell to tell me the time!

To what end? Just get to the railway station.

Intent on merely passing through her old neighbourhood, Mary Jane remained fearful of being seen by the black-eyed man or Jack the Ripper. She looked for a weapon as she moved.

A right into Fournier Street.

The lighted clock on Christ Church ahead and to her left said ten till four o'clock in the morning.

Hours had passed since Mary Jane left her room in Miller's Court.

Gabby must be dead by now.

Or she lingers as Jennie did, suffering, hoping help will come.

She thought of Daphne Michaels. The woman had found and taken Mary Jane to the infirmary after the man attacked her in Cardiff.

Without that aid, I might have died.

Though she hated Gabby, Mary Jane had nothing but regret for employing the ordinary cove.

Reaching the crossing at Commercial Street, she saw a broken wheel spoke in the gutter by the kerb. Mary Jane paused briefly to pick up the hard oak shaft. One end had splintered off sharp. She tucked that end under the waistband of her top skirt.

Hopping over the spreads of rutted "mud," she hurried across the street through slow, light traffic, and found herself turning toward Dorset Street.

She stopped, holding her head in her hands.

Something in me wants to go back to Miller's Court!

She didn't know when after half-past one o'clock in the morning the black-eyed man had intended to implement his plan.

Should I try to help Gabby, I could be killed.

I did not try to help Bell when Stuart Brevard attacked her. She were lucky a bystander did help or she might be dead now. The shame of that had kept her from visiting Bell in the infirmary, and had troubled her since.

Mary Jane found herself walking again, past the Ringers and turning right into Dorset. Few people on the street.

Despite knowing the time, she still did not know if she would be too late to help or too early and hurrying into danger.

Gabby caused so much suffering.

Yet I am not blameless.

Imagining Jennie's pain and fear, tears rose up, and Mary Jane stumbled half-blinded until she wiped them away.

I put her on the streets.

Still, should I suffer for that?

I hurry to my doom!

Why can't I stop myself?

Her steps faltered.

Because I cannot live with myself if I do not try.

What would have become of me if Jennie hadn't had the courage to swing that laundry sack?

Luck had been with me then, as it had been when I fended off Harris Brevard's attack.

Luck will be with me again.

Should I be careful in Miller's Court, no one shall know I'm there.

Reaching through the window, I could let myself in silently. If there is danger, I might still take the advantage, like I did with Joseph.

Mary Jane picked up speed.

Fear of darkness stopped her again—she saw not fifty feet away the opening to the Miller's Court passage.

SEVENTY-SIX

Dry kicks the door full open and lunges...

And the man has moved. An eight inch knife is in his hand, blocking Dry's thrust. The edge is dark with blood. He has speed, this one, and animal senses. Dry spins on his heel and ducks low so that the riposte goes above his head.

A bare half inch above it.

Dry's blade is reversed, driven down into the man's right boot, piercing the leather and the arch of the foot. A hiss from the other.

Recover and away, ready. Dry has his back to the hearth; the killer to the wall opposite, by the bed. The body upon the bed is a shambles of ripped and mutilated flesh. Gorse's face has gone, and much of the belly.

"What is this?" The tall man twists his lip up at one side. "Sent his apprentice, has he, the guv'nor from Deptford? His messenger boy means to test my mettle. Or do you have your own ambitions—maybe to steal Jackie's glory?"

Dry does not speak. Speech uses breath, concentration. He calculates, judging the man's next move. He might seek to use height and weight on the smaller man, or...

The open door. The Whitechapel Murderer is planning to escape. He does not care to fight an armed man, it appears.

He will not be given the choice tonight.

Dry leaps and slashes at the first twitch of movement, a cut to the other's knife-arm as the man charges for the door, but both are in motion and the cut is too shallow. Cloth and a sliver of skin. The killer is away into the courtyard, but not towards the passage to Dorset Street. Tenements line both sides of the short courtyard until it ends in a blank wall and the rear of taller buildings on Brushfield Street, to the north. Only the rooftops offer escape that way...

So Dry's quarry also has a head for heights.

A drainpipe creaks but holds, propelling the pursued man to the angle between the wall of another building and the Miller's Court roofs; Dry takes to the rope that he left in place, climbing up the side of the courtyard wall and along the tiles. The soles of his boots, painted with latex for this purpose, are almost silent.

Seven, eight paces between them.

SEVENTY-SEVEN

Cautiously approaching the dark opening, Mary Jane heard a scuffling of feet coming through the Miller's Court passage. Unwilling to be seen by those who might be within, her view of the part of court illuminated by the gas lamp remained obscured. Fancy told her that someone had stumbled on the way to the privy, or that a murderer had positioned himself out of sight, preparing to surprise her.

While the sound further stoked her fear, she looked for reasons to prop up her courage, thought of the day her mother had drowned and died. Mary Jane had allowed the treed thicket to stop her on that day, to keep her from hurrying downstream to help Mum. She'd retreated, looking for help, and yet later passed through the thicket successfully. Too late!

If I'd had the courage to push through the difficult patch quickly, I might have saved Mum.

Fear shall not stand in my way now.

Mary Jane took quiet steps, pushing forward through the corridor, listening.

No one in the court. Quiet now, but for the murmur of the sleepless city all around.

She paused just past her room to listen more carefully.

The door to the privy stood open. Dim light reflected into its interior showed no one within.

A person on Dorset Street walked past the opening to the passage into the court.

No light came from either window of her room. The curtains were drawn over them.

Mary Jane crouched down beside the small window and tried to peer in around the edge of the curtain, her heart pounding in her throat, her vision speckled with stars that appeared briefly with each pulse. She realised she was holding her breath and let it out slowly.

The coat Maria had left behind further blocked Mary Jane's view. She had to put her hand in and push the garment aside.

Hearing the cloth of her cuff brush along the glass, she flinched, yet avoided cutting herself.

She became still, heard nothing from within.

Any moment, one inside the room would cut her arm, her hand, or grab Mary Jane and pull her through the window into the room.

Her flesh prickled, the hairs standing up, as she slid her arm between the sharp edges of the broken pane, and reached to unlock the door.

Some relief when she withdrew her arm. A smell of night soil emerged from the hole in the glass.

Curious—I left nothing in the chamber pot.

Mary Jane stood, drew her sharp wheel spoke, moved to the door, and turned the knob slowly. Even taking care, the mechanism made a small clicking sound, and she knew she would have alerted someone inside. Did he wait patiently in the darkness within?

Even so, she pressed forward, opening the door. Mary Jane gripped her spoke more tightly. The light from the gas lamp outside sent a broadening rectangle of illumination into the room.

The odour of slops grew stronger, along with a smell of metal, iron possibly.

Ready to change course in an instant, dash through the passage and out into Dorset Street, Mary Jane instead held her weapon out before her, and slid a foot forward.

Blood on the floor beside the bed! The clothing Maria had left behind and Mary Jane had placed on the floor had been scattered. The petticoat, now bloodstained, lay beside a leg of the bed.

Still, nothing stirred within. She took another step, turning, trying to see into the shadowed corners.

Someone—Gabby—lay upon the bed. Mary Jane wanted to speak, but couldn't find her voice.

She turned toward the table, fumbled for the matches and lit the candle in the broken wine glass.

Mary Jane lifted the glass and turned toward the bed, hoping to give aid, fearing the worst.

No hope!

"Oh, Murder!" she cried.

She wanted to fold in the middle and loose her roiling gut. She retched uselessly, holding herself, trying not to drop her source of light.

Finally she knew what he'd meant—the black-eyed man had indeed christened Gabriella Gorse!

Her face gone, the skin and muscle cut away. Her blue eyes, so much like Mary Jane's, shown dully from the shambles of her mutilated features. Smears of red glued once beautiful, flaxen hair to the bedclothes.

Her gut had been laid open, her cunny, posteriors, and dairy gone. One leg, like a a joint of lamb brought to the table too many times, was carved to the bone. Butchered flesh had been piled upon the table, blood everywhere.

The ordinary cove is a madman!

Mary Jane hastened to blow out the candle, stumbled back, and set the wine glass down.

The starlings of her thoughts spooked. They flew in all directions at once, the flutter of notions and concerns too swift to have meaning, a great, grey rushing sound in her mind, followed by a wide-eyed calm. She lost track of time, standing motionless as she considered what had led to that moment.

A useless effort—I have been a pawn in a ghastly scheme of murder!

Then, a moment of clear thinking.

Get out!

Hurrying from the room toward Dorset Street, Mary Jane ran into someone in the passage. He clapped a hand over her mouth. She struggled, swung her weapon uselessly. Her heart beat too fast. She grew dizzy. The more she wriggled, the tighter he held.

I shall die, Mary Jane thought, suddenly wishing it.

The thought brought relief, a hope for release. She let go of life in that moment, became limp in his arms.

Yet life did not let go of her.

"Tis Joseph," came the familiar voice, whispered close to her ear. "We must lock the door. Your key."

"Gone," Mary Jane said, gasping.

"Go," he said. "I have a betty." Joseph shoved her in the direction of the street.

Glancing back, she saw him in the gas lamp light, crouched down beside the door, working with the tool. He didn't know about the broken window.

Unsuspecting, a couple walked past the opening to the passage without looking in. The woman laughed at something the man said.

Mary Jane hurried out into Dorset Street, and stumbled away along the lane, becoming increasingly lost within herself, her ongoing fright and thoughts all-consuming. She had little awareness of the world around her.

SEVENTY-EIGHT

Dry gains as the other man struggles by a rusting gutter pipe, heading high and east towards Christ Church, but the footing in this corner is uneven, uncertain—missing tiles and crudely patched gaps; lead unseated or stripped away by local entrepreneurs. With a glance behind him, the man drops down into the next courtyard, staggering as he lands. He has begun to favour the foot pierced by Dry's knife.

Dry is down after him, knees bent to take the shock, springing up to follow.

Six paces.

This yard leads through another arch and onto Commercial Street, an open stretch of tramlines and occasional traffic. The delivery men will be about their rounds soon.

The hands of the Christ Church clock, not so far away, stand at almost four in the morning.

In her Southwark lodgings, Catherine Weatherhead had lost her sight.

She could feel the crumpled linen of the bed beneath her, but she could not see the bed, her hands, her room. Her nostrils pricked to the smell of the Whitechapel streets—night-soil and horse dung, urine in the alleys, damp clothes hung across narrow streets. Cheap beer spilled in doorways, long with vomit.

She was possessed by the sight of two men, two monsters.

Let bishops debate whilst the workman does his job.

London town must provide…

The moon is near its first quarter, a bright crescent barely clouded now. The silver wound of it illuminates Commercial Street and the ways beyond. Almshouses and chapels, slum tenements and public houses, some showing a faint light. Mile End in the distance; breweries and rookeries around.

Dry's quarry slows, twists into Wood Street and Princes Street, past the synagogue and the old Yiddish Theatre. Four storeys of red brick and blank windows—no way to the roof ridges here. Brick Lane and back on himself, back towards the church. The man clearly knows the habits of the local police—he is dodging between routes where the constables

445

trudge.

It is a strange pursuit.

Neither man wishes to be seen by others, and they move in silence. The pursued slows as two drunks stagger down the road and gape around, then speeds forward once the drunks have passed; the pursuer follows in the same fashion, but always closer.

Four paces.

Christ Church ahead once more, the white spire etched against the thick sliver of the moon. His man is tiring; there are occasional spots of blood on the pavement from his foot. Dry sees him vault into the churchyard, perhaps meaning to slip behind the rectangular bulk of the church and lose his pursuer. Great porch and Tuscan columns gleam ahead, but are not reached.

Two paces between them, and Dry is the faster.

He slides low on the damp grass, right arm outstretched, and his blade slices across the back of the man's left knee, cutting into the tendons. The man staggers, curses—the first sound he has made since the room in Miller's Court.

Dry has said no word since his misdirection to the prostitute, Gorse.

A limping turn by the Whitechapel Murderer. Left leg weak, right foot bleeding.

"Your guts, then, errand boy" says the man, steadying himself and raising his own knife.

Wet turf, the faint humps of old burials, a broken bottle or two and discarded protections from trysts behind the walls. The lawn of the churchyard is more treacherous than the cobbles of Commercial Street.

Dry has danced before; will dance again. Feint and thrust, the recover, the sudden break to one side, and turn. Never be still, when the opponent has strength and reach. His mind trusts his hands; his hands trust the blade.

The tall man has no formal skill in the fight, but he brings long, powerful arms and the will to survive. He brings growing anger, enough that in the next moment of their dance, he manages to slash Dry along the shoulder, the blow not so deep, but painful.

He does not remember when an opponent last cut him, but memory—and pain—must wait.

The killer takes a ragged breath. "Your master knew his business when he took you on. But you'll see that I am worthy. Concede, and we'll *finish splitting the bitch together."*

Dry gives no answer as they engage again; another wild blow comes close to his gut, but he pivots and is elsewhere. The killer is so very unschooled that he cannot easily be predicted, and Dry takes measure of that. The energy which drives his opponent is the same loathing that fuelled the deaths of five women. He knows, however, that he can outlast this brute.

Blades clash once more, without result. Both men step back, and in the heartbeat that they pull apart, an owl, of all things, calls across the churchyard.

For reasons which will never be known, the other man looks up.

"Enough, I believe," says Dry, and slashes deep across the tall man's wrist, making his opponent drop his knife. Before the other man can react, he leaps high and slams the weighted pommel of his weapon into the centre of the man's forehead, dropping him to his knees.

Dry lands steady and poised.

It is interesting. He has used such a blow before, and taken a man's consciousness with it. This one is dazed, but still aware.

"You," the other gasps. "You are no messenger. You are The Tradesman, the Deptford Assassin."

"The newspapers call me so."

Dry kicks the fallen knife far from reach, and shifts his own blade to the other hand, the undamaged arm.

"But I have...I have admired your work."

"I am indifferent to your admiration. You yourself are..." He pauses, considering the words. "An inconvenience."

The man on his knees looks confused, unsure.

"You wanted them, the whores? I said, we could share—"

"I want for nothing."

A dazed half-movement to rise; an iron-toed boot cracks the man's undamaged knee. He moans and sinks again.

They are silent statues in the moonlight, facing each other. The Whitechapel Murderer coughs, and lifts his head. His look is sly, a last search for some form of control.

"So, you have the advantage of Jackie boy, but who is Jack?" Blood trickles down his forehead, the skin broken where the pommel struck. "All London wishes to know who I truly am, my story. Am I judge or Jew, doctor or docker?" The man laughs. "All London seeks me. And my name *will be remembered, for—"*

The exquisite blade seeks its target. Up through throat, tongue and palate, deep into the brain of one who liked to be called "Jack."

"All London seeks a clean privy," says the Deptford Assassin to the body which slumps before him. "Hardly a recommendation. As for your true name, I have no interest in the matter. It is dust, and will stay there."

He slides the blade free, wipes it on the man's coat and inspects the edges. Sharp as ever, and un-notched. Only now does he notice that his breath is tight with exertion. A rare occurrence. His hat is askew, and his jacket will have to be replaced. The slash in the cloth at the shoulder would make an ugly mend, even for a tailor of some talent.

But he is satisfied.

If he were a beast, a primordial force of nature, he would raise his face to the moon and howl his triumph. And the world would shake, that such as he walked this sorry Earth and held dominion over it. When he chose to.

He is, however, Edwin Dry. He brushes down his lapels, and makes sure that the encounter has caused no damage to his hat.

He has standards.

In the shadow of Christ Church, he drags the corpse upright and gets one arm around it. Cumbersome, but not impossible to transport. If any other should be walking the streets, they will see a drunk being escorted home by his friend.

He could leave the body here in plain view, a mystery for the police to consider, but why give the killer that grace? The man, even dead, offends him. A common murderer at heart, an amateur with an unpleasant weakness. Not even fit to be called an apprentice.

Not so far from here is a pig-yard, much like the one where someone once practised on a sow's carcass. The animals will be hungry.

The coarse teeth of pigs will rend the body—tainted meat, but they will not care. They will not wonder who he was.

By dawn the Whitechapel Murderer will be ordure in their sty.

She was bleeding, her stomach hot and cramped. The moon's gift, a few days early, the same night she saw Edwin Dry at his work and the death of the Whitechapel Murderer—as if blood could bring blood. Confused, she managed to find a sanitary bandage in the drawer of her night-stand and press it between her legs. Some part of her was still in Whitechapel, a lantern show of fading images...

The pigs are fed, and mighty pleased they were with an early break to the night's fast.

Small tasks remain to be completed.

Dry must return to Miller's Court without delay, and ensure that the scarlet scene of another's butchery serves its second purpose, one which completes the commission. If Kelly wishes to be presumed dead, the body in Number Thirteen must not be identifiable. Gorse the understudy will step forward into a final leading role.

The Whitechapel Murderer has already conducted a frenzied mutilation—a savage progression from his earlier work. No one would know this woman, apart from hair and height. Little more will need be done with the bloody corpse. A few errant items can be disposed of on the low fire which still crackles in the grate, and the room arranged to suit those who will discover the scene—neighbours, creditors or constables. The details always matter.

Better if he could have put an end to the killer nearer Dorset Street— the chase has eaten into the time allotted. Each minute lost increases the chance that someone will look in through the cracked window of Thirteen Miller's Court before he wishes it.

He will retrieve his rope, and remove any other sign that he himself has been in the vicinity, leaving by the rooftops once more. The stage, when Dry has gone, will show only that a man entered, killed, and cut the woman who lived there.

For the newspapers and their readers, their "Jack" will have struck again. A select few, when he has reported his main commission done, will comfort themselves that the killer who so vexed them is gone.

"Mary Jane Kelly" will be the last victim of the Whitechapel Murderer.

Catherine gulped down water, and wondered if she should call out for Mrs Bessovitch. Her legs were shaking, and she had no more brandy in her room...

He is satisfied. All trace of Edwin Dry has gone from Miller's Court and Dorset Street. No one has marked his passage between the crooked chimney pots. He eases the body of Gorse's escort—a detail delayed but not forgotten—into a ruined cellar a few streets away, even as wagons stacked with milk churns begin to clatter on the streets. The tenement above is uninhabitable, even by East End standards, and will be demolished in the next few days, bringing all down upon the anonymous corpse; the November weather will keep it until then.

One single and signal item remains, some streets away. The knife of the Whitechapel Murderer lies in Christ Church yard, worthless now in the long grass which covers so many dead.

This he will leave for others.

SEVENTY-NINE

Later Mary Jane would be told that she'd somehow got away from Joseph and wandered until the pubs opened. Then, she visited several of them, drinking and talking with others. She wouldn't remember any of that.

With her next awareness, she found Joseph escorting her out of the Horn of Plenty. He hurried Mary Jane across Crispin Street to Raven Row and into Artillery passage. Entering the thin corridor, she grew afraid. She suddenly saw the world around her more fully. Daylight had come.

She struggled to get away from him. He pulled her right arm up behind her back. "Walk calmly and quietly through the passage," he said. "You will hurt if you don't." He demonstrated with a tug on her arm. The agony too much, she pinched her mouth shut. They passed others using the thin lane, no one appearing to suspect that Mary Jane was being forced to do Joseph's bidding.

At Sandy's Row, just across from the Hoop and Grapes pub, a carriage pulled up. The door opened and Thomas Morganstone leaned out to help her in.

Mary Jane resisted. "You worked for the black-eyed man too."

His confused look said he didn't know who she meant.

"The cove," Joseph said. "Our *Guv'nor.*"

"Yes, all three of us have worked for him," Thomas said. "He is nothing like the evil he just vanquished."

Jack the Ripper? Isn't the ordinary cove just as wicked?

Again, Mary Jane struggled against Joseph's grip. Surprising herself, and him, she got away, and started running back through Artillery Passage.

Oddly, with her ability to run so well, she wondered at the need to do so. A thought out of place had occurred to her: *My boots! Why give me tidy boots if he meant me harm?*

A small thing. A foolish notion in the swarm of maddening thoughts on that day, but it stopped her in her tracks.

Yes, they had all three worked for the ordinary cove. He'd never lied to Mary Jane, and had been true to his word in all their business. He had no cause to harm her if she could not be located.

Though afraid of him, she'd trusted the strange black-eyed man until animal fear took away rational thought.

Mary Jane turned around. Thomas and Joseph had come for her, yet made no threatening move. Joseph reached slowly to take her arm. Thomas laid a hand on his shoulder. "Stay," he said simply.

They remained still for a moment.

Mary Jane no longer saw menace in their motives.

Then, she found herself in Thomas's arms. She'd not felt the few steps that took her there. She hugged him and wept quietly.

Her arms and legs had become useless. She sagged into his embrace, felt him lift and carry her. He placed her on the seat in the carriage, and Mary Jane knew no more for some time.

EIGHTY

Warm arms held Catherine; the lullaby sang in her ears, a little cracked and tuneless but so welcome. Her lap felt damp, and when she looked down, she saw that Mrs B had removed her undergarments and wiped her clean, wrapping an old petticoat around her waist.

"You say things," murmured the landlady. "You dream, and say 'Christ Church.' It is vision, da?"

"Da. Yes." Catherine swallowed. "He has…I cannot say it. Yes, another vision, a terrible one."

"This man in bowler hat—he does bad thing?"

"Bad? I no longer know. A wicked thing or a marvellous one. A necessary one, I pray."

"This is world. Some times, is many years later when we know which is which."

Catherine eased herself free of her landlady's arms. "I must wash, dress. I will have to send word to someone. What time is it?"

"Almost eleven in morning. Can I take message for you, Katerina?"

"You are a dear, but it is my responsibility. I have passed coin to the Devil, and bought what I had to."

Had she wanted to eat, there would have been no time. Before she had finished dressing and bound back her hair, someone was at the door. Catherine heard low, guarded speech from her landlady, then Mrs Bessovitch was on the stair.

"I think you come, Katerina."

The visitor was a slim, middle-aged man with a long brown coat. "Mr Swanson would see you. At the infirmary."

Catherine gripped the balustrade.

"Inspector Mallick—"

"Will you come with me, miss? The Chief Inspector is waiting." Crisp, but not unfriendly.

"This is not arrest?" Mrs Bessovitch stood close, formidable.

"No. An urgent, quiet word, that is all."

She was helped into the cab, to be followed by the slim man.

"You are with the police?"

"I am with Mr Swanson." He would say no more.

The cab driver took a fair pace through the morning traffic, depositing them at the main infirmary doors. Swanson's man gestured to her.

"Inspector Mallick is well. Mr Swanson has been sitting with him, but would speak to you alone. There is a room, to your left, a former porter's office. You should wait there."

The night had left her confused, unsure. She went where she was told, and for want of anything else to do, sat down on a linen box in the corner of the room. Shelves were piled with bed-linen in crisp white order and folded uniforms—nurses' garb, perhaps.

Swanson arrived soon after, turning and using his weight to slam the door shut behind him.

"I might apologise, lassie, but time is short. If we meet here, then none will ask—all do ken that I visit Eden Mallick, ay, to check his progress. The one who brought you will nae talk." He paced, his boots coming down heavily on worn floorboards, deep furrows above the bridge of his nose. "When is it to be done, for God's sake? Yuir man…there's been anither, a rare cutting-up that will give the newspapers joy and bring down more talk on oor poor necks, as though—"

"It is over, Chief Inspector."

He had not seen her face as he rushed in. Now he looked, and looked again. She knew from her wash-stand mirror that the night had left its marks. Her eyes were shadowed, bloodshot; her lips were pale.

"Over? What dae ye mean? A woman has been murdered, off Dorset Street."

"That was the last, I swear. The Whitechapel Murderer is dead."

"At the hands of…yuir hound from Deptford?"

"Yes."

He gritted his teeth, lost for a moment in unknown thoughts. "The guid Lord knows, I had my doubts on all o' this. Ye swear he's gone, this Jack?"

She could not tell him how she had seen it, felt it, but she must convince him. Men like Swanson were fond of facts…

"The killer was taken straight after his deed at Miller's Court. Yes, I know what has happened, and where. But I assure you he was served justice. One knee—the left one—slashed, the other shattered.

A long blade thrust into his wicked head, and the end swift after. Dead, Mr Swanson." Fragments of that other place spun behind her eyes. "Do you know Christ Church, in Spitalfields?"

"Aye, I ken it well enough."

"Send your man outside to that place. Or an officer you trust. In the churchyard, ten paces from the oldest yew to the east, and half-hidden where the grass has not been cut. You will find a knife there. If you have a police surgeon with tight lips, let him examine it. It is the one used at Miller's Court, and on most, if not all, the other women. It will not be used again."

Swanson let out a breath which sounded as if it had been held for weeks.

"Ye swear? No, I cannae keep asking that." He leaned against the shelving, fingers pressed to one temple. "Ye tell me that we have grand victory, and few will know."

"They will know eventually, when no more mutilated women are found on your streets."

"Aye. True enough. I'll ha' the body, then? Many will wish to know who he was."

"That is also gone, and the name with it." She looked up at him. "Better this way, Mr Swanson."

"How so? Am I to be swindled?" An angry, petulant touch to his voice.

It was something which had weighed on her, had grown as she read yet one more newspaper's speculations, or seen yet another supposed identification of the murderer in the spiritualist journals. Dry had also influenced her feelings on the matter, she supposed. The man they called Jack was nothing, and worth no one's time. Any care, any consideration or debate, should be saved for the poor women he had slaughtered.

But perhaps there was another, practical argument she could use on Swanson.

"What is your Scots saying, Chief Inspector? Wheesht a moment, and think about what you say. His identity died with him, and so did what might have followed."

"What might have followed?"

"Yes. Consider it. Were he to prove a Jew, a Pole or German, there would be demonstrations, even riots. Mobs would seek out others of his kind. Prejudice would feed, and innocents would suffer."

His frown brought thick eyebrows so close together they might have been one.

"And were he to turn out to be of high station or rank," she continued, "Then you would face worse, in other ways. Deceptions and concealments would be in order—or scandal. Would the women be less dead for that? Would your job be easier?"

Swanson's scowl remained. "Ye have a point, lassie. But—"

"It is done. Let us be thankful."

They stared at each other, challenge or assessment. Catherine could not tell. He was the first to look away, though.

"I will arrange to send you the remainder o' the fee. If the knife is where you say, and all else tallies."

"It will. And the man will find me to receive his due, I have no doubt." She clutched her arms around herself. "I wonder though—I cannot help but wonder…we have done something, set a hound on a hound, as you would have it. Are we the better for using such a dreadful device?"

He looked away from her.

"There are two or three folk above me," he said. "High above me, ye ken, not those at Scotland Yard. They approved when I told them what I might do—yuir name was not mentioned, if ye feared that. But lassie, they approved so quick that I have ma doubts as to their games. This man, the Deptford Assassin, as the papers call him. I asked once, should we no be hot on his heels?"

"I would question as to whether or not he could be taken."

"Aye, there's that, but listen tae me. I was told, and didnae like it, that I should look elsewhere. Why, I asked? Because there are times, they said. Because there are times."

"Such as now?" Catherine rose from the linen box. "We shall never know who has called on him before, Chief Inspector. How many villains or innocents he has claimed."

"It galls me, lassie."

"Then you are a decent man. I have summoned the monster twice, and must live with it. You have only done your duty. What will you do next?"

Swanson sighed. "There are names I can throw around, to please others. It will dae nay harm. And there will be false claimants, and those who would copy what has been done. We cannae be so sure that all were by the same hand. Those above will hear the truth; the rest o' us will carry on oor work. We will speculate and cast blame aroond, pretending I had never met ye. Oor single comfort is yuir certainty."

"My word is good."

She did not want to see Eden Mallick as unkempt as she was, She would come another day. All Swanson could tell her was that the inspector might yet keep his arm—the surgeons were more hopeful than before.

The Chief Inspector's man outside still had the hansom close by, and offered it to her. She accepted. It was early in the afternoon, but she needed to sleep—and prayed that it would be dreamless.

Two men, two wicked men, had died—Frederick Caille and the Whitechapel Murderer—and it was Mardy Cath Weatherhead of Fell Lane, Keighley, who had done for them. Not by her own hand, but by her word. Which was not always good, but surely held purpose.

As the hansom took her back to Mrs Bessovitch and safety, with a clatter of wheels on cobbles and the annoyed cries of the cab-man, Catherine sat back, her mind elsewhere. She had revulsion, doubt, and satisfaction at war within her.

And perhaps—in dark and solitary moments to come—there would be a touch of fear in there as well.

He has her scent.

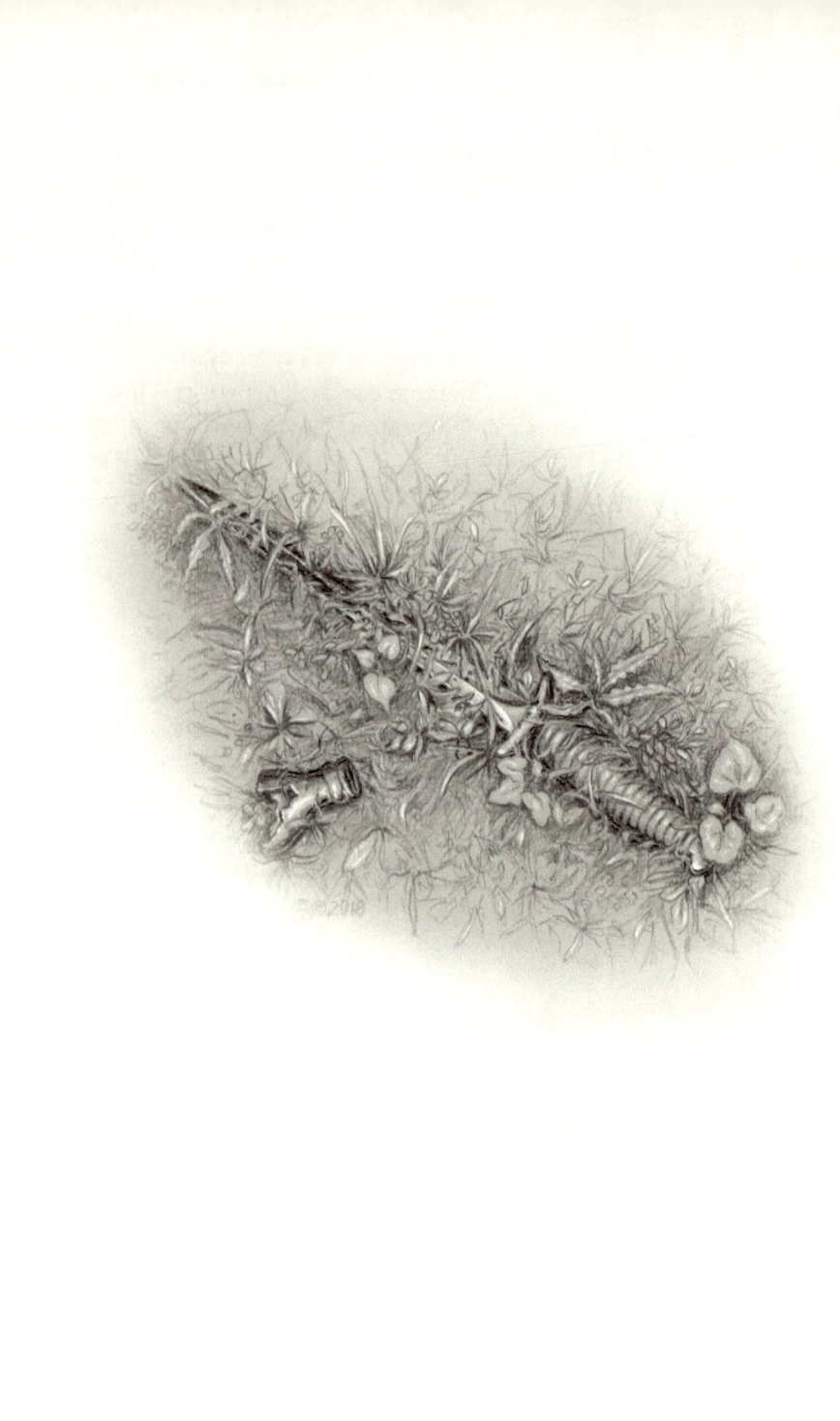

EPILOGUE

Carmarthen, Wales, 1890

A great length of rail passed beneath me, and the life of my flesh began anew in Wales.

I put it that way because I do not truly live while Gabby's remains occupy my mind's eye. I have few moments in which I am not reminded of her in my bed in Miller's Court. I eat little, and certainly no meat, as the sight of anything rent with teeth or knife takes away hunger and brings a lasting revulsion. I carry a sachet of lavender—a safe smell—held close to my nose most of the time, because I never know what other odour might carry me in recollection back to my old lodgings in Spitalfields. Any period of silence, should it be a lasting one, drives me mad. The worst silences are at night, when only severe fatigue allows me to sleep.

In October of 1888, in a scheme much more complicated than I had imagined, Thomas and Joseph had retrieved the emerald and platinum necklace from the top of the armoire in my old room at the Phoenix gay house. Fleming sold the jewellery to a fence. He gave me the funds. Once we'd arrived in Carmarthen, he and I were married and took a room together. Molly Fleming, I am now. We had every intention of exploring the love we clearly had for one another.

"You will recover your good spirits with time," he assured me.

I wanted to believe that, yet I suffer a severe melancholia that frustrates every effort toward happiness. Whilst being told and reassured many times that Jack the Ripper's career has ended, I fear that he might find and kill me. I have also feared that, after my performance on the streets and in the pubs of Spitalfields the morning of November 9, 1888, the ordinary cove will be forced to cover his tracks and kill me.

Indian Harry, John McCarthy's man, found Gabby at 13 Miller's Court that same morning when he came for the rent about eleven o'clock. The police were alerted.

Despite several witnesses speaking up to say they'd seen me that morning, common belief held that I died at 13 Miller's Court. Though the witnesses' reports appeared in print, eventually the newspapers seemed to come around to the belief that I had indeed perished.

"They say that because the police and the coroner say it," Joseph told me. "Seems some efforts were made to hasten the process of examining the

murder. Whether our strange assassin had anything to do with that or not, I don't know, but I have my suspicions. He had a police commission. I believe he returned to your room after we left to tidy it up. Whatever the case, we're safe here."

He said those things well over a year ago. In the fall of 1889, Fleming left me when he could no longer take my sensitivities; my sudden bouts of anger, my cringing in fear over things as simple as the sight or smell of blood. I do love Joseph, and hold no hard feelings.

Dear Elen Morganstone took me in.

"Two broken women together make a whole," she says.

Confined to her chair, she is much more capable than I. Her mother, Peggy, having passed away in the winter of 1888, Elen finds me useful. Thomas says she considers me a godsend. Help whenever needed, I do. I cannot believe I'm good company, and I am lucky to have her.

Crying out while having nightmares, I regularly disturb her sleep.

Thankfully, I do not remember the dreams once awakened.

Perhaps Gabby sends them for revenge. I hate her still for what she did for the Gully Bleeders that led to Jennie's death.

I also love her like a sister. How could I not—we died together in the same room.

Possibly the black-eyed man also visits my dreams.

Despite his unwillingness to say as much, it seems he had indeed been working for the police in some capacity. What of his dealings with me were considered with his police commission in mind? Although Joseph never said it outright, his words had implied that the assassin had been given the task of dispatching the Whitechapel Murderer. Had the ordinary cove sought a way to satisfy that commission and his contract with me simultaneously? I suspect I will never find an answer to that.

Did he indeed get Jack the Ripper? The killings did stop.

I hated the black-eyed man for what he'd done to Gabby. He had surely been the one to christen her corpse, yet I don't know if he'd been her killer. "You will learn little of my plan," he'd said.

Without seriousness, I've wondered if he owes me two and a tanner. I would laugh at that if I could.

I hate myself more. Set the events in motion, I did, what led to Gabriella Gorse's death.

I am her murderer.

I occupy a room at the back of Elen's tidy house on the edge of

Carmarthen. Well fed, kept in comfort, and even loved, I feel little of it.

When things get difficult for me I retreat to another room at the back of the house, where Elen installed Thomas's miniature town, the one we'd all worked on together as children. The small village is a pleasant one where nothing bad ever happens. The single ladybird, a ghost really, what walks the streets, is respected, and always treated well by her clients.

Some of the walls inside the houses still need paintings, and some of the figures could use better clothes, should I need distractions.

At the beginning of this record, I wrote: "Should I have another life, give me one of hardship and hatred or one of comfort and love, but not both. The knowing between the two is where true cruelty lies."

I know as I watch Thomas today, I would not truly want that. He is building a little fountain in the garden just outside my window to provide a continuous, soft noise in the night. If life had been purely pleasant, his gesture would mean little.

With the gentle sound, perhaps I shall sleep better.

John Linwood Grant is a professional writer/editor who lives in Yorkshire with a pack of lurchers and a beard. Widely published in magazines and anthologies, he writes strange period fiction, including the Mamma Lucy tales of 1920s hoodoo, the Last Edwardian series and contemporary weird stories. He is also editor of Occult Detective Quarterly, plus forthcoming anthologies, including 'ODQ Presents' and 'Hell's Empire', the incursion of the Prince of Darkness's forces into Victorian Britain. News of his projects can be found on his popular website greydogtales.com, which explores weird fiction and weird art. And lurchers.

Alan M. Clark grew up in Tennessee in a house full of bones and old medical books. He has created illustrations for hundreds of books, including works of fiction of various genres, nonfiction, textbooks, young adult fiction, and children's books. Awards for his illustration work include the World Fantasy Award and four Chesley Awards. As of summer of 2018, he is the author of 18 books, including twelve novels, a lavishly illustrated novella, four collections of fiction, and a nonfiction full-colour book of his artwork. Mr Clark's company, IFD Publishing, has released 45 titles of various editions, including traditional books, both paperback and hardcover, audio books, and ebooks by such authors as F. Paul Wilson, Elizabeth Engstrom, and Jeremy Robert Johnson. Alan M. Clark and his wife, Melody, live in Oregon. www.alanmclark.com

IFD Publishing Paperbacks

Novels:
Of Thimble and Threat, by Alan M. Clark
Baggage Check, by Elizabeth Engstrom
Bull's Labyrinth, by Eric Witchey
The Surgeon's Mate: A Dismemoir, by Alan M. Clark
Siren Promised, by Jeremy Robert Johnson and Alan M. Clark
Say Anything but Your Prayers, by Alan M. Clark
Candyland, by Elizabeth Engstrom
Apologies to the Cat's Meat Man, by Alan M. Clark
Lizzie Borden, by Elizabeth Engstrom
A Parliament of Crows, by Alan M. Clark
Lizard Wine, by Elizabeth Engstrom
The Door that Faced West, by Alan M. Clark
The Northwoods Chronicles, by Elizabeth Engstrom
The Prostitute's Price, by Alan M. Clark
The Assassin's Coin, by John Linwood Grant
13 Miller's Court, by Alan M. Clark and John Linwood Grant
Guys Named Bob, by Elizabeth Engstrom

Collections:
Professor Witchey's Miracle Mood Cure, by Eric Witchey

Nonfiction:
How to Write a Sizzling Sex Scene, by Elizabeth Engstrom

IFD Publishing EBooks

(You can find the following titles at most distribution points for all ereading platforms.)

Novels:
The Prostitute's Price, by Alan M. Clark
The Assassin's Coin, by John Linwood Grant
13 Miller's Court, by Alan M. Clark and John Linwood Grant

Guys Named Bob, by Elizabeth Engstrom
Apologies to the Cat's Meat Man, by Alan M. Clark
Bull's Labyrinth, by Eric Witchey
The Surgeon's Mate: A Dismemoir, by Alan M. Clark
York's Moon, by Elizabeth Engstrom
Beyond the Serpent's Heart, by Eric Witchey
Lizzie Borden, by Elizabeth Engstrom
A Parliament of Crows, by Alan M. Clark
Lizard Wine, by Elizabeth Engstrom
Northwoods Chronicles, by Elizabeth Engstrom
Siren Promised, by Alan M. Clark and Jeremy Robert Johnson
To Kill a Common Loon, by Mitch Luckett
The Man in the Loon, by Mitch Luckett
Jack the Ripper Victim Series: Of Thimble and Threat by Alan M. Clark
Jack the Ripper Victim Series: The Double Event (includes two novels from the series: *Of Thimble and Threat* and *Say Anything But Your Prayers*) by Alan M. Clark
Candyland, by Elizabeth Engstrom
The Blood of Father Time: Book 1, The New Cut, by Alan M. Clark, Stephen C. Merritt & Lorelei Shannon
The Blood of Father Time: Book 2, The Mystic Clan's Grand Plot, by Alan M. Clark, Stephen C. Merritt & Lorelei Shannon
How I Met My Alien Bitch Lover: Book 1 from the Sunny World Inquisition Daily Letter Archives, by Eric Witchey
Baggage Check, by Elizabeth Engstrom
D. D. Murphry, Secret Policeman, by Alan M. Clark and Elizabeth Massie
Black Leather, by Elizabeth Engstrom

Novelettes:
The Tao of Flynn, by Eric Witchey
To Build a Boat, Listen to Trees, by Eric Witchey

Children's Illustrated:
The Christmas Thingy, by F. Paul Wilson. Illustrated by Alan M. Clark

Collections:
Suspicions, by Elizabeth Engstrom
Professor Witchey's Miracle Mood Cure, by Eric Witchey

Short Fiction:
"Brittle Bones and Old Rope," by Alan M. Clark
"Crosley," by Elizabeth Engstrom
"The Apple Sniper," by Eric Witchey

Nonfiction:
How to Write a Sizzling Sex Scene, by Elizabeth Engstrom

IFD Publishing Audio Books

Novels:
The Door That Faced West by Alan M. Clark, read by Charles Hinckley
Jack the Ripper Victim Series: Of Thimble and Threat, by Alan M. Clark, read by Alicia Rose
Jack the Ripper Victim Series: Say Anything But Your Prayers, by Alan M. Clark, read by Alicia Rose
Jack the Ripper Victim Series: The Double Event by Alan M. Clark, read by Alicia Rose (includes two novels from the series: *Of Thimble and Threat* and *Say Anything But Your Prayers*)
A Parliament of Crows by Alan M. Clark, read by Laura Jennings
A Brutal Chill in August by Alan M. Clark, read by Alicia Rose
The Surgeon's Mate: A Dismemoir, by Alan M. Clark, read by Alan M. Clark
Apologies to the Cat's Meat Man, by Alan M. Clark, read by Alicia Rose
The Prostitute's Price, by Alan M. Clark, read by Alicia Rose

www.ingramcontent.com/pod-product-compliance
Lightning Source LLC
Chambersburg PA
CBHW020922020726
47495CB00002B/296